Heatshield

Don Anderson has been
a motoring corresponde
a reporter for BBC Television News in London, a television producer, a commercial radio programme controller, head of BBC radio in Northern Ireland and presently works for Independent Television.

Bought 23rd Feb 1990

Don Anderson

HEATSHIELD

PAN ORIGINAL
Pan Books
London, Sydney and Auckland

First published 1990 by Pan Books Ltd,
Cavaye Place, London SW10 9PG

9 8 7 6 5 4 3 2 1

© Don Anderson 1990

ISBN 0 330 30981 1

Printed and bound in Great Britain by Richard Clay Ltd, Bungay, Suffolk

ONE

Tarasov had only ninety minutes of life left to him.

So had everyone in the small group making its way towards the Alouette helicopter on the apron of Shannon Airport in the first glimmers of light of a May morning. Some stopped to watch an Aer Lingus 747, inbound from New York, drop with deceptive slowness onto the runway. Besides themselves, it seemed to be the only thing moving. As international airports went, Shannon was sleepy.

The men were beginning to relax. The Russians beamed at their Irish hosts, who returned the *bonhomie* when they weren't worrying about logistics and protocol.

The negotiations had gone tolerably well for both sides. Aeroflot, the Russian national airline, was to continue the terms for leasing fuelling, landing and staging rights at Shannon in the west of Ireland. In its heyday, Shannon had functioned as the first and last stepping stone for planes crossing the north Atlantic. Few now needed such a stepping stone. Just the Russians.

Tarasov was shaking with laughter, waving his new purchase from an airport shop in front of the Irish. 'It's an Irish tea-cup,' he said.

The Irish nodded with tired and tolerant grins.

'The handle is on the inside.' Another convulsion of laughter shook the fat on the Russian's body like the sound insulation on a road drill.

The senior official of the visiting delegation didn't join in his colleague's unrestrained merriment. He had noticed the subdued reaction of the Irish.

'I must apologize. . . .'

'No need,' Colm Fitzroy interrupted. 'It's just that we've seen the joke before. After all,' he winked at the Russian, 'it now counts as one more export success for Irish manufacturing.' Now everyone could laugh, Tarasov

5

louder than them all. He had turned the cup over and read, '*Made in Taiwan*'.

They boarded the helicopter. As the rotors began to spin, Colm Fitzroy told them that he wished his Russian guests had had more time for sightseeing at the conclusion of their mutually beneficial negotiations. He assured them that the cliffs and mountains of Ireland's shores should really be experienced at ground level, among the rugged people who lived there.

Tarasov leaned towards his colleague in the seat beside him. 'What people?' he muttered under cover of the rising engine whine. Tarasov preferred cities with bright lights – preferably red – and action, to the sparsely populated outer edges of an under-populated island. 'This is a KGB plot to stop us even thinking of defecting.'

The Alouette took off for the last time and headed north.

Major Petr Fedorovich Stukalin of the Soviet Air Force would have prayed if he had known how.

He was a mere five sunrises and four sunsets into the proving flight and suddenly all the lights had come on and all the screens had gone off. He stared, immobile with disbelief, at the panels and then stabbed the warning light re-set buttons in a flickering hope that the warning mechanisms were themselves at fault.

But they told an awful truth. His sleek craft was dying. Somewhere beneath his feet there had been a massive surge throughout the power distribution circuits. System after system had closed down in quick succession until only a small emergency battery supply of electricity was left.

Automatic altitude control was lost and the craft began to tumble slowly. Soft moonlight and earthlight played silent shadows on the pale wings, useless in the airless void of earth orbit.

Also lost was the automatic stream of telemetry being re-layed to ships and land-stations below. Briefly he thought of the panic on the ground as the pinnacle of Soviet aerospace technology was reported lost to control at Tyuratam on the other side of the world.

Radar would not locate him. Not this special machine. Stukalin was on his own.

He could not ask for advice because he was under the strictest orders not to reveal the nature of the flight to potential enemies of his country. Anyway, he would want his remaining electricity for other more profitable uses. His options were few. He could stay in orbit, watching his meagre battery power dwindle to the point where he would be unable manually to position his craft for re-entry into the atmosphere. If that happened, he would be dead before eventual uncontrolled re-entry and cremation.

Or he could do what the training manual called for — leave orbit immediately and re-assess the situation when the spacecraft had become an aircraft. Unlike the Ameri-can shuttles, Stukalin's prototype spaceplane had an air-breathing jet engine for use in the atmosphere after re-entry.

Stukalin's on-board computers had died, so it was back to a pocket calculator, tethered to the flap in the breast pocket of his tunic to prevent it floating into some nook or cranny. He found pressing the little buttons and sorting the calculations extraordinarily difficult.

Too little practice, Stukalin admonished himself. He should have simulated the manoeuvre more often on the ground, but it had been difficult to manage this. The design engineers had said that a catastrophic electrical failure like this was a 'worst case scenario' which could only happen if the spaceplane hit something.

And, they had told him, if it hit something that big, the pi-lot would probably die immediately. The spaceplane hadn't hit anything, but the power had nevertheless collapsed, leaving the pilot ill prepared for the spaceflight equivalent of Bleriot conditions.

Stukalin swore that he would survive long enough to have 'Worst Case Scenario' written on some design engineer's headstone.

He set to work manually operating small jets to make the spaceplane fly tail first so that the rocket motors were pointing forwards. When he was satisfied, he reached for the control that would determine whether he lived or died.

He flicked the orbital engine-burn switch. At the same time, he started the countdown on the calculator.

The engine fired. He felt the reassuring shudder and pressure as the thrust cut the speed which was keeping him in orbit. It had to burn for one minute and forty-three seconds. No more. No less. Thirty seconds. One minute. One minute fourteen seconds. The engine faltered. He felt the thrust drop. Then it picked up again. How much thrust had he lost? Without full instrumentation he could only guess. He could feel perspiration sticking the calculator to his palm. He guessed at two seconds' worth of extra burn. A minute forty-five. Cut.

One way or another, Stukalin's fate was now sealed. He would soon learn whether the spaceplane was going too fast or too slow for controlled re-entry.

One final manoeuvre was needed. Slowly Stukalin spun the craft round so that it was facing forward once more with the nose pointing up at thirty-three degrees. Another piece of guesswork, but he had five degrees of latitude either side to play with. At this angle, the heatshield on the undersurfaces would protect the frame as the friction of the atmosphere reduced his speed from seventeen thousand kilometres per hour to eight thousand.

Minutes later Stukalin could see a dull, red glow emanate from the leading heatshield surfaces. It was a good sign. If he was lucky, he would emerge hot and fast somewhere high above the north Atlantic, heading east towards Scandinavia and northern Russia. And that exhausted almost the full extent of his navigational knowledge.

* * *

Colm Fitzroy was noted in Irish administrative circles as a man with good attention to detail. He had therefore left the flight plan of the sightseeing tour for the Russians to the last minute.

The route would be dictated by the very latest weather and coastal reports. As they say in Ireland, if you don't like the weather, wait a moment.

Colm sat beside the pilot, a sheaf of weather telexes clipped to his diary, his constant companion. He was unfamiliar with the characteristics of occluded fronts and such like. The pilot interpreted for him.

'Clearer weather is coming down from the north. If I were you, I'd go north over this cloud first and then drop to a low altitude for their cameras.'

Colm nodded. It was good advice.'OK. Take her up and head for Inishowen.' The helicopter flailed through the layer of cloud and broke into a bright pink dawn glow. Colm turned to the Russians.

'We'll begin the real sightseeing in about an hour. By that time the cloud will have cleared where we're going.' The Russians nodded. The pilot rolled his eyes. He hadn't guaranteed absence of cloud over the hills and mountains of County Donegal.

Conversation lapsed. Some caught up on sleep. Flying over a fluffy carpet of cloud was soporific, except for the pilot, who noted with satisfaction that the cloud layer was floating higher in the atmosphere as he flew north. He could entertain the hope that the cloud ceiling beneath would soon clear the mountain tops.

'We've arrived.'

On the pilot's announcement Colm Fitzroy scowled at the cloud. 'Are you going down into that?' he asked dubiously.

'We're just about over the coast. Don't worry. We're quite high and I'm not going to hit anything.' The pilot was still smiling when he dropped the Alouette into almost zero visibility and into the path of a radar-invisible projectile.

9

They were not granted the mercy of a quick death. The deafening bang, the racing of the engine, the dizzy rotation of the cabin, the screams of those who could gulp in the blast of cold air, the centrifugal force pinning them, the glimpsed blurs of sea, land and rock.

It was a hell which seemed to last an eternity. Tarasov mouthed a woman's name in what he knew were the last seconds of life.

The final smash on a hillside. Silence. Until a lark continued its briefly interrupted song.

TWO

No air. Except in the bubbles. Panic. Remember the training. The training in water.

Stukalin gasped for breath as each north Atlantic wave momentarily swamped his goldfishing mouth. He controlled his breathing until his battered senses recalled the buoyancy aid round his neck. He pulled its inflation cord. His head now remained above the water and the remnants of panic began to subside.

His eyes focused on the automatic radio-rescue beacon, its aerial radiating signals on the international distress frequency. He swore.

Flailing his arms, now hampered by the flotation collar round his neck, he wallowed and thrashed towards the bobbing transmitter. When the high-whip aerial came within his grasp he yanked it horizontal and snapped it off cleanly at the base. From one of the pockets of his clinging grey overall, he wrenched out a knife and savagely breached the radio's waterproof casing. It sank, to his evident satisfaction.

Only then did he strike out towards the beach a few hundred metres away. Beneath the closely cropped hair, his face was grim and determined, with no residue of earlier mental disarray. It was the face of a commander who had taken command of himself. It was also the face of a man who was grateful for an unusually calm sea and for the dawn of a warm spring day.

He staggered up the long beach, his eyes professionally surveying the sparse heather-clad hills dotted with abandoned cottages. One of them would give him cover and respite while he thought about what to do next.

The receding splash of the waves gave way to rising birdsong as he progressed. There were no sounds of alarm and no sounds of curiosity, like a car or tractor engine.

'I can't be that lucky,' he thought as he scrambled through the gorse. 'Somebody must have seen what happened.'

Stukalin wasn't sure where he was. He had never heard of the Inishowen peninsula at the very north of the Republic of Ireland. It was a lonely place. That much he was already learning.

The stone remains of the cottage walls were evidence of what had been a solitary lifestyle for some peasant farmer and his family a generation or more ago. Grass-covered furrows showed where the soil had once been tilled in a field now given over to sheep-grazing. There was no obvious evidence that anybody had visited the place recently, so the Major relaxed a little.

He badly need to unwind. The tension of re-entry had just been subsiding when his airbreathing jet engine exhausted its fuel. He had been prepared for a crash landing, but had not been prepared for the collision.

At first he sat at the base of a wall, the victim of an inactive fatalism brought about by exhaustion and shock. But the peace and beauty of his surroundings began a quiet process of recuperation. By mid-morning he had garnered enough confidence to strip and wash his clothes free of sea-salt in the little stream trickling past a roofless house, which had become his hiding place.

His growing feeling of security admitted his bruised body to slumber, curled up like a cat in hay under warm sunshine.

A noise! His eyes opened wide. Every muscle snapped to attention, his security and his sleep ruptured by a sound instantly identified by his subconscious. It was the swishing pounding of helicopter blades approaching at low level.

In a split second he was on his feet, scrambling for a corner of the stonework. Against the outer wall was a pile of peat, covered with a tarpaulin. It was too late to retrieve the overalls and underclothing, incongruously and conspicuously laid out to dry beside a house with no roof.

He cursed his carelessness and covered as much of himself as he could with the tarpaulin. A searching helicopter could hardly fail to detect the signs of his presence.

The rhythmic beating, the high-pitched whine and the loud thundering seemed to stand still in the air. But it was an illusion, for the helicopter neither slackened speed nor changed direction as it flew almost overhead. He stared after it in disbelief as the machine followed the contours of the land until it breasted the hill on the far side of the glen. It disappeared from both his sight and his hearing.

Dumbfounded, the Major gathered his partially dry clothing into a bundle and hid it. After a few moments of bewildered thought, he retrieved most of it and dressed.

While he did so, he tried to make sense of the helicopter incident. He hadn't recognized the markings, but he didn't need to. They were not British. 'Irish flyers must have Braille instruments,' he muttered.

The relief was momentary. Questions for which he had no answer flooded his mind. How were Headquarters and Control reacting to his disappearance? How much did they know about what had happened to him? What was he expected to do now?

He knew that he must not force their hand. If Control wanted to tell the Irish of his presence, that must be their decision, not his. So far, it appeared they had not done so, or the beach below him would by now be swarming with people and the helicopter would have landed on top of him.

If he was right, then he should rid himself of identification and identifying possessions. The labels of his clothing, his footwear, his pens, even the pencil torch all testified against him.

Only now did the Major began to think seriously about the next move. First, he thought, must be reconnaissance. Silence had fallen once more on a landscape of stone-walled fields patterned on hill and mountain. There was no sign of life, except perhaps below him where a large caravan was parked on a grassy patch near the beach, half a kilometre away. Nobody approached it or left it. As far as he could see it was deserted.

He was also waiting. In the distance he occasionally heard a tractor, a church bell, an airliner. Sometimes he heard the receding sound of the helicopter. He waited for a search that never materialized. Maybe the plane had been radar-invisible, but he wasn't yet convinced beyond all doubt.

The evening fell slowly, just as it did at home. He began to move. The sky was clear and the bright moonlight was annoying, although it helped his progress towards the caravan. He lay still for a long time beside the dry-stone wall near the caravan, just close enough to sense any slight movement or sound. When he was satisfied, he quickly and expertly broke through the window above the towbar.

His first find, by the light of his pen torch, was a windfall. It was a tourist map of Ireland, which he spread on the table. The Major began examining the map and placed upon it what navigators call the circle of probability – an imaginary circle within which his position probably lay. Electronics working from satellite signals had revolutionized naviga-tion to the point where, if Stukalin had been carrying one of his own military instruments, it would have registered his position change if he'd walked the length of the caravan.

For thousands of years navigators had dreamed of such magic as they struggled with circles of probability sometimes hundreds of miles across. As Stukalin's navigation instruc-tor had put it: when Columbus set out he had little idea where he was going, on arrival he didn't know where he

was and when he returned he didn't know where he had
been . . .

Stukalin was better placed after his own Atlantic crossing.
Despite large patches of cloud cover, he had been able to fix
his line of travel from his vantage point on high. If he had
kept to the emergency plan, if the second misfortune hadn't
occurred, he could have crossed Scotland after skirting the
northern-most point of Ireland.

He had already narrowed his position to an area covering
the western isles of Scotland and the very north of Ireland
before seeing the markings on the helicopter. He was on
the north Irish coast – in the Republic of Ireland rather than
British-controlled Northern Ireland.

That was good luck. He was aware that the British were
fighting in Northern Ireland and he had no intention of getting mixed up in that mess. Fighting armies were alert armies, with informer networks which made hiding harder.
He knew that from his own experience in Afghanistan.

The small torch beam roved over the map's unfamiliar
shapes and words. He picked out roads, railways, main
towns, Dublin the capital, and the land frontier with
Northern Ireland. But the map couldn't tell him exactly
which part of the coast he was on. All he could do at this
stage was learn place names, and the shapes of headlands
and sea inlets, so that when he saw any of them later, he
could pinpoint his position.

Obviously he would have to travel south towards Dublin
and the Soviet Embassy. He couldn't risk telephoning on the
assumption that all lines to his country's diplomatic mission
would be tapped and he might have to describe his predica-
ment openly to a doubting duty officer.

Then something caught his eye on the map, closer to the
north coast than Dublin. A pictogram of an aircraft and beside it the word 'Shannon'. He moved the light to the bottom
of the map to pick out the scale.

An airport. Only a hundred and sixty kilometres away.
He frowned. The name was familiar to him, which meant

that it must either be a military field, or perhaps a fully equipped passenger facility.

His face changed as he brought a clenched fist crashing down on the table, which collapsed under the blow. Hissing his exasperation, he flung himself onto a seat.

The old doubts about the scientists' claims had returned. Very small radar signature was how they put it, especially from dead-ahead. Shannon approach radar would have been illuminating the plane in profile, which presented the largest return radar signal.

He looked out at the sea. The moon was reflected in a stream of silvery light on its surface, pointing fingers of radiance into little bays, capturing little islands in silhouette.

As he stared he repeated the word 'Shannon' to himself again and again. Why did he know that place? He would have recognized only a few place names from Ireland, like Dublin, Belfast, or Derry because they occurred in news items about IRA fighting and tortuous Irish politics.

Shannon, Shannon, Shannon.

He pocketed packet soups from one of the cupboards, then a tin of condensed milk. His mind turned momentarily to food: what he really wanted was fresh food, and the smell of good cooking. No tins, no packets.

Cuba! A flight plan to Cuba. That was where he'd seen Shannon listed. Flights from Moscow to Havana stopped at Shannon to refuel and resupply. More important, the planes stopped at Shannon on the return journey, so there was an Aeroflot office at Shannon with a direct flight to Moscow at its disposal.

He pounced on the map again. Yes, it was feasible to travel there. There would be friendly faces at Shannon, secure communications and a speedy, smuggled passage on a plane home. At last the Major began to believe that he could escape fast enough for his data to be useful.

There was a new lightness in his touch as he opened the remaining cupboards of the caravan. A final discovery presented him with a decision.

Should he arm himself? Under one of the bunks lay a double barrelled shotgun. He picked it up and examined it. The barrel could detach from the stock, so he could carry it inconspicuously in two pieces. Inside one chamber was a single cartridge and he could find no more ammunition.

He made his decision. Then, with renewed vigour, he set about disguising himself. Drawing once more on the resources of the caravan, he pulled on a pair of slacks from the musty wardrobe, an old shirt which had been rolled in a ball, a jacket that smelt of fish, a shapeless light raincoat and a battered pair of training shoes. Except for the shoes, none of the clothes was a good fit. He deftly detached the barrel of the shotgun from the stock. That way it could be hidden in the folds of the coat.

In the middle of the floor he made a pile of his outer clothing, his papers, his plastic identity card, and his knife — everything in his pockets that bore his own name or that of his organization. On a shelf beside the cooker he had found a packet of cigarettes and matches. He broke one of the cigarettes in half, lit it and placed it inside the box of matches. When the glowing tip reached the match-heads, there would be a flare.

His final act before leaving the caravan was to open all the gas taps on the cooker and on the wall lights. He was well away when the fireball lit up the bay, obliterating the tracks of test pilot Petr Fedorovich Stukalin. Soviet Air Force Major. Cosmonaut. Fugitive.

Three thousand miles away from the Inishowen peninsula and on the other side of the north Atlantic, an Irishman called Faloon glanced up at the departure lounge clock yet again.

Faloon was agitated. Any minute now the shuttle flight from Washington DC to New York would close. There would be another flight in an hour, but he wanted to be in New York for early evening. Where the hell was Sarah?

At first glance Faloon didn't look European. In his

particular line of business, distinctiveness in appearance didn't pay dividends. During the past months, Faloon had begun to like the Americans and many things American. The shoes, for example, in which he now paced impatiently, were no longer the delicate Italian slip-ons he once wore. He now favoured a heavy brogue. But not in speech. In speech, he now favoured longer vowels.

The fact that the American men seemed better shod than Europeans perplexed Faloon. Americans walked only to and from their cars.

So Faloon was in the process of assimilating the best of Stateside taste with that of the European. His monogrammed shirt, restrained tie, well-cut sports jacket with toning slacks gave him the air of a junior White House aide leaving Washington DC for a weekend's pleasure in New York.

Faloon was, of course, looking in the wrong direction when the shrill female voice yelled, 'Faloon!' He spun on his heel to greet the woman.

She was roughly the same age as Faloon, about thirty, with dark curly hair, a bit like Faloon's. Her sober dress and marching gait signalled that she was an executive working woman in authority somewhere. Beside the tall Faloon she appeared smaller than she really was.

'For chrissake Sarah,' bellowed Faloon. 'You're always late. Procrastinating woman.' He bent down and grabbed her suitcase, pushing her towards the air bridge to the aircraft.

Sarah was unrepentant. 'There you go again. Using big words to make us poor Americans feel inferior. Anyway that's no way to speak to your boss in public.'

He fished for the tickets and shepherded her through the gate, relief written all over his face, amusement written all over hers.

Only one passenger remained in the departure lounge after Sarah and Faloon had left. He got up, walked past the gate and stood at the window looking at the plane at the ramp.

'The flight is closing now, sir'.

'I'll catch the next one. I'm waiting for someone. Must've been caught in the traffic,' the man replied to the stewardess without taking his eyes from the plane. When he saw the aircraft begin to taxi, he left the lounge quickly and stopped at a phone. He punched a New York number.

'They're just leaving. No delays so far.'

'OK,' said the voice at the other end and rang off immediately.

Faloon grumbled as the plane climbed. He was uncomfortable. They had not been able to get seats beside the emergency exits with the leg room Faloon liked. He gripped his nose between his finger and thumb and blew, making his cheeks puff and his eyes bulge. 'Have a sweet, you big Paddy. It's better for pressurization than making yourself look like a rare tropical fish.'

'Don't call me that.'

'A tropical fish?'

'You know what I mean . . .'

She grinned and resumed poking about in the box of chocolates he had uncharacteristically given her.

Faloon's name had always given him trouble in the US. He didn't like his first name, and wouldn't let anybody in the FBI use it. Everybody tried Paddy, but usually only once. Faloon loathed being called Paddy and he was big enough to make his preference stick.

In the FBI files he was listed as Patrick Faloon, seconded, parent department, G2 Dublin, Irish Republic. Generally speaking, first names were used in FBI circles, so when confronted by someone who appeared to hate his first name, the whole office had a problem. Faloon hadn't been much help in the beginning. He said he wasn't a Paddy, and wouldn't supply an alternative.

The FBI was not without its resources in such matters. Over the teleprinter circuit to the G2 building in Dublin had gone a simple enquiry, agency to agency, using a diplomatic code.

'What first name do you call your man Faloon if you don't

want your nose broken? Answer soonest. Illegal Alien Dept. FBI. Wash. DC.'

Back came the Irish capital. 'Two rules about Faloon. Rule one: On everyday occasions, call Faloon Faloon. Rule Two: On all other occasions, refer to Rule One. Personnel Section. G2. Dublin.'

Faloon looked out of the window as the aircraft emerged into the bright sunshine above the clouds. Mentally he was opening his palms and counting to ten. He was not going to give Sarah the satisfaction of needling him with the 'Paddy' purely to divert attention from the fact that she'd almost caused them both to miss the plane.

So he set his features into a hint of a smile and projected his thoughts far away in space and time. It was easy to slip back into that raucous smoky Friday night pub near the Dublin office, downing pints of Guinness.

A distortion of nostalgia. In reality, there had been few Friday nights of carefree revelry after a week in the office. The pub faded, driven out by images of the things he might really have been doing on a Friday night in Ireland as a member of G2.

The country had been partitioned over sixty years ago after a dirty guerrilla war against the British. In Northern Ireland the IRA Provos – terrorists or freedom fighters depending on the point of view – were fighting to take the last six counties of Northern Ireland out of Britain and into the independent Republic of Ireland.

The fact that most of the people in those six counties did not want to become part of a united Ireland complicated things for everyone, including Faloon and G2. In its constitution, Ireland laid claim to Northern Ireland, but there was little a nation of three and a half million people could do to make good the claim. An invasion into British Northern Ireland by the small Irish army was out of the question.

Over the years therefore, successive Dublin govern- ments granted Northern Ireland a *de facto* recognition

19

while maintaining the claim to jurisdiction. This infuriated extreme nationalists, from whose ranks emerged the Provos, or Provisional IRA, dedicated to the violent overthrow of British rule in Ireland. However, it meant that if the British government was the Provos' number one enemy, the 'quisling and puppet' Irish government was their enemy number two.

If the situation in the Republic of Ireland had remained merely a war of words, then G2 would have continued with casual sentry duty. After all, what happened across the border in Northern Ireland was not of immediate concern. Until the inevitable happened. The Provos needed arms, explosives and money to fuel their war against the British and pro-British Irish. But stealing them in Northern Ireland became increasingly difficult as effective counter-measures came into force. The police and army were everywhere. So the IRA Provos began pillaging south of the border, raiding on soft targets in the Irish Republic itself.

They raided Irish quarries for explosives, robbed Irish armouries for weapons, held up Irish banks for money and when they encountered resistance, began killing Irish policemen and soldiers – all in the name of Ireland. Suddenly in Dublin, counter-insurgency became a priority.

Sleepy G2 shook itself and began recruiting new men who demanded new strategies, new equipment and new methods.

Faloon had been taken from the final year university class of Trinity College, Dublin, to an old house about thirty miles outside the capital. In this secluded place the new G2 had lectured him, played games with him, let him be an overgrown boy scout, teased him, frightened him, and allowed him to get drunk while they recorded what he said.

At different times, they saw Faloon as the man out front, sometimes the man who could hardly be seen, Faloon the loud-mouth, Faloon the whisperer, Faloon the talker, Faloon the listener, Faloon the clown. Then the enforcer. Then the executioner. Faloon was the completely credible actor and that quality made him consistently effective in the field. His reputation grew, as did the list of his enemies in the ranks of the IRA Provos.

'Chocolate?'

Faloon turned away from the window back to Sarah. 'Sorry. I was miles away.'

Sarah looked at him severely. 'I hope you weren't thinking of that old emerald sod again, were you? You're supposed to be thinking of the dirty weekend ahead, which I've helped you fix on FBI expenses.'

He looked about him with mock apprehension. 'Quiet,' he hissed. 'This plane is bugged and the passenger list riddled with CIA.'

'Why is it that the only time you are serious is when you are not speaking?' she said. 'And when I ask for your thoughts, I get a load of blarney. That's Irish for bullshit.'

'OK OK. I was dreaming. I think I'm frustrated.'

Sarah smiled and put her head on his shoulder. 'Good. That's a condition this weekend is designed to relieve.'

He took a chocolate but began speaking before it reached his mouth. 'No, Sarah, now I'm serious. I've been over in the US for nine months and what have I done? I've sat behind a bloody desk day in and day out. I'm getting soft.'

'Don't exaggerate, Faloon. There aren't all that many files that you haven't closed satisfactorily. My reports on you so far have been glowing.' She scanned him proprietorially.

Faloon laughed. He knew that if it had not been for her skilful handling he might have cut short the year's secondment. G2 had sent him for a year to Washington to learn about the use of computer systems in the Federal Bureau of Investigation.

He had greeted the initial offer of a year in America with open arms, quickly reverting to suspicion and alarm when told he had to sit at a desk and bring back hands-on experience of 'information technology' as it applied to the world of terrorism and counter-terrorism.

Sarah smiled and munched a chocolate. She was accustomed to these occasional outbursts of protest against hours at the keyboard and masses of printout.

'Anyway,' she continued, 'am I right in thinking you have a lap-held down there, and a cuddly little modem to go with it?'

Faloon pulled a face and made a playful attempt at slapping her hand. A 'lap-held' was a standard issue small portable computer and a modem was a smaller device for connecting it to any telephone. With the modem, the computer could be connected to any computer in the world – as long as the entry codes were known, and, of course, as long as the other computer was also connected to the phone. Very useful indeed.

Sarah was poking fun at Faloon because his conversion to the devices had reached the point where he felt naked without one. But he did not like being reminded of the fact.

The captain interrupted to tell everybody he was going to fly round thunder clouds. Faloon and Sarah looked through the window at the towering anvils of vapour and snapped on their belts. Neither of them particularly liked flying.

'You seemed to change your attitude to computers quite suddenly, Faloon. You weren't the easiest guy to lead to a keyboard. Mind if I ask at what point on the road to Damascus you saw the light?'

'The phone. That's what did it.'

'I'm not sure I'm with you.'

'When I connected an FBI box of chips to a British box of chips on the others side of the Atlantic with an ordinary phone line, I began to see the light.'

There was a moment's silence as the import of Faloon's words made their impact on Sarah, as they were meant to. Sarah was frowning in earnest. 'You mean you used British data to help smash the Green Boys?' Her face had lost its sparkle. Now she was both angry and puzzled. 'But the files you threw up on screen were all US origination.' She looked at him with mounting suspicion.

'They are now. Just call them a present to Uncle Sam from John Bull through the good offices of a leprechaun.'

She exploded. 'Faloon! What have you been doing? We've specific agreements with the British on the exchange of computer data and you know that.'

Sarah's face was flushed. She was a section leader with an unblemished record and good prospects of promotion. She had just learnt that the piratical Faloon had stolen British secrets, albeit in the good cause of uncovering a cell of Irish Americans running arms over to Ireland for the Provos.

'Somebody's going to have my ass for this,' she said with her index finger stabbing in Faloon's direction like a hand gun. 'To tap into British files unauthorized is bad enough. To do it for data they might have given us above board is fucking crazy.'

Faloon shook his head confidently. 'They won't be able to trace the leak. At least not easily. I did it with a lap-held from outside the FBI, then transferred the files from the lap-held into the Bureau's Big Daddy computer. When you access those files from here on, you'll find the additional data credited to me here in New York or Boston. Not from anywhere else, like England.'

Sarah wasn't looking at Faloon now. Her mouth was set as straight as a steel rule. 'I said why didn't you simply ask the Brits?'

In his most superior manner he replied, 'I did, in a manner of speaking.' As he spoke, he leaned over to take another chocolate from the box on her lap. She snapped the lid shut and stared very coldly at him. A symbolic act, thought Faloon. He had better change tack if he wanted the box to open.

The captain interrupted again through his treble speaker to say they were about to land at New York's LaGuardia airport, where it was raining.

Faloon turned to bring his mouth alongside Sarah's ear. He smelt her perfume, her hair and her body. He lowered his chin to feel the rise and fall of her breathing.

23

No reaction.

'Sarah, did you hear about the Pan Am pilot coming into Shannon?'

He paused. Still no reaction.

Imitating the accent and tone of their captain, he intoned, 'Ladies and gentlemen. We are about to land at Shannon. Please fasten your seatbelts, extinguish your cigarettes and put your watches back fifty years.'

No reaction at all. Maybe she'd heard it before.

A man stood impatiently on the ground, watching through the rain for the jet to drop out of the low cloud.

THREE

Slieve Snaght is the highest land on the triangular Inishowen peninsula. Halfway up it sat Major Stukalin, relaxing on a smooth rock in the warm sunshine.

In front of him he had spread the tourist map. Beyond the map stood a large curious sheep with an untidy splash of red marker dye on its back. The stranger and the animal eyed each other. Slowly the Major executed a shallow military bow, an impish grin on his face.

'Greetings, my red woolly friend. Greetings from the Central Committee of the Union of Soviet Socialist Republics, the Ministers and Presidium of the Supreme Soviet, not forgetting the Academy of Sciences.'

The beast bolted and the Major feigned insulted pride. Despite the traumatic events of the last twenty-four hours and the physical demands made upon him, his spirits were high. During his first night on the move he had not travelled far, preferring to halt when the lights of a large village appeared both ahead and below him. He wanted to plan before moving further.

The new dawn spilled shafts of orange and gold along the pleats of the hills all around him. He looked back towards the north and saw far below, not more than five miles away, the beach that had been his introduction to Ireland. From this distance, there was little to distinguish it from the dozens of others nestling between majestic rocky headlands. Only the Russian knew why that particular bay had become unique.

From this vantage point the stranger could pick out coastal shapes and match them to the map. He now knew precisely where he was. The Inishowen peninsula.

The spine of the peninsula was a line of bald hills down the east side, hiding the eastern shore and the land beyond, which was British territory. From the map Stukalin could see that he was within ten miles of the border. At all costs, he reminded himself, he must stay within the jurisdiction of the Irish state.

The soft, heather-perfumed air filled his lungs and with that came renewed gratitude for being alive. There had been moments when he believed he had seen his last dawn, so this one he savoured with almost spiritual intensity.

No trees, he thought. None except for geometric man-made patches of conifers. He was thankful that the Irish seemed to have cut down most of their native trees. This simplified cross-country navigation, as long as the good weather continued. With that thought in mind, he looked to the west and saw a horizon of hills shrouded in mist and rain. The wind was westerly, so the present bright sunshine would not last. He estimated that he had about an hour, perhaps ninety minutes, of good weather left. A maritime pattern of changeable weather was not what he was accustomed to, but his predictions nevertheless would be accurate.

Stukalin was optimistic and turned his attention once more to the map, doggedly determined to cover the hundred or so miles to Shannon Airport. But his optimism did not displace a realistic recognition of his plight. He cursed his unpreparedness; he was less at home than the sheep he had just talked to. He wondered how he was going to reach

Shannon fast. There was no rail link, which would have been his first preference.

Major Stukalin did a profit-and-loss account of his position. Against him was his lack of local knowledge, and the fact that he had had to steal and destroy. Those activities would leave a track. His English was good, but the map told him that there would be an Irish variant which might prove difficult – how on earth was Slieve Snaght pronounced? He had been taught to speak English with an American accent. Finally, as a man with some sense of style, he knew that he probably looked a bit odd in his hastily acquired wardrobe.

On the credit side, he became increasingly convinced that the Irish did not know what had happened and were therefore unaware of his presence. There was still no sign of unusual high-level search activity. The helicopter was back in the early morning air, but nearly always along the same route. In other words, it was not conducting a search.

A cloud passed over Stukalin's face. He knew why the helicopter was in the air. There would be investigators who would eventually discover enough to begin a search. But for the moment, he had a head start.

He also had a gun, which, with its single cartridge, would be a weapon of last resort. The advantage for Stukalin would lie in its possession, not its discharge. He carefully folded the map and headed towards the road below him. He had thought of a plan.

Stukalin was now in a hurry. Keeping to the walls of fields, he headed towards the road. The ground was sometimes rock, sometimes peaty bog. Time and time again he found himself sinking almost to his knees, bringing progress to a temporary halt. To make up time, he ran where he could, his eyes on a road intersection below.

He should have kept his eyes on the ground. He missed the rabbit hole with his eye – but not with his foot. The hole tumbled him to the ground, twisting his ankle badly.

Grimacing in pain, he instantly realized that his options were reduced further. The plan he had formulated high on the hillside would need to work first time, because overland travel on foot was no longer a realistic option.

Sometimes crawling, often hopping, he cut straight for the nearest part of road. His first idea had been to wait for a car to stop at the junction he had seen from further up the slope. The junction would have either slowed or stopped a vehicle, giving him time to examine it and its occupants before pouncing.

The twisted ankle meant that it would take too long to reach the junction. Time was not his ally. He would have to take the first car that presented itself. Ideally he wanted a car with only one compliant person in it.

He scrambled as best he could over the wire-net sheep fence by the side of the road. The single strand of barbed wire on the top tore his clothes and made him bleed.

Would the people of these parts be curious enough to stop if they saw an unshaven man in a torn coat, with blood from scratches dripping from his fingertips, with his lower parts liberally covered in black mud, standing on one leg, using a shotgun as a crutch? The Major decided not to leave it to chance.

He hobbled back along the road to examine something he had seen from the hillside with his scavenger's eye. It was the discarded remains of an old bicycle lying in the overgrown bottom of a ditch. It had no saddle or front wheel, but it remained recognizable as a bicycle.

He heaved and tugged. The undergrowth of years was reluctant to part with it. When it was free, he cleaned away most of the remaining vegetation and set the rusty relic in the middle of the road. Stukalin then draped himself across it in a manner that served to hide the fact that the front wheel was missing.

Finally, he dabbed blood from his fingers over his forehead and placed the shotgun in his right hand, hidden under the half-open coat.

Then he waited.

Insofar as he had a choice, he had selected a point in the

road where it dipped between two small rises, allowing an oncoming driver enough time to stop before hitting him, but not enough to allow long examination. Stukalin wanted the driver to jump to the conclusion that a man had fallen from his bicycle and was hurt.

The rusty old machine made an uncomfortable bed as Stukalin lay on it, waiting for the sound of an engine. For a long time, all he heard was the wind in the gorse bushes and the baying of sheep, sounding like mocking laughter. The clouds were gathering above him. He shivered. Were there no people in this God-forsaken place?

Then he heard it. The unmistakable sound of a car travelling south towards him – the direction he wanted. He made final, unnecessary adjustments to his position and gripped the shotgun near the base of its stock. This meant he could wield the weapon single-handedly like a pistol.

The car appeared over the rise. The Major slipped off the safety catch and hung his head, as if in a daze.

He watched tensely and surreptitiously. A small green saloon with at least two people in it began to slow down.

It came to a halt a cautious distance from the apparent accident.

Good, thought the Major. The condition of the bicycle would not be so obvious from that distance. For a moment nothing more happened. The Major began moving with a slight rocking motion as if in pain. He dipped his head as further evidence of distress and the people left his field of vision.

But it seemed they were taking stock, which was not what he had expected. They should by now have sprung from the car, instinctively eager to help an accident victim.

'Come on, come on,' he urged under his breath.

Stukalin could hear the car engine on tick-over and above it, the sound of discussion. The words stopped. The car doors opened, both together. Two sets of footsteps were approaching. They would soon see the suspicious state of the bicycle. It had to be now.

Very suddenly he sat up, whipping the gun from its hiding place.

'Stop.' His voice rang the command loud and clear. The word echoed into the hills. 'Don't move. Not a muscle. If you move I will shoot and at this distance with this type of gun I cannot miss.'

They were a couple in their mid-twenties. The man had unkempt hair, an open necked shirt over which he wore a sweater and a shapeless brown jacket. Blue jeans completed his garb. The woman was slimmer and more stylish. She too wore jeans, tight fitting, as was her black high-necked jumper. On her feet were short, leather boots.

Both did as they were told. Neither spoke as Stukalin climbed painfully to his feet – or more accurately, to his foot. Lying on the ground for so long without moving had stiffened his body, and his ankle was badly swollen. He moved away from the old bicycle towards the side of the road to lean against a fence-post. The road must be cleared quickly before another car turned up.

'You,' he barked at the man and pointed at the bicycle, 'move that back to the ditch.'

The man moved slowly forward, never taking his eyes off the gun, held in one hand and following his movement, pointing low. The man stopped at the bicycle but made no move to pick it up.

The Major looked at his eyes and saw danger. The young man was not afraid. He was calculating, just like Stukalin himself.

The plane banked and turned in the thick cloud, its engines rising and falling in pitch as it positioned for its final approach to New York's LaGuardia airport.

Faloon hated being in a plane when it was flying in mushroom soup. He hated putting that much trust in instruments, especially when flying into somewhere with buildings sticking up over a thousand feet.

Normally he would have struck up a conversation with his neighbour to cover his nervousness, but the smouldering Sarah was ignoring him. He thought she was over-reacting to the little matter of his burglary of British computer files.

Too much imagination. That was what the G2 instructors had told him during initial training. If you want to use that imagination of yours, they'd shouted at him, then imagine what your enemy might do — and do it to him first. But Faloon never discovered how to command his imagination.

In the end, the instructors accepted Faloon as he was. They suspected that the idiosyncratic Faloon mind, which occasionally made him a menace to his friends, would always be a menace to his enemies. Sarah had yet to learn that fact. She had only seen Faloon behind a desk learning to use a computer and its stupendous ability to sift information. It was an unfamiliar environment for a man who hitherto had ranged free, crawled through ditches, staked out lonely farmhouses, and occasionally extinguished lives when he had to.

That was something Sarah had never seen. Faloon's deep unassuageable and cold anger. One day she would see it. Briefly. In the meantime, for Sarah, Faloon was an attractive hunk to hang on her arm. That was why she was travelling to New York with him, why she had manufactured professional circumstances which required them both to be in New York over a weekend.

It had not been too difficult for Sarah to convince her own boss that there were loose ends to tie up after Faloon's excellent work against the Green Boys and their gun-running to Ireland. Perhaps the boss suspected what she really had in mind, but thought she deserved a break. In the FBI, it was easier to give her that kind of break than a bonus.

The plane sank from the cloud over the grey waters of the harbour, which yielded only at the last moment of the flight into concrete and runway. Faloon saw that the arrival had begun to thaw Sarah. She was still ignoring his verbal advances but she did hand him her luggage and allowed him to drape her raincoat over her shoulders. That was communication of a sort and would suffice for the moment.

It was good to be back in New York. It was Faloon's kind of city.

'Stay here a moment,' she ordered, breaking the silence. 'I'm going to freshen up.' She stalked off towards a lavatory.

'Have a pee while you're in there,' he joked, instantly regretting opening his mouth as she turned her flame-thrower expression on him. She disappeared into one of the lavatories off the large concourse.

Faloon, ever active, scanned for something to occupy his mind. That was when the car inside the concourse caught his attention. It looked like a vintage convertible Mercedes, immaculate in its two-tone chocolate paintwork, chromed wire wheels, exhaust pipework and large headlamps. A splendid machine displayed expensively and incongruously on carpet beside a shoe-shine boy and a cigarette machine.

The car turned out to be neither a Mercedes nor old; it was a clever replica made by fitting fibreglass panels over a modern chassis and engine. Faloon inspected it at close quarters and thought of his own real sports car, chocked up on blocks in his garage in Dublin. He stepped over the dainty cotton rope fence, threw his baggage into the rear, and himself behind the steering wheel.

Faloon was a purist in the matter of vintage cars and had little regard for replicas. He had to admit, though, that the workmanship was impeccable and the whole effect quite amusing. It had a wooden steering wheel, proper, round dials set in a veneered dashboard, vertically pleated hide-seating, rear-view mirrors everywhere. There was a mirror on the far-side windscreen, the middle of the screen and the near-side screen to give the driver cinemascopic view of where he had just been.

He could see the door of the ladies' lavatory. Sitting comfortably in real leather was a better way to keep watch for Sarah's reappearance than kicking his heels around that

31

door, just like the guy leaning against the lavatory wall reading a magazine.

The hint of a smirk fell from Faloon's face. Maintaining his watch in the mirrors, he had seen the man with the magazine lower it and stare for a few seconds straight at the car.

The man's eyes had focused directly upon the back of Faloon's neck. After a few seconds, he had slowly raised the magazine to hide his face once more.

Faloon pondered. The fake Mercedes was very conspicuous. Even more conspicuous when a passing traveller was trying it for size. The man's interest was normal, not abnormal, Faloon chided himself.

The door of the ladies room opened and Sarah emerged a few steps. The man with the magazine did not lower it from his face.

Why? Faloon wondered.

If the man had been waiting for his own woman to emerge, of course he would have looked at the person who came through the door. Faloon decided to sit still and watch.

Sarah too remained still, her head moving from side to side in search of her man. Inevitably, the car also caught her attention and then she saw Faloon. With a look heavenward to ask God to give her patience, she headed towards him.

At that point, the man lowered the magazine, then deftly slung it into a litter bin. Faloon watched him, knowing he had only seconds to do so unobtrusively. He was probably in his early thirties, with short ginger hair and moustache, wearing a black leather jacket, corduroy trousers and black calf-length boots. Why calf-length boots? Odd attire for air travel.

'Faloon! How did you expect me to find you. You're not supposed to do that.' She seized a small notice board and turned it round to face him. Faloon wheeled as if surprised at her sudden appearance. The notice board in her hand read in big capital letters, 'Do Not Touch'.

'Put that notice down, Sarah. Can't you read that you're

not supposed to touch it.' She had to laugh and the chill in their relations evaporated, which pleased Faloon enormously. He might need her full co-operation in the next few minutes.

They both set off towards a news stand and selected a newspaper. He stopped and pretended to be studying a rack of magazines.

'One of us is being followed, Sarah.'

She looked at him with the smile still on her face. Then the smile faltered. The joke had gone. Faloon's grip on her arm had lost its gentleness.

'Faloon,' she began slowly and deliberately, 'don't fly off the handle when I say what I'm about to say. You've been backrooming it now for much of a year and I know you feel more at home in the rough and tumble outside offices. Isn't it just possible that you're imagining things?'

'That's possible, Sarah. So let's set up a little test.'

'What kind of test?' she asked dubiously.

'We'll walk towards the exit near the cabs and go through the door. Just outside, we'll stop.'

'Oh don't be stupid, Faloon. I'll guarantee a dozen people follow us through the doors. Want me to arrest them?'

Faloon ignored her sarcasm. 'On my cue, we will suddenly turn back inside as if we've forgotten something. You head for the Eastern Airlines inquiry desk over there and ask them something.'

'Meanwhile you'll be arresting a dozen people. Is that it?'

Faloon was not rising to the bait. He continued his instructions. 'I'm splitting from you and will end up over there at the phones.'

'What am I supposed to do?'

'Stay near that airline desk. That'll look natural and give you a chance to look for the man I think is following us.'

At last Sarah remained silent. She did not ask how she was supposed to pick out the man.

'Luckily he's distinctive,' Faloon continued while thumbing his way through a magazine. 'Short reddish hair with a moustache to match, black jacket and big black boots. Got that?'

'Where did you see him? Are you sure . . .?' He cut her off.

'I'm sure of nothing. I'm going to find out whether or not I'm imagining things. That, my girl, is how I've lived this long. Let's go. You know what to do?'

She nodded affirmation, looking worried. Faloon took her chin in his large hand and guided her lips to his for a quick peck. 'Now smile. Part of our job is acting.'

She nodded again and after a pause, smiled uncertainly. Not great acting, thought Faloon as they turned towards the concourse, but it will suffice for the moment.

Faloon's eyes roamed in almost every direction without conveying an impression of urgency or concern. He picked up his quarry standing alongside the fake Mercedes, looking at it intently. The man did not cast so much as a glance in their direction as they headed for the exit.

The automatic glass doors opened before them and they were once more in the fresh air.

'Has he followed us?' asked Sarah, not daring to look around.

'Did you pick him out. He was over beside the car?'

'No.'

Damn, Faloon said to himself.

The next moves should reveal something. He squeezed her arm and they both turned at once and swept back through the terminal doors.

A few feet through the doors, coming towards them from the right, Sarah saw the ginger-haired man. She could not take her eyes from him.

Faloon jolted her with an exaggerated gesture and pointed out the Eastern Airlines desk, forcing her to look elsewhere. The man walked past them, through the doors and disappeared in the crowd outside.

34

Faloon and Sarah separated as planned.

Faloon was exasperated. All agents, whether destined for a lifetime at a desk or not, should be given some training in undercover techniques. The man with the ginger moustache might have picked up Sarah's inept interest. Faloon ran to another set of exit doors and went through them.

Remaining close to the wall, he slowly walked down the outside of the building towards the other exit doors where he had last seen the target. Clusters of travellers were looking for cabs or embarking upon large coaches. They gave Faloon cover as he cautiously made his way forward.

Faloon by now expected to see nothing of interest and his expectations were fulfilled. The man was nowhere to be seen.

He growled angrily and returned to Sarah at the airline desk, where she was playing her role passably well. She had picked Faloon out of the crowd. 'Well, Sarah,' he sighed. 'You did see the man.'

She was excited. 'I did, and he was exactly as you described. I saw him immediately as we came through the doors. Didn't you see him?'

Faloon looked at her to detect yet more sarcasm but there was none. An innocent abroad, thought Faloon, closing his eyelids and uttering an oath.

'The trick, my dear Sarah, is to see without looking. But he's not here now. Let's go.'

They shared a cab with two other people also going into Manhattan, so uninhibited conversation between them was impossible. In a way, Faloon was glad of the silence. It gave him a chance to savour one of the sights he would remember forever: the sun going down over Manhattan.

The thundershowers had cleared. Coming in from the east at the close of day presented that fabulous skyline of extraordinary buildings in silhouette against a flaming curtain. Sunsets usually reminded Faloon of home. This sight never did. Instead, it reminded him of the rest of the world, which was a good thing for most Irishmen.

Because of his big frame and long legs Faloon had been directed into the front passenger seat of the cab. He turned and smiled at Sarah, who smiled back. He threw a precautionary glance past her into the traffic stream behind, and saw nothing that alarmed him.

He turned in his seat and pulled down the sun visor. As he hoped, there was a vanity mirror on the back of it. He used it to keep a partial watch on following traffic. Sarah worked out what he was doing.

The other two passengers misunderstood. They glared at Sarah and at Faloon's back, believing that he was watching in case they interfered with his ladyfriend. The silence became a little oppressive. Faloon whistled a happy tune.

The cab drew up outside the Algonquin Hotel with only Faloon and Sarah as passengers. The others had been dropped off first. The driver let them pick up their own baggage from the back of the cab. Normally he would have been their willing porter but he figured that there was not going to be any large gratuity from a couple who had shared a cab from LaGuardia, notwithstanding the prestigious destination.

Sarah was in good form again. There was the evening in the city to look forward to and Faloon was good company in any city. Faloon was also in good form, despite a nagging worry about what had happened at the airport. It all could have been an overworked imagination feeding on the circumstantial.

The Algonquin in West 44th Street was Faloon's favourite address and he always tried to stay there when in New York. The FBI did not use the Algonquin for employees of Faloon's rank, or even Sarah's. But for Faloon it was worth the extra expense from his own pocket.

The red-brick façade and cast-iron bay windows hinted back to the twenties, when it was a literary salon of the city. Dorothy Parker and others had long since departed and the tastefully panelled lobby was now crowded with people like Faloon.

Businessmen and tourists still met to talk in its elegant

winged chairs, thus preserving a little of what had once been. And West 44th Street was a good street, home to the New York Yacht Club and the Harvard Club. In short, the area had the kind of style that Faloon liked.

When the cab driver saw the tip he had been given, commensurate with Faloon's annoyance at being seen to handle his own baggage outside such an establishment, he hurled an insult at the pair. Suddenly Faloon turned and ran back down the steps.

'Oh ignore the man, Faloon. You're not going to brawl on the street, are you?'

Faloon was not in the least concerned with the outraged driver. His total attention was directed at a motorcycle, accelerating away from them.

Astride it was a man in a black jacket and black calf-length boots.

FOUR

There were just the three of them on the lonely stretch of road along the bottom of the valley. Stukalin standing apart with the shotgun, the girl, motionless, and beside her the young man who was daring the stranger to shoot.

Stukalin knew that with only one cartridge, he had lost as soon as he pulled the trigger. He had to bluff. It was a card game. The Russian stared back unwaveringly into the eyes of the cool opponent, but he kept the barrel of the gun angled downward, held in one hand. 'If I pull the trigger,' he said with deliberation, 'the gun will jerk up to discharge into your stomach. Now move that bicycle fast before I run out of patience.'

Stukalin looked at the girl and back at the man, before continuing. 'I need transport. If I have to, I'll shoot both of you to get it. Now move the bicycle.'

The young man measured that threat. It wasn't the

words in the strangely precise American accent that alarmed him. It was the way the gun was held. An amateur would have the gun already pointed level at him. So whoever the older man was, the young man judged, he was dangerous.

So the young man capitulated and picked up the bicycle. He vented his defiance in the disgusted way he flung the rusty relic forcefully over the fence back into the field.

Stukalin felt the adrenalin in his system. He was beginning his journey home. 'Back to the car, both of you. I want you, sir, to drive. You will get into the driver's seat first. Then I will get into the back. And the woman will enter the front passenger seat last.'

As they walked back to the car, the Major spoke to the girl. 'Don't try to run off. I will simply shoot him, and then you.'

There was no reply and when they reached the car, they complied. The Major told them to drive south towards Buncrana, the place whose lights he had seen during the night.

As the hills rolled by, the Major estimated they would be at Shannon in a matter of hours. He turned to the woman. 'Give me your handbag and his wallet.'

The woman complied silently and handed over their possessions. From their driving licences Stukalin learnt that the man was Richard O'Donnell and the girl Moira Strain. Between them they had over two hundred and fifty pounds.

Lying at the bottom of the woman's handbag was a small mirror. In it Stukalin saw that his face was a mess. Using tissues from her bag and saliva from his mouth, he cleaned up. He still looked haggard, but no longer a hospital case.

Leaning forward, Stukalin glanced at the fuel gauge. A quarter full. Not enough, he guessed. 'How much is a litre of gasoline?' he asked. The couple exchanged puzzled glances.

'They're still dishing it out in gallons, if it's petrol you're talking about,' O'Donnell answered gruffly and lapsed back into silence. The Major quickly put the gun to Moira's head.

And O'Donnell quickly gave the information Stukalin wanted.

'When you come to Buncrana . . .' The Major was interrupted by the sniggers of the couple.

'Alright. How do you say it?' They told him, amid more sniggering.

Sniggering? Their mockery unsettled Stukalin. He issued more orders. 'Stop at the pumps and fill the tank to the top.' Again the two exchanged glances. Stukalin was becoming alarmed. This couple should be shaking in their shoes, not making jokes at the expense of a man holding a gun to their backs.

The Major needed to establish his authority. He injected greater harshness into his voice. 'And while you, sir, are buying the gasoline, this gun will be below the passenger seat, pointing upwards. Are you clear about the consequences of a stupid action on your part?'

There was no answer from either of them. On the outskirts of Buncrana, they came to a filling station. O'Donnell looked at the Major, who nodded. The car drew up at the pumps and they waited. Nobody appeared.

'Is this place open?' demanded Stukalin.

'It's self-service. You put the petrol in yourself.'

'OK. Put petrol in and remember where the gun is pointed.' O'Donnell nodded, got out and made towards the pump.

As he did so, a man appeared from inside the little shop alongside the filling station. 'It's alright, Dick,' he said loudly with a smile. 'I'm here. I'll do that for you.'

O'Donnell made no reply. He stood beside the pump like a de-activated robot.

'Greet him,' Stukalin hissed at Moira.

'Hiya Arthur,' she called out the window, waving but without a suitable accompanying expression on her face. The pump attendant hesitated for a moment, looked from

Moira to O'Donnell, and without answering, began dispensing petrol.

Richard O'Donnell stood leaning against the back door of the car, apparently watching the operation. The Major seethed and leaned forward to catch O'Donnell's eye with a look of deep threat.

O'Donnell looked away but didn't move. He had seen the remains of a broken Coca Cola bottle near the base of the pump. Without moving his hips, which the Major could see, O'Donnell carefully used his foot to draw the jagged base of the bottle towards the car.

The attendant saw what was happening and imperceptibly slowed the delivery of petrol. O'Donnell used the extra time well. With precision, he manoeuvred a spike of glass ahead of the back tyre. He paid for the petrol and resumed his position at the wheel.

The pump attendant went back to his small shop without looking back. O'Donnell raced the engine, but slipped the clutch for a slow acceleration. The noise masked the sound of the crunch of glass as a piece embedded itself in the tubeless tyre.

If it had not been a tubeless tyre, deflation would have been immediate, but fate and modern tyre technology were favouring the Russian. The tyre casing gripped the glass sliver tightly, allowing only a slight leak.

The Major knew nothing of this as the car drove through the main street of Buncrana. His mind was racing. The pump attendant had been suspicious; he was sure of it. Stukalin turned and looked back. No one was following. It was still early in the morning and few people were about.

There was something he needed to do urgently.

He leaned forward to get a better view ahead. O'Donnell turned on the wipers as the first drops of rain fell. Suddenly the Major saw what he was looking for.

On the right was a long inlet of the sea, Lough Swilly, according to his map. There were tracks down to the beach through low sand hills.

'Slow down,' he shouted.

O'Donnell, startled, lifted his foot immediately.

'Turn off there.'

The car lurched and sagged as it bounced along an undulating track of wet packed sand until it was out of sight of the road behind a low dune. It stopped on the Major's order and the engine was turned off, leaving no sound but the gentle lapping of the waves.

The couple looked at each other, and then at the Major. 'Can you drive, Moira,' Stukalin said gently.

'No,' she replied immediately. In an instant reaction, Stukalin lashed her violently across the face with the back of his hand. O'Donnell turned as if to attack but the Major had raised the gun. Moira didn't utter a word as her face acquired a lop-sided blush. O'Donnell remained immobile, his face set in hatred.

'If you look in your handbag,' Stukalin said, tossing it back at her, 'you will find your driving licence under the box of tampons. Are you also going to tell me that you don't menstruate?'

He waited for some reply and when none came, he turned to O'Donnell. 'Slowly, I want you to get out of the car.'

Richard O'Donnell did so and stood facing the Major.

His next instruction was addressed to the woman. 'Lie down on the floor of the car. I want your head on the floor.' At long last, a look of subservience crossed her pretty face. She did what she was told.

'Now, Mr O'Donnell, walk slowly back and down into that hollow, below that overhang of sand.' He complied woodenly.

'Turn round and face that wall of sand, then kneel.'

Stukalin saw what he wanted in O'Donnell's face. It was fear, real fear. Moira began to sob wretchedly. O'Donnell shook uncontrollably.

'That filling station was not self-service, Mr O'Donnell, and your gas-pump friend's name, Moira, is not Arthur.'

The Major stopped speaking and allowed the acidic silence between Moira's muffled sobs to eat away the last remnants of their confidence. He broke the shotgun, briefly giving Moira the appearance of checking that both barrels were loaded and snapped the weapon shut. It was an unnecessary act which served to raise the tension to an unbearable pitch.

'It is not given to many men to see the earth in which they will be interred. You have no time to pray. Goodbye.'

With that Stukalin fired. The sound of the shot inside the car was deafening, but superimposed upon it was a long ragged scream from Moira.

Faloon hardly spoke as they checked into one of the Algonquin's double rooms. He ripped open his baggage and took out a small computer with a standard typewriter keyboard.

Sarah stopped unpacking and stood behind him as he typed words on to its small screen. It was a message to the large FBI computer back in Washington, giving a description of the ginger-haired man and where he had been seen.

'Throw me over the modem and call up Big Daddy, Sarah please.'

Sarah grabbed a small grey box that had been packed with the computer and went over to the telephone. She called a Washington FBI number and was answered by a duty officer, the day office staff had long since gone home. After a short conversation, dotted with passwords, she was connected to the mainframe computer, confirmed by a long and constant siren tone.

'Big Daddy is on the line and wants to know who's calling,' she said. 'Are you ready?'

Sarah clipped the phone into two rubber cups on the modem and connected the modem to the computer. With a few keystrokes, Faloon opened a channel and entered his own codes allowing him access.

As a final check, the small computer was interrogated electronically by the mainframe, known to all as Big Daddy, and it automatically disgorged further access codes unknown to its human operators. Thus the way was cleared to allow Faloon and Sarah to receive the information they needed.

Through the modem, now connected to the phone, Faloon sent the queries he had already typed down the line to Big Daddy as a series tone. The answer was swift, as always. Four people answered the brief description, but only one of the descriptions raised their alarm. During much of the preceding nine months Faloon had inflicted a lot of damage on the Green Boys.

He had destroyed their ability to buy arms in the United States, to collect them over a period in secret armouries and then send them across the Atlantic in ocean-going trawlers or tramp steamers, mainly from Boston.

But he had not completely destroyed the organization itself, at least not the core of it. Like a stubborn cancer, a few cells remained, so that reactivation was always a possibility.

From this point, the FBI could only try to identify people round whom a new Green Boys operation could coalesce. That was the present stage of the game, and the excuse Faloon and Sarah had used to justify their expenses-paid trip north to New York.

The pair had not planned to do much work, but it now looked as if the work had come to them.

'So there we have it, Faloon,' said Sarah glumly. 'I suppose I ought to apologize to you, if not for what I actually said, then for my suspicions.'

'Somehow they must have picked us up at Washington and were ready for our arrival here.'

Faloon stuck his hands deep into his pockets and went over to the window.

'Some day we will have to tackle the root of this problem, which is a Provo sympathizer mole somewhere in the FBI.'

'I thought we'd put that suspicion to rest for all time,' replied Sarah. 'You're not going to re-open old sores. It demoralizes the section.'

Faloon sighed. 'The section will be unable to take further action against the Green Boys unless the source is cut out. Somebody had accurate information about our movements. And that could be lethal.'

He crossed the room back to the small computer and read its information yet again. The ginger man was Martin Riley, suspected as the main organizer of the gun-running traffic, but against whom the FBI could not assemble a case because of insufficient evidence to present to a court.

Convictions against Irish terrorist activists in the New York and Boston areas were notoriously difficult to achieve because of an underlying Provo sympathy among the large Irish American communities. Very hard evidence was needed, and Faloon could not get it against the expert Martin Riley.

'Somebody had to tell them when we were leaving for New York. And they had to follow us to the hotel because I couldn't leave a forwarding address like the Algonquin. The accountant would have blown a fuse.'

Sarah was now operating the computer, scrolling the information up the screen. 'Look at the number of times he's been across to Ireland and back. Can't we get him excluded as an undesirable alien?'

To answer her own question, she scrolled back to the beginning of the file, looking for nationality.

'He has a USA passport, hasn't he?' said Faloon, seeing confirmation of the fact in Sarah's face. 'That was one of the first ways I thought of dealing with this particular worm, but you can't deport a US citizen. Strong though his contacts with the old country remain, he is now an American.'

'With your contacts, why couldn't you get him excluded from Ireland? That at the very least would have made things difficult for the Green Boys and their hard-working little organizer.'

'I thought of that too, but it means presenting evidence in an Irish court. Riley could portray himself as a political or humanitarian activist and make the facts fit. In short, I face the same problems in the courts on both sides of the Atlantic.'

'Well what's the bastard up to now?' exploded Sarah.

'I think I know. If I'm right, there is a little birdie inside the FBI telling Riley all about me. In that case, he knows my role in collapsing the Green Boys. He'll know precisely why I was brought over from G2, and what I did in Ireland against his friends, the Provos.'

'If he knows that, then the leakage could be on the Irish side. . . .' Sarah waited for more. Faloon rarely mentioned what he had been doing back in Ireland.

'Possibly. Either way he'll know,' Faloon conjectured, 'that I've been able to add expert manipulation of computerized files to my many other outstanding achievements, and will have come to the conclusion I myself would've reached in his place.'

'We'll have to ask for a larger room,' said Sarah sarcastically. 'This one isn't big enough for the three of us – you, me and your head. What would you do in Riley's place?'

Faloon smiled. 'If I was a Green Boy, I'd want the arms shipments resumed. I couldn't do that effectively with Faloon following me with his big computer.'

'You don't have to be a genius to get that far. You're not irreplaceable, you know.'

Faloon was very serious. 'I agree nobody's irreplaceable. But it would take time to replace me and the Green Boys need time to regroup, time to reorganize. They could buy time.'

'How?' said Sarah in a small voice.

'By killing me. I think they'll try to kill me this weekend.'

FIVE

They lay fully clothed on the bed, listening to the sounds of the Algonquin. Faloon had fixed his eyes on the ceiling, Sarah on the folds of the sheet. Neither had spoken for a long time. It was not how they'd imagined spending their time.

They had come to New York to enjoy themselves and each other. Instead, Sarah was tense, all the more so because she saw Faloon reverting to type. She had a career plan for him; he was to be somebody she had nurtured, somebody she had convinced to come inside, not because he was getting too old for the game outside, but because he was still relatively young, active and good.

Sarah had argued for immediate retreat back to Washington or to another hotel, Faloon for staying and fighting. He'd said that the Green Boys would catch up with him somewhere, and it might as well be here and now. At least this time he knew they were on their way.

'Get up, girl,' he said suddenly, hitting her rump a playful smack, 'let's go out and get drunk or something.'

'Or something,' she replied. 'We are going to need all our wits about us.' She looked at him and added, 'And if we remain together, you will have one wit about you.'

'Very funny. But you're improving. When I first met you, a situation like this would have caused severe depression and hysterical weeping.'

Sarah didn't know whether she had been complimented or not.

'I figure it will take them some time to get their plans together' he said breezily. 'After all, they didn't know where we would be staying until they followed us here, so they've still some planning to do. They were never all that fast.

I guess we've until tomorrow before we need to become paranoid.'

'Christ, are you always that confident?' she snapped. After a moment, she added quietly, 'We'd better tell the boss we're facing up to them. The Bureau don't like freelancing.'

'And what are we going to tell them, Sarah? All we have is a sighting.' He rubbed his brow. 'We're short on detail and very long on conjecture. Now listen. If you yourself took some convincing, what do you think that headquarters lot in their button-down shirts and their brownstone college attitudes are going to think?'

Sarah remained silent. Faloon sat up and leaned over her, warming to his theme. 'The duty officer will order us back to Washington. We'll have proof of nothing except a little panic on our part. I'll survive because sometime soon I'll return to Ireland and G2, but you'll be stuck here with this episode on your personal file.'

Sarah looked bleak and Faloon felt a little sorry. He hadn't meant to display vulnerability, at least, not quite so starkly.

Pulling her to him, he said, 'I'll compromise. I will leave a little message for Big Daddy to deliver fresh on Monday morning.'

He took the computer onto his knees once more and Sarah set up the phone link. Faloon typed a message saying that they'd possibly made contact with Martin Riley, last heard of in connection with the Green Boys. Nothing about feeling they were under threat.

'Happier now?' She nodded.

They showered and dressed for a night on the town. As they were leaving their room, Faloon took a sheet of newspaper and placed it on the floor across the threshold, half inside and half outside their room. He pulled the door until it was nearly closed, then reached round and set a paperback book on the newspaper on the room side.

When both of them were in the corridor, Faloon shut the door and gently pulled the newspaper towards himself from under the door. Inside the room, the book on the newspaper was drawn up against the inside of the door.

Finally, he consigned the newspaper to a wastepaper basket and hung a 'Do Not Disturb' sign on the outer handle.

Sarah was scornful. 'What'll all of that accomplish?'

'It's not foolproof but it will do. If somebody enters that door the book will be pushed into the room. Unless the bastards are really good, they won't give a book on the floor a second glance. But I will. I've left the light on inside. When I return, I'll look under the door and there'd better be the shadow of a book.' He winked at her.

They went through the lobby, each pretending they were not looking for ginger hair and moustaches. Faloon was carrying the small case containing the computer and modem and he paused to lodge it in the lobby safe. Once in the street, they turned and headed for Sixth Avenue.

'Aren't you going to hail a cab, Faloon?'

'No, let's walk. We can see if anyone is walking with us.'

'Faloon, you don't have a gun.'

He hailed a cab.

They got out a short distance away in Times Square. No one had followed them either by car or motorcycle and they both relaxed.

Times Square was another of Faloon's favourite places. It managed to combine decay and vitality, like a jungle of weeds sprouting from a compost heap. The vitality sprang from the movement. Everything in Times Square moved, from the giant neon signs to the street hawkers, selling everything from one-dollar watches to heroin or sex. The roadways and the sidewalks never stopped.

The backdrop was a mixture of bars, cheap eating houses, peepshows and electronic shops, all open for much of the night. Street theatre in the middle of theatreland.

'A corny city you Americans have here. A New York square, and I mean a square-shaped square, is called a park. A triangle like this is called a square. Did you know that, Sarah?'

'No,' she said flatly.

Minutes later they were snaking their way towards an empty table in a steakhouse. Faloon liked American steaks. He also wanted somewhere with plenty of bustle.

This steakhouse meal fitted Faloon's requirements very well, since it offered unlimited salad of great variety along with unlimited Californian wine. Faloon pretended to drink more of it than was really the case. It all helped Sarah to relax and forget.

Forty Second Street was for the rip-off trading, picking pockets, snatching bags, buying and selling drugs, buying and selling sex. And yet in Faloon's eyes, there was a brotherhood of an unholy kind on the street, a conspiracy which stopped dog eating dog. The Faloons and Sarahs of the world would be the targets, chosen not through personal malice but because they were outsiders. Faloon accepted that condition. It seemed to have more honour than his own trade.

A cab drew up and disgorged rowdy passengers. Faloon and Sarah got in. The streets back to the Algonquin were emptier; manholes in the carriageways gave off steam, fleetingly suggesting to Faloon that the city was sitting upon a live volcano that could erupt at any time. Sarah lay back in the shiny plastic seat, silent and smiling. Happy at last.

Faloon paid the driver and Sarah went ahead into the hotel. Faloon saw her heading for the bar. He was about to join her when it occurred to him that he should check their room. He asked for his room key at the desk.

'Two friends called while you were out, Mr Faloon.'

'I wasn't expecting anyone. Did they leave their names, by any chance?' Do pigs fly, he said to himself.

'I'm afraid not, sir,' smiled the clerk.

He began to run to the elevator, then checked himself to a quick walk. After all, what was the hurry. The room had probably been thoroughly searched by now.

Faloon approached the bedroom door with stealth along the deserted corridor. He knelt and put his ear to the ground. That way he could use one eye to see if his book was still in place, silhouetted against the room light.

No silhouette. The room light had been switched off. Someone had been in their room.

A useless observation, because the door suddenly whisked open.

Towering above him was the man with the ginger moustache. In his hand was an automatic pistol, with a silencer.

Altogether a humiliating situation for G2's bloodhound. And a dangerous one, because the man with the gun Faloon now knew to be Martin Riley, Green Boy, gun-runner and prime enemy. He was the man he'd fought on the computer screens. He'd hoped to meet him face to face some day, not buttocks to face.

Quickly, but gently so as not to eject the cartridge automatically, the Major broke open the shotgun, removed the spent cartridge manually and gave the appearance of reloading.

A low moan came from O'Donnell's prone body, lying half buried in sand which had fallen from the vertical face in front of him.

O'Donnell had felt the sand fall and his imagination worked overtime. The cool dampness became the seeping of his lifeblood from a gaping hole in his back. The weight upon him was the final ebbing of his strength. With numbed fingers he cleared a space round his nose and mouth for his last breaths. The movement of sand stopped and he remained motionless.

Moira felt the warm barrel against her cheek. She stopped screaming. The stranger was motioning her out of the car.

She emerged, barely in control of herself. She saw her man lying immobile and half buried. She urinated and the dark stain spread down her jeans.

'Go and get him,' Stukalin roared. She now accepted that she would die beside O'Donnell and in her terror, simply wanted to get it over with. She stumbled forward and pushed the sand from round his head, crying.

'You're alive!' she yelled and immediately regretted it. She turned and looked wide-eyed at the Major, who was still sitting in the back of the car, the shotgun poked out through the window in their direction.

Stukalin spoke, very softly. 'Yes, this time he is alive. Next time you try to trick me, I will not shoot into a sandbank. I will kill you both.'

Neither of his captives moved. O'Donnell continued to play dead until the meaning of Stukalin's words sank into his badly shaken brain. He let Moira help him to his feet. He hugged her passionately.

The Major looked on dispassionately and said eventually, 'We will be spending the day in this car and I would like it to be as pleasant as possible.' He reached forward to the front seats and grabbed her handbag. 'You have spare pants inside. Go down to the sea and change. Wash your trousers. They can dry on you.' He tossed the bag onto the sand.

Moira broke away from Dick, picked up her bag and set off towards the sea, her face streaked with tears.

O'Donnell stood where he was, his head no longer high. The Major noted the absence of defiance and felt the exercise had been very worthwhile. He cast a glance in the direction of Moira, who had removed her clothing below the waist and was washing herself and her jeans in the sea.

Then he checked the beach. No sign of life other than themselves. The shot had been deadened by being fired inside the car.

'Turn the car,' Stukalin suddenly snarled at O'Donnell. 'And if you stick it in the sand, I'll assume that to be a deliberate action.'

'It will stick,' O'Donnell replied hoarsely, still not recovered from his ordeal. The Major brought the gun up to O'Donnell's stomach, holding the weapon in both hands this time. O'Donnell reacted by pointing at the rear wheel.

The Major opened the car door and got out. The back tyre was flat. Stukalin began a Russian oath but controlled himself in the nick of time. Must have been something on the rough track, he thought savagely.

'I hope you carry a spare wheel.'

'It's in the back.'

The Major limped over to the sandbank beside O'Donnell, then motioned him towards the flat wheel. 'Change the wheel, fast.'

O'Donnell moved quickly and opened the back of the car.

'Stop,' shouted the Major. 'Back away.' O'Donnell moved away from the car. Stukalin stepped forward and looked into the boot space. There were a few articles of clothing in cardboard boxes. These he emptied onto the sand. The spare wheel and tools were strapped into a side compartment.

Stukalin grunted his satisfaction and resumed his position at the sand bank. From there he could both supervise O'Donnell and keep an eye on the girl on the beach.

The Major revelled in the new attitude exhibited by his captives. The girl was doing exactly what she was told. The man was working in the boot of the car, bent over in his frenzied labour to free the spare wheel, assemble the car jack and find the wheel spanner. The spare wheel bounced out of the boot. We mustn't get another puncture, the Major thought.

His eyes panned to the girl. She had moved up to the head of the beach and was trying to dry her hips with tissues. She was attractive. Her thighs were lightly tanned, her buttocks had no hint of sag and her stomach was enticingly flat. She was indeed a pretty woman.

Stukalin's mind drifted back to those final months of his training and the puritanical regime it had required. He had a woman back home whom he wanted and needed. He allowed himself to wonder what making love to Moira would be like. Hardly likely to happen, he thought. His foreplay had been somewhat brusque.

The shot, when it came, deafened Stukalin and tumbled him off balance. The shotgun fell from his hands – an involuntary act that may have saved his life, for when he looked up, he found himself staring at the wrong end of something frighteningly familiar.

'Don't move.' O'Donnell's voice rasped. 'I feel like killing you so don't move.' The Major remained very still on the ground.

Stukalin gaped at O'Donnell who was crouched at the back of the car. In his rock-steady hands was an Avtomat Kalashnikov AK-47 automatic assault rifle.

The Russian immediately recognized the standard issue weapon of Warsaw Pact armed forces. It was also a favourite weapon of the IRA Provos, but Stukalin was unaware of that.

Before he could recover, Faloon was yanked by the scruff of the neck into his own hotel room and the door quickly slammed.

Faloon tried unsuccessfully in the semi-dark to see where the second man was.

'Put your arms behind your back, clasp your hands and hold them away from your body,' came the hoarse whispered order.

A webbing belt with a self-holding buckle was slipped over his upper arms and tightened. He was hit heavily in the back, sending him spinning over a chair.

Before he could recover, a second belt was round his legs and tightened with a pull. He was now helpless and he stopped trying to move, preferring to lie on the floor and examine his captor.

Riley turned on the room lights and looked back at him, pocketing the gun since it was no longer needed.

'What are you waiting for?' Faloon roared, hoping to attract attention.

'In my own time, Faloon. You're in no position to call the shots. And don't try shouting again or things will get unpleasant.' He paused to light a cheroot, inhaling deeply.

Riley seemed to be in no hurry. Faloon wondered why. Oh hell! Sarah! He's waiting until she appears.

Faloon tuned his ears to the corridor outside. Once he heard Sarah, he would shout a warning. Riley hadn't thought of gagging him.

'I want to talk to you, Faloon,' Riley said quietly as if they were meeting in a bar. 'Consider yourself lucky that some of us thought you worth talking to, otherwise you'd be dead by now.'

Faloon's one thought was somehow to get Riley to leave before Sarah appeared. She would begin looking for him soon. Faloon nodded and Riley con tinued.

'We want to meet you on our home ground, and you, of course, would know where that is.'

'Boston, I suppose,' said Faloon. 'But since you are talking now, what is wrong with the present.'

'It isn't yourself we particularly want to hear from. It's your little box of tricks. Your computer chatterbox that has nearly ruined us. We think it can be made to work for us, but not from here.'

Faloon was stuck for words. In fact, he was astounded. So Riley wasn't after his blood. Well not yet anyway. It was the computer files.

'We have searched this room and couldn't find the computer.' Riley smiled at Faloon, though hardly with warmth. 'I presume it is in the hotel strong room. No matter. Make sure you bring it to Boston with you.'

Where was Sarah? Why was Riley so self assured? Faloon knew Riley had seen Sarah with him at the airport. But his attacker was not waiting for the door to open. It dawned on Faloon that Riley was not expecting Sarah to appear.

Only then did the answer surface from amid the confusion in Faloon's head. The hotel clerk said there were two men. Where was the other? With Sarah?

As if he had been reading Faloon's thoughts, Riley said, 'You won't see her for a while, and not ever if there is trouble with you.'

He leaned over Faloon. 'Listen carefully because I'm not writing this down for you. Fly to Boston tomorrow and bring the computer. At Boston airport, go to the Hertz desk and hire a car. It's already been reserved and a further message has been left for you.'

He waited for some reaction from Faloon. There was none.

'You'd better follow those new instructions,' Riley said coldly. 'At a place we'll tell you about later, you will use the computer to reveal certain files for us. If there is a problem, any problem, then Sarah will pay.'

The man is a fool, Faloon thought.

'First we will access files whose contents we already know. That way we will discover if there's been any tampering.' He brought his head closer to Faloon's. 'From the state of those couple of files – and you don't know which ones – we'll know if you have set us up, Faloon.'

Not such a fool, thought Faloon, but here was confirmation that there was a Green Boy source inside the department, somebody with limited access to computer files.

Riley walked over to the door. 'Your girlfriend will have a message for you to ensure your co-operation.' With unnecessary violence, he kicked away a paperback book lying in his path on the floor and let himself out quietly.

Faloon immediately began wriggling, bucking like a freshly caught eel. It was five or six minutes before the cursing Irishman could free himself. He had thought of using the phone to raise the alarm but quickly changed his mind. A stupid act on his part could harm Sarah.

He flung himself out of the room and down the staircase, then round the lobbies, the bars and ground floor rooms.

Breathless, he collapsed into one of the winged chairs with the hotel night staff peering at him intently from behind pillars. There would be little point in asking any of them for details of Sarah's departure. She had gone and that was all he had to know. He pulled himself over to the reception desk and reclaimed his computer. Clutching it to him like a small boy with a teddy bear, he left in despair for his room.

He went straight to the closet for his small suitcase, which was on the floor beside Sarah's. That was when he noticed that Sarah's case was not there. A quick search revealed that few of Sarah's belongings remained.

Very thorough and very well prepared, thought Faloon grimly. The Green Boys, who were no longer thought capable of effective action, had counter-struck by activating a mole in the FBI's Undesirable Alien Department. This was the only reasonable explanation to account for the accurate monitoring of Faloon's departure with Sarah from the Washington office and their arrival in New York.

From that point he had played his hand badly. In spite of what he'd said to Sarah, he'd not taken the Green Boy threat sufficiently seriously.

The FBI would be less than pleased. He had left Washington unarmed, leaving only vague details as to what he was doing and where he was going, and had allowed his boss to be kidnapped by enemies he was supposed to have neutralized.

Clever Green Boys. In a business where your reputation is only as good or bad as your last job, he would be ruined.

The thought of Colonel Grundy, head of G2 in Dublin, standing before him with a report of this shambles made him shudder almost as much as Martin Riley with a gun.

56

Nor would Colonel Grundy relish hearing that the Green Boys had penetrated computer files on his own side of the Atlantic.

Faloon set the computer on his lap and began composing a message. It was a very different one from that sent earlier. This message accurately reported what had happened, outlined his proposed course of action and asked unashamedly for help.

When he had finished, he went over to the window and closed the last crack in the curtains, latched the security lock on the door and went into the bathroom, taking the computer with him.

Rummaging in his washbag, he produced a small screwdriver and his electric shaver. With a flick of his wrist he removed the shaving head from the shaver and exposed the workings. Someone very familiar with electric shaver design might have discerned a small oblong object that did not belong. Faloon carefully prised it away, allowing it to fall gently into a folded towel.

Picking the object up between a finger and thumb, Faloon examined it carefully, paying special attention to its eight small metal legs. It resembled a rectangular black beetle.

An electronics engineer would have recognized it as a microchip. This was not FBI issue; it was a G2 chip. It was Faloon's magic lamp by which he could call his own genie at times of extreme trouble.

Turning the computer upside down, he removed three small screws and a plate to expose the circuit board. The board had sockets for microchips. Faloon removed an FBI chip and replaced it with his own, refastened the plate and went back into the main bedroom.

Security agencies never fully trust one another, even when co-operating. Some say, especially when co-operating. In the final analysis, Faloon was a G2 operator and the chip by which he had just modified the FBI computer gave him secure communications back home.

The chip, which was a mini-computer memory, contained a means of encoding text in a variation of the Hayhanen code. To encode his message, Faloon had only to type in four memorized words and the computer automatically changed the text of his message into a list of numbers, hidden inside which was the number for decoding.

For his next message, there would be another four words, different ones *ad infinitum*. It was a devilish code, invented by the Russians, giving in effect a different cypher for every message. Since each key was used only once it was difficult to break.

'Put it this way,' Faloon's instructor had said back in Dublin, 'by the time anyone broke it you would be well away. Even though the FBI captured the Russian spy who gave his name to the code back in 1957, they never managed to break the code.'

A comforting thought for Faloon. This was one message which he did not want to fall into FBI hands.

He dialled a Dublin number. In a nondescript tower block in Dublin and in an office which appeared to have a role in the field of exports. It was six o'clock in the morning and Faloon's call was answered immediately.

'O'Brien here,' said Faloon. 'I have some sales figures for you. Can you connect me appropriately.'

'Please hold, sir. Connecting you.' No further human voice was heard on that line. Faloon listened for a burst of tone which was his signal to press a button on his computer. The machines on different continents whistled to each other, and Faloon whistled to himself.

He was a little happier now. His message had included his present phone number and he expected an answer within ninety minutes. That gave him time to think.

His first thought was about Sarah. Poor Sarah. A college girl whose experience of combat was academic, who had had an unexciting upper-middle-class childhood and adolescence in Connecticut, and who now was in the hands of a very determined section of the Provos.

Faloon began to feel more and more uncomfortable. Sarah, as Faloon's boss, had access to even more computer files than he had. Martin Riley had taken her, but had made only a half-hearted attempt to take the computer that ought to have gone with her. Either they had their own computer, and since it was a standard commercially-available computer with a small modification, that might be possible, or . . .

Or they wanted something that only Faloon could provide, and Sarah's abduction was just the means to another end.

What end?

SIX

Colonel Henry James Grundy, Head of G2, was awakened by the telephone early on Sunday morning. In the last few years, he'd become accustomed to a leisurely Sunday in his upmarket home in the Wicklow Hills to the south of Dublin. This Sunday would be different.

A lean-faced man of about fifty years of age, he had an agile frame and a head of black hair without a trace of grey. He was generally taken to be ten years younger than he was, a fact that was a source of pride to the colonel and a slight source of annoyance to his wife.

Colonel Grundy walked with a slight limp. Under a United Nations banner he had seen action in the Congo, in Cyprus and more recently in Lebanon. Keeping two sides apart, or as in Lebanon, three or four sides apart, had never been satisfying soldiering for Colonel Grundy. It always seemed that his guns were pointed the wrong way, politically or militarily.

When the grenade was thrown at him, he was facing the wrong way and was left with a limp and a new resolve to develop eyes in the back of his head.

Colonel Grundy needed eyes everywhere in his position of Head of G2. He had a small team of special operators whose main task was aspects of internal security and counter espionage, particularly where there was an external and military ingredient to the threat. Routine internal security was the job of the police.

Life was sometimes complicated for the Colonel and his department. The Republic of Ireland in its constitution claimed the six counties of Northern Ireland, which had opted to remain part of Britain. For some people, that constitutional claim gave the IRA Provos a spurious legitimacy; in others it gave rise to ambivalence – a state of affairs that exasperated Colonel Grundy.

The Colonel wasn't in the least ambivalent towards the Provos. He regarded them first and foremost as enemies of the Irish state, because they sought to impose, by very nasty means, their own solution of the Irish problem on the Irish government.

All of this affected relationships with the United Kingdom and with the Americans. There were more Irish-Americans than there were full-blooded Irish. If the British hadn't driven so many Irishmen out of Ireland over to the United States in the last century, then Americans influence on the situation might not have counted for so much this century.

But that was wishful thinking. Grundy had today's problems to deal with, and doubtless the ringing telephone would be one of them. He thought he could guess which . . .

The Colonel's wife groaned from under the blankets. 'Oh James. Stop that thing ringing. It's going right through my head.'

'It's probably something more on that helicopter crash.' Grundy groped for the phone. 'The Russians have been kicking up a fuss. Our people don't understand why. You'd think we'd killed them deliberately.'

'Tell them to take all the Russians and. . . .' The rest of her advice on the matter was muffled into incoherence as she put the pillow on top of her head.

Doing something to all the Russians in Ireland would be quite an undertaking, thought Grundy. He didn't think that Ireland justified the very large Russian presence in the country. They had a splendid embassy in Dublin, and a fuelling facility on the other side of the country at Shannon Airport. What did they all do, he often asked himself. From time to time other people also asked him that question and he was supposed to have an answer.

'Nightwatch here sir. I wouldn't trouble you, sir, but . . .'

'Oh get on with it, man. Of course you wouldn't trouble me unless you deemed it necessary.' The nightwatch continued, but in the formal and approved manner.

'A PET, sir. Cat one.'

'I'll be down immediately. Send the car.'

'Already on its way, sir.'

Grundy grunted and put the phone down.

'Well,' said his wife, taking her head from under the pillow. 'Has the Red Army occupied the Post Office?'

'I don't know. It's a cat one PET.'

'Give it some milk and go back to sleep.'

Grundy didn't laugh. He had heard it too many times before and a Priority External Teletext, category one, was never a joke.

Grundy's car sped through the deserted streets of Dublin. If only it was always so easy to glide through this Georgian city. On weekdays the traffic was chaotic. If Grundy were ever to plan a military takeover, he would time it for four o'clock on a Friday afternoon. At that time the capital of Ireland is bound and gagged by its own carriageways.

However, Grundy's mind was not mulling over anything as frivolous as a putsch. He was increasingly concerned by the puzzling sequence of events stemming from a helicopter crash on the north coast.

The conversation at last night's party with the Foreign Minister had unsettled him further. He tried to remember the exchange.

61

'James,' the Minister had said, drawing him aside, 'what do we know about this chopper, eh?' The Minister had just filled his pipe, which was providing a smoke screen behind which they both withdrew.

'Not much yet, but then at first we didn't think we'd be involved.' Aware that this might sound a little callous, he continued. 'Of course the deaths of our two Aer Rianta people and the pilot were very unfortunate. Colm Fitzroy was a rising star, by all accounts. A pity, but I suppose it's the death of the Russians that is involving your department.'

The Minister nodded confirmation. 'Yes. The Russians are being very difficult. You'd think that a minister of theirs had gone down in that chopper. Their ambassador at the very least.' He stopped to relight his pipe and Grundy waited to hear more. Grundy wondered why his political boss had begun to talk about 'choppers' when the machines had been 'helicopters' to him for decades.

'They've asked that a team of their own experts be allowed to visit the crash site,' the Minister went on once his pipe was glowing. 'Even went so far's to say that a team could be flown into Shannon on one of their planes before the day was out!'

'How did you react to that?'

The Minister peered into the bowl of his pipe as if surprised to find there was something burning in it. Grundy had sometimes thought of taking up pipe smoking. It gave one time to think.

'Diplomatically, I told them to get stuffed,' he said, then noting the look on Grundy's face, he added, 'Don't worry. The dead Russians were not high rankers that would involve me directly – that's if they were who they were meant to be. Your department, I think, Grundy.'

Grundy smiled to himself. His department was where all the nearly unanswerable questions were directed. 'I ran routine checks immediately. I automatically assume that every Russian can have an intelligence or KGB function.'

'Find anything?'

'Nothing very surprising, but I'm asking friends in the business if they know anything.'

'Did you get anything from the Americans?' he asked sharply.

'Nothing new on the names.'

'Look, James, use this information carefully.' Grundy looked a little pained but the Minister ignored that. 'Today the Americans asked if they could help with investigations into the cause of the crash. And do you know what they were offering?' Grundy shook his head, as he was supposed to.

'They said they could have an investigation team flown into Shannon before the day was out.'

'Are you saying both the Americans and the Russians want to examine the site of this helicopter crash? Bloody hell, what's going on?'

The Minister nodded in sympathy.

'I'm right in thinking, Minister, that this helicopter was an Irish aircraft, being flown by an Irish pilot and well inside Irish airspace?' Grundy was half talking to himself.

'You are indeed. That's why our government is becoming a little shirty, first with the Russians and now with the Americans. Any thoughts?'

In the middle of the party and with his head in the centre of a large cloud of tobacco smoke, the G2 chief had been unable to think clearly. Afterwards he had spent most of the night thinking. Now in the car in the early morning, he still had no coherent answers.

Helicopters were subject to catastrophic failures from time to time. There'd been no suggestion of sabotage, at least not until the Russians and then the Americans began showing unnatural interest. But who would want to kill Aeroflot middle managers negotiating re-fuelling facilities?

Irish experience at the hands of more powerful neighbours, notably the British, coloured their expectations in situations like this. When the British wanted something inside Ireland, they might first ask for it. If they didn't get it, they sometimes sent in their own people to take it. Some of G2's counter-espionage work was directed at maintaining national integrity against the British. It was a game they played with the British, sometimes with horrendous results. The possibility of having to deal with superpowers acting in the same manner was daunting.

Whatever the reason, the Russians seemed to want something in that crash wreckage very badly. The Americans must now know about it as well and wanted it equally badly. Colonel Grundy now considered it a possibility that the Russians and the Americans would begin to infiltrate agents or use embassy staff already in place, and that Ireland was about to become a secret battleground between the competing giants.

Grundy didn't say as much to the Minister, but he suspected that the man had already worked that out for himself.

These then were the thoughts running through Grundy's head as he entered the G2 offices. The nightwatch attempted to stand at his desk, but his chair caught in the carpet and his stance became a crooked caricature of a smart snap to attention. Grundy wasn't in the mood to notice.

'Hope you left that teletext in the memory, nightwatch.'

'Yessir. I knew you would want to decode immediately. You can take it on your own workstation.'

'Who's it from?' He pulled his coat off his shoulders and flung it across an empty desk before heading towards his desk.

'Faloon.'

Grundy stopped and turned.

'Faloon! Oh hell. What kind of hole are we in now?' He resumed his march towards his office. Without turning or slowing, he shouted back, 'Did he sound elated? That bastard only talks to us with either very good news or very bad news.'

'Hard to tell, sir.' Faloon could be the bearer of his own bad news.

Grundy began decoding behind the locked door of his own office. He sat at a desk with a screen and a keyboard, entered a series of memorized key sequences which gained him access to special decoding chips in the circuitry – the partners to the chip that Faloon had inserted into his computer.

The Colonel typed with one finger because keyboards were a late entry into his life. On his appointment to the department he'd seen the dire need for more resources. Increasing the number of employees was one possibility, but this ran against the prevailing climate in any government office. In addition, he could not recruit security personnel like doorkeepers. It took time to winkle out the right people and Grundy was short of time.

Contrary to popular belief, most espionage and counter-espionage work is boring and repetitive. At the heart of intelligence work is the painstaking assessment of huge amounts of information, much of it openly available in various publications.

The man with the cloak and dagger still had his place, of course. But Grundy's great contribution was to recognize that the core of his operation was the filing cabinet.

Computers are huge filing cabinets with inbuilt lightning cross-referencing, so Grundy installed a network of computers, all connected to 'Bimbo', nickname of the Irish Central Data Processing Services computer system.

Grundy read the decoded text and buried his head in his hands. He'd enough problems without Faloon adding to them. His priority was clearing up the mystery of the helicopter crash without crossing swords with both the CIA and the KGB. Faloon's problems were a side-show.

It didn't take a man like Grundy long to make up his mind. He was going to need Faloon. For all his escapades, he was the best Grundy had. The return message, which the Colonel encoded himself, was brutally short. The list of numbers was passed to the nightwatch workstation with instructions to send it to Faloon immediately and confirm receipt.

Grundy rose from his desk and leaned against the window. High above him in the delicate early morning light a trans-Atlantic jet billowed its trail westwards. How long, he wondered, would it take for the Russians and Americans to mobilize their forces?

What the hell did they want?

He went back to his desk and organized round-the-clock surveillance of both the Russian and American embassies. Turning his attention to the airports, he trebled the team at the immigration desks at Shannon and Dublin. When he had done that, G2 had no more men to allocate. No reserve.

Except for one man. Faloon, who was on the other side of the Atlantic pining over an empty bed.

Grundy went back into the outer office, where the nightwatch was still trying to connect with Faloon.

'If you're speaking to him, don't say I'm here.'

'There was a phone call for you while you were in your office. I didn't want to interrupt. It was the police in Buncrana. Wouldn't talk to me. Wanted my superior officer. I said you'd call back. The number's on the pad.'

Buncrana! That's near the crash site, Grundy reminded himself as he grabbed a phone. It couldn't have started already, could it?

Major Petr Stukalin lay on the sand near Buncrana looking down the muzzle of a Russian gun.

The first to move was Moira. She pulled on clean knickers and jeans. Her partial nakedness had served its purpose by drawing Stukalin's attention away from O'Donnell. She scampered behind O'Donnell to the boot of the car, moved some objects and emerged with a pistol in one hand and a magazine in the other. She snapped the two together in a manner that impressed the Major.

Throughout, O'Donnell kept the Kalashnikov pointed at

the Major, who stayed still as instructed. Though his face appeared blank, the Major's mind was running through permutations of his inadequate scraps of knowledge of Ireland. None seemed to make much sense, so he tried for more information.

'Who are you?' he began hoarsely.

Neither the man or the girl answered him. Instead they talked to each other as though the Major wasn't present.

They spoke in a torrent of fast English and Irish which the stranger was unable to understand. From the inflexions and interrogative interchange between the two, Stukalin guessed that they were exploring options about his future – if any.

Stukalin's guess was almost correct. The stranger's future depended on his identity. Moira was convinced that the man in front of them was a British undercover agent sent into the Irish Republic either to abduct or eliminate known Provos.

O'Donnell was unsure. The American accent was wrong for a start. Moira countered that the number of nationalities and races in the lower ranks of the British Army made it something more akin to the French Foreign Legion. The man was a Canadian, she said, probably of Ulster Protestant stock from a place like Toronto where the bigoted bastards like that tended to gather in the new world.

Stukalin was also desperately trying to identify. His first guess was that the pair in front of him were the Irish equivalent of the KGB, or some kind of special border police. This accorded with his own experience, but doubts crept into his mind when he remembered that the rifle in O'Donnell's hand was a Kalashnikov. He knew that the Irish armed forces were equipped with NATO-compatible weapons, though Ireland was officially neutral. That much be remembered from staff college.

He decided to remain silent and see what happened. If they had been ready to kill him, then the Kalashnikov's first shot would have gone through him instead of past him.

Moira was smarting in the wake of the terror and humiliation Stukalin had inflicted upon her. 'Who else could he be but a Brit,' she asked, slowing the delivery of her words and lapsing into English alone as her confidence returned. 'He was taking us towards the border. Isn't it obvious that it's a long range snatch squad? He's a bounty-hunter.'

Unfortunately for Stukalin, leaving the Inishowen peninsula by land necessitated approaching the border with Northern Ireland. The importance of this fact was lost on the Major.

Moira looked as if she might shoot Stukalin on the spot. The Major wished he had been nicer to her when he had the gun. And with that thought, he unwisely allowed his eyes to drop to the shotgun lying beneath him. The glance was intercepted by the wild-eyed Moira.

'Move away from the shotgun,' she yelled. Even O'Donnell jumped at her sudden eruption and Stukalin feared that the Kalashnikov might be fired accidentally. He defused the tension by moving away from the gun. Moira retrieved the weapon, making sure she didn't obscure O'Donnell's firing line.

'What's a Brit?' inquired the Major.

'It's not the time for humour,' O'Donnell snarled quietly. 'I'll tell you what we're thinking, which may cut your capacity for joking. We think you're a member of something like the SAS and you've come over the border for Provo prisoners, perhaps dead or alive. Well you've failed, Britshit, and you are a prisoner of the Provos.'

'And outside British jurisdiction,' Moira gloated. 'At the very least we can cause an international incident by simply parading you. Even the Dublin Government start shouting when you SAS types invade our country. Maybe we should shoot him and parade the body.'

'Take it easy, Moira,' O'Donnell warned her. 'This catch could be important for us. We could exchange him for one of ours inside. Either way, I'm thinking carefully about the next move.' The man is in command, thought the Major.

'Yes, you're right. We could get some information from this bastard,' Moira added with menace. 'Lie face down. Turn your head away.'

She approached him and knelt on his back. Deftly she grabbed his hands, brought them together and tightly bound his thumbs together. He was hauled to his feet and pushed towards the car.

'You drive, Moira. I'll sit in the back with our guest, whoever he is. Head for Fahan.' He gave her the rifle. 'Give me your shooter and put the Kalashnikov in the boot.'

'I'll put the shotgun in the boot as well,' she said, looking at it closely for the first time. She broke it open and gasped in surprise. 'It's not loaded!'

They both looked at the Major in astonishment. O'Donnell quickly ran his hands over his prisoner's clothing, taking everything out of his pockets, the map, the food. All the items he had taken from the caravan.

'No ammo. He didn't have any more,' said O'Donnell. He took the shotgun from Moira, held it to the sky, looking up the barrels. 'Only one shot ever fired. The other barrel is clean,' said O'Donnell, perplexed.

He confronted Stukalin. 'We know Her Britannic Majesty's government is not the last of the big spenders, but sending out its soldiers with a shotgun and a single round is daft. In fact,' he added, turning away and looking at the sea, 'I don't believe it.'

Moira glared at the Major with even more anger. The Major stared back at her and she felt the strength of his gaze. She needed to hate him because she had retribution to exact. O'Donnell was unaware or ignored their silent duel and continued to contemplate the waves. He came to a decision.

'I don't know who he is and I don't think we're going to find out on this beach.' He turned to the Major. 'Even if you don't talk, it'll be interesting to see who comes searching for you. That'll tell us something, like whether you are valuable or not, and to whom.'

Moira added, 'If you are lucky, you will turn out to be valuable to us.' She turned to O'Donnell. 'Perhaps we should stay here until dark.'

But O'Donnell was already at the car, checking the contents of the boot and closing it. 'No. We could've been seen coming here and the shots could've been heard by someone who doesn't think it's duck shooting. I know it's risking a VCP, but we should move.'

The Major was bundled into the back of the car with O'Donnell.

'Are the police friends of yours, stranger?' O'Donnell asked.

'That depends of how much of an enemy you are. What is a VCP?'

'Another of your jokes?'

'No. I don't know.'

Moira in the driving seat spun round to face the Major in another explosion of anger, but was arrested by the Major's expression. He looked sincere.

O'Donnell too had noted Stukalin's expression and said, 'A VCP is a vehicle checkpoint and everyone on both sides of the border knows that.' He motioned to Moira to start driving.

'So you are on the wrong side of the law. Why?' asked Stukalin.

'Maybe the bastard is just an ordinary criminal,' Moira suggested, as she started the engine.

'Do you really believe that, Moira?'

She didn't answer. Instead she scowled again at Stukalin, who was wearing a funny smile.

'What's so funny?'

'You've forgotten something quite important,' Stukalin answered.

'Like what?'

'Your car has a flat tyre.'

SEVEN

When Stukalin had finished changing the wheel Moira rel-
ished tying his thumbs together again. Very tightly. It was
the only revenge O'Donnell was permitting her for the time
being.

The car lurched and sagged as it negotiated the undulating
lane through the sand dunes back towards the road. In the
back seat sat the Major. Beside him, O'Donnell was holding
the pistol but not directing it at his trussed prisoner.

Stukalin was now aware that he had blundered into
the jumbled and confused world of Irish terrorism. The
word Provo – or even 'Provisional IRA' – meant little to
him.

The IRA, he began to remember, were anti-British and
occasionally were accorded friendly analysis in *Pravda*.
This could be an important factor in the crucial decision
of whether to reveal his identity. If they searched him
properly, they would realize his nationality anyway. The
IRA could be allies.

O'Donnell also began to analyse. His prisoner behaved
as if he'd had military training. He had used the shotgun
professionally, even to the point of firing his only round of
ammunition to bluff them into submission.

If, as Moira was insisting, the man beside him was a British undercover soldier, sent clandestinely across the border
to capture them, he'd have been properly armed for a start
and sufficiently well briefed not to let them poke about in
the boot of the car without thoroughly searching it himself
first. The boot was the obvious place to hide weapons,
wasn't it?

Therefore, O'Donnell argued to himself, the stranger
didn't know they were likely to be armed. It followed that
he did not know who they were.

That in itself did not convince O'Donnell fully that the man was not an undercover British soldier. He could have been after somebody else; he could have bungled his mission, lost his proper weapons and could have been trying to regain the border.

He turned to look at Stukalin. The Major turned away. O'Donnell saw that a few days ago this man had been neat. And sunburned. His chin was unshaven but his hair was neatly cut. The jacket and coat were such a bad fit they drew attention. No undercover person would think of presenting himself so oddly.

And then there was the stranger's language and the way he spoke. They'd heard him begin to swear in a foreign language. From intimate and hostile contact, the Provo knew that the British army was, as Moira had stated, a melting pot of races. O'Donnell had studied modern languages and recognized that his prisoner was speaking English grammatically — which was unusual. He was sure that English was not the man's first language, though his command of it was excellent.

He could still be a British army spy and British Special Air Service kidnapper, but there was something was missing from his vocabulary, raising doubts in O'Donnell's mind. The stranger used no military jargon words in his English. But more significantly, he did not appear to recognize them. Men who share a mess, or a safe house, as O'Donnell had done for a period of time, begin to mingle their vocabularies. Even enemies like the IRA and the British army had some common jargon. O'Donnell knew it was an involuntary process and it had sometimes amused him. That had not happened to the stranger, therefore he was very new indeed to Ulster.

So who was he? Somebody on a first mission? So new he didn't know what a VCP was? Of course, he could be a consummate liar, couldn't he? It still didn't add up.

The uncomfortable motion of the car ceased when it regained the road running parallel with the shore.

72

'Keep your eyes peeled, Moira.' O'Donnell was once more staring through the windscreen, sometimes behind.

Moira saw his movements in the mirror. 'There won't be any *garda*,' she said. 'They don't usually get out of their beds this early on a Sunday,' The task of driving had relaxed her somewhat. A long, straight section of the road revealed no threat. Just empty road.

'There was a disco last night at St Eugene's,' she went on, 'and most of the *garda* were there. Those that weren't outside vomiting were inside finding women to sleep with. Either way, this morning they won't be in the best form for being policemen, never mind playing at soldiers.'

O'Donnell said nothing. He had argued enough with Moira and there was nothing to be gained by clashing with her again. Despite her words, both of them would be looking out for police.

As a man who had studied the habits of the guards, or *garda*, in their Gaelic name, O'Donnell knew that only the young guards had been at the disco, and that only the younger of those had drunk themselves sick. They would grow out of that.

Their officers would not have been to the disco and it was they who would determine action or inaction. Were they, O'Donnell wondered, searching for the stranger? If so, the roads could be dangerous.

'Untie my thumbs. The blood circulation to them is restricted.' Stukalin was addressing O'Donnell but Moira responded. 'Stick them up your arse,' she rasped.

Suddenly she lifted her foot from the accelerator and almost froze behind the wheel. The vehicle check point, the VCP, had been skilfully placed. It lay within a short straight stretch of the road, long enough for a safe deceleration, short enough to prevent detection from afar. Stukalin moved slightly to see past Moira.

Two groups of uniformed men with their vehicles formed the road check. At the centre were a couple of blue cars, police cars, parked obliquely across each half of the road, leaving a narrow chicane for traffic to pass. Charging through at speed would be impossible.

The policemen were gathered round their own vehicles and were separate from the second group, to whom the Major quickly diverted his attention. These were soldiers, clad in camouflage and, unlike the police, were armed with automatic rifles and sub-machine pistols.

The soldiers were protecting the policemen and to the Major's professional eye, were well positioned. Their field vehicles were parked ahead and behind the police. A soldier was in the middle of the road, signalling Moira to halt.

'Smile, Moira, we've nothing to hide from this man. Relax him. Wait until we reach the police.' While he spoke, O'Donnell quickly stretched behind Stukalin with a penknife and cut his thumbs loose. As Stukalin began rubbing his painful thumbs, O'Donnell threw an overcoat over his shoulders.

'Not a word, stranger,' O'Donnell warned Stukalin. 'And not a move or my first shot will take you out.' The gun disappeared into the folds of O'Donnell's clothing.

By the time the car had finished its deliberately slow approach to the first soldier, both Moira and O'Donnell had pleasant expressions on their faces. Stukalin's face was a mask.

'Good morning, madam.' The soldier paused, looking at the empty front passenger seat.

Moira seized the initiative. 'God, but you look a bit rough. Were you at the dance last night? You look as pale as most of the lads in Buncrana. The ones that are out of their beds, that is.'

'No, no.' The soldier laughed. 'This is the way I look every time I'm ordered out of bed at three in the morning.'

The soldier had straightened up, his attention focused on Moira's smiling lips and flirting eyes. She's cool, thought Stukalin, but how far are we going to get?

Moira kept the questions coming. 'Has something happened or is it just routine?'

74

'The army makes a routine of taking me from my warm bed at ungodly hours. Nothing much has happened since that helicopter crash. And no one walked away from that, God rest their souls.' Behind them, another car had come round the corner and queued for the soldier's attention. He resumed his duty. 'Just go up to the police car, madam, if you please.'

Moira gave him a cheery wave and an extravagant smile that could be seen by everybody, as it was meant to be. The other soldiers had also taken their cue from the first soldier, so as Moira drove slowly towards the police cars, where the real interrogation would take place, no one was paying them undue attention.

'Good girl.' O'Donnell was leaning forward in his seat. 'Tell them this man drank bad poteen last night at the dance and we must get him to hospital fast. He's very ill.'

'Poteen?' hissed Moira.

'Don't argue. Do it.' He sat back in his seat, casting a warning look in the Major's direction. Stukalin had never heard of poteen, but he guessed that it must be an illegally distilled liquor. That happened in Russia too.

'Good morning, madam.' The policeman looked into the car, at the empty front seat and then suspiciously at the two men in the rear. 'Driver's licence please.' As he spoke, he was looking at Stukalin.

He examined her licence, lifting his eyes frequently from the document to the three people in front of him. O'Donnell cursed his decision to sit with the stranger in the back. He should have sat him in the front passenger seat with a gun at his back. If Moira didn't say something, he knew the policeman was going to pull them over for a thorough search.

'It was a bit of a wild night in Buncrana last night, wasn't it?' Moira began with the trace of an apologetic smile. But the policeman didn't take the bait and silently waited for more from her.

'We're on our way to the hospital in Derry. Our friend back there took bad poteen and he's pretty sick,' she said.

This produced a reaction from the policeman. He bent down and looked hard at Stukalin. This particular policeman was not going to be side-tracked so easily. O'Donnell had his foot on top of the Major's and was pressing down hard as a physical warning.

'He needs attention fast,' Moira pleaded.

'If you don't mind, madam, I'll be taking a closer look.' He looked behind them and saw that several cars were now waiting beside the first soldier. He wanted to clear the way. 'Pull over, please.'

'I'll just move closer to the verge. Our friend keeps vomiting,' Moira answered, slipping the car into gear. To the guard's consternation, she began driving through the chicane of police cars, passing the road check's bottleneck. The guard made a half-hearted attempt to stop her but changed his mind and pointed to a parking place just beyond the police cars.

Moira was driving at walking place and no alarm was being raised. But since the car had been singled out for a search, several guards began converging on the vehicle.

She did not stop behind the first police cars. Instead, at slow speed, she got the car past them. The soldiers on the other side of the check were the problem now. The guards who would mount the search had not yet reached the car, and were expecting it to stop any moment.

'Keep driving ahead quite slowly,' O'Donnell ordered quietly. 'We'll keep them off-guard and guessing as long as possible.'

Now that they were on the other side of the road check, O'Donnell noticed that oncoming cars were waiting on this side of the check point. In an instant, he knew how they might yet escape.

O'Donnell's car was now moving away from the nucleus of the checkpoint followed by a group of guards, who were expecting the slow-moving vehicle to stop for them at any moment.

'Keep crawling like this until I give the word and then drive like hell for those waiting cars up ahead,' O'Donnell whispered, the adrenalin pumping. 'Once you pass them, tuck in behind them as you go for the corner.'

That was as much as O'Donnell had time to say. One of the policemen shouted at the car to halt. The following policemen broke into a run. O'Donnell fixed in his gaze the soldiers in front, who were unslinging their weapons.

'Go, Moira, go.' he yelled.

Moira crouched low over the wheel as the car accelerated fast in low gear. O'Donnell grabbed Stukalin and pulled him towards the floor of the car, throwing himself on top. For the first few moments, nothing could be heard inside the car except the high note of the racing engine.

The first shots were fired.

O'Donnell was gambling on these being fired high as a warning, which seemed to be the case since none hit the car. He felt the car lurch as Moira carried out his instruction to weave in behind the queue of waiting cars. They were now accelerating away from the check point on the wrong side of the road, with the parked cars in the line of fire of most soldiers.

The first shot to hit the car passed through the back window and the windscreen, which turned opaque. Moira smashed her fist through the screen and it exploded in a splash of tiny glass pieces.

An unsuspecting motorist came round the corner towards them. By now the soldiers had recovered their line of fire and shots began to hit the car repeatedly. The gamble had been lost. They were unlikely to survive a fusillade.

It was the terrified oncoming driver who saved them. Moira, no less terrified herself, drove straight at him and for a few seconds the soldiers behind were unable to fire without the risk of hitting an innocent person.

The innocent person, the oncoming motorist, swerved and braked at the same time, skidding to a halt broadside across the road.

'Go over the grass!' O'Donnell screamed. When Moira left the road, she cleared the field of fire and the shooting started again. Several more shots hit the rear of the car. Two thumped into the back of the passenger seat and into the dashboard. Moira didn't flinch. The car seemed to fly for short distances as she drove it over the bumpy verge at breakneck speed. The noise was deafening.

Suddenly the firing stopped. Moira had brought the car back onto the road, this time behind the broadside car which now sheltered them. They rounded the bend and were gone.

'Moira! Were you hit?' O'Donnell levered himself up off Stukalin's bulk on the floor. She shook her head, speechless. O'Donnell put his arm on her shoulder and squeezed. She had done well.

Stukalin hadn't moved and was still on the floor where O'Donnell had thrust him. The Provo saw the blood. He pulled his prisoner upright and saw pain and shock in his face. Blood was pouring from the Major's left arm.

Moira looked round. 'How bad?'

'Hard to tell.' O'Donnell felt roughly through the clothing. 'But I don't think the bone is broken.'

'I'll look at it when I get a chance. See if you can get a tourniquet round it.' Moira was a trained nurse.

The car faltered.

'Dick,' shouted Moira. 'This car is sicker than any of us. Those shots must have hit something in the engine.'

O'Donnell glanced out of the star-crazed rear window. He was looking for signs of pursuit but he saw something else. A trail of liquid. It didn't matter whether it was water, oil or petrol; the loss of any one of them spelt the imminent end of their transport.

He looked again at his prisoner. The Major was ashen-faced and lay slumped in the corner of the rear seat holding his upper left arm tightly with his right hand. Blood seeped between his fingers.

On the floor of the car were an old pair of boots. O'Donnell ripped the lace out of one of them, tied it into a large loop and threaded it up the Major's injured arm above the wound. He took a pen from his pocket, inserted it into the loop and twisted. This tightened the lace round the arm and stopped the flow of blood. Finally, he put Stukalin's right hand, the good one, on the pen.

'Don't let that untwist, my friend.' He turned to Moira. 'Whenever you like, turn this car across the road and block it. I've an idea.'

'It'll have to be now.' The engine was beginning to chug to its final halt. She threw the wheel over and stopped the car astride the road. The Major groaned as he was thrown about during the turn. O'Donnell quickly got out.

'Get him over to the side of the road. Seat him on that wall and look at his arm.' They had the road to themselves but scarcely for long.

Moira helped Stukalin over to a low wall. 'Do you want him out of sight?' she asked.

'No. Very much in sight. And I want his bleeding to be seen. We have a little time before those bastards gather themselves and come after us. In the meantime, they won't allow anything else to follow.' He turned his attention to the road ahead. 'With a bit of luck, someone will come towards us and they'll think we've had an accident.'

Another gamble, thought Moira, but they had no choice. She silently prayed for an oncoming car and then looked at Stukalin.

She knelt beside him. Her anger at him had been set aside and she became the professional nurse. 'He's in shock. The wound isn't as bad as I thought but he may need blood. Do you want to leave him?'

She turned to O'Donnell for an answer but his attention was elsewhere. In his hands was a cardboard box, taken from the boot. Into it he was throwing large loose stones from the top of the roadside wall. When it was full, he covered the contents with newspaper.

A vehicle was approaching. It was coming from ahead, not from the direction of pursuit. Moira's prayer had been answered and O'Donnell had only seconds to complete his task.

Inside the boot, he ripped the plastic cover from the back of a rear light cluster, gripped the multi-strand wiring tightly and ripped a length free.

He raced to the box on the road behind him and thrust the ends of the wires, still attached to the bulb-holder, deep into the cardboard box. When he was finished, he had before him a large heavy box with electric wires leading from it.

'They'll be expecting a bomb so I've given them one. That'll keep them busy for a while.' As he spoke, O'Donnell removed the rifle and shotgun from their hiding places and placed them at the foot of the wall. He kept the pistol in his pocket.

The approaching car came into view as O'Donnell joined Moira and Stukalin beside the wall.

Couldn't be better, thought O'Donnell as he looked up and saw a well-polished Mercedes saloon slowing down, a middle aged woman at the wheel. She stopped, accepting immediately that there had been an accident. O'Donnell walked briskly over to her.

She wound down the window, looking past O'Donnell at the injured Stukalin. 'Oh dear. What's happened?'

O'Donnell opened the driver's door. 'We need your car to get this man to hospital immediately.' Moira was already helping the Major towards them.

'But of course,' said the woman her face full of concern. She checked that the rear door was unlocked and O'Donnell opened it. Moira pushed Stukalin in first.

The woman was being helpful. 'Keep that rug underneath him. It'll keep the blood off the seats. Is it just his arm?'

Before any of them could answer, the sound of frantic engines, squealing tyres and a police siren reached their ears. O'Donnell ran back to the wall.

'What's going on?' shrilled the woman, as she focused on O'Donnell returning with an armful of guns.

'Move over, lady.' She froze in panic. O'Donnell kicked her. She whimpered and clambered clumsily into the passenger seat, aiming for the door handle and escape. O'Donnell threw the rifle and shotgun over the back seat and drew the pistol.

'Stay where you are,' he bellowed and she froze once again. As he took over the wheel he passed the pistol to Moira. 'Shoot the bitch if she's any more trouble.'

He turned the Mercedes back the way it had come and away from the fast approaching police and army. Smoke poured from the rear tyres as the full power of its big engine spun the wheels on the tarmac. The Mercedes was round the corner before the first police car skidded to a halt at the sight of their target vehicle across the road with its boot open.

Soldiers and police tumbled from their vehicles into the fields alongside the road, making wrong assumptions that their quarry had taken off on foot.

The Mercedes came to a halt at the edge of Fahan, a hamlet of a few private houses and a couple of restaurants. It was still early on a Sunday morning and nobody was about. It was a small community sleeping in a fold of silent hills, overlooking the Sound between the mainland and Inch Island. A jetty and anchorage completed the chocolate-box scene.

Sitting in the front seat of her own car, the woman sobbed, tears washing her make-up down to her neck. O'Donnell grabbed her handbag.

'I haven't got much money with me,' she pleaded.

O'Donnell opened her wallet, removed her driving licence and put it in his pocket without looking. Only then did he speak.

'I want you to drive away from here and don't come back today. You're not to go to the police and if they come to you, you're not to give them a description of us.' He stopped to allow his words to sink past the woman's immediate fear. He needed to frighten her deeply. 'If we ever think you informed, my many friends will know your name and your address.' He patted the pocket containing her driving licence.

She nodded, dumb and wide-eyed. O'Donnell took a tissue from her handbag and gave it to her. As she wiped her eyes, he took a cigarette from her bag and lit it with her lighter. He put the cigarettes and lighter back into the bag and handed it to her, putting it on her lap when she refused to grip it.

Finally he took the cigarette from between his lips and put it between hers. She drew deeply and gratefully on it.

'We will leave you now. It's over.' He turned to Moira. 'This is where we change cars. We must get back over the border fast. Get out.'

Moira was puzzled but obeyed O'Donnell by helping the Major out onto the footpath. O'Donnell motioned the woman back into the driving seat. Once in position, she sat motionless, staring ahead. O'Donnell recognized immobility brought on by fear. He had seen it happen to new recruits on their first active service and had learnt how to deal with it.

He had to get this woman and her car away from Fahan and themselves.

'Seatbelt,' he said gently and the woman began moving. Her shaking hands buckled the belt but that simple action switched her brain into automatically following a familiar sequence.

She restarted the car and drove out of sight.

When the Mercedes had disappeared, Moira asked, 'What bloody car?' She was draping the coat once more round the Major's shoulders, keeping him as warm as possible. She loosened the tourniquet for a short while, to prevent the limb dying.

'There is no car,' said O'Donnell, 'but that woman believes there is. She'll eventually talk to someone, of course, and I want her to talk the search away from here. Start walking.'

'We're not going over the border either then?'

'Too right we're not.'

Nobody paid any attention to the small group walking down the pathway towards the jetty. O'Donnell went to an upturned rowing boat, righted it, inserted the rowlocks and dragged it into the water. He rowed over to the steps of the jetty, where an uneasy girl and a sick Russian were boarded.

He rowed in the direction of the moorings, towards an unremarkable fishing boat lying placidly to a weed-infested buoy.

EIGHT

In Faloon's early days at G2 his instructors had warned him about his sunny disposition. 'Faloon,' he remembered them saying, 'if you're going to hurt someone, maybe even kill them, stop laughing first.'

In the Algonquin Hotel bedroom, in the centre of Manhattan, in the middle of New York, Faloon had stopped laughing. He looked again at the screen of the small computer, willing the words to read differently. Grundy's message, which he had just decoded, remained the same.

He had been ordered back to Dublin by the fastest route possible. He was to report immediately to base headquarters. There was no advice, no message of support, not a word about the kidnapped Sarah. He was reacting badly. To hell with Grundy and to hell with G2. Faloon was a man with conflicting instructions to follow, those from his legitimate boss, others from Martin Riley and the Green Boys. He didn't wish to follow either. If he obeyed Grundy, something unpleasant, perhaps terminal, would happen to Sarah at the hands of Riley. If he obeyed Riley, something nasty would happen to himself at the hands of Grundy.

Faloon connected the computer to the telephone again. This time he called up an American electronic database and called up the airline schedules. A plan was beginning to form in his tired and depressed mind.

The computer screen now told him that Aer Lingus, the Irish airline, had a flight out of Boston to Dublin that evening. That was a full working day away.

It was not the first flight between America and Ireland, but a booking on it would serve to make Grundy think he was obeying instructions. At the same time, Faloon's arrival in Boston would cause the Green Boys to believe he was following their instructions. What happened in Boston would depend on what he found when he got there.

He could use the computer to buy a ticket on the first shuttle flight to Boston, debiting his FBI credit card expense account. He also bought a ticket to Dublin via Shannon on FBI expenses. The thought of Grundy sorting that out with the FBI administration lifted his spirits a little. Finally he tried to snatch a couple of hours' sleep.

Faloon left the Algonquin at dawn in a cab, heading back the way he had come so breezily the previous evening. Again he faced the sun and again he watched the traffic, becoming twitchy whenever a motorcyclist appeared.

Once inside the LaGuardia terminal, Faloon was determined not to be caught off-balance a second time. He examined everybody who came into his view. He stared at all those who were suspicious because they were staring at him. Then at all those who were suspicious because they were not staring at him. Only his pride prevented his locking himself in a toilet cubicle until near his flight time.

At a news stand he bought a copy of the *Irish Times* to catch up with home news. It was several days old but could have been several years old if the headlines had been anything to go by – up and down the Emerald Isle, the devout declared that Madonnas were physically moving in their shrines. Faloon thought it was small wonder the northern Protestants wanted to remain separate from the rest of the country.

The aftermath of the helicopter crash was by then an inside page story. Ireland had never endured many air crashes, so the item caught Faloon's interest. Furthermore, it had crashed on the Inishowen peninsula, which Faloon knew well from childhood holidays. He read the names of those killed. In a country with a small population, he might have known one of the victims.

But he recognized none of the six names. Three of them were Russian, Faloon noted, and he wondered what were they doing at Inishowen. Grundy wouldn't like that since it took them too near the new microwave communications link with Scotland and Northern Ireland. It existed as part of the new telephone system, but the dishes also carried classified military communications.

The flight was called and Faloon was first through the gate.

The final approach at Boston was over the sea, though a tense Faloon was unable to appreciate either the harbour's beauty or its history. At that moment, Boston for Faloon was an Irish city in the hands of his enemies. On landing he threaded his way to the Hertz desk.

'Faloon's the name, I understand you've a car for me.' His mood was thunderous and his manner unappealing, but the lady was professionally pleasant. She smiled.

'Good morning, Mr Faloon. One moment please.'

Faloon watched her closely and impatiently. This transaction should give him his first contact with the Green Boys in Boston. Until that happened he couldn't begin to plan Sarah's escape.

'Yes. Here's your reservation. There's a message here for you as well.' She handed him a white envelope with his name typed on it.

'Oh good,' said Faloon, trying hard to match her pleasantness. 'You didn't, by any chance, see the person who left this?'

'I'm afraid not, sir. I wasn't on duty last night.'

'It hardly matters.' He smiled to hide his frustration. 'I'll know as soon as I open this.' He pocketed it unopened and lifted the rental documents. His face clouded over and the Hertz lady raised her eyebrows.

'I wonder if you could change this car,' he said. 'It's a two-door and I really need a four-door automobile.'

'No problem.' Good thing about the Americans. They lived in a land where the customer was right. In Ireland, the customer was right only if he stood his ground.

Faloon walked away quickly, heading for a small general store off the concourse. From behind a rack of postcards of old Boston, he looked back at the Hertz desk. The receptionist was busy sorting through documents; no one else had approached her and she was making no telephone calls.

So she was not telling anyone about his last-minute change of car. Disappointed, he concluded that the Hertz lady was not a possible pipeline to the Green Boys. He looked around to see if anyone was watching him. He saw nobody.

At the back of the small store he opened the envelope. It contained nothing more compromising than a tourist map of the city. Settling into a seat in the middle of the concourse and in the middle of many other people, he spread the map and examined it, looking every inch the exploring tourist.

Then he saw the simple message. Boston owes its existence to its superb natural harbour, formed by the confluence of three rivers. The rivers meet in the inner harbour, an historic cradle out of which the city had grown. With a ballpoint pen, someone had ringed a piece of that

86

history, 'OLD IRONSIDES, US FRIGATE CONSTITU-TION'.

Nothing else had been written on the map. No name, no time.

Faloon searched the recesses of his memory. The old battleship had been built in the early eighteen hundreds to harass the British in a short war – a piece of symbolism that wouldn't be lost on the Green Boys. Faloon knew some of this, partly as a residue from his schooldays, partly out of a keen interest in sailing and the sea.

Back home he had crewed on many an offshore racer and had been roaring drunk in every Irish Sea harbour. He had also had a passing interest in maritime history and had scuba dived on wrecks along the Irish coast.

The frigate *Constitution* was now moored permanently on the edge of the Charlestown naval yard as a museum and tourist attraction. That was where he was next to make contact with the Green Boys.

Next time, the meeting would be on more equal terms. His first visit would be to a Boston gunsmith. As he walked towards the exit and the rented car park, he folded the map back into the envelope.

In his imagination, he was already strangling Martin Riley in the rigging of Old Ironsides, prior to rescuing his maiden in distress. He knew nothing would be that simple. The Green Boys had all the time they needed to prepare for him. Unless Faloon could think of something, it was going to be their show, not his.

'I beg your pardon,' Faloon apologized. While still in his dream world, he'd walked into an on-coming couple. The baggage trolley being pushed by the woman behind then ploughed into his upper heel, knocking him off balance. Helping hands restored his equilibrium and further apologies soothed his exasperation.

Outside the terminal building, with the fresh breeze blowing in his hair, Faloon began looking for a signpost to the Hertz carpark, at the same time searching his pockets for the Hertz documents that would tell him the number of his vehicle.

They were not in any of his pockets. He must have left them at the Hertz desk. Annoyance furrowed his face as he picked up his case and began walking back into the terminal, still searching his pockets.

Then it dawned on him with fury. The envelope with the map was missing too and he knew that he hadn't left that document behind. He'd fallen for the oldest trick in the book. His pocket had been picked. Not for his wallet. For the envelope and the map.

He was now running inside the terminal, his eyes peeled for any of the four people he had apologized to. He headed in the direction of the Hertz desk. Standing at the desk were two of the people he was searching for. He leapt into action.

'OK, you two. Let's have my property back.' Faloon had the man's arm in a tight grip. The man's arm didn't move. It was like steel.

'You're the guy who bumped into us at the door. You're not causing more trouble, are you.' The man glared very threateningly at Faloon and the Hertz receptionist saw the prospect of big trouble on her doorstep. She picked up her phone. 'I'm getting security.'

The last thing Faloon wanted was involvement with local police. The most serious charge he could levy was theft of a few bits of worthless paper, most of which were probably the property of the Hertz company anyway. Time to retreat.

'No, forget security. I'm sorry sir. A case of mistaken identity.' Faloon turned to the Hertz lady.

'Do you have another set of documents, please? I have just had mine stolen.' There was a pregnant silence. 'I mean I've just lost them.'

She hesitated, looking from the man to Faloon and back again, then took her hands from the telephone.

'Certainly, Mr, er, Faloon, isn't it.' He nodded and the new documents were handed to him with a 'have a nice day' smile. The man with the iron muscles was still scowling as Faloon backed off.

For some moments, Faloon scarcely realized the full significance of what had just happened. In mitigation, he was very tired after a night that had seen celebration, then defeat, disappointment, and very little sleep.

Faloon was as worried as ever he'd been in his professional life. He was in trouble with G2 and Colonel Grundy in Dublin. And the tone of Grundy's gruff message ordering him home with unseemly haste could be interpreted as meaning he might also be in trouble with the FBI.

This time Faloon found the car and threw himself in behind the wheel. He headed towards the centre of town. The episode of Boston Airport had been a mistake, but with one good effect. Faloon was fully alert and in a cold, dangerous mood.

Who had confronted him at the airport? Not the Green Boys. They knew what was in the envelope.

Who then did not know and might try surreptitiously to find out? There could be only one answer: the FBI.

'Grundy!' Faloon bellowed out loud. 'You're a devious bastard ... bastard ... bastard. You shopped me to the FBI. They must be tailing me.'

He clenched his fist and punched the steering wheel in frustration. He thought of Sarah. Would Grundy's warning have reached the ears of the Green Boy source within the FBI? If so, what was waiting for him at 'Old Ironsides'? Would it be Sarah's body?

He drove into a multi-storey car park near the centre of the old city and dumped the car on an upper storey. It was useless to him; possibly it harboured a radio bug.

He was beginning to lose faith in his ability to go anywhere unseen. His adversaries, official and unofficial, were good.

Faloon would have liked Boston if he'd been in the mood. The city was old enough to have meandering streets

89

like the old cities of Europe. Old houses and graveyards co-existed with tall office towers. The old buildings gave the new architecture a human scale. How different from Manhattan, where huge buildings were made to look small by the vast ones. Faloon wished that something in Boston could make him look small. He needed to hide in the brickwork.

He also needed a gun. The FBI, whom he presumed now had the map, would have drawn the same obvious conclusion as himself from the circle. They would have the area round the old frigate staked out long before he could reach the spot. If the Green Boys knew what was happening, his mission was already doomed.

Retrieving Sarah was becoming an ever more remote hope. The Green Boys might just shoot Faloon in retaliation, before, during or after their assignation with him. At a best guess, they would keep Faloon alive until they were certain he'd yield nothing to them. Then they'd shoot him.

Of course, the FBI might have deduced what the Green Boys were after and might shoot him first as a preventative measure, Faloon thought grimly, mentally hurling another curse across the Atlantic at Grundy. But not as a first option, as he'd seen.

The FBI's first option clearly had been to find out where Faloon was to meet the Green Boys and to interfere. They'd tried to do so without alerting either Faloon or the Green Boys. The agency could also have arrested him at the airport, but had deliberately chosen not to, not even when he made a fool of himself at the Hertz desk. He saw the gunsmith's shop, its window filled with the full range of the hunter's needs. Guns, ammunition, crossbows, waterproof clothing, traps. Traps! Faloon smiled humorously. It occurred to him that he was the bait in an FBI trap.

He always carried with him his FBI identification and a valid firearms certificate so preliminary formalities at the gunshop were short. Most of the hand guns on offer were target pistols, which were too big, too fragile, and too small a calibre for what Faloon had in mind. He wanted something that would stop Martin Riley in his tracks. He didn't want a revolver, an old and trusted design of hand gun which still held a high place in the affections of Americans. However, tucked away at the back of the shop Faloon saw what he could use. It was a Walther PBK 9mm pistol, favoured by police forces in Europe and light enough for a pocket. He was able to buy a spare magazine and a box of ammunition far too large for his purposes. He hoped.

He loaded both the pistol and the spare magazine in the shop, making a present to the nonplussed shopkeeper of the remainder of the ammunition. Putting the Walther in an outside pocket, and the spare magazine in another, he left in a cab, ready for battle.

Faloon told the driver he was a tourist who wanted a tour of the old buildings and sites of the city. He leaned forward to pass the driver a fifty dollar bill.

'I'm an impulsive sort of guy. If I see something that I really like I'll just jump out. You keep the change.'

In a city like Boston, this did not greatly surprise the driver and he accepted the instruction phlegmatically. He didn't even turn round when Faloon suddenly left him at the Old South Meeting House and darted down a sidestreet, then down another and yet another until the angry Irishman had lost his own sense of direction. He hailed the next taxi that crossed his path.

'Nice city you have here,' Faloon said breathlessly. 'Take me to Bunker Hill.'

In the short time he had had to study the map given to him by the Green Boys, Faloon had noticed Bunker Hill. It overlooked the Charlestown Navy Yard where Old Ironsides was moored and possibly offered the best reconnaissance.

Bunker Hill was a disappointment to Faloon on several counts. Most crucially, it did not give him the high view of the navy yard he needed. Surprisingly, he found it devoid of a sense of history. It hadn't been accorded the dignity and style he felt should mark the first engagement of the American War of Independence. Bunker Hill was a scruffy piece of grass surrounded by nondescript housing. The site had been robbed of the very view that had made it a defensive position against the British two centuries ago.

He started walking. Halfway down the hill, he caught a partial view of his target. He could see the masts of the frigate and a queue at the end of its gangplank. Behind the queue was a large parade ground surrounded by low buildings. There were people and parked cars in abundance and only one way in or out. Ideal for what the Green Boys wanted.

He knew that someone, or some two or three, would pick up his trail at the gate, but Faloon's chance of establishing their identity was remote. Nor was there any point in trying to sneak up unseen to the entrance. He had to cross open ground and broad highways to reach it. He had no option but to enter the trap set for him by the Green Boys – and modified by whatever the FBI had up their sleeves.

He made a final check of the pistol and spare magazine, deciding to transfer the pistol to his trouser pocket. That way he could keep it in his hand all the time. He should have bought a camera. Everybody else had one.

To the untutored eye, Old Ironsides, or the USS *Constitution* as the US Navy preferred to call her, looked very much like any other early nineteenth-century battleship. Faloon knew that the ship had been at the forefront of war technology in her day. She had been smaller and more manoeuvrable, better armed and better armoured than contemporary European ships and proved formidable in action. Faloon was willing the same attributes upon himself.

Inside, the old ship was more pristine and doubtless smelled a lot better than when in service. Under the low deck heads, young ratings, pressed into duty as guides, gave word-perfect explanations, dotted with over-rehearsed jokes.

Not that Faloon was listening; he was waiting, the only role left to him. At least the FBI had been discreet. He was unable to pick out an obvious tail. In fact, he'd been unable to pick out anyone suspicious except himself.

It happened as one of the ratings was describing the sequence for firing one of the cannons. Faloon felt a smooth and small hand gently grasp his own and smelt a waft of perfumed air. Beside him, standing with assumed intimacy, was a slip of a girl, hardly more than nineteen, wearing blue jeans and a blouse covered with a bulky sweater. As Faloon stared at her, she appeared tremendously interested in cannons until the rest of their small group was ushered to the next point of interest.

'Have you seen the museum ashore?' she said, looking at him intently. 'It's got things you'd find very interesting.'

As she spoke she was leading him towards the upper deck and the gangplank. Climbing the steep steps, Faloon worried about who this girl represented. Where was he allowing himself to be led? Green Boy or FBI? Was he making contact or being arrested? She could be an ordinary hooker, of course.

NINE

Side by side they walked across the parade ground towards one of the buildings.

'Where is she? Is she here?' Faloon began.

'I don't know.' The girl didn't slacken her pace or even look at Faloon. 'I'm a messenger, just a messenger.' She sounded proud of herself and Faloon wondered if this was the first clandestine act of her short life. No matter, she was a Green Boy. He'd made contact at last.

'What's your name then, messenger?'

'Messenger will do just fine.' She smiled for the first time. Faloon didn't respond.

'Sarah had better be available in one piece or heads will roll, bloodily. That's a message, messenger.'

The girl shook her head. 'It's no good getting uptight at me. I don't know Sarah; I've never seen her and I don't know very much about what you're talking about. My job is to help you give us some information and help you get some in return. That's all.'

'What the hell is it that you people want? Let's get it over with right now.'

'Not yet. I've been told you'll need convincing that we mean business.'

Faloon looked across at her for signs of sarcasm but came to the conclusion that she was telling the truth as she saw it. She was too young and inexperienced to hold much authority in the nefarious organization she represented. They lapsed into silence and Faloon used the remaining time before they reached their destination looking for the girl's hidden back-up.

'Expecting company?' She glanced about nervously. 'Because I hope not, for your Sarah's sake.'

'How am I to know that Sarah is OK? If I don't see her I've no guarantee that she's even alive.'

'I've a message from her. You'll see it when we reach a more private place.' Some of the messenger's confidence had returned.

Led by the girl, the two of them entered the museum and began an infuriatingly slow tour of the exhibits, mostly devoted to demonstrating seafaring life in the 1800s. Inside there was not the same freedom to talk. In museums, galleries and libraries, a hoarse whisper can sound like a parade ground order. Their communication dried up. They went upstairs. The girl stopped in front of a row of television sets with keyboards in front of them. 'Do you like computer games?'

Faloon was too exasperated to answer. The girl shrugged and began to play. It was a text game in which the player took on the role of the captain of a man o'war. The computer displayed options and the player chose. Marks were awarded for the right decision.

Faloon wished life was as simple. He didn't think he'd been aggregating many marks over the last few hours in his own game. The girl continued playing. Playing for time. What was she waiting for, Faloon wondered?

In the next instant, he found out. The girl was waiting until they had the gallery to themselves. She beckoned Faloon to follow and skipped to the far corner, to a door marked 'private'. With one last check to ensure no one was a witness, she opened the door and pulled Faloon through.

Faloon found himself in a dark corridor which traversed the building. It opened out to reveal a narrow rear staircase. She led him down two flights and into a little-used cellar and store room. When she switched on the light, Faloon saw that he was in a long room, filled with redundant display material. In a recently cleared corner stood a table and upon it, a video recorder, a portable television set and a portable cellphone.

Faloon's heart sank. What he was looking at told him that the only contact he was going to make with the Green Boys in the flesh was this girl. He resolved never to let her out of his sight. If necessary, he thought grimly, two could play the hostage game.

As the girl went forward to the video recorder, Faloon pulled out the Walther. 'Right, madam, your bag please.'

She turned and looked at him, more angry than surprised. 'You're simply delaying things. You didn't really think that they were going to send me here with a bag full of things you might find useful, did you?'

She didn't look at the pistol, but straight into his eyes. One day she'll be good, thought Faloon. Pity she's started on the wrong side. She dropped her bag onto the floor.

'Move away from the bag. Go over to the wall, turn and face it.' She complied slowly. Faloon bounded towards her and pushed her roughly against the wall, then pulled her back again just over a metre.

'Put your hands against the wall at a height just above your head,' he commanded. 'And move your feet wide apart.' In that position, she was steeply angled against the wall, sufficiently off balance to make a quick movement impossible without plenty of warning.

From behind, Faloon searched her thoroughly, not sparing her blushes, if she had any. She gasped as he made sure that her breasts were flesh and blood. Reticent searching in Belfast had led to many a shop disappearing. He moved to her thighs and hips, though he thought there was hardly enough room inside her jeans for a dollar bill to be inserted.

Finally, he made her take off her shoes. Only then was did he turn his attention to her bag on the floor.

He carried it to the table and tipped it out. It contained only two objects. A purse with a small amount of money, and a video tape.

She was looking back at him when he spoke. 'What were your instructions at this point?'

'Can I move now?'

He nodded and backed away from the table. She picked up the video tape and dropped it into the video player. 'I was told to play this message from Sarah,' she said, turning on the television set.

They both stepped back as the picture settled down. Faloon turned the television sound up full, but there seemed to be no sound recorded on the beginning of the tape. He was soon to discover why.

The camera had been in a fixed position, as if high up on a tripod. It looked down on an old army-style iron bed, minus its mattress. At the foot of the bed was a watering can and some coiled wires.

There was movement into the picture from the left. Two men and a woman appeared, wearing hoods that left only their eyes uncovered. The two men were half dragging, half carrying Sarah between them. She was completely naked, red-eyed and looked frightened, though she wasn't struggling.

Sarah was positioned on the bed face up and held spread-eagled as her wrists and ankles were strapped to the corners of the bed. The two men retreated out of the picture.

The hooded woman picked up the watering can and sprinkled Sarah's body from head to toe, concentrating on her head, breasts, hips and feet. In a single motion, she replaced the watering can and picked up the wires, untangling them as she looked at Sarah's face.

Faloon was speechless when he realized what was about to happen. He shot a glance at the girl beside him and her face told him that she was also probably seeing this for the first time. When his eyes returned to the screen, Faloon saw that the wires resembled those on an electric welder. One of the wires ended in a crocodile clip and this had been attached to the toes of Sarah's right foot. The other wire ended as an insulated probe in the hands of the hooded woman. He noticed she was now wearing heavy rubber gloves.

Holding Sarah's head by the hair, she touched Sarah's ear with the probe.

The effect on Sarah's body was instant as the electric current travelled the length of it. Her head was thrown back and her legs arched clear of the bed in a rigid spasm.

After a few seconds, the probe was withdrawn and Sarah's body collapsed like that of a puppet whose strings had been released.

The woman looked at Sarah's face and said something unheard to the unseen men. One of them stepped forward and gave her something. It was a boxer's gumshield and it was pushed roughly between Sarah's lips. The woman was bringing the electrode down to Sarah's breasts when Faloon leapt forward and pulled the video player's plug from the wall. A symbolic and futile act.

He turned on the girl messenger and brought the pistol

97

up to eye level. She saw the emotion in his face and was terrified.

'I didn't know. As God is my witness, I didn't know,' the girl messenger sobbed. 'I was left the tape at a pick-up point with instructions to bring you to this room. That's all. Honest. I don't even know where they have her.'

She collapsed to her knees and the line of Faloon's aim followed. His hand shook. He closed his eyes and opened them to dissipate some of the fury and rage and helplessness bottled up within him. He knew he must remain calm. The aim of the video was to unnerve him and he mustn't succumb.

'The rest of your instructions, what are they?' demanded Faloon harshly.

The girl struggled to her feet, her face streaked with tears. 'I'm supposed to telephone a number.'

'Give it to me.'

'I can't. It's in the telephone memory as last-number-redial. You push the button with the asterisk on it, but I don't know what the number is.'

'Clever bastards,' Faloon fumed. He pressed the asterisked button. The phone was picked up the other end on the first ring but nobody spoke. Faloon broke the silence with a single word.

'Faloon,' he snarled.

'Hang up and wait,' came the crisp answer from a woman and the line went dead.

They waited. The girl was in control of herself once more. Faloon was living on his nerves. His hands were shaking so much that he put the Walther on safety in case he shot the wretched girl without meaning to.

The phone rang and he snatched it to his ear.

'Hello Faloon.' It was Riley's voice. Faloon struggled for self control. 'You've seen your girl. She's quite a good conductor, isn't she?'

'You are an animal, Riley. When I reach you I'll give you worse than an animal's death. That's a promise.'

'Save your hot air, Faloon. You're a traitor to Ireland and so is the government you serve. Your Sarah is a traitor's woman.'

'She's not part of all this, Riley. Let her go.' Pleading with the likes of Riley was sticking in Faloon's gullet, but he was not in a good negotiating position.

'Her return is in your hands, Faloon.'

Faloon tried another tack. 'Look, Riley. You know something about me. I've a girl in every port – ships passing in the night. There's a limit to what you can get out of me using her.'

But Riley mocked him. 'Faloon, you're wasting time. I know all about you and darling Sarah. I know how often you screw her, your favourite position, her favourite one, and some of the other things the pair of you amuse yourselves doing.'

Riley pressed home his advantage. 'She's so keen to keep away from electricity she begins answering questions before we finish putting them.' He chuckled.

'In that case, you will have got all the information you want. Let her go.'

Riley's answer to that plea was immediate. There was a rustling sound as a hand covered the mouth piece; muffled knocks and then the sound of distressed breathing.

'Faloon, is that you?'

'Sarah! Oh God, Sarah.'

From the background a harsh order by Riley interrupted. 'Read it, woman.'

There was the rustle of paper and Sarah began reading. 'A forty-three year old Englishman arrived in Boston Harbour late last night after an eleven week Atlantic crossing in his small sailboat. He was . . .'

Sarah's trembling voice halted in obedience to an indistinct order from Riley. A further pause and it was Riley back on the phone. 'You're a sailing man, aren't you, Faloon. If you want the full story you can read it in today's paper, so now you know she's still alive, alive enough to hurt and keep hurting. He was interrupted by a long scream.

'Faloooooooon.'

'Get her out of here.' Riley shouted.

Faloon heard Sarah being removed. Riley resumed speaking.

'Right Faloon. Now you know the score, let's get down to business. If I get what I want, I'll release the woman. I'll have no further interest in her and I'll keep my side of the bargain.' Little chance of that, thought Faloon despairingly.

'If she's told you everything, then you've got everything. There's nothing for me to add.'

'There is, Faloon. There is something that she doesn't know, but you do. Are you listening, Faloon?'

'Yes,' replied Faloon tersely, for he was listening with all his concentration in case he heard any peripheral sound over the line that might lead him to where Riley was speaking. Faloon had forgotten about the girl at his end and wasn't watching her. But she was watching him. Riley continued.

'We aren't terribly interested in what the FBI has got on us. They aren't the real enemy. The British are the enemy. It's the British computer files that are doing us great damage and the fact that you can get into them.'

At long last the nightmare was beginning to make sense to Faloon. The Green Boys had wrested from Sarah the news of his breach of British security data bases in Northern Ireland. The stakes were very high. Faloon was being caught in a vice.

'We want two things, Faloon. First the present protocols and codes for entering the computers at the British Army Northern Ireland HQ. Second, we want a name. The name of the tame programmer who gave you the information in the first place.'

Faloon desperately needed time to figure a way out of this mess, if there was one. 'You're wrong, Riley. The British computers aren't constantly connected to telephone lines like the FBI ones. You can't access the data by phone except by arrangement.'

'Stop fucking about, Faloon. Some of the British material can be directly accessed. You know that; we know that. The codes, Faloon, or do we start running up our electricity bill?'

'I can't give you the information now. It's not the kind of stuff I walk about with. You can understand that, can't you. Secondly, even if I did have it, it's too complicated to give over the phone.'

'I don't believe the first bit. I agree with the second, so we have a dead letter drop already planned. Take down these details.'

In the turmoil, Faloon had forgotten about the girl. He had the telephone in one hand; in the other, the gun, with its safety catch still on. He put the gun on the chair behind him and, holding the phone to his ear, reached inside his coat for a pen and something to write on. The girl pounced on the weapon.

Faloon stared at her, his hand frozen immobile inside his coat. The girl had backed away from him, holding the Walther in both hands at arm's length, pointing it at him. She didn't utter a word, but continued to back away from him towards the door.

As Faloon opened his mouth to speak, the door behind the girl burst open. Framed in it were four men, two standing, two crouched, all with handguns pointed at Faloon and the girl.

One of the men was also holding a badge. He shouted as the girl began to turn, 'FBI. Freeze.'

The men saw the girl swinging her aim from Faloon to themselves, or so it appeared. They fired. The short lethal bursts flung her body back to Faloon's feet. The men followed fast. One seized the fallen Walther. Another grabbed Faloon and put him against the wall. The third turned the girl's body roughly over and said unemotionally, 'Dead.'

The last one had the phone to his ear. 'It's dead too,' he said.

'You stupid bastards,' Faloon erupted. 'You've fucked this up in a big way. If you shoot first, asking questions after is useless. She was our only lead.'

Faloon was overwhelmed with a mixture of bitterness, despair and frustration at the knee-jerk reaction of the FBI men. 'She was a stupid girl who thought the Green Boys would give her a little adventure. She didn't even know enough to take the safety off the Walther.' The FBI man holding the Walther examined it and nodded confirmation of what Faloon had said to the captain.

The captain was in no mood for recriminations from Faloon. He was expecting gratitude and relief, both notably absent. He met Faloon's anger with his own.

'She had a gun. She was about to fire on us. That's all we could tell. All she had to do was to stay still.'

'The gun was mine.'

'And the inexperienced girl had gotten hold of it, Faloon. You're an asshole. We've got plenty of questions, Faloon, and somebody to give us an answer.' He jabbed his gun in Faloon's direction.

One of the men pressed a button on the video player and when it didn't work, investigated and replaced the power lead. The television flickered into life, picking up the picture where it had left off. The hooded woman continued her action and applied the electrode to Sarah's breast. The tortured body twisted and arched. The men watched in stunned silence as the torturer, with a woman's knowledge of a woman's body, touched sensitive parts, pausing only to make sure that her victim remained conscious. When she at last lost consciousness, the video ended.

The captain turned to Faloon. He was much less hostile. 'That was Sarah, wasn't it?' Faloon nodded.

'Did this girl know the address where those bastards did that?' He inclined his head in the direction of the body crumpled on the floor. The girl's thick sweater was soaking up the blood that oozed from numerous holes in her chest and back.

Faloon sighed. 'No, I'm pretty sure they had kept her in the dark. She brought the cassette but I don't think she knew what was on it until she saw it here. Poor little cow.'

'It's our woman I'm worried about. Who were you on the phone to?' The captain looked hard at Faloon.

'Riley. Green Boys.'

'Yeah. You left a vague message about him from New York. So Martin Riley is behind this. We'll find him. But, while we're doing so, it would be a great help if we knew what he was after? It must've been something very special to go to these lengths. This,' said the captain, pointing at the video, 'was meant to apply pressure on you. So what did they want?'

'Material I was gathering on the Green Boys and other Irish republican groups helping the IRA Provos here,' Faloon lied.

'What did you give them?' snapped the captain sharply.

'Nothing. I gave them nothing. Riley had just reached the point of outlining his demands when you burst in.'

The captain looked at Faloon in a manner that revealed he didn't really believe the Irishman.

'I would've given them nothing,' Faloon went on, 'whether you'd appeared or not. Once they get what they want, Sarah is dead. I can keep her alive for a while by keeping my mouth shut. Though whether she'll stay alive now that this has happened . . .'

Faloon's voice trailed away. The captain nodded, seeming more satisfied.

'OK Faloon, you can go.'

'You're letting me walk away?' Faloon sounded amazed.

'No, Faloon, fly away. You're a bundle of trouble in this place. Your guys in G2 want you back home fast, though I can't understand why. You can tie up a whole agency by just belonging to it, seems to me.' He put his hand in his pocket and handed Faloon his own passport.

He continued, relishing the effect on Faloon. 'We packed your things. Your suitcase is already with Aer Lingus at Boston airport. Now we're packing you to go along with it. This is your bag, isn't it?

He was pointing to Faloon's overnight case, which he had carried with him throughout. He'd expected to need the computer. When Faloon nodded, the captain nodded in turn to one of his men. The case was picked up, opened and the computer withdrawn.

'Now, Mr Faloon, your FBI identification and credit cards please, and your firearms permit.'

Faloon's much lighter bag was now put into his hands. Two of the FBI positioned themselves on either side of him and began ushering him towards the door.

'And don't take your eyes off him until that plane door closes,' the captain ordered. 'I don't want to see the creep again.'

'What about Sarah?' Faloon shouted over his shoulder.

'She's our problem now. Keep away from it, Faloon. That's an order from me and an order from your people in Dublin. But I wish I could keep you for a while, because you haven't told me the truth. The Green Boys are not putting the screws on you for FBI material. They've got Sarah and she'll give them all the information they want under that treatment.' The captain moved up to Faloon until his face was very close. 'They picked up Sarah to get something else. Something only you know, that's my guess. Am I right, Faloon?'

The captain was indeed right and his words set Faloon wondering about an untidy detail in the events so far. The Green Boys and Martin Riley wanted access codes into British files. That is what they had wanted right from the beginning, from before they had picked up Sarah. How the hell had they known . . .

Something was wrong, but there was nobody he could talk to about it. Maybe he had been thinking along the wrong lines all along about the leakage. There was now another possibility. The Green Boy mole might very well be a full-blown IRA mole – somewhere on the other side of the Atlantic. Somewhere within British intelligence.

TEN

'Have you heard? Faloon's on the way back here.'

'That so? I thought the blue-eyed boy had another few months swanning in the United States to endure.'

His colleague leaned over the desk conspiratorially. 'He should've had, but the news is that he has crapped in the nest over there and there's been a bloody great row. I hear that our American cousins told Grundy to recall Faloon or they were going to lock him up and throw away the key.'

The other man nodded. 'Serve the over-privileged bastard right. Grundy thinks the sun shines out of his arse, even at midnight. Whatever happened over there, if it convinces our grand old man that Faloon shits like lesser mortals in G2, then good will come of it.'

The office door behind the pair slammed with unusual vigour. Both men turned a little red. It was the boss, Colonel Grundy, and he was in a dark mood.

'And if you two didn't sit on your arses so much,' Grundy muttered, 'maybe I'd see a bit more sunshine round this place.'

Grundy threw his coat across an empty desk, and himself across another. He had not meant to succumb to the temptation to retaliate to the overheard words of his two G2 staffmen.

He knew that his men had been working flat out watching both the Russians and the Americans, while trying to keep up with some of the routine work. He also was aware that his men scarcely knew what they were looking for.

'Look for something unusual,' had been Grundy's general instruction, but since they had not been keeping a close eye on the comings and goings of the Russian and American embassies recently, recognition of the unusual was not easy. Nevertheless, reports from the embassies were pouring in, along with those from the airports. It was boring, repetitive work and ill-tempered conversations like the one Grundy had overheard were perhaps the least to be expected.

Colonel Grundy should have gone straight to his office to deal with the mounting paperwork. He cast a baleful glance at the screens, the keyboards and printers. The computer consultant had told him that computers were leading towards the paperless office. Ballocks! They were knee-deep in print-out.

But this morning, Grundy decided to forego an early start behind his own desk, partly to undo his hasty last words to the two red faces in front of him and partly to seize the opportunity to talk to some of his men. From his army days he knew the value of informal contacts with the troops.

Grundy was as frustrated as the rest of G2 in Dublin and the rest of Ireland. Something was happening, but he and G2 didn't know what. As yet there was no explanation for the helicopter crashing on the north coast nor for the highly unusual interest of first the Russians, then the Americans. He had asked his CIA contacts for information, but had been fobbed off with a few patronizing sentences, even including an infuriating 'way out of your league; let the professionals do the job!'

Grundy knew that the two men working for him were professionals, even if they were not playing on the world stage like the CIA. Like most of his staff, neither of them had delivered the scoops that Faloon had; on the other hand, neither had landed him in the kind of trouble that Faloon could generate. It was only human for others in the service to feel that the Faloons of this world had their sins too easily forgiven.

However, there were times when people like Faloon paid a greater price for their favoured status than many others in G2 knew. Betrayal could be part of the price. Grundy had betrayed Faloon to the FBI chiefs. He hadn't allowed Faloon the time he implored to rescue his woman and Grundy wondered if Faloon would survive what he'd done to him. An early morning call had told him he had, but at a price. Everything had a price.

The boss had betrayed his own man because the overall priorities had demanded it. Grundy felt he had to ensure that G2 had as many friends among sister agencies as possible in preparation for a clash with both the CIA and the KGB. To undermine the CIA he might need the FBI in Washington, so Faloon was sacrificed on that altar. Grundy would need other friends as well, like the British.

'Any important messages overnight, nightwatch?' Grundy began quietly. He leaned forward to offer the man a cigarette from an old-fashioned silver case. It was a peace offering and the atmosphere relaxed.

'As far as I can gather, sir, it's routine stuff.' The man paused, giving Grundy the opportunity to leave. Grundy nodded without moving. The man wanted to talk further and Grundy was staying to listen.

'Colonel Grundy, this is the biggest turnout we've had in years and we all know it's not the usual stuff of closing the border and hunting the Provo. Who's the enemy? Is it the Russians and the Americans at the same time? Surely they're not both helping the Provos?' He paused again, not knowing whether he'd asked for more than he should know.

'No, they're not.' Grundy smiled, stubbing out his cigarette. 'At least, I don't think this has anything to do with the IRA. All I can say is that we're pretty sure the Americans and the Russians are somehow going to meddle in our jurisdiction.'

The two men brightened. This was very different and they were all ears for Grundy's words. 'We think, just think, that they are scrambling for something, but . . .' and here Grundy brought the palms of his hands slowly down onto the desktop in a gesture of frustration, 'we don't know what, we don't know why, we don't know when and we don't know exactly where.'

This was what the men wanted to hear. Enmeshing with big battalions of the intelligence world was an intriguing and rare prospect.

'So that's why Faloon is returning,' said the nightwatch, avoiding Grundy's eyes.

Grundy rose and headed towards his own office. 'Faloon is coming back to have his arse kicked. I'll risk a sunburnt foot.'

They both sniggered. Another little betrayal of Faloon, thought Grundy, but all in the interests of the Service. And now he would deceive the pair in front of him for the same reason.

He added, 'And when he does come back I'll put him on something routine for a while. Which reminds me, anything more from the Inishowen area and the roadblock bust?'

The nightwatch shuffled through papers on his desk. 'Yes sir, a little. First you won't be surprised to hear that those responsible got away.'

Grundy grimaced but said nothing. Nightwatch continued. 'But the *garda* got a look inside the car before and after it left them. The occupants were two men and a woman, the woman in the driving seat and the two men in the back.'

'Why?' asked Grundy, his journey to his own office postponed as his analytical mind slipped into top gear.

'They told the men at the scene, before they managed to drive through them, that one of the men in the back was ill because he'd drunk bad poteen at a binge in Buncrana the night before. They said they were taking him for urgent hospital treatment.'

'Any of them recognized?'

'Not sure, but two of them, they think, were Provos. One of the men they did not recognize at all. Never seen him before.'

'Anything special about the stranger?'

'It's not in the report sir, but when I was chatting to the officer concerned on the phone, he told me that the man who was supposed to be ill had a deep suntan, even under an unshaven chin. He didn't look ill. The combination of all these factors, including the seating arrangement, made the officer suspicious.'

'But not suspicious enough to put a gun on them immediately,' Grundy snarled. 'Kidnap? Could the man in the back have been a kidnap victim?'

'Possible, sir, but there are no reports of anyone missing.' The man stopped speaking for a moment because Grundy looked so angry. 'They caught up with the car and it appears that at least one of them was hit by gunfire. There was blood on the back seat,' he added.

'And I don't suppose that collection of fine policemen were able to follow the blood anywhere interesting after finding the car? How far did that car get from the road block anyway?'

'It would appear . . .'

'Nothing is appearing,' Grundy exploded. 'Everything is disappearing. Give it to me straight, man.'

'The car was damaged by army gunfire, sir, and it got only a few miles down the road. The police and army on the spot found what they thought was a bomb in the boot, so they closed the road. . . .'

'Never mind that. Where are the people who were inside that car?'

'They don't know, sir. They've lost sight of them.'

Grundy rubbed his brow with his hand. Perhaps none of this mattered anyway. Perhaps it was a routine dust-up between police and Provos.

The nightwatch added his own conjecture. 'It would be my guess that these people hijacked another motorist and buggered off fast while the hoax bomb kept everyone else busy for a while.'

Grundy snorted. He thought fleetingly of the Israeli Mirage fighters he had watched over Lebanon, casting flares behind them as they streaked across defended targets. The heat-seeking missiles fired from the ground went for the decoy flares and the planes flew on to safety.

'Nightwatch. Get onto that phone and tell the police to look for some frightened person who's keeping his mouth shut about a hijack. Or find out if someone in the area is missing.'

The nightwatch responded sluggishly. 'They won't like us for telling them their business,' he said reaching for the phone but Grundy was already heading for his office. He entered and closed the door, swearing under his breath.

Then he had a thought and phoned the office he'd just left.

'Put nightwatch back on.' he ordered curtly.

'He's on the other line, sir.' In the background Grundy could hear a heated exchange between nightwatch and some police officer.

Grundy sighed and said, 'Then see to this yourself. I want you to check and double check that all the bodies in that helicopter crash on Inishowen are accounted for. Check with our team at Shannon. I want all the Russians there accounted for, dead or alive. Got that?'

At last Grundy turned his attention to the paperwork. On top of the pile was a message from Arthur Semple in London, returning Grundy's previous call. Both men were busy, and both were engaged in the same type of work.

Arthur Semple and James Grundy had been bumping into each other throughout their careers. Like Grundy, Semple had been a serving army officer but unlike the Irishman, had gone on to be a diplomat, at least to outward appearances. Grundy was a captain in Africa when he first came across Semple, who at the time was a junior military attache. The two men had taken an instant liking to each other, sharing a common interest in military history, chess – and spying.

Grundy and Semple were to meet again in the Near East, Grundy as a Unifil Colonel commanding the Irish contingent of the United Nations peace-keeping force, Semple as a senior military adviser on special assignment to the British embassy in Beirut. For Grundy, even a battered Beirut had its attractions when normal existence was a dusty dug-out in southern Lebanon. The city became more attractive for Grundy when he discovered that Semple was in it.

They began meeting regularly, renewing their friendship, tacitly accepting that they could feed professionally off each other with mutual benefit. From Semple, Grundy got a good idea of the mood of the Israelis, who were the dominant military power in his area. Semple in return received intelligence about the state of the militias and their current intentions.

At about the same time as Grundy's appointment as head of G2 in Dublin, Semple had been posted back to London. It was some months before it filtered through to Grundy that his old friend had become a prominent member of the British DIS, the Defence Intelligence Staff. Once again the two began communicating professionally and personally.

The British DIS co-ordinated all army, navy and air intelligence. It also had a finger in economic, technical and scientific intelligence. There had been the odd occasion when Grundy had used this important link to warn Semple of impending trouble. Usually that some British intelligence initiative in Ireland against the IRA was about to be publicly exposed.

British covert action on the territory of the Irish Republic was a very touchy political issue in Ireland and potentially could wreak havoc in the delicate relationship between the two countries. The Irish were very sensitive about their sovereign rights.

Grundy, as a professional, was able to perceive the intelligence imperative behind limited operations by MI5 in Ireland and therefore might, out of self-interest, chaperone bungled MI5 jobs out of harm's way. He usually had MI5 agents arrested and secretly bundled back across the border. Normally he had found himself dealing with MI5, even though this agency's job was British internal security and counter-espionage. However, since MI5 had an important station in Northern Ireland to counter the IRA, their field of action frequently reached out over the border of the United Kingdom, which was usually MI6's responsibility.

Lately the British had been reckless. They had poured agents into Ireland without telling Irish counterparts during the last two Provo IRA kidnappings of British businessmen. Irish Special Branch had been tripping over them. When that happened, the whole business was likely to become both public and political. Sometimes Grundy found himself arguing on behalf of the British in secret meetings where MI5 was, in effect, on trial.

These episodes were very much to the fore of Grundy's mind as he asked his secretary to get Semple on the line. Grundy normally had won his cases on Britain's behalf on one condition – that he let the British know how hard he had fought to keep British spooks out of Irish court rooms. In other words, some day there would have to be a quid pro quo. For Grundy, it was quid pro quo day and Semple must know it.

'Pawn to king four. Checkmate,' said Grundy into the mouthpiece, smiling broadly. Semple didn't need to be told who was on the line. Only Grundy would open like that.

'Grundy, you old reprobate. I thought they'd moved you over to the Irish Sugar Board or something sweeter. Don't tell me the defence of the republic is still relying on your fast-failing faculties?'

'Indeed it is, until my political masters can find someone more devious, ruthless and unpleasant.'

'Then your masters have a great problem with the succession. Now was I calling you, or you me. I've lost track of just who made the first call.'

Grundy was not slow to seize an advantage. 'I'm returning your call.'

'It really doesn't matter,' laughed Arthur Semple. 'We want to see each other and I think I know what about.'

Grundy was mildly surprised and remained non-committal. 'I agree we need to chat to each other, Arthur. Your place or mine? I'm not fussy.'

'Let's make it mine. I don't want to be seen outside the country just now. It's far too easy to be seen on your patch, Grundy. How soon can you get over to London?'

This alarmed Grundy, as Semple knew it might. Only on the odd special occasion did Britain accord Ireland 'most favoured nation' status in the field of intelligence since the Irish were not part of NATO.

Grundy had charged at the door guarded by Semple only to find that it was already open. At such moments, the unprepared and inexperienced fall flat on their faces. Grundy was neither.

'I can be with you for lunch.' Grundy said simply.

'Northolt?'

'Yes. Let's keep this quiet.' He rang off.

Grundy called in his secretary. 'I want to get into RAF Northolt as fast as possible. See if the official jet is free and if it isn't, get the Foreign Minister's office to free it for me.'

Grundy rarely threw his weight around and when he did, he usually got what he wanted.

He was driven to Baldonnel Aerodrome, the military airfield serving Dublin. Grundy didn't want to be seen either leaving or arriving.

The flying time between Baldonnel and Northolt was forty-five minutes and Grundy spent that time wondering what Arthur Semple was about to spring on him. He'd originally placed a call to Semple to ask the British Army to watch the border from their side. He'd hoped to be able to make the request without having to answer too many questions.

But Semple wasn't asking questions. He seemed to be giving answers without even bothering to find out Grundy's questions. Did the British know what the Russians and the Americans were up to in Ireland? If so, were the British going to ask permission this time to cross the border?

Grundy hoped not. He knew that the political climate in Ireland would generate a negative answer.

In that case, Grundy wondered, would the British ask G2 to operate on Britain's behalf, arguing that the interests of both countries could be served? In the past Grundy had done this, but without telling the politicians.

But this time the politicians already knew too much and the risk would be too great. Grundy remembered that it had been the Foreign Minister himself who had begun to harbour suspicions about the Russians and the Americans.

Suspicions about what? Grundy wondered if he was about to be humiliated in London. An old friend Semple might be, but he could hardly resist the temptation of revealing to Grundy what was happening in Ireland. Grundy felt as if he were playing chess able to see only half the pieces.

The landing was uneventful and Grundy disembarked from the Hawker Siddeley 127 into what looked like an ordinary London taxi-cab. A Semple plaything.

Semple enjoyed travelling in these special cars and took every opportunity of showing them off to Grundy. The lumpy diesel engine had been replaced by a smooth petrol unit with an equally smooth automatic gearbox. The front seat space now held elaborate communication gear, disguised as luggage. The windows were heavily tinted and Grundy assumed he was entering an empty car to be driven to Semple's office in south London. Halfway into the spacious rear compartment, he stopped and grinned. Arthur Semple was tucked away in the corner.

'Shut the door, Grundy, there's a draught.' Grundy opened his mouth to say something but changed his mind. Settling himself in the comfortable upholstery beside Semple, Grundy noted that Semple had added some extra electronic toys and that the glass soundproof partition between themselves and the driver was tightly shut.

'Good flight?' beamed Semple and without waiting for an answer motioned the driver to proceed.

Semple looked older than Grundy, but then, most of Grundy's contemporaries did. He had a mass of silvery grey hair immaculately combed. His dark eyes sparkled with good humour.

'Arthur.' Grundy used Semple's forename because he found the English habit of calling associates by their surnames uncomfortable. 'Arthur, why do I qualify today for the red carpet? To be met by one of your precious cars was honour enough. To find you inside it is an unexpected, not to say, disconcerting honour.'

If Grundy was hoping Semple would say something to disperse the fog Grundy felt all around him, he was disappointed.

'I would like to say that you always merit such treatment,' said Semple, 'but you wouldn't believe me, would you?'

Grundy shook his head.

'So, Grundy, I've decided to take the afternoon off and lunch you to mark your birthday.'

'It is not my birthday, Arthur.' Grundy had decided to play whatever game Semple was playing.

'I leave it to the unimaginative to mark your birthday on its anniversary. I am marking it today. Now sit back and enjoy yourself.'

So Grundy decided he would sit back and enjoy himself. The car had not turned towards London on leaving the airfield. Instead it had turned right and had joined the M40, taking them in the direction of Oxford. Grundy guessed they were heading for the NATO command centre when they slowed down and took the High Wycombe exit. But he was wrong and out of the corner of his eye Grundy saw Semple smile as the car turned south towards Marlow and the Thames Valley.

It wasn't yet time to talk seriously, so the two friends chatted about inconsequentials and shared memories. The car joined the Great West Road on the outskirts of Maidenhead and headed towards Reading.

Grundy would not have allowed anyone else to have taken him on a mystery tour, but he knew Semple's sense of fun rarely deserted him. Semple was trying to force Grundy to ask where they were going – and Semple would have told him immediately. But Grundy knew that if he asked, he would have lost the game.

Grundy almost lost the game when the car turned into a narrow road called Honey Lane. It was clear from Semple's small preparations that they were approaching the end of the journey.

The car rounded a corner to bring into view the Dewdrop Inn. A little pub isolated among the fields and trees, tucked away out of sight of the twentieth century.

'A ploughman's lunch and a bottle of wine, Grundy. It'll serve to remind us what we're plotting to save,' said Semple with uncharacteristic portentousness.

The game had ended. Grundy still had no idea what he was plotting to save, but whatever it was, it was changing Semple's normal behaviour more than anything Grundy had experienced before.

ELEVEN

They were early for lunch and the Dewdrop Inn wasn't crowded, but for these two men, three was a crowd. Semple and Grundy carried their lunches outside to the picnic tables.

'James, Ireland has suddenly become very interesting to a lot of people. Did you know that?'

Grundy noted that Semple had reverted to using his forename, a sure sign, if another were needed, that matters were indeed serious.

'I know that we're under a lot of pressure from both the Russians and the Americans,' Grundy said simply. 'I have to confess that I don't understand fully what they are up to. I've a theory, of course.'

Semple raised an eyebrow. 'Would you confide in me, James, because I am about to confide in you completely. It would be a great help if I knew how far you'd got.'

Grundy nodded. Naturally he did not believe for a moment that Semple would completely confide in him. This was a spy-speak way of saying that they should distrust each other less than usual for a while. Semple and Grundy would never tell each other everything, but information was a traded commodity. Both knew that the dividing line between an act of necessary co-operation and an act of treason was very narrow.

They were clearing the table for dangerous consultation. Grundy began. 'Last week, Arthur, a helicopter took off from Shannon for a joyride round part of our north coast. The Russians had been negotiating for an extension of their Aeroflot refuelling facility at Shannon. Three of these Russians went sightseeing in the helicopter.' He stopped to taste the wine, and to see if Semple was interested.

Semple was so interested Grundy imagined he'd stopped blinking.

'Of course, no one asked G2 first,' he went on. 'Almost certainly the Russians were members of the KGB's Directorate T and I don't like them anywhere near those microwave links on the north coast. We're supposed to be neutral and I don't want the Russians finding out that they carry a NATO reserve communications chain.' Semple waved his hand in a silent light manner, perhaps to indicate that he didn't want to acknowledge what the Irish were secretly doing for NATO.

'Anyway, that helicopter fell out of the sky killing everybody on board. Now the Russians and the Americans are trying to examine the wreckage and crash-site.' Grundy paused to pop a lump of bread and cheese into his mouth.

'Have you taken the chopper wreckage apart?' asked Semple quietly.

'Of course we have,' Grundy replied somewhat testily. 'And combed the crash-site and retrieved most of the wreckage. There was nothing on the helicopter that shouldn't have been on it. No unusual test gear, no clandestine signal monitors, no funny notebooks. Nothing. Nevertheless, we're missing something. It's infuriating.'

Grundy withheld from Semple that he was beginning to suspect that there was a fourth Russian involved in the episode, that this man had escaped death and been captured by the IRA Provos.

Grundy believed that somehow the Americans must have found this out, and now the Americans and the Russians were racing each other to get him. Such conjecture still did not answer the big question for Grundy. What did this mysterious fourth Russian possess which was so important? The microwave link information was important, but not that important. The Russians may already have their suspicions about the big aerial dishes.

Semple began slowly. 'I think I can give you part of the jigsaw. Usual conditions, James. I've not been talking to you.'

Grundy nodded.

'Does the name "Shield" mean anything to you?'

Grundy looked blank.

'Then, my friend, take a deep breath and listen.'

* * *

The rowing boat bumped clumsily against the wooden hull of the fishing boat, rocking gently at her moorings in the little bay at Fahan.

'Stay still while I make fast,' ordered O'Donnell. 'It's very easy to capsize a dinghy.'

Moira looked as frightened as when she had been under fire at the checkpoint. At the other end of the dinghy sat Stukalin, pale and strained. He needed one arm to keep the tourniquet in place on the other. He had no hand free to steady himself.

O'Donnell climbed onto the deck of the fishing boat and secured the rope from the dinghy to the larger boat. He grabbed a shorter length of rope and tied the end in a loop.

'Put that round our friend, under his arms,' he said.

Bringing Stukalin up the side was a difficult balancing act for a frightened girl and an unwell man but it was eventually accomplished. Moira knew from the look on O'Donnell's determined face that her fear of the water was of no account to him.

Once on deck, Moira looked around bleakly. 'Do you know who owns this boat or is this another one of your brainstorms?'

But O'Donnell was already engrossed. Kneeling by the side of the anchor windlass, he retrieved a small magnetic box of the type used by motorists to hide spare car keys about their cars. Moira watched as he withdrew a key and opened the wheelhouse door. Only then did he speak to her.

'Bring him in here and then through the hatch to the main cabin below. Everything we'll need is on board.'

Moira was sceptical. To her eyes, the boat looked every inch a dirty working boat. The best she expected to find below decks was the smell of dead fish and perhaps a rusty tin of food whose label had disappeared in the damp. She helped Stukalin to his feet and through the wheelhouse door.

She was surprised. The inside of the boat smelt antiseptic and was spotlessly clean. Militarily clean. Furthermore, the wheelhouse walls were covered with electronic equipment of every kind. Moira did not recognize any of it, but the Major did, through his purposely half-closed eyes.

'In here,' called O'Donnell, already down in the main cabin with his arms outstretched to lend a hand to the others. The wounded stranger was laid out on a bunk.

'Here's a chance to practise your nursing, Moira. I want him fixed up. I don't want him sick and I don't want him dead.'

119

The Major smiled grimly at these comforting words. Patch me up, IRA man, he thought, but for my plan, not yours.

Moira began removing the clothing from the Major's chest and arms. She confirmed for herself that one of the shots at the roadblock had ripped through the muscle tissue of his upper left arm without hitting the bone.

'I can't treat this properly,' she said. 'The wound may already be infected and isolated on this boat I'm more helpless than a witch doctor.'

O'Donnell moved across the cabin.

'What about this, Moira?' He was holding open a locker crammed with medical supplies – bottles, bandages, disposable syringes and sterilizing equipment.

She took a deep breath. 'I think there's enough in that cupboard for a small hospital.' She was pushing her hands deep in exploration of the locker. She opened the next locker and found yet more.

O'Donnell watched her with amused satisfaction. 'That's exactly what it is, Moira. It's an emergency field hospital provided by the Army Council of the Provisional IRA. Provo soldiers need Provo medics.'

He shot a quick look out of a port-hole before continuing to satisfy Moira's curiosity.

'The Brits don't think we retreat into Inishowen because the peninsula is an obvious cul-de-sac. This boat changes that. We can hide it anywhere around this ragged coast for quite a while, in a bay or in the middle of a fishing fleet. There's enough food, fuel and medical supplies for a month.'

Still disbelieving, she darted from locker to locker, verifying O'Donnell's words. 'There's enough here to treat the stranger properly. More than enough.'

'Right, girl, so get on with it. I'll get the guns from the dinghy and tie it up properly. And give me the pistol. I don't want our friend jumping you and arming himself again.'

120

'I don't think he's capable of overpowering anyone right now, do you?'

Stukalin closed his eyes, on cue like any good actor. He was going to be helpless and listless until his chance came. It might come sooner if he appeared more incapacitated than he thought he was. He watched O'Donnell pocket Moira's pistol and wondered if he would ever catch him off guard again.

O'Donnell went up the steps to the wheelhouse and opened another locker. From it he took a set of well worn overalls and a waterproof smock. Dressed like that he was indistinguishable from the hundreds of fishermen who worked that coast in similar boats. O'Donnell had fished alongside his father from the age of nine and could play the part convincingly.

O'Donnell's movements on deck therefore did not betray him as he prepared the boat for sea. The dinghy was untied from the big boat and secured independently to the mooring buoy and the fishing boat's big diesel was started. It fired within the first few turns of the starter, for like the rest of this special boat, it had been maintained properly.

O'Donnell let the engine warm up while he sat in the wheelhouse. He reached for binoculars and surveyed the shore in front of him.

If there was an awareness of the beauty of the mountain behind him, or of the shimmering water of the sea lough, then it didn't show. Nor did he glance at the seagulls which hovered expectantly above his head. No titbits from gutted fish this time for them.

O'Donnell stared at the road near the shore. A police car, its blue light flashing and its tyres scrubbing the tarmac, tore into his field of vision. And just as fast, roared out of it again.

Time to move, thought O'Donnell. One day, some policeman or some soldier will look at the sea and begin to think. But it mustn't be today.

121

O'Donnell left the wheelhouse and untied the ropes securing the fishing boat to its mooring buoy. The motion of the boat changed perceptibly as it was given its freedom. Propelled by the light breeze, it fell back from the buoy and from the dinghy attached to it.

He allowed the boat a moment's liberty in the chop. With a nonchalance born of an easy skill, he ambled back to the wheelhouse and crunched the engine into gear.

O'Donnell smiled to himself, pleased with his performance during this odd day in his life. He had won yet again, and, he suspected, a greater personal victory might yet be in store. That depended upon finding out the identity of his prisoner. The strange man who did not fit any easy pattern.

'Dick,' Moira was shouting above the noise of the diesel. 'Come down here.'

'Don't be daft, Moira. I'm navigating a channel.'

'Haven't you got one of those automatic pilot things?'

'Aye, but it only steers in straight lines and I'm threading through the moorings.'

'There's something down here you ought to see.'

'Then bring it up to the wheelhouse because I can't go down.'

O'Donnell thought he had been answered by silence, but the engine was drowning what was really happening. The stranger appeared at the hatch, minus his outer clothes and partially supported by a wide-eyed Moira.

The stranger's upper left arm had been bandaged and the rest of the limb was still stained with blood. He was supporting himself on one leg and both legs were caked in mud. But what claimed O'Donnell's attention was the stranger's garment. An armless one-piece suit, tight fitting, light grey, with electrical connections hanging from several points.

And emblazoned on the chest were the letters 'CCCP'.

For what seemed a long time, nobody spoke. The boat chugged on.

122

'I am Major Petr Fedorovich Stukalin of the Soviet Air Force. It's time we talked to each other.'

Grundy's heart raced as he waited for Semple to continue. At last, under an English apple tree in the garden of a little English pub, Semple might give him the vital clue about what was happening. The old-boy network was scoring again.

'Shield is the code name of a big OTH radar system we are perfecting with American money.'

'OTH? Arthur.'

'Short for "Over The Horizon". We've developed a radar that will allow us to look over the Earth's curvature. Normally radar is straight-line. With OTH radars we could see almost across the narrowest part of the Atlantic with this radar.'

'I thought this technology already existed. Isn't there a working model yet?'

'I'm coming to that, James. A few miles down that Great West Road at a place called Cricklade, we – that's ourselves and the Americans – have an experimental but fully working radar. The range is about three thousand kilometres. It's beamed out over the Atlantic. It'll eventually be just a part of a full system, tied partly to cruise missile targeting and partly to service general defence and intelligence needs.'

'And why are you telling me this? Has Shield seen something of interest to me?'

'Could be, James, could be. Last week Shield obtained a trace of an aircraft flying very high far out over the Atlantic. It was on the very altitude limits for aircraft, somewhere around a hundred thousand feet and on a straight-line course that would have taken it across the north of Scotland. In other words it was heading for our airspace.'

'Friend or foe?'

'Not friend. Realistically only the Americans and the Russians could have a craft like that, and from the way the

Americans were reacting, it definitely wasn't one of theirs. In fact, our American friends were very upset.'

Grundy didn't see where all this was leading. 'I suppose you weren't able to do much, even when it did enter your airspace,' Grundy probed. 'You haven't got anything except missiles that could attack at that height. You didn't shoot it down, did you? Was it a reconnaissance aircraft?'

'That's just it. James. We didn't shoot anything at it. We didn't get a chance. It disappeared.'

'Disappeared!' Grundy voice rose an octave. 'I thought you said Shield worked,' he scoffed. 'How could the plane be lost?'

'Two points. This new radar is set for long-range detection. We've found that at shorter ranges, the beams tend to skip over targets. In other words, for shorter ranges, we still need conventional radars.'

Semple interrupted himself to eat.

'I take it that the aircraft came inside the area of unreliability of Shield, but was still outside the range of ordinary radars?'

'Correct, James,' Semple mumbled with his mouth full.

'Have you built any shorter-range Shield radars yet?'

'Yes. We've had one running for a while in Wales with a range of about two hundred kilometres.'

'North Wales?'

'No. The entrance to Milford Haven in the south.'

Grundy mulled over what he'd just been told. Milford Haven was more than two hundred kilometres from Malin Head and the Inishowen peninsula. That radar would be of no help. He put another question.

'On a projection of that plane's course, would it have entered Irish airspace?'

'If it had continued to travel in a straight line, it might very well have clipped your most northerly point, somewhere about Malin Head.'

Grundy took some cheese. He hoped Semple could not see excitement mounting in his expression. Semple was back to playing games and would release more information, but only if asked the right questions. They were not talking about coincidences.

'Was the plane flying at a constant height when last monitored?'

Semple gave Grundy a broad grin and Grundy knew he'd played Semple's game correctly.

'Bravo, my friend. It flew at a constant very high level for about three hundred kilometres. Then it began descending, maintaining its north easterly course.'

'Alright Arthur, stop the teasing. You say it disappeared. That means it didn't reach Scotland. What do your experts think happened to it?' ·

Semple breathed in heavily. 'I said that there were two caveats with the Shield radar contact. One is its close-range unreliability as I've said. The other is that the mystery echo was very weak. During tracking, it disappeared altogether for minutes on end, so that when it finally disappeared, we weren't certain whether this thing was still in the air or not!'

'Was this wonder-machine of yours working properly? You did say Shield was experimental.' Grundy was disappointed. It seemed that Arthur Semple didn't have all the answers.

'We have a theory. Want to hear it?' Grundy nodded glumly and Semple carried on quietly.

'You've probably heard of "stealth" techniques, as applied to warplanes.' Semple was being careful of Grundy's feelings now. 'You will know that "stealth" is the collective term for a number of ways to make aircraft less visible to radar. Special paint, special fuselage shapes and special materials in construction and so on. We think this was a Russian experimental "stealth" craft deliberately probing the detection capabilities of Shield. The thing appeared faintly from nowhere and disappeared to nowhere. It's very worrying for NATO, as you can imagine.'

'Why are you telling me this, Arthur? I don't see how G2 is involved.'

'Be patient, my friend, because things get a little complicated from this point. You may be involved.' Semple broke off to make sure that nobody could overhear. He had deliberately chosen an outside meeting place to aid privacy.

'It is entirely possible that the Russians have got their "stealth" perfected to the point of our own capability. This bloody plane of theirs may be back in Russia, and now they're waiting for a reaction from us to indicate whether we saw it or not. So far, we've kept our mouths shut. We want them to think their present techniques are perfect and should go from prototype stage into production.'

'I understand that. Go on.' Grundy grumbled. Semple was leading him somewhere and patience was not his prominent characteristic.

'There exists, however, the possibility that Shield was a true, if slightly imperfect witness, to what happened. We postulate the following. From the sudden dip we think the plane could have suffered a flame-out – engine failure. Let's assume that to be the case.'

'In which case, the thing is in the Atlantic somewhere,' Grundy said.

Semple nodded. 'It was travelling very fast, about Mach three point five. Projecting from that, and from the glide angle, it should have ditched off the coast of Scotland. We had a Polaris sub waiting for it – the only thing we could get to the point in time that could escape detection.' He pulled off a lump of French bread but made no attempt to eat it.

Fascinated, Grundy waited for him to continue.

'But our mystery craft didn't turn up, Grundy. That means it could be anywhere, including Russia if the engine restarted.'

'And if the engine didn't restart, it could be somewhere else. Even Ireland . . .' said Grundy softly.

'Quite so, James.' They both sat back and refilled their glasses. At last, Grundy was getting a picture, but Semple hadn't yet finished.

'Your helicopter crash is a convenient and coincidental blind. The Russians may be interested simply because their nationals were killed — or they are desperate for an excuse to get to Inishowen without alerting us. That makes the Americans think it's Inishowen and also want to tramp all over your peninsula. What are you going to do about it, my good friend?'

'Are we so sure it has come down?'

'Think of the Russian reaction and try to account for it any other way. Or the American one, for that matter. That was no ordinary plane. We think it was a prototype which got into trouble.'

'Yes, but the Soviet land mass is huge. Why were they testing over a potentially hostile sea? Any answer for that one, Arthur?'

Semple looked at Grundy and shook his head. 'None, except that they may have finished all the tests they could do over their own territory and felt confident enough to test in operational conditions. The answer may be in the wreckage, wherever that is. Or with the pilot, if he survived.'

As Semple said that, he examined Grundy's face. Grundy countered by burying his nose in the wineglass, fighting hard to give nothing away. He fixed his eyes on a distant church steeple. He thought of the men who had built it and of the dates on its headstones. Anything to stop the man beside him reading his mind.

He had it. Grundy now knew where the extra Russian in Inishowen had come from. He knew why the Russians and the Americans wanted to get to Inishowen. The only fly in the ointment was that the Provos had the pilot.

Grundy now knew more than Semple. It was a wonderful warm feeling.

'Delightful lunch. Now I really must get back to Dublin.' Grundy said suddenly. Too suddenly for Semple's liking.

'Who was it who first said there's no such thing as free dinner?' Semple leaned forward and put a lightly restraining hand on his guest's shoulder. Semple would pay for lunch, but so would Grundy, one way or another. 'There's one thing I thought you'd ask me. Now I'm wondering why you haven't.'

Grundy raised both his eyebrows by way of reply. Whatever you say, say nothing, he quoted to himself.

'You should be asking me why I've told you all this, because your good friends the Americans have not trusted you sufficiently to do so.'

'What do you want?' asked Grundy.

'Depending on what you find, we might pay a high price. If substantial parts of this remarkable craft have survived somewhere on your patch, and you let our scientists at Farnborough loose on it before anyone else, then it's possible there might be some movement politically on Northern Ireland. In the Irish direction, of course.'

Grundy remained impassive, so Semple added, 'The secrets of that plane might allow us to skip a generation of research and development in air defence technology. That's billions upon billions saved in the defence budget. The knowledge is no use to the bloody Irish. You don't even build crop-sprayers.'

Had it been anyone else speaking, Grundy might have been affronted, but Semple was simply spelling out negotiating positions.

He had been given a secret message for the Irish government.

Grundy would deliver the message and when he did so, the pressure upon him to find the plane before the Russians and the Americans would be intense. He had one great advantage. Both the British and the Americans could do nothing openly without revealing to the Russians that the West had spotted their plane, however imperfectly.

Now the British were ready to go behind the backs of their American allies, suggesting a deal by which G2, the agency with the greatest operational freedom, would act on behalf of Britain and the politicians could sort out the price.

'I have Her Britannic Majesty's Government to thank for the ploughman's lunch then,' said Grundy, draining his glass.

'Indeed,' said Semple. 'It will feature accurately on my next expenses.'

It had been an unofficial official contact between the two countries. Very Irish, thought both men, lost in their own secrets as they made their way to a London taxi cab, incongruously waiting outside the country pub.

TWELVE

Faloon was feeling raw.

He had hit the bottle after being bundled into an Aer Lingus Boeing 747 by two large sullen FBI men at Boston. After that indignity, the cabin staff had treated him like the criminal they assumed him to be.

'The service on this flight is atrocious,' he had remonstrated. 'Give me a complaints form.'

'Drop dead, sir.'

His fellow passengers had assessed his status similarly. Those allocated seats beside him asked for other seats and were granted them, with one beneficial effect. It allowed the exhausted Faloon to lift the armrests to make a bed of three seats.

Unnoticed, one man's eyes bored into Faloon with particular intensity.

Faloon was thankful that the flight from west to east rushed towards the dawn of a new day at six hundred miles an hour, shortening the night. He wanted to see the end of that particular day.

He lay awake under the dimmed cabin lights, enduring the snores and wheezes around him, the occasional crying of a baby, or the hoarse whisper of another insomniac apologetically ordering another drink. Faloon was worried.

He had been thrown out of the United States by the FBI, the agency with which he was supposed to be fashioning fraternal links. Inexplicably he hadn't been allowed to help rescue Sarah even though he'd been the man on the spot with great experience in dealing with the Green Boys. He imagined that Grundy had something to do with that turn of events, so he was not looking froward to meeting his boss.

The only bright point on the bleak horizon was the strong deductive evidence Faloon now possessed pointing to a Green Boy source inside the FBI. He would deal with that matter from G2's offices in Dublin.

But that single small achievement could not obliterate his sense of defeat. He was unused to defeat. Not defeat on this scale.

He rubbed his eyes and squinted at his watch. Not long now to a landing at Shannon, the first port of call in Ireland. Then a short hop across the country to Dublin, and to some of the answers he sorely needed.

He needed sleep. Faloon as a child used to imagine he was blind by closing his eyes. Later, when exploring the lime-stone caves of Sligo, he had experienced real darkness for the first time and discovered that complete absence of light is something few normally sighted people ever experience.

Psychologically he tried to re-create the peace of complete blackness and it wasn't working. Light seeped through his eyelids. From time to time, fellow passengers would slip by silently and Faloon could record the passing of each through his leaky eyelids.

Another shadow. This time it didn't pass. It had stopped motionless in the aisle beside him. He waited. No movement. No sound. No passing of the shadow. Someone was looking at him, long and hard.

I'm becoming paranoid, Faloon cautioned himself. But he remembered that even paranoiacs can have enemies and began, imperceptibly and without disturbing the slow rhythm of his breathing, raising an eyelid by a millimetre.

The view through the tiny slit and trembling eyelashes was not very clear, but enough to confirm that he was indeed under scrutiny. The man looking at him was tall with powerful shoulders. He was wearing a navy double-breasted blazer and grey slacks. From his position, Faloon was unable to distinguish any facial features without opening his eye further and risking confrontation. At this point, he preferred the watcher to think he was asleep.

The man began to move away. As he did so, the back of his right hand came into Faloon's view at the optimum height for his observation. Faloon partially opened an eye and saw a scar. A large star-shaped scar on the back of the right hand. Accident or enemy action, wondered Faloon.

Why had this person spent so much time looking so intently at him?

Feigning emergence from sleep, Faloon sat up to see where the man in the blazer had settled, but he had already disappeared down the long fuselage.

Plenty of time, thought Faloon. Anyway, why should he be alarmed? Half the people on the flight had seen Faloon being marshalled to his seat in a highly unorthodox manner. Hardly surprising that he was an object of curiosity.

Nevertheless, time for a walk. Faloon rose, taking care not to disturb the inert bodies around him. He headed for the most distant toilet to give himself the chance to find all the large men in blazers on the flight. He decided to go up one aisle and return down the other.

In the lavatory Faloon sat just long enough to make the visit seem natural. Alone, he wondered if the Green Boys had put a tail on him. They might have had access to the passenger list through local contacts in Boston. The rest would have been easy.

Faloon stood up and unlocked the door. He was off-guard.

The instant the door was unlocked, a fist like a small barrel punched through the aperture to hit Faloon's solar plexus. When a second more ferocious blow followed the first, Faloon's defences were in disarray. He sagged to the floor semiconscious.

A large, clumsy man pushed his way into the cubicle, closed the door rapidly, locked it and knelt. From the inside pocket of his blazer the attacker withdrew a pouch labelled 'Diabetic Insulin'. Working fast and expertly, the man filled a syringe and began injecting Faloon's thigh through the fabric of his trousers. The pain roused the dazed Faloon. He twisted, wrenching the syringe out of his skin.

His attacker did not attempt to inject the rest of the insulin. Instead, he calmly stood up, stepped outside and pulled the door behind him.

There was no witness to what had happened; no one waiting outside. In the early hours of the morning, with the lights of the plane dimmed, nearly all passengers were asleep, or trying to be.

The man in the blazer took full advantage of his opportunity. Producing a small screwdriver on a keyring, he locked the lavatory door from the outside, using the emergency facility incorporated on the latch.

It was the change of pressure popping his ears that brought Faloon fully back to the world of the living. He staggered and vomited.

'Are you alright in there?' It was one of the air hostesses, calling him through the door. 'We'll be landing shortly at Shannon. Do you require assistance? You must resume your seat.'

'I'm fine,' replied Faloon hoarsely. 'Just a touch airsick. I'll be out in a moment.'

Faloon tidied himself as best he could. An anxious steward posted outside the toilet escorted him back to his seat, assuring him that the flight would soon be over. Faloon scarcely registered the plane landing at Shannon.

Despite his protestations, Faloon was held back by the cabin staff until almost all of the passengers had disembarked. Most were travelling the remaining short distance to Dublin, though everybody was encouraged to leave the aircraft to spend money in the duty-free shop at Shannon.

Faloon was fading. His breathing was becoming heavier and his brow was speckled with beads of perspiration. He needed help to reach the toilets for another bout of nausea. He had hoped with diminishing optimism that not enough of the drug had entered his thigh.

Faloon made a feeble attempt to look about him for the man with the blazer and a scar on the back of his hand, but the images reaching his mind were becoming blurred. Words formed in his mind to tell his helpers what had happened, but he couldn't get them past his lips.

He felt sick again. He rambled. The cabin staff became increasingly alarmed as they listened to disjointed words about a man named Grundy, about the Green Boys, about tortured women, a man in the lavatory, Old Ironsides, the bastards in FBI and the bastards in G2.

A stewardess came running down the aisle from the direction of the toilet that Faloon had been in. She had the remains of a small glass phial in her hand. 'Can you hear me, Mr Faloon?' The chief steward was leaning over him. 'Are you diabetic?' But he saw that Faloon's eyes were beginning to roll.

'Get an ambulance. This is serious.'

'Welcome to Ireland, Viktor Losev,' the KGB resident officer gushed, pumping the new arrival's hand in extravagant greeting.

The Russian station in Aeroflot's offices at Shannon was a pleasant if somewhat boring KGB posting. Losev's arrival was a welcome break from the monotony of counting Russian nationals into the staging post and counting the same number out again.

Losev's perfunctory response to the effusiveness alarmed his host until he followed Losev's gaze through the office window. In the distance someone on the tarmac was being carried off the Boeing on a stretcher.

'Trouble?'

'A G2 man stationed in the United States that I was told to look out for. He was on the same flight. That could not be a coincidence so I immobilized him.'

The Shannon officer was alarmed. 'That's not your line of business. He'll lead them straight here.' He swore.

'Not until I'm well away. I am a diabetic. I dazed him and pumped him full of my insulin. He was badly disorientated when I left the aircraft, unable to think. Unless they diagnose fast, agent Faloon is heading for a coma.'

The Shannon KGB man looked at Viktor Losev with new respect. 'Was there any hold-up with the G2 men going through immigration?'

'Not at all. By the time I reached them, they were consumed with the problem of a sick G2 man on the plane.' They both laughed.

'You'd better leave immediately, Losev. Good luck with your mission.'

Viktor Losev departed from Shannon Airport and began driving north towards Inishowen.

Colonel Grundy's heart sank. Was this the man he had sent to the USA as an example of the cream of G2? Faloon didn't look like the cream of anything. His hair was tousled, his shirt collar looked as if the Boeing had parked on it, his clothes were crumpled, his shoes had traces of vomit on them, his eyes were red, sunken, black-rimmed and set in a gaunt visage. He was breathing painfully through a fragile ribcage.

Against medical advice, Faloon had discharged himself from the hospital in Limerick. Because the broken phial had been found, the effects of the insulin overdose were reversed before too much damage had been done.

Nevertheless Faloon had emerged weak and drained from the ordeal. As soon as he could walk, he presented himself at G2 headquarters. If he was nursing a faint hope that his frail physical condition would engender his leader's compassion, the thought vanished on seeing Grundy's stony face.

On Grundy's desk was a telexed report of what had happened in Boston. Faloon had disobeyed FBI standing instructions by operating without authority and without informing the agency. The FBI, in spite of Grundy's help in tracing Faloon, still suspected that Faloon was following secret instructions from Dublin. Relations between the two agencies therefore were cool.

'Right, Faloon, let me hear your side of it – and it had better be good.'

Faloon winced. As he spoke, he knew there was no hiding of the fact that he had disobeyed Grundy by spending the day in Boston grappling unsuccessfully with Martin Riley and the Green Boys.

'Are you surprised that the Feds kicked you out?' Grundy shouted.

'I'm surprised you shopped me. You must've known what I was trying to do. And I might've got to Riley if you'd have kept quiet about me.'

Grundy was apoplectic with anger. 'Do you think the world revolves round your priorities, Faloon? I'm beginning to believe that your disregard of orders is too great a disadvantage to ignore any longer. I needed the FBI as an ally.' Grundy paused for breath and added, more for his own benefit than for Faloon, 'I'm going to have to rely far too much on the British.'

'I don't understand.' Faloon was shaking his head. 'And don't trust the British with anything until we've had a quiet word with one or two people . . .'

But Grundy wasn't listening. 'Of course you don't understand, Faloon. You've messed up more than you could possibly know.' There was a silence and Faloon knew better than to try to break it. It was Grundy's court and Faloon was in the dock. He would talk about the possible British leak when things cooled down a little. Grundy obviously had something else on his mind at that moment.

'Some days ago,' Grundy bellowed, 'a helicopter carrying Aer Rianta people and two Russian negotiators from Dublin on a joyride fell out of the sky for some reason.'

'Yes. I saw an *Irish Times* piece about it.'

'What you don't know is that behind the scenes, first the Russians and then the Americans have been breaking all conventions of international behaviour by trying to investigate the bloody crash.'

Faloon blinked and tried to focus on helicopters, Russians and whatever else was occupying Grundy's mind. In the circumstances, that was proving difficult, but he persevered.

'The microwave dishes, sir. Are we putting anything special through them at this time?'

'No more than usual. Anyway the Russians already suspect, if they don't know for sure, that NATO material is sometimes transmitted. That wouldn't bother them too much unless they wanted to cause an internal political rumpus here. I don't believe that's the game, not now anyway.'

Another thought appeared to cross Grundy's mind. He picked up a typewritten report from his desk. 'That goon who floored you in the plane. Ever seen him before?'

'No. Never. He might have been the man I saw looking at me sometime earlier, but to be honest, I don't know. It's all in my report.'

'Had you come across him or his likeness in the FBI files?'

'No. That scar on his hand is too noticeable to be missed.'

'And you think, Faloon, that this man was following you.'

'I'm now certain of it. The Green Boys seem to have new backbone. Breaking into British computer files in the North is a prize worth a few risks. What's more, Riley and his thugs must've thought that I'd set a trap for them in Boston and they're out for revenge,' Faloon lowered his head. 'Have the FBI located Sarah or her body yet?'

Grundy gestured in the direction of his in-tray while shaking his head. 'If they have, they didn't tell me, but then I'm no longer their favourite son.'

Grundy had little sympathy for the man before him. Anyway, he was still thinking about the man Faloon described in the plane. 'If access to British computer files was so important to the Green Boys, Faloon, that they took the extreme risk of capturing and torturing FBI agent, why did they send a man to follow you and disable you on the plane? Are you trying to convince me they risked that attack in the closed environment of a plane purely for revenge? That doesn't fit the pattern, Faloon.'

Faloon was feeling worse than ever. This was the time to tell Grundy that the Green Boys might now suspect that Faloon had deduced the existence of an IRA agent within British intelligence. Here was good enough reason to shut him up as soon as possible. But before he could say anything, Grundy was back on the warpath.

'Let's go over all this again,' said Grundy. Faloon was in no position to argue. He began back in Washington, and took the narrative through to his imprecise recollections on the Boeing. Grundy stood with his back to him, listening and sometimes interrupting to clarify a point. Faloon knew that his job was on the line.

When Faloon had finished, there was silence once more. Faloon had never wished so earnestly for the end of an interview.

'Faloon,' began the colonel once more, very quietly, 'you say you gave the FBI back their computer before they kicked you out. Correct?'

'It was their computer. I could hardly bring it back with me.'

The Colonel maintained his quiet tone, its menace bypassing the tired Faloon.

137

'And the chip, Faloon, our code chip? Naturally you had an opportunity to remove it before handing the computer back to the Feds?'

Faloon sucked his breath and closed his eyes. 'No, Colonel Grundy, I left it in the computer.'

The words sounded like the beats of a funeral drum.

The colonel spun on his heel. 'You know what you've done, don't you. It's the equivalent of handing over our code-books.' Grundy pounded the desktop. 'That's it, Faloon. You've pushed me over the edge. The latitude left to me in this matter is now very small. Our codes will have to be changed throughout the organization and the diplomatic service.'

Faloon was speechless. He simply hadn't been prepared for the FBI suddenly re-possessing its computer before he had removed the G2 code chip. When that did happen, he had been too preoccupied to realize what he had really lost.

With little conviction, Faloon tried some damage limitation. 'You know as well as I do that the chip contains only the core of the code. Without what's in my head, the chip is useless.'

Grundy was not mollified. 'If the FBI have the core, the codes cannot be regarded as secure. We may not have too many earth-shaking secrets in this little country of ours, Faloon, but it's my job to safeguard those few we do have. G2 operatives do not, repeat not, hand out our code chips like sales samples.'

Grundy stalked round the edge of his desk to deliver his verdict.

'There'll have to be a full internal inquiry. I'll have to report this to the foreign affairs people and the minister may even press for an external inquiry. You're suspended, Faloon. Now get out. Take a holiday, far away from me. Out.' Grundy turned and barked into a desk intercom. 'Collect Mr Faloon's identity cards on his way out. Promulgate his suspension from duty until further notice.'

138

He looked up to fire a parting shot but Faloon was already stalking out through the outer office, flinging his cards at the frightened secretary.

In the corridor, Faloon's dejection quickly gave way to a cold calculating anger. Then he remembered his instructor at his initial training telling him, 'Don't get angry, get even.'

Easier said than done. He was on his own now, he reminded himself grimly, digging his hands deeply into his trouser pockets.

Then he smiled – the kind of smile film cartoonists reserve for the villain who thinks he has found a way of ruling the world. Faloon bounded down the staircase to the floor below and to an office marked 'Stores'.

'Hello, Mr Faloon. I didn't know you were back with us. America seems to be a rough place, by the looks of you.'

'Jet lag, Eddie. That and having to attend to the needs of all the hostesses all night at thirty-five thousand feet.' He laughed and gave Eddie a big wink. 'Look, old son, I'm back in harness and I'm back to our own little computers now. Have you still got my old one gathering dust on one of your shelves back there?'

The storeman went to a locked room, entered and re-emerged with a small lap-held computer, the same make as the one Faloon had used in the Algonquin Hotel.

'It's not your old one. This newer model has the telephone modem built in. Have you got your authorization, Mr Faloon, please?'

'It's with my passport in the Colonel's outer office. I've to return there and on the way down I'll drop it into you.' Faloon turned his maximum charm on the good-hearted Eddie who, against his momentary better judgement, succumbed in the face of the false promise.

But he safeguarded himself. As Faloon turned to leave with the machine, he said, 'You haven't forgotten that it's only an ordinary computer without the code chip. No chip until I get written authorization.'

'Of course, my good friend.' Faloon's reassuring smile won again.

'That's be just fine, Mr Faloon, just fine,' grinned Eddie, giving a bad imitation of southern American drawl as Faloon disappeared.

Faloon, still smiling, skipped down the staircase and wondered what was happening to the little FBI computer he had been using.

He wondered if it was now sitting on a Washington storeman's shelf after the code-chip had been taken out and lodged separately in a safe. Would the storeman have recognized the chip as not being an FBI one? Faloon doubted it. He would have a few days' grace.

And how long would it take Grundy to discover what he had overlooked? Faloon dug his hand into his pocket again and closed his fist round a small oblong object with little legs. Grundy had forgotten that if Faloon did not have the G2 code chip, he must have the FBI one!

Faloon disappeared into the confusion of Dublin with renewed purpose and with the means of accessing FBI computer files by telephone.

THIRTEEN

The room in Moscow's KGB headquarters was too warm and the atmosphere too chilly. Stepan Yanovich Yermash, First Deputy Chairman of the Presidium, was preparing to chair the latest of a series of crisis meetings.

There were about a dozen men in the room, including Bulgakov, head of the KGB.

'Gentlemen,' Yermash said briskly, 'the Presidium meets tomorrow and we'd better have some options to put before them.' He broke off and cast a furrowed brow in the direction of the papers before him. 'The report from our people in Ireland is sketchy, to put it mildly.'

He turned to Zotov, the GKNT chief, or, to give his full title, the Chairman of the State Committee for Science and Technology. 'Zotov, First question. Do we know yet for certain if the spaceplane came down on land or sea?'

Zotov scratched his head. 'No change in the data available. You will remember, sir, that there was no in-flight positional data telemetry transmitted . . .'

'Yes, yes. We know all that. And we are presuming that the spaceplane re-entered the atmosphere because we can't find it in space. At our last meeting you said that a computer analysis might give us a more precise point of impact.' Yermash broke off to light a cigarette, giving the spokesman for Soviet science a chance to redeem himself.

Zotov continued. 'You will also remember, chairman, that the craft was well off course and almost undetectable.' He looked ruffled and Bulgakov, who was sitting opposite, smiled to himself.

'Then I take it,' Yermash snarled, 'that you are telling us in a long-winded way that the maximum precision we can achieve is a sausage-shaped area, sixty kilometres by twenty, just off, or is it on, the very north of Ireland.' He studied his papers to confirm the figures.

Zotov chose not to follow his line of inquiry. 'We quickly diverted a surveillance satellite to make a pass over the area and to give us a speedy film canister drop.'

'Why didn't you use a television satellite? It would have been far faster,' sneered Bulgakov from across the table, just waiting for the right moment to show what was in the file in front of him.

Zotov cast a baleful look in the direction of Bulgakov. 'The advantage of film, as my State Security colleague well knows, is very high definition. Much better than television.' From a folder, he withdrew a set of large photographs, selected the top half dozen and spread them in front of Yermash.

His manner became more confident as he watched Yermash and others poring over the selected prints. He saw Bulgakov out of the corner of his eye and assumed that for once, he had subdued the KGB man.

'These photographs,' he explained, 'are of the remains of an Irish helicopter which crashed coincidentally at almost the same time as our craft, and almost at the same place. Three Russian personnel on board were killed. They were from our Dublin embassy and their mission need not concern us.

'I'm showing you these photographs, chairman, to illustrate that if our craft had come down anywhere in this piece of land, we would now have photographs of the wreckage with the same detail as these ones. We therefore believe the craft didn't impact on land. All of it crashed into the sea.'

There was no disguising the general relief that their machine was at the bottom of the sea.

'Mr chairman.' It was Bulgakov, who wasn't sharing in the general feeling. The meeting quietened. 'Mr chairman, we've lost one of the most advanced craft ever built by Soviet science. It contains equipment, electronics and materials, which, if they fell into the hands of the West, would gravely compromise the security of the whole Socialist community. And where it is all now? At the bottom of a Western-controlled sea. That's where it is.' He thumped the table in anger.

Yermash drew deeply on his cigarette. He loathed tub-thumping blusterers. 'What the KGB chairman has said is accurate. However we should be thankful for small mercies. If it's in the sea, our enemies don't have it. Not yet, anyway. Nevertheless,' and here Yermash turned his gaze on the representatives of the defence and foreign ministries, 'we must formulate a plan immediately for the location and retrieval of the spaceplane. An outline plan should be ready for tomorrow's Presidium. We'll meet again in two hours.'

Yermash gestured the end of the meeting. He looked worried, though the outcome was slightly better than he had expected.

'One moment, Mr chairman, if I may,' interposed Bulgakov. 'I am not fully satisfied with the situation.'

Zotov reacted defensively. 'Is the KGB questioning the findings of my technicians?'

'Not at the moment, no. We haven't had time to fully examine the prints, but I believe a full examination will confirm that the remains of our spaceplane are not on that Irish peninsula.' Zotov was mollified.

'However,' Bulgakov· went on, 'our fishing fleet reports that a brief burst of about forty-five seconds was transmitted from the spaceplane distress beacon, heard by three vessels. Subsequently, I diverted Aeroflot flights to Shannon over the whole area and no further beacon transmission was picked up. Why did the beacon stop?' Bulgakov threw his weight back into his chair to await an answer.

One of the technical advisors accompanying Zotov looked first at his boss and then at Yermash. Yermash nodded and the man volunteered timidly, 'It must have been a faulty beacon, or most likely was damaged on impact.'

'What genius designed a maritime distress beacon which is damaged on impact with the sea?'· Bulgakov sneered. 'Let's hope this useless thing with its brightly coloured flag is not found by our enemies.' He looked at the unfortunate technical advisor, who wisely decided that he had said enough.

Zotov leaned forward to bring the Minister for the Maritime Fleet into his view. 'I take it that the forty-five seconds was not enough for even a vague position fix?'

'Quite so,' came the reply. 'If we had been warned to be on the lookout, it would have been a different matter.' Everyone was passing the buck.

Yermash was anxious to bring the meeting to a close and looked at the KGB chief to see if he was finished. He was not.

'I think we're in a real mess. Let's start with the Americans and what they might know,' thundered Bulgakov, 'because within the past hour our sources in Ireland began to relay information which is alarming me. Crucially, I am told that the Americans have offered to help the Irish with the helicopter crash investigation. The offer has astounded the Irish and made them suspicious about what is happening in the Inishowen area.'

The atmosphere, already tense because of Bulgakov's menace-laden probing, became heavier.

'Do you think the Americans know much?' Yermash asked anxiously.

Bulgakov exhaled noisily and impatiently. 'My own guess is that their information is flimsier than ours. I think they know roughly where it came down and they've conducted the same exercise as ourselves.'

'You mean satellite photographs?'

'Possibly, but we know for certain that a British reconnaissance aircraft has overflown the peninsula. That's a bad sign.'

'And what did the Irish do about that?' It was a question from the Foreign Ministry people down the table. The Defence Ministry representatives snorted. One jeered, 'They threw stones at it.' This raised a few chuckles.

'Don't laugh,' cautioned Bulgakov, 'because the game isn't being played with military hardware. The situation needs the most subtle handling. Can we find our plane without disclosing its existence, or without revealing its secret, and finally, without a monumental loss of face?'

The question appeared to be put to Zotov, who refused to be provoked.

Yermash, the Deputy Chairman of the Presidium, looked distressed. His committee was supposed to present the Presidium with answers and policy alternatives.

144

'What steps are being taken to find our spaceplane?' he demanded in an effort to cut through the obfuscation.

It was the turn of the Maritime Fleet Minister. 'A specialized seabed survey vessel has been despatched from the Baltic and should reach the area north of Ireland within the next day or so. We are confident that we will be able to locate the target.'

'What then?'

'We already have the *Aleksandr Tortsev* in the area on her way back from Africa. That ship is a large landing craft and is equipped to bring heavy items to the surface in shallow water. She has a large crane mounted amidships.'

If we can find the damn thing, Yermash thought to himself, once more ready to close the meeting. But Bulgakov wasn't finished yet.

Bulgakov drew himself into an erect position in his seat. 'My greatest alarm stems from inquiries being made at our embassy and at the Aeroflot base at Shannon. Grundy's organization, tiny G2, has put all its meagre resources into watching our installations – and those of the Americans. They're also watching ports and airports. Something else has alarmed the Irish.' He stopped infuriatingly to fill a glass with water from a decanter on the table.

'G2,' he went on, raising his voice slightly, 'believes we had a fourth man on the crashed helicopter – and that he walked away from the accident. Now why on earth do they think that, comrades?'

Whatever they were thinking, no one round the table dared voice their thoughts. So Bulgakov voiced them.

'Whatever the reason, if the Irish think there is a fugitive Russian at large in the Inishowen peninsula, then it simply cannot be anyone from the helicopter.' Yermash closed his eyes. At last he could see the bombshell about to be dropped by the KGB chief. Like a Russian tank, Bulgakov ground on, 'But the man could be Major Stukalin. Stukalin did not have a parachute, so his plane must have landed softly enough for the pilot to escape unharmed. My guess, gentlemen, is that our machine is near the shore, relatively intact and in shallow Irish territorial waters. Soon the Irish could have both man and machine.'

The meeting closed with a single whispered expletive from Yermash.

FOURTEEN

Faloon lay beside Nuala.

'Faloon,' Nuala said hesitantly, 'it is said that the three best things in life are a drink beforehand and a cigarette afterwards. I don't smoke; you didn't bring me any duty-free booze and your battered body didn't come up to expectation in the middle. What has matriarchal America done to you?'

Nuala Gallagher immediately regretted opening her mouth. Faloon had appeared at her Dublin flat earlier in the day, pecked her in a sisterly way on the cheek, told her he was going to stay awhile and finally threw himself into her bed and slept. He was not yet ready for her barbed humour after uninspiring lovemaking.

Nuala Gallagher and Faloon had known each other for over ten years, ever since Nuala had joined G2 as a junior typist. Her Irish republican family background, her personality, university education and artfulness had resulted in speedy promotion. At the age of thirty-three, Nuala Gallagher had become a private secretary in the office of the Foreign Minister of the Irish Republic.

In that office, her hours were irregular and she was often granted time off work as compensation for the burning of midnight oil, usually after accompanying the ministerial entourage to Brussels. Fortunately for Faloon, she had time off to cope with him.

Nuala had put her career first. She was a feminist be-cause she had decided early in her adult life to use men

146

the way she saw men using women. With her long auburn hair, deceptively submissive watery blue eyes, she had little difficulty in attracting men. Most fled in disarray when their ritual advances were repulsed with deriding wit. Nuala Gallagher did not suffer fools, gladly or otherwise.

Faloon had been different in his approach in those heady early days. He had noticed her in the office, and she had noticed him. Each had been conceited enough to consider themselves the best in their respective fields. That common factor had been sufficient to guarantee that they would explore each other. True to Nuala's expectations, Faloon had advanced.

'May I appeal to one of your foremost attributes by inviting you out to dinner?' he had asked, standing well away from her, seemingly engrossed in his expenses. It was a well-laid trap and she knew it.

'You don't know me, Mr Faloon. Me or my attributes, foremost or background.'

'I stand corrected, Miss Gallagher.' He had turned to face her with an impish smile. 'I should have further qualified my reference to your attributes with adjectives such as "assumed" or "apparent". You can't stop people making assumptions about you, just as I can't stop you making assumptions about me.'

'Assumptions are the product of thought, Mr Faloon, and I have made none about you because I've not thought about you for a single second.'

'I am greatly relieved. Nevertheless, my assumptions about you, made necessarily at a distance, must stand.' He had returned with feigned concentration to his expenses. In the end, she had found the bait irresistible.

'What to you is my foremost attribute?' she replied, surrendering a little.

'Your loneliness. You are not a girl's girl and you stand apart from the rest of the women in the office. You are not a man's girl, because you mock the male. Sustained remoteness like that is something special. You must be lonely.'

'You know only what you interpret from seeing me in this office, Mr Faloon, and I have a life outside the office. A life you know nothing about. That's the way I like it.'

Faloon nodded. 'Yes, I agree with you. Social lives should be kept separate from working lives. Less complicated that way.'

And with that, the conversation had ended, though neither of them wished it. That evening, as Nuala had been walking towards her bus stop, Faloon had drawn up in his open Morgan sports car.

'You didn't say, Miss Gallagher, whether you would join me for dinner. I've put all assumptions through the confidential waste shredder.'

She climbed in.

'Put on a headscarf or your hair will be wrecked,' he had said.

'In this traffic, Mr Faloon, your car will not be fast enough to wreck my hair. And later, neither will its driver.'

That had been almost ten years ago. Faloon and Nuala had since evolved an easy and frank relationship peculiar to themselves. They saw each other from time to time, even lived together for short periods, but each accepted that there would be other partners. Jealousy never arose between them and they talked freely about their other relationships. Their friendship was a secret between them. They didn't trust anyone else to understand it.

So when Faloon fled from the G2 offices with the computer he had half stolen and the aims half formed in his mind, he went to Nuala's apartment. She hadn't asked too many questions when she saw his disturbed state. When he had slept, she had slipped between the sheets beside him and soon discovered that he was uncharacteristically uninterested in lovemaking. But he did want her beside him.

'I'm sorry, Nuala. It's not your fault, it's me.'

'I haven't seen you like this for a long time. Is it anything you can tell me about?'

And so he told her some of the things that had happened. He told about Sarah, that his bungling could have led to her death, that he was probably going to be fired from G2. When he had finished, Nuala could only respond by hugging him more tightly, each lost in their own thoughts.

'Grundy asked me a question and I didn't have the opportunity to answer.' Faloon said suddenly into the growing darkness of the bedroom. 'He asked me to give a reason why that thug on the plane floored me if he was following me. He said it didn't make sense.'

'It would've made more sense the other way round. You trying to stop him.'

Faloon raised himself on his elbows. 'Good thinking, Nuala. Maybe I've been looking at the episode the wrong way round. Did Star-scar think I was following him!'

'Now that's out of the way, will you put a little happiness in my life,' whispered Nuala, but a little gentle exploring told her that if Faloon was getting excited, her nakedness had nothing to do with it.

'Why on earth did he think I was following him?' Faloon asked, addressing himself. 'The Green Boys knew where I was going.'

Nuala became more interested. 'Faloon, what if it wasn't a Green Boy, if it was someone else altogether?'

'I'm not involved at the moment with any other factions or any other cases. Unless it was simply an old score being settled.'

'You yourself may not be involved in any other cases, but the rest of us are, and that includes the rest of your department.'

'What are you talking about? What do you know?'

Once again, Nuala faced a conflict between the demands of the confidentiality of her office and her friendship for Faloon. She tried her best to resolve the conflict.

149

'Faloon, when you got out at Shannon, did you notice anything?'

'Nuala, some bastard had pumped me full of chemicals and my mind was wandering on the moon. What should I've seen?'

'You should've seen too many G2 men. Lucky for you, Faloon, that they were on hand at Shannon. They may have saved your life.'

'Were they waiting for me, Nuala?'

'Christ no, you conceited bastard!' Nuala exploded.

Faloon shut up while he applied more thought to what Nuala was trying to tell him. She said nothing more to help him. They rarely talked shop and both knew the reason for that. At last Faloon spoke.

'Too many of our people on duty. Doubling up everywhere. Round-the-clock by the looks of it. Are they watching other places as well, Nuala?'

'I wouldn't know, Faloon. Remember, I don't work there any longer.'

'Well, if they are, then Grundy can't have too many people on reserve. What on earth has caused this flap?'

Faloon began to squirm uncomfortably as he remembered more of Grundy's outburst in the office.

'The helicopter crash! Grundy was ranting about the helicopter crash. He wasn't interested in the Provos or the Green Boys or about any of the things I wanted to talk about. He was wittering about Russians and Americans. And about having to rely too much on the Brits. For what? What happened to the chopper?'

Faloon felt Nuala's relief and knew therefore that he was on the right track. He pressed on with his line of thought.

'We didn't shoot down our own chopper just to get rid of a couple of Russian spooks, did we?' he ventured. 'Grundy told me that the Russians probably know already about the microwave dishes.'

'Careful, Faloon, don't tell me too many things I'm not supposed to know. I won't tell you things that you aren't supposed to know. You've guessed correctly that G2 is very stretched. You're not correct about why the chopper crashed. Publicly, we're saying that the reason for the crash is not known, and I think we're telling the truth. We don't know why the Russians and the Americans are so excited.'

This drew Faloon up short. His imagination had run away with conjecture about the helicopter being shot down.

Nuala did some prompting. 'Think along these lines. You say Grundy betrayed your mission to rescue Sarah. Knowing Grundy as we both do, that is very possible. But you haven't thought of a reason.'

'He saw a mess and wanted his man out of it as fast as possible. He wanted to keep things sweet with the FBI. That might be reason enough.'

'True, but he also wanted the final defeat of the Provos and their Green Boy friends in America. After all, that was one of the reasons you were sent there. No, Faloon, it's possible that he sent for you because he needed you desperately for a bigger battle back home. When you went your own way, you may have betrayed him.'

'And when I lost our code chip to the FBI, I betrayed him again,' said Faloon softly.

Nuala groaned. 'Oh Faloon, don't tell me any more.'

'I'll tell you one more thing. I'm borrowing your car.'

'Where are you going?'

'Inishowen.'

'What for?'

'To have a look at where that helicopter crashed. There's something that we're all missing. Every time I hear about this trouble over here it begins with the helicopter, so that's where I'll start.'

'Start what, my dear Faloon?' Nuala looked at him wearily. 'Give it a rest. If you want to be nice to Grundy, just lie low, and here on my bed.'

'Sure I want to be nice to Grundy, but not that nice. Where's that car of yours?'

'Have it your way, Faloon, or nearly your way. You can have my car, but I come with it. And don't tell me I can't because it's official duty. I know differently, don't I?

Faloon opened his mouth to argue and then shut it. His mouth had got him into enough trouble for one day.

In the sea on Lough Swilly, off the coast of Inishowen, the fishing boat's engine chugged with a constant and regular beat. O'Donnell's heart did not.

O'Donnell was looking from Major Stukalin to Moira with a mixture of astonishment and interrogation.

'I think he's telling the truth, Dick. Everything he's wearing underneath his outer clothes is strange. The labels look Russian, though I suppose I wouldn't know the genuine article.'

'Look round his neck. Is there an identity tag?'

Stukalin made no move to prevent her searching round his neck. She located the fine chain and pulled it until the shining metal disc came into view.

'It's Russian. I can't make it out.' Moira looked helplessly at O'Donnell.

'Let me see it.'

Moira tugged the tag roughly from the Major's neck, much to his annoyance. O'Donnell took it and looked at it, dividing his attention between the identity tag and keeping the boat on course.

The fishing boat was by then navigating the main channel of Lough Swilly on a northerly course. The sea in this sheltered inlet was placid. O'Donnell's mind was in turmoil. Was he to believe this evidence or was this a new trick by British intelligence to trap them? If so, what was the form of the trap? How on earth was it to be sprung? The questions overtook each other unanswered.

O'Donnell addressed the Major directly. 'What did you say your name was?'

'Major Petr Fedorovich Stukalin of the Soviet Air Force.'

152

'Like hell. You expect me to believe that? What are you doing here?

'It's a long story, O'Donnell, and I'm in no condition to stand half naked on a boat deck to tell you. But I do assure you, my embassy would be very pleased to hear from me – or from you about me.'

The Major's reference to his condition reminded the nurse in Moira that he had a painful gunshot wound in his left arm and that he appeared to have sprained an ankle. He had begun to shiver.

'I'm taking him below, Dick. Russian or not, as you have said, he's valuable property.' Moira was still smarting from the treatment Stukalin had meted out to her on the beach. He was property rather than a patient.

Stukalin allowed Moira to help him. He thought that her attitude towards him had softened a little. Did she believe him, he wondered. Before he disappeared below out of O'Donnell's view, the Major spoke again.

'Do you believe me, O'Donnell?'

'I don't know.' O'Donnell turned from the sea towards Stukalin. 'I just don't know. I'll have to think of some way of testing your words.'

'But you think I could be telling the truth?' pressed Stukalin.

'You could be. It would explain a lot I couldn't understand about you before. But then again, it all could be a well-rehearsed plot.'

Stukalin, still holding Moira for support in the hatchway, shook his head and smiled mirthlessly. 'This country must harbour more exquisite conspiracies than Moscow. And with the world at my feet, I had to land in such a place.' He disappeared into the cabin.

A few minutes later, Moira reappeared alongside O'Donnell and followed his eyes over the bow of the boat.

'What have we got ourselves into, Dick?'

'I don't know. It's been a long time since I've repeated that phrase so many times and meant it. I'm inclined to believe him, but he's going to have to come up with more information. I mean, how did the bastard get here? He had no money, no wallet, a coat and trousers that hardly fit him, and underneath a garment with electric wiring.'

'If he's not what he says, then who is he?'

'He could be a plant. The British might think that somebody like him could end up meeting the top command of the Provisional IRA. Then he'd leave with . . .'

'We're being stupid, Dick. The helicopter crash! Remember there were Russians on the crashed helicopter. That's where he came from.'

'Moira, the reports say they're all dead.'

'And we know all about newspaper reports, don't we.' Moira was pleased with herself. For once, Dick did not have all the answers.

'You may just be right, Moira, but I want to be certain. Why would an ordinary chopper passenger be wearing fancy gear like that under his ordinary clothes? It was supposed to be a joyride for business partners. When the British threw me into one of their bloody helicopters, only the pilot wore that kind of gear.'

Moira pulled a face. Dick was making difficulties just because he hadn't thought of it himself, she pouted to herself.

'What now?' she asked.

'I need somewhere quiet to think and to talk to our friend. I'll head for Macamish.'

Moira shrugged. 'Never heard of it. Where is it?'

'You're not of sea-faring stock, my pretty lady.' O'Donnell admonished gently, his spirits rising. 'Macamish is an anchorage in a little rock-infested bay on the opposite side of Swilly. I can hide behind a spit of rock watched over by nothing more menacing than a Martello Tower.'

He looked to the left and pointed out the Martello Tower in the distance.

'The tower isn't manned, is it?' said Moira, reaching for the binoculars.

154

'No.' And O'Donnell smiled a rare smile. 'No. That tower is what's left of another age of British security worries.'

The reference to the Napoleonic wars was lost on Moira. 'I've been shot at enough today,' she grumbled. 'I just don't want to sail into the marine equivalent of a checkpoint.'

O'Donnell realized that the events of the day had drained Moira. She needed time to recover. They had almost been killed back on the road and had escaped more through luck than anything else.

'Neither do I,' said Dick in a soft reassuring tone. 'I want a quiet spell to do some thinking after an active day.' He grinned at the understatement. 'When it gets out that Dick O'Donnell allowed himself to be hijacked, they'll laugh from here to Connaught.'

A grin returned to Moira's face, much to O'Donnell's satisfaction. He went on. 'I knew there was something odd about that man down there, and it wasn't just his American accent. In other ways he didn't seem to fit the usual mould of undercover Brit.'

He suddenly raised his arm and pointed. Moira followed his direction and saw a pair of seals basking on the rocks. When the sound of the engine came too close, they slipped into the water and disappeared.

'One other thing. At the roadblock, he didn't seem to want to announce his presence, and it wasn't just because I had a gun on him. He's a cool customer and probably worked out that when we were right up close to the police and soldiers, I daren't use the gun. If he'd been a Brit, he'd have chanced something, because he'd have known that undercover Brits don't stay alive too long if we get hold of them.'

O'Donnell paused to change course towards Macamish. 'Check that our Russian guest isn't tunnelling his way out through the hull, Moira.'

Moira swung her head into the cabin and out again. 'No. He's lying down on the bunk. I don't think he's in any condition to go anywhere.'

'Take no chances, Moira. I think he's as tough as they come.'

To reassure both of them, Moira stuck her head into the cabin again, then decided to go below. As O'Donnell threaded his way among the rocks, drawing on the knowledge gleaned from his boyhood games in this bay with an old rowing boat and from scuba-diving as a teenager, he smelt coffee.

'How do you manage to make instant coffee smell so good?'

'I throw a little on the gas flame.'

'Smells like Russian coffee,' Stukalin suddenly joined in.

'I thought it smelt good,' shouted O'Donnell.

'I could bring you to Russia and let you see for yourself, O'Donnell. Would you like that?'

'I've heard that some people who go to Russia have trouble getting out again.' He turned to Moira. 'Moira, as soon as I drop the anchor, get some food cooking. While we eat, Major Stukalin can give the details of any offers he wants to make to us.'

They heard the Russian mumble, 'And some people who come to Ireland have trouble getting out again.'

O'Donnell went forward to drop anchor. The boat drifted back gently, taking up the slack of the anchor chain and digging the flukes into the sandy bottom. When he was satisfied that the boat would stay where he intended, O'Donnell shut down the engine, cast a final look over the deserted shoreline, then joined Moira and Stukalin in the cabin.

'Now we have peace to talk, and all the time in the world,' he said to the Major.

Far to the north of them, in the cold seas between Ireland and Iceland, a ship with a crane on it hid itself in the middle of a Soviet fishing fleet. Teams of sailors suspended on gantries began painting its hull green. Others were building wooden structures on deck to disguise the ship's profile and to hide its weapons. The flag of the Soviet Union was replaced with that of Greece. When preparations were complete, it set a course for the Inishowen peninsula. O'Donnell did not have all the time in the world.

FIFTEEN

The red light inscribed a circle in the darkness and rain. It was a police signal to the car Faloon was driving.

Nuala lay curled up asleep in the front passenger seat. The rhythm of the wipers, the drone of the engine had relaxed her.

'Wake up, Nuala. It's a police roadblock.'

Nuala struggled reluctantly into wakefulness. 'Which side of the border are we on?'

'The southern side. I've lost my gamble.'

If there had been more time, Faloon would have driven round the border of Northern Ireland towards the county of Donegal and Inishowen, thereby staying within the Republic of Ireland. But the direct and the fastest route to Inishowen lay across Northern Ireland, or British-occupied Ireland, as the IRA was prone to call it.

Whatever it was called, the border spelt trouble for people who wanted to move from place to place discreetly. On both sides of the frontier police and army patrols operated to intercept weapons, ammunition and explosives being smuggled into the North. Normally Faloon was part of that security screen, but not now, not as a freelance undercover man with a stolen computer and an unsanctioned half-baked idea of a mission.

Faloon's gamble lay in crossing into Northern Ireland in bad weather, on the basis that security patrols would sit in their warm dry vehicles in driving rain. There would be no trouble from the customs. The customs officers on both sides of the border went home each evening, leaving the roads open.

Faloon drew to a halt beside the policeman.

'Any identification, sir?'

As Faloon reluctantly pulled out his driving licence, he saw the number of his car being entered on a sheet of paper on a clipboard. His name, address and licence number were added.

'And your destination, sir?'

'Donegal. We're taking a few days off for an early holiday, before the real holiday-makers.'

'And what line of business are you in?'

'The tourist business. Bit of a busman's holiday.'

The policeman shot a look at Nuala and decided that no further questions were necessary.

They drove on, Faloon's face reflecting his dismay. Nuala attempted to distract him.

'They probably think we're off for a dirty weekend. If I have my way, that's exactly what it'll be.'

Faloon remembered how another woman on the other side of the Atlantic had said something very similar to him only days ago.

'I don't care if those clod-hoppers think I screw sheep.'

'Thanks,' Nuala said.

History was indeed repeating itself.

'Nuala, please. I'll always prefer you to a sheep.'

'Sometimes your sense of humour is asinine.'

'I draw the line at donkeys.'

Suddenly changing mood, Nuala asked, 'Why didn't you invent another destination for that checkpoint? Why tell the truth when a lie will do just as well?' It was an old department joke.

'If G2 and Grundy start checking the files – and their computers should have those checkpoint lists number-crunched by coffee-time tomorrow – they will know I'm heading for Inishowen. If I lied, they would look for the reason. As it is, there's a chance Grundy will think I'm taking a holiday, as ordered.'

Nuala gazed thoughtfully out into the cone of light fashioned by the headlights. They had crossed the border and were now on a good open road in countryside once more. The rain had stopped and there was no sign of military or police presence on the British side.

'Faloon, Grundy knows you well enough to think that you are going to Inishowen to meddle.'

'Possibly. But he's too hard pressed to divert much thought in my direction. He'll jump to conclusions when he sees you're with me.'

Faloon threw a reassuring glance at Nuala, but neither was very convinced. When Grundy discovered that one of his small computers was in Faloon's baggage, the idea of Faloon on holiday would linger like a stray cat in a dogs' home.

The sun was just beginning to rise as they motored along the banks of the River Foyle towards Londonderry. They passed a signpost which read 'derry', the prefix erased by local nationalists.

On the outskirts of Londonderry, just inside Northern Ireland, Faloon pulled into the car park of a hotel incongruously named the Everglades.

'I need to do a little work and I'd better do it here through the British telephone system. Grundy's people will be listening to all computer tones on the Irish side, if what you've told me is correct.' He held the car door open for her and took their bags.

'Are we booking into a room?' she asked, looking at the baggage as they walked towards the hotel entrance.

'Yes, for a while. You can get some proper sleep. I'll try connecting the computer to other friendly machines. Depending on what they say, I might be able to get some sleep too.' He gave her a big wink, put his arms round her slim waist and led her towards the hotel entrance. On the wall was a large coat-of-arms of the city. It featured a skeleton. They both looked at it with distaste.

'Why don't you take an hour's rest first, Faloon, and then connect up your box of tricks?'

'No. I want the telephone networks when they are free of most business traffic. Anyway, I couldn't sleep with so many questions on my mind.'

Nuala watched him unpack the small computer. 'Are you about to do anything illegal with that thing?' she demanded.

Faloon looked across at her, wondering if she was joking. 'Everything I'm doing is illegal. It could be very messy. Do you want out?'

'It's too late for that. I'm already in deep enough to be thrown out of the Minister's office. I'm now banking on you doing a superman act and bringing us all back to dry land.' She paused and then added, 'Without a code chip you won't have access to anything useful.'

Faloon put his hand into his coat pocket and withdrew a matchbox. He carefully removed a computer memory chip from it.

Nuala was aghast. 'Oh shit, Faloon. Where the hell did that come from? So you didn't lose it after all.'

He smirked. 'Oh yes I did. This is not a Grundy chip, Nuala. It's the FBI's equivalent. And I'm banking on my old G2 chip being mistaken for an FBI one in Washington to buy me some time.'

'They'll have your head for this, Faloon.'

'G2 or the FBI?'

'Both, you idiot.'

'I don't think so. When the time comes, they'll quietly exchange them. Anything else would be too embarrassing, don't you think?' Faloon grinned as he up-ended the computer, unscrewed the back panel as he had in the more prestigious Algonquin room, and inserted the chip.

Nuala looked on disapprovingly. 'Are you going to plug into the FBI computers?'

'I am.'

'You're mad.'

'I need information. I can get it from the FBI central computer – and even from the British, if needed.'

'The British!'

'Yes. The FBI computers allow limited communication with some British computer files – part of the international agreement against terrorism.'

Faloon dialled the Washington numbers he knew by heart and asked the switchboard to connect him to the main computer bank. As he had expected, his sudden departure from the FBI had not yet been notified to the FBI switchboard. That was the good thing about big organizations, you could rely on mistakes like that.

As he waited, Faloon covered the mouthpiece and turned to Nuala, who looked a bit shocked.

'Let's see if they've emptied my electronic mailbox,' said Faloon, in gleeful anticipation.

'Let's see if your codewords are still in operation,' she answered grimly. 'I'm hoping not.' She half believed that any minute the door would burst open and Faloon would be carried off.

But neither her hopes nor her fears materialized. Nobody burst in and Faloon's codewords were still operative. Faloon began communicating with the big American computer from a hotel bedroom in Ulster.

'Message from Grundy for me.' Seconds later it was scrolling past his eyes. He snorted in disgust.

'Grundy telling me again to come home immediately. This mail is a bit late.' He moved further into the message, rapidly losing interest. Suddenly he leaned forward with renewed concentration.

'I wish I'd seen this before I was put on that plane in Boston,' he muttered, gesturing at the screen. 'In a guarded way, Grundy was telling me that both the Americans and the Russians were showing an odd interest in the chopper crash.'

He scratched his head. 'I wonder,' he said, thinking aloud, 'whether that message was meant for me or for Uncle Sam. Grundy must've known that a mailbox in an FBI computer can be read by someone in the FBI.'

He stabbed the keyboard and more of the message was revealed on the small screen. 'That's funny,' he growled.

'Nothing's funny,' Nuala replied. 'I'm worried about what's going to happen to you when they find out what you're doing.'

'I think that in a roundabout way Grundy was warning me about the Americans. Could that be so, Nuala?' Faloon persisted.

Nuala closed her eyes. He knew her problem. If she answered his question, she would be breaking a trust and breaking the law. However, she did answer. Her muffled voice reached him with the information he wanted. 'G2 is ranged equally against the Americans and the Russians. And yes, I think Grundy was trying to warn you.'

For a brief moment, Faloon didn't move. Suddenly he stood up and swore volubly. He went over to the bed and sat beside her. 'Sometimes I'm a fool. My FBI codewords are intact. Do you know why?'

Nuala shook her head.

'Well maybe it isn't bureaucratic sloth. And maybe it wasn't FBI carelessness that left me with an FBI chip which works.'

'What are you saying, Faloon?'

'I'm saying that the Americans are keeping track of me. Right now they know exactly where I am. And soon they'll know my immediate concerns.'

Understanding spread across Nuala's face. Her eyes fell on the little computer and its connection to the telephone – to the FBI.

'Disconnect!' she yelled.

'Too late. The FBI Big Daddy has already logged this number.' He closed his eyes. 'And I thought I was being so bloody clever. They were several steps ahead of me – and Grundy.'

He swung back to his small computer and jabbed at the keys once more.

Nuala stared in disbelief. 'The damage is done,' Faloon explained. 'So I might as well continue. First I'll find out who that gorilla on the plane was, the one who filled me with insulin.'

Faloon knew what kind of data banks he could access. First he tried the Green Boy data base, asking the computer to throw onto the screen anyone listed with a prominent scar on the back of the hand. No match, said the screen.

'Does that rule out the Green Boys?'

'No, it simply reduces the likelihood. Maybe whoever entered the data didn't include anything in the "distinctive marks" box. That happens, you know.'

He tried the FBI personnel files, next in line of suspicion. Access denied, said the screen.

'Surprised?'

'Nope.'

'I suppose you'll ask for KGB personnel files next,' she mocked in an effort to divert Faloon from digging his professional grave by continuing with illegal searches of FBI files. Her words had the opposite effect.

He looked up and blew a kiss at her with both hands. 'Not a bad idea,' he said. 'KGB files – no. But diplomatic files – yes.'

It didn't take Faloon long to consult the diplomatic files. Most of the information was a matter of public record, but the FBI listed all those either known or suspected to be intelligence people in addition to their day job. Faloon entered the approximate age, a few lines of general description and finally, the details of the very distinctive star-shaped scar. Who matched all that, he asked.

He waited. The computer searched.

'Jackpot!'

The answer was Viktor Losev. Losev was on the scientific and technical staff of the USSR's embassy in Washington. Little was known of his background except previous postings in other countries. The injury to his hand had occurred several years ago while working on a defence project at a place called Tyuratam in the Soviet Union. After the accident, he had transferred from technical operations to the Soviet Union's scientific and technical diplomatic staff.

Nuala stood behind Faloon to watch the information arriving.

'Some diplomat,' she growled, 'assaulting unsuspecting people in aeroplane lavatories.'

'A scientific spy who seems to have had little difficulty in lifting the hem of Grundy's security curtain and sneaking inside. G2 thought the Russians would be coming from the east.' Faloon laughed.

'You've nothing to poke fun at, Mr Faloon. It was the Colonel who correctly guessed that Star-scar might be nothing to do with the Green Boys. He more or less told you that when you were being fired.'

'Suspended, woman. I'm just suspended.'

'And we all love a bit of suspense.'

Faloon busied himself again. He called up the passenger lists of those leaving the USA, culled from the airline computers. For the Aer Lingus flight ex Boston onto which Faloon had been bundled, there was no Viktor Losev.

'Well, at least we're sure that he is up to no good, Nuala. He travelled under an assumed name. I wonder why the Americans let him out.'

Nuala walked over to the wardrobe and took out a couple of clothes-hangers. 'Has it struck you, Faloon, that they deliberately let him out, and then deliberately put you onto the same plane with maximum publicity? Has it occurred to you that the FBI might have thought you'd already received Grundy's warning about the Russian interest in yourself? Were they not hoping you'd follow him, or that he'd follow you? Either would serve the American purpose.'

Faloon gave her a sidelong glance. 'You could be very good at this type of work. But what do you know about the American purpose? And why the Russians despatched a technology specialist? Losev is an engineer.'

Nuala shook her head.

He returned to the screen, scratching his chin, scarcely noticing Nuala stepping out of her clothes and leaving to take a shower. As the sound of the shower reached him, he replaced the telephone receiver and returned the computer to his suitcase.

Nuala stood in the bath under the shower head, feeling the healing warmth trickling down her body, carrying away the discomfort of the night. She didn't turn as she heard the shower curtains open and close, nor when a pair of hands appeared round her body, working up a rich lather with her perfumed soap in her body hair.

The long fingers rubbed into muscles from the nape of her neck to her hips. She closed her eyes and threw her head back on Faloon's shoulder. He turned her and pulled their bodies tightly together. He kissed her, longingly, tenderly, demandingly.

Later, still wrapped around each other, but with their passions spent, they slipped into sleep. Neither opened an eyelid until mid-morning, which was later than Faloon had planned.

Nuala began packing. 'What now, Faloon?' she asked. 'There mightn't be anything at the crash-site for you to pick up. Whatever everybody is after, they haven't been able to find it. One man with a stolen computer is not going to succeed.'

'But many people think there's still something to find, and Losev may be one of them. I think Losev followed me onto the aircraft at Boston. He must've thought I'd been tipped off about him didn't want me on his tail after landing, I suppose.'

Nuala wondered briefly if the Americans had originally intended using Sarah to keep track of Faloon and then had to improvise when the Green Boys interfered. Her private speculation was interrupted when Faloon suddenly darted to the phone, his contact number book in hand.

Seconds later the phone in the Accident Investigations Department at Baldonnel Airfield was ringing. Faloon asked for the man in charge.

'How do you know it's not a woman?' interrupted Nuala, her feminist sensibilities ruffled.

'Because I've met the guy.'

'Absolutely sure it's a male?'

'As sure as I can be without sharing a shower with him.'

That left Faloon in peace to make his inquiry.

'Hello, Brendan. Faloon here. Just breezed in from the States and they've got me back in harness already.'

Nuala listened as Faloon created the illusion that he was working officially on the chopper crash, that he hadn't yet had time to read everything in the file, that he was being pressed to do the impossible in next to no time and could Brendan spare him a few moments of informal background. Of course Brendan could, and he must hear all about America when Faloon was buying him the drink he owed him.

'From the files I've read, Brendan, they don't know anything. They don't know why it dropped out of the sky.' Faloon winked at Nuala.

'You're partly right, Faloon,' Brendan began. 'On this particular helicopter there's been at least one accident caused by an inspection hatch on the tail pylon opening in flight and hitting the tail rotor. It takes bits out of the blades, which then become so badly out of balance that the tail rotor wrenches itself right off the end of the helicopter.'

'Can't helicopters do without a tail rotor long enough to land safely?'

'Not normally. Without a tail rotor, the body of the helicopter will spin in the opposite direction to the big blades. It goes out of control. The impact damage at Inishowen was consistent with the fuselage spinning when it hit the deck.'

'Didn't anybody know that this hatch could bring the whole machine down?'

'Everybody did, Faloon. Information like that is exchanged between operators. Aer Rianta knew about the problem and had fitted, not one, but two modifications to prevent that happening.'

Faloon listened as Brendan unfolded a few last details, after which he thanked the investigator copiously and replaced the receiver. He told Nuala what he had just heard.

Nuala thought for a moment before asking a question. She was in front of the dressing table mirror, finalizing her make-up. Falcoon was standing in the middle of the room with his back to her, stark naked, and gazing into the waters of the River Foyle.

'Faloon, why don't Brendan and his accident investigation people know for sure that it was the hatch? The odds on its being anything else are very slim.'

Faloon sat on the bed and began dressing hastily. 'It seems we've found practically the whole of the helicopter, except the last few feet of the tail pylon. No hatch, no tail rotor. And Brendan says the point of fracture leads him to believe privately that the whole last section of the tail was ripped off. But without a few more bits, it's just guesswork.'

'Ripped off? But that would mean it hit something,' Nuala responded.

'Or something hit it.'

Faloon had dressed and in a hurry.

'We know something odd was happening,' he said, 'and both the Americans and Russians are playing a cat-and-mouse game? I wonder if either of them gave the IRA a portable SAM?' Faloon conjectured.

'What's that?'

'Surface-to-air missile.'

'God forbid.'

They were too late for breakfast and too early for lunch. Nuala complained hungrily as she was hustled into her own car and driven once more through the border just outside Londonderry, and onto the Inishowen peninsula.

Not far behind them, a car hired at Shannon was also being driven towards Inishowen. The hand on the wheel bore a star-shaped scar.

SIXTEEN

Colonel Grundy was unhappy, unhappier than he'd been for a long time. He was outside the office of the Foreign Affairs Minister, sitting in a plush chair in an area reserved for distinguished visitors. The secretary was doing her best to make the head of G2 comfortable, but to little avail.

Grundy was being kept waiting much longer than ever before. He knew why, and so did the unfortunate secretary. Both knew that displeasure was being communicated to Grundy. It might have been easier, Grundy grumbled to himself, if the familiar Miss Gallagher had not been on leave.

At last the Minister would see him. With an involuntary and needless adjustment of his tie, Grundy fixed the ghost of a smile on his face and marched into the office.

The Minister had two smartly dressed aides with him and they were just putting the final touches to some task. During their interchanges, Grundy's presence was not acknowledged. He was forced to stand, not presuming to take a seat, as yet another level of reprimand.

As the two smart young civil servants left, nodding

affably to Grundy as they passed, the Minister's countenance changed from generous approval to dark displeasure. He motioned Grundy to be seated. In the past, the Minister had always come round the desk to talk to him. On this occasion, he sat behind his desk, his hands clasped in front of him.

'Colonel, I have always had the greatest faith in your abilities and have always felt that G2 could not be in better hands.'

'Thank you, Minister.' Grundy accepted this opening kick in the teeth.

'But the events of the past few days are serving to bring into question your whole method of operation.'

Grundy's face had become a mask. The Minister, normally a friend to G2, was not relishing the interview either. He offered Grundy a cigarette from a small, ornate box. Grundy shook his head in refusal. The Minister then continued.

'I am led to understand that your total resources have been devoted to this Inishowen business. Now, don't get me wrong. You'll probably be anxious to point out that it was I who first alerted you to very unusual interest from both the Russians and the Americans in this helicopter accident.'

Grundy coughed. 'If you'll forgive the interruption, Minister, there remain strong indications that something very unusual is going on. Your instincts in the matter were accurate.'

The Minister held up his hand to indicate that he was not in the mood to allow interruptions, particularly ones like that. He was trying to claw back his position. Being reminded of previous contrary positions was an unfriendly act.

'Grundy, the Baldonnel investigation people say that there was a design fault in the helicopter. A similar accident occurred some years ago in a North Sea oil field. Am I not correct?'

'Indeed, Minister, but . . .'

'So we can isolate the crash itself as an accident. We found nothing in the remains, human or technical, to cause any alarm. It's therefore safe to assume that the unusual interest from the superpowers was due to some internal pressures in both countries, or indeed, pressures arising from their mutual rivalry.'

At this point, the Minister became more emphatic. He was about to lay down the law. Grundy became very apprehensive.

'With respect, Minister, you do not have vital additional information . . .'

'Enough, Grundy. I am beginning to think that the whole episode has gone to your head.' He reached across his desk and grabbed some sheets of paper. 'Do you know what these are, Grundy? Complaints, Grundy; unprecedented complaints from both the American and Soviet embassies. In essence, they are accusing G2 of harassing them. They're asking me if there is anything I want to discuss. The answer, Grundy, is negative.'

The Minister threw himself back into his chair and angrily tossed the papers back into a tray. But he wasn't finished.

'Then I return from Brussels and a mauling at the hands of our European friends, to find that all our codes must be changed because one of your operatives carelessly made a present of code information to the Americans. And, I hear on the grapevine, this happened as the Americans were throwing him out. If we keep on this course, Grundy, South Africa will have more friends than Ireland.'

For the moment, the harassed politician seemed to have shot his bolt. He looked at Grundy grimly. Grundy took his time. He felt that if the Minister had any further thoughts, better that he heard them all at once. When nothing more was thrown at him, Grundy began.

'The following information I could only give you in a personal and private interview like this, Minister. You were not wrong in your first reaction to the Inishowen crash. There is something funny going on and you were absolutely right to feel that in your bones. I now have evidence to support that statement.'

Although he hid it well, the Minister was becoming a little apprehensive. When he had spoken earlier of his faith in Grundy, he had really meant it, so when Grundy stood his ground and told him to listen, he usually did so. He had vented his anger.

'I hope this is not another bombshell, Grundy. I've had quite enough for one week.'

'It is a bombshell,' said Grundy, hiding the satisfaction the words gave him.

The Minister thought for a moment, reached for the telephone and asked for coffee to be sent in. Then, as if to stretch his legs, he stood up, walked round the desk and sat on a chair beside a long, low table. He motioned Grundy to the chair opposite. Grundy began slowly.

'You've heard me speak of a man called Arthur Semple from time to time.'

'Yes, a friend of yours. Englishman. Diplomat at some of the places you did your soldiering. Yes, vague memories. What about him?'

'Well, he's now in the same line of business as myself. He's an important man in the British Defence Intelligence Staff and he's confirmed your suspicions to me.'

'Look, Grundy, you've always had friends in certain places. I've known that but I don't want you telling me officially. Your links at a high level with British intelligence services could be an albatross round the neck of myself, and indeed, this whole government. You understand that, don't you?'

'Fully. And I want you to understand the risk I'm taking in telling you the source of some extraordinary information. It's important that you believe what I'm about to tell you, because I believe it.'

A knock at the door announced the coffee. When they were once more alone, Grundy began his account of the meeting in Berkshire with Semple. He told him of the Shield experimental long-range radar and what it had picked up and lost off the northern tip of the Inishowen peninsula. He said that the British were peeved because the Americans were keeping information to themselves. The British thought the lost aircraft must be Russian.

'Hence,' grinned the Minister, 'all this interest from the superpowers. The helicopter crash was a coincidence. A remarkable coincidence!'

'You appear to have been correct right down the line, Minister,' replied Grundy, peering intently into the bottom of his coffee cup.

'There's more,' he continued. 'It's not an intelligence or security matter. It's political and I'm acting, as was Semple, as an unofficial channel of communication between our two countries. Are you willing to accept a message on that basis?'

'Normally no. Definitely no. But presuming you think I should do so on this occasion, go ahead.'

'The race to find this high-performance plane, or the bits of it, is no longer between the superpowers alone. The British are now runners and want to go into partnership with us.'

'Why?'

'Semple argues that if we get hold of it, we'll have to sell its secrets because the technology will be beyond our capacity to emulate.'

'I can see that, but we could go into partnership with any-body. The Americans would pay enough to make inroads on our foreign debts, the French are technology-hungry and I need some bargaining power at Brussels. And the Russians themselves – they might consider a trade deal over a considerable period of time. That means the British will have to join the queue.'

'Semple says the British have something we want.'

'And what might that be, Colonel?'

'Northern Ireland.'

The Minister said nothing. He got up and walked to the window.

'Grundy,' he said quietly, 'this window faces north, and it is about the only thing in this office which does. We can't afford to abandon re-unification as an ultimate national goal. Nor, as things stand, can we afford Northern Ireland itself. Surely that doesn't shock you?'

'No. In intelligence, I'm required to have faith in almost nothing.'

Grundy was smiling when the Minister turned to face him.

'You may smile, Grundy, but politicians like me have to deal with realities.' Grundy had scored. 'The most we want is some face-saving movement from the British, but all the time hoping they won't shift their ground on sovereignty. Not yet. That bunch of bickering sanctimonious bigots up there would bleed us dry. If I could think of a foolproof way of doing it, I'd fund political Protestantism to stop it losing more ground.'

'And that, my dear Minister, is probably why you're already thinking of a way of selling this plane – if we ever lay our hands on it – to a combined Anglo-American bid. The British can give you something politically. The Americans could come up with cash.'

'You've known me too long.'

'Well don't move yet, Minister. I need hardly remind you that we've nothing – nothing at all. If the plane is in our jurisdiction, we don't know where. The Americans and the Russians must have a more accurate picture but they're not telling us. In fact, they're obscuring as much as they can.' Grundy gestured at the complaints in the tray on the desk. 'They're trying to make sure we are kept in the dark. Meanwhile, the Russians have moved somebody into the country, and the Americans will also try, if they haven't already succeeded.'

The Minister looked alarmed.

'I thought that all your precautions were meant to prevent the KGB and others getting in.'

'They are, but I can't close every door. All our years coping with the Provos would have told you that.'

'I don't know whether this lost plane will be of any value to us politically or otherwise,' the Minister barked, 'but I do know that if we don't find it and somebody else does, it will not go well for the government – or its servants who might be held responsible. Do I make myself clear?'

'Perfectly, Minister.'

'We must find it, Grundy, before anybody else does. Not the Russians, not the Americans and not the British. I'm going to swamp Inishowen with police and army. You'll have to make your embassy-watching more discreet.'

He pulled out his pipe in a flurry of satisfaction with his own decisiveness. 'Oh yes,' he added. 'I want the book thrown at that idiot who annoyed the Americans and lost our codes. Connive with Semple and the British if you must, but if that ever becomes public, even around these offices, I'll disown you, Grundy.'

'Hmph. Just when I need a friend in high places.'

'Grundy, my dear man, I am your friend, otherwise I wouldn't have cleared your decks!'

The Minister, grinning all over his face, was back behind his desk. Grundy turned and left, unspeakable thoughts about politicians tumbling through his mind.

In the fishing boat's main cabin Major Stukalin suddenly chuckled, taking O'Donnell and Moira by surprise.

'Has the wine gone to your head, Major?' scowled O'Donnell. 'Because whoever you are, it's a safe bet that you're not where you should be. Hardly a laughing matter for you.'

'I agree with what you say, Mr O'Donnell, but the situation is not so desperate that I am prohibited a joke.'

'What joke?'

174

'Because your marvellous marksmen shot my arm, I must eat with a fork, just like an American. That is funny for a Soviet officer.'

'No funnier than speaking English with an American accent,' Moira chipped in.

'International English is American English, not English or Irish English. American English is what foreigners are taught. You two can be very difficult to understand sometimes.'

'We understand each other,' growled O'Donnell.

'And now it is necessary for us to understand each other. I must ask you again whether you believe I am a Russian and not one of your British enemies.'

Stukalin was looking hard across the small cabin table at O'Donnell as he put this question. The past hour had been almost convivial. The boat bobbed quietly at anchor; the breeze was light and warm, the sea gently rippling. Moira had lit a gas lamp, which provided some heat in the cool of the north Ulster evening.

In that atmosphere, the three of them had sat down to a passably good meal, all from tins, but tasty nevertheless. O'Donnell had also provided a bottle of red wine. But only one glass.

'We too are soldiers, Major,' O'Donnell had explained, 'but unlike soldiers in a regular force, we're never off duty. So we don't drink. We'll drink again when the war is over. The wine is for you, and you alone. I hope it's to your taste.'

For a moment Stukalin thought O'Donnell was being melodramatic. He shrugged his shoulders and drank alone. Silly man, thought Stukalin. Trying to get a Russian vodka drinker drunk on a paltry bottle of wine.

O'Donnell had steered the conversation away from matters of the moment. Instead he had talked about the history of Ireland, about battles throughout the centuries against the invader, always by inference and sometimes directly, justifying the present IRA action in terms of historical experience.

The conversation had become heated only at one point, when O'Donnell had compared the British presence in Northern Ireland with that of the Russians in Afghanistan.

'I did a tour of duty in Afghanistan. I didn't like it much, using jet fighters against villages, but we were called to the aid of the legitimate Afghan government. My country's policy is to help friendly governments against Western-backed counter revolution. Anyway,' Stukalin added as an afterthought, 'there were plenty of signs of your military presence once upon a time in that country. And your forces were further from home then than mine are now.'

'Our military presence!' O'Donnell had objected with unexpected verbal violence. 'The Irish have never been imperialists, only the victims of imperialism. That was a British army.'

Stukalin wiped his lips with the back of his hand. 'I looked at some of the old graves in Afghanistan, O'Donnell, and that is where I last saw your name. On a grave. There were Irishmen there, perhaps even your antecedents.'

O'Donnell was very angry and the Major was very cool. 'Are there Lithuanians and Latvians and Estonians in your army, Major? And are they being buried beside the O'Donnell in Afghanistan?'

Major Stukalin had paused to sip his wine and had decided that the exchange had served its purpose. He changed tack.

'It must be difficult for you to recognize that for most of the world, what is happening here is a sideshow. Please don't get angry again, because as an intelligent man, you know I'm telling the truth. Beyond these shores you will find most people think Ireland is part of England. On my school map, all of this was called the British Isles.'

He sat back against the bulkhead and waited for a reply from O'Donnell. When there was none, he went on.

'When the world is divided, capitalist against socialist, rich against poor, black against white, the people on this island are divided by issues that have no meaning for the rest of the world. Hardly surprising I know so little about your irrelevant little war.'

O'Donnell broke his angry silence.

'I don't expect the Russians to know anything, or care one way or the other. I just like your rifles and use them against my country's enemies. But they do know about us in America and we've a lot of support there. And whatever you may think of America, Mr Russian Major, it is a bloody big and important slice of the world.'

This was the point at which Stukalin had made his little joke about eating like an American. The purpose had been to soften the atmosphere. The Russian felt uncomfortable when the links between the Provos and the Americans were being paraded.

And when Stukalin had asked the question about whether his identity as a Russian was still in doubt, it was more to swing attention back to Russia than to gain information. Stukalin already knew his captors had accepted he was a Russian. But how much more could he tell them?

O'Donnell was answering his question. 'Yes, you are Russian, but you haven't told us why you are here. What's your mission, Major Stukalin?'

'Name, rank and number. I think that is all I am required to give you.'

'That's the fullest co-operation you may give an enemy. Are we enemies?'

Stukalin counselled caution to himself. O'Donnell was clever. He also had command of a means of escape. The Major had never thought of escape by sea. Forgivable in an airman, he supposed.

Stukalin was beginning to think he might need the pair in front of him if he was to escape from Ireland without tangling with officialdom. He was wounded, in the hands of brigands and the countryside was probably infested with Irish security forces looking for him — and the two people opposite him. His lack of knowledge about this odd country was partly responsible for his present uncomfortable plight. Time to use words skilfully.

'No, Mr O'Donnell, you're not my enemy, nor the objective of any mission. When I arrived here, the little I ever knew about the situation in Ireland I had forgotten.' Stukalin allowed himself a rueful smile at how he had tangled with the IRA. 'But now that I'm here I want only one other thing. I want to leave as soon as possible. I want to get back to Russia.'

'Then answer my question. Why are you in Ireland?'

Moira lifted the coffee pot from the galley stove and offered Stukalin a refill. The diversion annoyed O'Donnell and Moira noted the exasperation flitting across his face.

'You were in that helicopter, weren't you?' she said impatiently.

O'Donnell turned on her. 'Bloody hell, woman. Keep your mouth shut. Shut tight. I'll do the talking.' O'Donnell was enraged and was shouting at the top of his voice. Moira, Stukalin noticed, looked frightened. He waited until O'Donnell had regained his composure.

In the light of what had just happened, Stukalin thought very fast about how he should play his cards.

If he accepted the convenient cue provided by the naïve Moira, then he would need to know where the helicopter had come from and where it was going, who his fellow passengers were, whether it was civilian or military, and why it had crashed. Only the last question could he answer.

He looked across the table. Moira was white-faced and O'Donnell red-faced. Both awaited his answer.

'I was not on that helicopter. I know nothing about it.'

Moira's eyes widened and O'Donnell was mollified.

'I'm relieved you said that, Major Stukalin,' O'Donnell said almost in a whisper. 'I wouldn't have believed you otherwise and I'd then have called into question everything you've said so far.' He couldn't resist shooting a look of triumph in Moira's direction. 'Now pour some coffee.'

The short interlude provided both Stukalin and O'Donnell with some thinking time. Initially, O'Donnell had felt more by instinct than by deduction that Stukalin had not been in the helicopter. Later, he recognized that Stukalin's garb, particularly his undergarment, was not that normally worn by helicopter passengers, and Stukalin could not have been the pilot of an Aer Rianta helicopter. Logically Stukalin must have come from somewhere else.

Stukalin's thinking was different. He had begun from the viewpoint that O'Donnell was not an easy man to tell fairy tales to. He was formulating an escape plan but it depended on O'Donnell swallowing a big lie. To lie successfully, he needed to gain a reputation for truth.

O'Donnell had gone on deck to check that the anchor was not dragging. It was an unnecessary chore. The setting sun had washed the sky in vermilion, backlighting the hills and mountains of Donegal. The peaceful beauty was mirrored in the surface of a flat sea. The boat would have maintained its station attached to a bucket, never mind a seventy pound anchor.

Stukalin came up into the wheelhouse, where O'Donnell joined him.

'No more dancing round each other, Major Stukalin. Where have you come from? Why are you here?'

'I was flying over the north Atlantic, not far from your shores. My plane developed engine trouble and fell into the sea. I managed to reach the shore and stole clothes from a holiday caravan near where I landed. I got the shotgun with its single cartridge also from the caravan. I burnt the caravan to cover the theft.'

'And why did you hijack us?'

'I told you. It was for your car. I wanted to reach the Aeroflot base at Shannon Airport. From there I could quickly reach home.'

'And why not simply walk into the nearest police station and be sent home in style?'

'It was a warplane, illegally in Irish airspace. My country

does not look kindly on officers who start an international incident.'

'Why not, Major Stukalin? Your submarine officers cruise around Swedish harbours, and maybe Irish harbours for all I know. Why on earth should I help you escape?'

Stukalin held his breath. Time for the big lie. 'You like Kalashnikov AK-47 assault rifles, don't you, O'Donnell. Well, you can have more. Also rocket-propelled grenades.'

O'Donnell looked closely at Stukalin, whose face glowed in the light of the dying day, and said nothing.

'And SAM 7s.' Stukalin continued with a stock list for a terrorist supermarket. 'Heat-seeking surface-to-air missiles. Helicopter killers. Mines. Mortars. Grenades. Night sights. We have a lot to offer.'

O'Donnell looked into the sky and the hills. His nose sniffed the cool, evening air. His ears listened to the gentle lapping of wavelets against the wooden hull. Never accept a first offer, his senses told him.

O'Donnell directed Stukalin back down into the main cabin, where Moira was washing the last of the dinner utensils. The Major was led through to the forward cabin and shown a bunk.

'Bedtime, Major. Before you sleep, think of how you are going to communicate the deal to your principals.'

'I have already thought of that. There is enough transmitting power on this boat to make arrangements. You put to sea, meet a Russian ship, transfer me and take your weapons as a gift from a grateful Soviet Government.'

'I'll think about it, Major.' He shut the cabin door, locking Stukalin inside.

O'Donnell had already decided what to do. It was the most dangerous decision he had ever made. He returned to the table in the main cabin and lapsed into deep thought.

SEVENTEEN

The loss of the spaceplane was beginning to take its toll in the Kremlin. The first casualty was Yermash. The Presidium had not liked his emergency committee's report and in the prevailing climate of suppressed panic, scapegoats were needed. Where was the craft? Yermash could not be precise. Was Stukalin dead or alive? Yermash didn't know. Could the Western powers get their hands on the wreckage? The spluttered incoherence of Deputy Chairman Yermash conveyed the message that possibly they could. His resignation on the grounds of ill health was promulgated in a very small *Pravda* paragraph.

Conversely, things had gone very well for Bulgakov, the KGB chairman, who, though not a member of the Presidium, had been called into its deliberations about the lost plane. He had deftly managed to imply that a more positive report would have been presented if he had been in charge of the emergency committee.

The Presidium's actions were now dictated by fear of Soviet technology falling into American hands. They decided to back the ambition of the KGB chief.

Bulgakov not only replaced the unfortunate Yermash as the committee chairman, he managed to negotiate an expanded mandate allowing him more freedom of action, particularly in the foreign field. It was the greatest gamble he had ever taken in the snakes-and-ladders game of Soviet power politics, but if he succeeded . . .

On the other hand, Bulgakov knew that he had placed himself on a tight-rope, from which he might fall or be pushed. If he failed, he would join Yermash in rural obscurity — or worse, given the enemies he had collected during his career.

'We will open with the report of the T Directorate of the

KGB,' boomed Bulgakov. 'It has been tabled and the director himself will talk through the important points.'

The thin man in a grey suit and spectacles began talking. 'We have placed an operative from the directorate within Ireland and he is travelling towards the Inishowen peninsula as I speak. His name is Losev.'

'One man. Is that all?' came the surprised question from down the table.

'Our immediate objective is to find Stukalin because only he can tell us where his machine is. We may need to contact the local IRA and that is a job for one man, not a battalion.'

'So we still don't know exactly where the plane is?' came another question.

'I'm afraid so. Frankly we can't be certain that Stukalin is alive and in the hands of the IRA. But it's a good guess.'

At this point, the director broke off to reach for photographs. 'You each have copies of these photographs, taken by our planes over-flying the helicopter crash site and by satellites. You also have a copy of the Irish investigation report into the cause of the helicopter crash.' Everybody nodded. 'You will see that the Irish have blamed a tail pylon design fault for the crash. But they're lying. Look at the early satellite photos.'

There was a rustling round the room as photographs were shuffled and when he was satisfied that everyone on the committee had the correct photographs in his hand, he continued.

'The wide-angle low resolution shots show the tail pylon lying near the shore several kilometres from the main fuselage. Clearly the pylon broke free during flight.'

Many round the table exchanged puzzled glances. It was a spaceplane they were looking for, not the unfortunate helicopter.

'How do we know that fuzzy blob is part of the helicopter? It could be anything?' a brave sceptic asked.

'Precisely,' the thin man beamed. 'We thought the object

might have been part of Stukalin's craft, so we took high resolution pictures from the Aeroflot flights. The object definitely was the tail pylon.'

Zotov scowled. 'Why are we wasting time on this helicopter crash and the bloody Irish investigation? Who cares! It's our own craft we should be looking for.'

The T Director, still wearing a superior smile, paused to offer the rest of his report to his superior. Bulgakov accepted and took over.

'The Irish investigators want us to believe that an inspection hatch on the tail pylon opened, leading to the loss of the whole tail assembly during flight. This was an original design fault with this type of helicopter. But our high resolution photograph shows that the inspection hatch remained closed. It could not have caused the crash.'

The committee looked at Bulgakov. They still agreed with Zotov. Did it matter if the Irish had got it wrong? The thin man undertook the explanation.

'Think!' Bulgakov thundered. 'Let us say our spaceplane ran out of fuel for its jet engine because it came down too far from home base, and was therefore in a powerless glide. Our machine and the Irish helicopter seem to have crashed at the same time and in the same area. The conclusion is obvious.'

'They collided,' the T director said simply.

Zotov spluttered his disagreement. 'That's too much of a coincidence for us to believe. The chances of that happening must be astronomical.'

'Agreed,' Bulgakov said promptly. 'But we know that the Irish removed the tail from public gaze before any other piece of wreckage and in their report ask us to believe they don't have it. Preposterous! The Irish have constructed an elaborate lie, good enough to fool the rest of the world, but not us. The circumstantial evidence that Stukalin hit the helicopter, probably in cloud, becomes overwhelming. No other explanation fits these extraordinary facts.'

Zotov could think of nothing else to fit the facts and

acknowledged defeat with a wave of his hand. 'Then it's in the sea,' he said resignedly, 'near that point and close enough to the shore for Stukalin to reach land. The Irish know more than they pretend.'

Bulgakov nodded to the T director to continue.

'As we've heard,' the thin man started up again, 'the Irish have recalled their top man from the United States. We can assume that the Americans and G2 are working closely together. This man, called Faloon, may have been following Losev from Boston with instructions to stay close to him, hoping to be led to the precise crash site.'

'Can Losev break loose of Faloon?' Zotov queried.

'Losev disabled Faloon. Faloon has detailed knowledge of both the Inishowen peninsula and of the IRA. He may be the only credible means by which the West could find our craft before our own ships do so. He continues to be a possible danger.'

Bulgakov added, 'Losev was correct not to kill Faloon on the plane. That would have led to an investigation of everyone on board and Losev would have been uncovered.'

The KGB chief exchanged a long look with his T director. An order had already been given privately and explicitly. If Faloon went to Inishowen, Losev was to disable him, permanently and finally.

Faloon and Nuala drew up outside the police station in Buncrana in Inishowen, making no attempt to conceal their presence. They had crossed the border once more just outside Londonderry, and were logged on a British computer as they did so.

Everybody's computers knew exactly where Faloon was.

'I don't feel happy near police stations any more,' Nuala said. 'What are you up to now?'

Faloon looked inscrutable. The shock of having fallen from being G2's most favoured son to being its greatest liability was wearing off. The buccaneer element was back on top.

'I'd like to know what's going on here.' He peered at the heavy presence of soldiers and policemen. An unusual sight in Buncrana. 'Inside that police station is Sergeant Michael Higgins. Mr Higgins and myself are old friends.'

'Hadn't you better check in case Grundy has already set the hounds on you?' Nuala looked worried. 'Old friends in the *garda* must still obey orders. They can't all be like you.'

'This one is. That's why he's still a sergeant.' Faloon left the car and walked into the police station with a confident spring to his step. He was greeted as a long-lost friend by several policemen and told that Michael Higgins was not immediately free. He would meet Faloon at the usual pub in a few minutes.

Faloon led Nuala to a small pub along the street, its walls darkened by decades of nicotine. When Sergeant Higgins joined them, he gave Faloon an ebullient welcome, and Nuala a look of surprise.

Higgins was everybody's picture of the country policeman; overweight, jolly and sympathetic. Everybody knew Higgins, and he in turn knew everybody.

To Faloon's surprise, he ordered a cup of coffee. 'Daren't drink on duty,' he said, displaying a professional piety which surprised Faloon. 'We've been inundated with so many commandants and other exalted police persons that I've taken to calling everybody "sir", just to be on the safe side.' He glanced at Nuala.

'Nuala is another old friend, Michael. You could trust her with your poteen.'

'That's more than I'd trust you with.' He grinned acceptance at her. 'And what brings you to this part of the world? Don't tell me you are on holiday, because even with this charming lady by your side, I might find it hard to believe in the circumstances.'

Faloon sipped his coffee. 'What circumstances, Michael?'

Sergeant Higgins sniffed. 'You know, Faloon, even though the Provos occasionally use this place as a launch pad for attacks on Derry, it preserves a sleepy quality which we both liked. You can get used to the Provos, so long as the mess they make is somewhere else. Now don't raise an eyebrow at me, for when you came up here to relax, the last thing you want me to point out is a Provo, unless he's between you and the next drink.'

'Things never got that bad,' interrupted Faloon with mock seriousness.

'Well, they're worse than that now. It all started when three of them in a car burst through the checkpoint the morning after the big dance here. We were looking for whoever broke into a holiday caravan and then deliberately set fire to it, not bloody Provos.'

'Did you know these three?' Faloon asked.

'Dick O'Donnell and Moira Strain,' said the sergeant, shaking his head and looking into the distance. 'Oh yes, we knew they were Provos but they'd always been very careful not to cause any trouble this side of the border.'

Faloon leaned over the table and lowered his voice. 'Two questions, Michael. Why did they break cover and burst through a cordon? And why have you not mentioned the third person in the car?'

'Are you on duty, Faloon?' Michael asked suspiciously.

'No, but it's a long story. Very briefly, I'm interested because I was mugged in a lavatory the other day, and I think there could be a link between that and what's happening here.'

Faloon could have expressed himself better and Higgins could not resist a guffaw. Faloon looked uncomfortable, impatience having banished his usual humour. He could hardly tell them now that his ribs hurt only when he laughed.

'OK, OK,' said Higgins, becoming serious again. 'I'm guessing now. I think the third person in the car was the reason why they burst through. Moira Strain was driving

186

and O'Donnell was in the back with the sunburnt stranger. To my way of thinking, the stranger was their prisoner.'

'Tell me about the stranger.'

Michael's brow furrowed. 'This is the part I'm very un-sure about. Rumour has it that he was a Russian from the helicopter crash. You know about that, don't you?'

Faloon nodded again and added, 'What do the Provos want with a Russian?'

'I hear they want to ransom him, maybe for weapons.'

'They'd better not try that,' Nuala said, stabbing the table with her coffee spoon. 'The Russians have fought shy of that kind of nonsense. Anyway, everybody was killed in that helicopter crash, or so it was reported. But I suppose somebody might've got out.'

Michael looked at Nuala in some surprise. Faloon smiled and said, 'She used to be in the firm, Michael. She knows a few things.'

Higgins resumed his train of thought. 'That chopper hit the ground very hard, Faloon. It was in pieces. I just don't see how anyone could have got out alive, never mind uninjured. They had to use jacks and spades to prise the bodies free.'

Nuala's expression showed her distaste. Faloon just looked mystified and asked, 'What are the orders to the police and army on the hillsides, Michael?'

'They want two things. They want a Russian, though God knows where he's supposed to come from. Then they want any remaining bits of the helicopter. Anything, no matter how small. Mind you,' Higgins' voice dropped to a hoarse whisper, 'the bit they've lost isn't all that small. They've lost the whole back part with the small propel-ler.'

Faloon listened carefully and then reached behind Nuala for a map of the Inishowen peninsula. Sergeant Higgins then pointed out the precise position of the helicopter crash. He also pencilled on the map a dotted line representing the course of the helicopter for the last few miles before

187

it crashed. This was based on police station chit-chat, but Higgins said he thought it reasonably accurate.

It was a sweep round Malin Head followed by a turn south that would have taken the aircraft over some of the scenic parts of the north west of the peninsula. In response to further questions from Faloon, who wanted to know everything, Higgins also ringed the site of the road check forced by the Provos, and finally the position of the burnt caravan, which had occasioned the original road checks.

As the three crossed the road back to Nuala's car, Michael Higgins revealed that in Buncrana itself, as distinct from the semi-enclosed world of policemen, rumour had it that the Russian had O'Donnell and Moira Strain as prisoners, not the other way round. Faloon shrugged.

With open distaste, Higgins surveyed the street, filled as it was with policemen and soldiers. 'If the hordes of official strangers were less patronizing to local policemen, they might get somewhere with their enquiries.'

Faloon had other things on his mind, so he said goodbye to Higgins and set off for the site of the helicopter crash.

At another time and on another errand, the sparkling glimpses of the Atlantic between gentle valleys would have induced a feeling of well-being in Faloon. But this was where six people had died. The flurry and bustle had moved on. It was like a visit to a cemetery the day after a funeral.

'Not much to see, Faloon.'

Faloon looked around him. Nuala was right. The investigators had removed every trace of the aircraft with the efficiency of a giant vacuum cleaner. Faloon thought he caught sight of something under a small whin bush and bent down to pick it up.

'Anything interesting?' Nuala shouted across at him.

'No,' he said, turning the object in his hands. And then, in a small voice to himself, he observed, 'If it had been an ordinary one, the handle would've broken off . . .'

and he dropped an Irish tea cup back into the foliage.

Nuala lingered a while, walking slowly until Faloon could think of something else to do..

'Nuala, let me look at that map Michael Higgins marked,' Faloon shouted through the quiet air. With his finger he traced the flight path of the helicopter. Then his eyes lit on the circle round the point on the coast where the caravan had been burnt.

'If somebody had aimed a weapon of some kind at the helicopter, they could've done so from here.' Faloon jabbed his finger at the pencilled circle where the caravan had been.

'And then burnt the caravan and any evidence it contained, you mean,' Nuala said.

'Yes. It's a favourite trick of the Provos, especially with stolen cars they've used in a shooting or a bombing in the North.' Faloon noted the quickest route on the map, crudely folded it and stuffed it back into Nuala's handbag.

'It's a long shot, but we haven't come up with anything else,' he said. They were both somewhat depressed as they returned to their car.

Further along the hillside, on a parallel farm track, there was another parked car. Leaning over its roof was a man with binoculars, keeping Faloon and his companion under very close observation. He watched the pair drive off. Then he climbed into his own car and followed, taking care to keep his distance behind them.

The route towards the burnt caravan led Faloon and Nuala through countryside even more deserted than the hillside they had just left. Whereas the hillside had shown signs of recent incursion by a throng of people, the field where the charred embers lay looked relatively undisturbed.

Not completely, of course. The police had been recent visitors. Faloon and Nuala could see a number of places where their boots had tramped down the grass during their cursory inspection.

The road beside the remains of the caravan was a rough track with a few broader places for traffic to pass. Faloon parked in one of these passing areas some distance away. Nuala got out of the car and began walking ahead of Faloon, towards the remains of the caravan.

Faloon held back and eventually sat on a hummock, looking silently at the blackened chassis and tyreless rims, then at the sky. It didn't make sense. No one, even the most inept Provo, would have chosen this place to fire a missile at a target in the sky. The caravan had been parked in a sheltered spot in a fold of the hills. In other words, at the lowest part of the little bay. There was high land all around. Anybody shooting down a helicopter would have done so from high ground, perhaps from the cover of one of the derelict cottages that his eye had been drawn to.

The caravan might have been a rendezvous point for the firing team, in which case the missile could have been aimed from the nearest cottage to the caravan.

An overgrown trail led uphill from the road alongside the remains of the caravan and Faloon set off towards it. Nuala ran to join him. 'I'd like a look at that old building on the hillside,' he explained. 'It's the only bit of substantial cover overlooking the caravan.'

The words didn't make much sense to Nuala but she said nothing for the moment. She sensed that Faloon was dejected. Her prophecy was coming true. There was nothing to discover in Inishowen.

They started up the hill. 'This must have been a very different place at one time,' Nuala mused. 'There would have been the sound of children.'

Faloon looked doubtful. 'Don't romanticize too much, city girl. Life here was hard. They didn't stay, did they?' He waved his hand towards other distant abandoned small-holdings. There wasn't another living soul in sight.

When they reached the roofless cottage, Faloon was already lost in another time, striding purposefully through the old doorway. Nuala didn't follow him. She moved to the side of the ruined building where a little stream ran. Doubtless the water supply of the long-forgotten family that had once given this cottage life.

She wanted to know what the sparkling water tasted like. Probably tasted of peat. She leaned forward to dip her cupped hand into the narrow bed, and something incongruously clean and new caught her fingers.

It was a piece of bright orange cloth. She grabbed it and pulled, but it was attached to something which held it fast. Exploring with her fingers, she found a rod weighted down and hidden by rocks and gravel. By pulling, pushing and digging with her hands, she triumphantly tugged free a long thin flexible tapering pole, taller than herself and topped with a fluorescent orange flag.

'Faloon!'

He ran back out to her, thinking that she had fallen.

'A radio aerial. Could this be part of a missile guidance system?'

Faloon examined it quickly. His face fell in disappointment. 'Missile launchers are camouflaged, Nuala, not day-glo orange. This looks like part of a new emergency marine beacon. Where's the rest of it, I wonder?' He was examining the broken base of the aerial.

'It could've been left by the troops searching for bits of the helicopter,' Nuala said slowly, clearly unconvinced by her own words. 'It had been deliberately hidden in the bed of the stream.'

'And troops aren't that tidy.'

'And I suppose their aerials aren't day-glo orange either . . .'

'So what else is hidden hereabouts?' Faloon wondered aloud, his heart beginning to beat faster.

Nuala's heart was not racing. She thought the artefact in Faloon's hands was odd, but since the hills had been crawling with police and army looking for bits from the helicopter lying on the ground, there could be a thousand innocent explanations for the hidden aerial.

Maybe there are soldiers and policemen who care for the environment and bury their rubbish, she said inwardly. She didn't want to say anything to Faloon. The discovery had re-animated him.

After a quick and fruitless search of the bed of the little stream, Faloon went back within the broken cottage walls. His eyes fastened on the neat pile of peat. Something was wrong with it. The tarpaulin! It was on the ground instead of being tied over the peat. He dived into the peat bricks, casting them behind him like a terrier burrowing for a bone.

'I've got them!' He turned triumphantly to Nuala. In one hand, an orange lifejacket, still inflated. In the other, a one-piece pressure suit.

Both clearly marked 'CCCP'.

That was when the first shot rang out. It blew a hole in the chest of the pressure suit.

EIGHTEEN

Stulakin's expression was a mixture of determination and satisfaction as he settled himself into his bunk. He heard the cabin door being locked. He heard Moira put a cassette into a player, and he heard Irish folk music for the first time. He liked it and relaxed. It had been a long day.

Dick O'Donnell and Moira Strain retired to the wheel-house, putting the main cabin filled with music between themselves and their prisoner's ears. Moira eased herself into a corner. 'Do you think he'll cause any trouble, Dick?'

O'Donnell shook his head. 'Not tonight. He has a nasty wound in his arm, he's very tired and I made sure his glass was well filled as he ate.'

'He doesn't look to me like someone who'd lose a drinking contest. I read somewhere that drinking was their national pastime.'

'We won't take any chances. One of us will be awake at all times. I'll take the first watch. You go and put your head down, girl. You look as if you need matchsticks to prop your eyelids open.'

She made for the hatchway, pausing as she came near him.

'Go to bed, go to sleep,' he ordered.

She understood his answer and went below. Turning to face him through the hatch, she began to undress. Unmoving and unmoved, he watched. When she was naked, her body a pattern of moonlight white and dark shadow, she moved one hand over a pool of black above her thighs, her eyes never leaving O'Donnell's.

He slowly rose, approached the hatchway, blew her a kiss from a smile and whispered softly, 'Goodnight, girl. Sleep well.'

Then he closed the hatch, paused for a moment with his eyes shut, opened them again and turned to one of several pieces of radio equipment fixed to the wheelhouse bulkhead. His thoughts had already left Moira, who did not have his degree of self-discipline. She buried her head in a makeshift pillow and dreamed herself to sleep.

On the other side of the bulkhead, in the forepeak where Major Stulakin was imprisoned, there was a corresponding silence. The Russian had risen from his bunk and was making sure that his activity had made no noise.

First he had searched the bulkhead for a peephole and had found none. Then, painstakingly in the blackness, he had begun his search. The top of the bunk was removed, the bottoms of the lockers underneath were prised up, the ribs and stringers supporting the thick timbers of the hull were brushed by the Major's hands until, eventually, he found something in the deepest part of the bilges.

Its handle was partly split; its blade was encrusted with years of rust. For all that, the Major's heart pounded as new possibilities flooded his mind. He was holding a medium-sized screwdriver. In the wheelhouse at the other end of the boat, O'Donnell was engrossed every bit as much as Stulakin. His hands were on the controls of a marine band VHF radio telephone. This one was not quite standard. In addition to its normal sixty channels, it had a number of private ones on special wavelengths. It was to one of these that O'Donnell had switched the set.

'MV *Kenny* to Islay Heather.'

Softly he repeated this call-sign into the telephone handset.

The man who answered was not on a boat called Islay Heather, as an eavesdropper might have assumed. He was in a house alongside a garage and filling station on a road outside Buncrana, whose lights O'Donnell could see across the placid Lough Swilly.

This garageman, while watching O'Donnell manoeuvre broken glass under his own tyre, had slowed down the flow of petrol to help him. He had then alerted the local IRA that O'Donnell was in trouble, perhaps kidnapped by a British undercover agent. That was the most favoured theory before news of the shooting at the road block filtered through.

More conjecture ensued among the Provos until it was learnt that O'Donnell's boat was absent from its mooring at Fahan. Only O'Donnell could have moved it, so an uneasy calm had prevailed until the pre-arranged time for communication. The garageman had been waiting on the correct channel to hear O'Donnell's voice.

The men talking to each other were aware that radio transmissions are broadcasting, not private communication. They spoke in code and in Irish to arrange an immediate meeting. The first stage of O'Donnell's extraordinary plan was under way.

Some minutes later, a small boat moved away from the shore in the half light of the early summer evening, the outboard motor on tick-over. No hint of hurry as the boatman steered towards the mouth of the sea lough, deliberately not heading towards the anchorage at Macamish, where O'Donnell said he was waiting.

When the garageman was sure that nobody was taking any interest in him, and that he was not easily visible from Buncrana, he opened up the outboard throttle and skipped at speed across the water separating him from the Provo commander.

O'Donnell's boat was a silhouette against the reflection of the sea. The garageman pulled out a pocket transceiver from his coat and spoke a single word in Irish. On the same channel, another word came back. He was clear to approach.

O'Donnell had ranged fenders against the hull, so the visitor's boat made contact silently. A rope was thrown expertly. Then another. Only when the men of the sea had seen to their craft did they greet each other.

'You don't know just how glad I am to see you, Dick. There are terrible rumours back in Buncrana,' blurted the garageman, giving O'Donnell a bear-hug that made him think of the Russian.

'They're very quick to write me off, Sean,' gasped O'Donnell, trying to avoid garageman Sean's bad breath without being obvious about it.

'At least this time you remembered to call me Sean,' grinned Sean. 'What bloody name did Moira call me last time?'

'Oh yes, you stupid bastard, I've forgotten what name it was. The first that came into her head. We were trying to warn you that we were in trouble and at the same time tell you to do nothing.'

'Didn't I do just that?' said Sean, looking miffed.

'Not well enough, Sean. The man in the back seat with a gun on Moira saw through you.' Then, noticing that Sean was taking all this very much to heart, he added, 'But all's well that ends well. We have the gun now and the stranger is in our hands.'

'Thank God for that, Dick. I was beginning to wonder when you'd get round to telling me about this

195

mysterious stranger. He's the subject of a lot of wild talk.'

O'Donnell didn't answer immediately. He had had enough of standing out on deck and he directed Sean into the wheelhouse.

'What rumours?' O'Donnell asked when they had settled.

Though Sean was yearning to learn what had happened to O'Donnell, he knew that his requirements came second to those of the man before him.

'I naturally told the lads that you were in trouble,' Sean began. 'I told them what I'd seen.' Sean paused here for a sign from O'Donnell that he'd done the right thing. O'Donnell nodded and Sean proceeded more calmly.

'First they were going to set up their own road-blocks, then came the news of the shoot-out on the road to Fahan. After that they decided to keep their heads down.' He looked in appeal at O'Donnell. 'They didn't have much option, Dick. The place was crawling with *garda* soldiery.'

O'Donnell again nodded once more in agreement.

'I asked about the rumours, Sean. What rumours about the man do we have?'

'It's round the village that you've one of the Russians from the helicopter and that you're going to sell him back to the Russians.'

'Who the hell's saying that?' O'Donnell's sudden anger startled Sean.

'Well I got it from one of the police I knew.'

Sean's eyes followed O'Donnell as he turned to gaze over the water. No words were spoken. Just the silence as O'Donnell adjusted to the possibility that if such a rumour was circulating among the lower ranks of the police, then more than likely it was a leak from the higher ranks. Getting the Russian anywhere was going to be difficult. But in his plan, moving the Russian was secondary.

O'Donnell turned sharply and faced Sean. 'I'm now going to trust you with one of the most important tasks you will ever perform for the Republican Movement.'

Sean's face became very serious. When O'Donnell spoke in such formal terms, he was about to command. O'Donnell never wasted his words.

O'Donnell took a note-pad and ballpoint pen from a shelf in the wheelhouse. He wrote several lines without stopping, speaking only when he had finished writing.

'On this piece of paper I have written what looks like a list of local phone numbers. Only the first two figures in each number matter. Taken together, those numbers will make up a number in the United States. The international code for phoning from over the border is included.' He waited for Sean to indicate that he understood before continuing.

'Make it a collect call. You will ask for a certain man and when you get him, tell him that our father is very ill and that he must come over to represent all the relations in America. Say that Dick needs him urgently.'

'If they're listening, Dick, the shits listening in won't have much trouble unravelling that message.'

'We'll have to take a chance, Sean. Make the call at a pay phone, from somewhere like a pub. I want that message delivered tonight. I want this man with us tomorrow. He'll probably land at Shannon. You be there to meet him and bring him to me. Immediately. Have you got that?'

'Yes. I've understood,' Sean said quietly, 'but I can't meet someone whose name I don't know.'

'Don't breathe this man's name anywhere. And that's a threat.' He looked into Sean's face, which twitched visibly. 'The man's name is Martin Riley.'

James Grundy was glad that he had crossed the border into Northern Ireland and come to Belfast. It got him out of the G2 office, away from the burden of waiting for something to happen.

He mingled easily with the throng travelling from the Republic of Ireland over the border to the north for cheaper prices in the shops. So his hotel room had bottles of alcohol and other items to smuggle back over the border, just like everyone else. Purely to maintain his cover, of course.

He had come to meet Arthur Semple and had booked into the same hotel as the English intelligence man. A meeting in Belfast became a possibility when Semple had let it drop casually to Grundy that he was going to fly to Ulster on business. Fine, Grundy had said, they could meet again.

Neither of them had given enough thought to their meeting, otherwise they might have warned their secretaries to avoid the Europa, Belfast's most obvious hotel, the place where everyone met, where journalists drank with politicians, policemen, soldiers, with other journalists – and with spies.

'I'm a commercial traveller in ladies' underwear. What are you?' Grundy grinned over the lip of a Bushmills single malt.

'I was going to be an evangelist until I found out that people in this God-forsaken place found that terribly interesting,' mocked Semple, morosely surveying a mixed crowd in the first-floor bar.

'Arthur,' said Grundy, to continue their fun, 'didn't anybody in your outfit tell you that evangelists are a rare sight in Ulster bars. So what's your new story?'

'I've decided to be an accountant. Tested it on a couple who tried to strike up a conversation at the bar. Said I was an accountant and they drifted away.'

'Sometimes that is the life I would gladly opt for, Arthur. Our business can be far too cut-throat for my taste,' Grundy lied glibly.

Semple sipped his gin. 'How well do you know this town, Grundy?'

'Well enough to be uncomfortable in this hotel in your company. Let's go.'

They drained their drinks, Semple pulling a face because he had forgotten that alcohol was sold in bigger measures in Scotland and Ireland.

The Crown Bar just opposite the Europa Hotel suited

their purposes better. It was one of the few pubs in the city which had retained 'snugs', partitioned sections, each with its own little door. With new atmosphere and a modicum of privacy, they got down to business.

'How far have you got, my friend? Have you found anything?' asked Semple.

'Nearly.'

'Stop prevaricating. What have you found?'

Grundy was not yet ready to play Semple's game. He knew that his government was not going to trade information for political concessions by the British in Northern Ireland. How would Semple react?

'We're not interested in any proposals from your side on the Irish question. Any such proposals can be placed openly on top of the negotiating table when the time comes.'

Semple looked puzzled, then a trifle angry. In common with many of his associates in London, he had thought that concessions from the British concerning Northern Ireland were always a trump card, always playable, above or under the table.

'So what do you want, Grundy?'

'Same as usual, only more considering the size of the prize.'

'But you don't know the size of the prize. Where is that bloody Russian plane? Are there any bits of it big enough to be a prize?'

'I think there may be, and inside our jurisdiction. I think the pilot survived in one piece, and this leads me to the conclusion that his plane did so as well.'

Grundy could not avoid feeling pleased with himself as he watched Semple become more and more agitated.

Semple reminded himself that the Irish reacted adversely to directness. Bit like the Arabs.

'Like another drink, James?'

Grundy nodded with satisfaction. A drink and his first name all in a single sentence from Semple. Such a rich diet. But then, his old sparring partner always was quick on the uptake. They both forsook spirits for draught Guinness.

Grundy brought the dark glass to his lips, then began speaking across the top of it. 'What would your reaction be if I told you that the Provos have captured the pilot and have hidden him away somewhere?'

Semple's reaction was to splutter, spilling a dribble of Guinness over the table and part of his jacket. 'That's a joke, isn't it, Grundy? An Irish joke in very bad taste.'

'My dear Semple, all Irish jokes are in bad taste. I'm certain that the Provos have got the pilot and that they probably have an idea of how important he is.'

Semple pulled out a handkerchief to mop his hand-finished suit but his mind was not engaged in matters sartorial. He turned to face Grundy with optimism. 'That must mean you have a fair idea about where the Russian plane is. Where is it?'

'You've asked that question before. We have a smaller search circle for the plane and an ever-widening one for the pilot. If we find the pilot, we could have a much better chance of locating his plane.'

'Forget the pilot for the moment, Grundy. Go for the plane. It has the technology we want.'

'The technology that Ireland wants, Mr Semple,' Grundy corrected. 'Then our respective governments can start talking and any deal will be made at a political level, not across a sloppy table in Belfast.'

Semple began clutching at straws. 'There must be some way we can be of help. If the Provos try to bring him over the border . . .'

'I thought you lot had learnt the hard way that the Provos aren't stupid.'

They both paused to sip their drinks and to think. Semple began to fish. 'At least you've sent your best man to the area. He knows the place inside out. If anyone can turn up something, he will.'

Grundy scowled. 'What man?'

'Oh for God's sake, Grundy, stop dancing round the

maypole. We spotted Faloon and his girlfriend Gallagher across Northern Ireland to Londonderry. We know where he's going and why. I thought you were actually moving him openly to tell us what you were doing.'

'Just testing, Semple, just testing. It's as good a way as any of finding out how fast you can process data,' Grundy laughed in a slightly forced manner, because going through his mind were doubts about how fast his own operation could extract data. He hadn't known about Faloon from his own sources.

Grundy had already guessed that Faloon would go to Inishowen with or without authority. He knew Faloon had taken a computer without a code chip, but he was annoyed that his own system had not thrown up Faloon's travelling.

Something else occurred to Grundy. 'You would tell me if the British had an operative in Inishowen? I don't want MI5 on my patch, particularly now. Are you tailing Faloon, Arthur?'

'Of course not. I'd hardly have introduced Faloon as a topic if we were keeping an eye on him. He is, after all, still the man most likely to succeed, is he not?' Semple smiled and motioned with his empty glass that it was Grundy's turn to buy. Grundy gathered the glasses and left the snug for more Guinness. Things were not going the way Britain wanted, Semple reflected. From what Grundy had said, the plane almost certainly existed. It could be a few feet under soggy peat in one of those bloody Irish bogs. If so, British technology aboard reconnaissance aircraft overflying Inishowen daily would find the plane. But time was needed, particularly with the Irish in their present mood of no deal with the British.

He was grateful that draught Guinness took so long to pour and was delaying Grundy's return. It gave Semple time to re-order his priorities. He now knew that the Irish had found the pilot – even if it was the wrong bloody Irish – and therefore his plane could not be far away.

When Grundy returned to the snug, Semple was absent.

Probably getting rid of the last lot of Guinness, thought Grundy. Wrong. Semple was talking on the payphone at the other end of the bar. He replaced the receiver and pushed his way back to the table.

'Just checking with the office. All is quiet, I'm glad to say,' said Semple as he squeezed behind the fresh Guinness.

'Anything of interest?'

'No. As I said, all quiet.'

'Were you transmitting or receiving information?' Grundy asked quietly, peering intently at the head on his drink, as if it were a crystal ball.

'Grundy, you have a nasty suspicious mind. May I remind you that you haven't come up with anything new. In fact, everything on your patch seems to be very stationary, except the Provos, who can find foreign pilots faster than the combined forces of the state. Has it occurred to you that the reason we haven't found the plane is because the pilot told the Provos about it, and they have hidden the damn thing? Who would the Provos in turn want to deal with?'

'I trust that the British authorities will not enter into a deal with the IRA.' Grundy's manner was now hostile.

'Not as a first option,' replied Semple, feeling the pendulum of advantage swing once more in his direction. 'But if we are forced into less favoured options, like buying Russian advanced avionics and materials technology from the Provos, we'll do it. But then I think you already know that.'

'If you do that, we would make such a deal public. It would weaken your position in Northern Ireland considerably.'

Semple laughed. 'That might make short term difficulties for us. But the great British public is pissed off with Northern Ireland – and so are your lot south of the border. The only people who want to fight for Ulster are the Provos and their Protestant counterparts.'

Grundy was very angry but held his tongue. Semple was infuriating him.

'Anyway, from what I just heard on the phone, all of this could be academic,' Semple pressed on, though in a more conciliatory tone. 'The Russians are not standing still. And I hear on the grapevine that our mutual friends the Americans are about to strike a deal with the Provos. We'll both be frozen out.'

Semple's final satisfaction was the apoplectic expression on Grundy's face.

NINETEEN

Faloon flattened himself on the ground alongside Nuala. He wondered why he never ever had a gun when he needed one.

Viktor Losev wondered why every time he attacked someone, he missed. He had almost missed Faloon with the insulin needle. He wondered how he would explain his marksmanship back at KGB headquarters – if he ever managed to get back to Moscow.

As he plotted his next move, another part of his mind was filling with excuses. He could plead with some justification that he was an expert merely in scientific and technical intelligence. He was a pen-pushing agent; he had never been good at the strong-arm stuff even in basic training.

Never before had Losev been required to shoot someone, or even disable someone as he had done on the plane. If headquarters had wanted a strong-arm stormtrooper, why did they send him?

Excuses would be of no avail. With whatever skills he could muster, he had to stop those two people reporting what they had found.

The hillside overlooking Faloon and Nuala's hiding place was crossed with drystone walls forming a patchwork of small fields. Losev began using the cover of the walls to advance towards his target.

Already the sun was beginning to slide behind the blue, grey and purple hills of Donegal and the walls running north to south were presenting Losev with the added cover of long shadows. He knew that if he delayed, Faloon and the girl would escape in the dark.

But Losev had also presumed that Faloon was armed. In the aftermath of his initial ineffectual action, Losev's tactic was to work himself unseen from his first firing position to another one higher up the hill, but at least ninety degrees of an arc away. That should leave his targets exposed. To ensure that they remained where they were, he emptied a magazine above where Faloon and Nuala were crouched.

As the rounds sang inches above their heads, Faloon and Nuala clung together, as if their proximity could shut out the danger. Stone chips and dust sprang from the wall behind them, mocking the frailty of their bodies. The powerful weapon in Losev's hands could cut them in half. All he had to do was get so close that even he could hardly miss.

Faloon edged forward to the remains of a garden wall. It was only a few stones high, but it was saving their lives. Like all the other walls on the hillside, it was drystone, so there were gaps between some of the stones.

'For God's sake, Faloon. Keep your head down,' Nuala whispered tensely. 'Those bastards want to kill us.'

Faloon moved his head to position his eye against a small gap. 'I think there's only one person. At least, only one weapon fired from one position. I wish I could find the position.'

'What for? You haven't a gun, so let's get out of here.'

'Good idea. Call a cab.'

Nuala pursed her lips in a mixture of fear and exasperation. She looked around her with fresh eyes.

The tiny stream had carved a small notch through the peaty soil. It was only a foot deep, perhaps eighteen inches in places, but it effectively hid the stream itself from only a few feet away.

'Faloon, the bed of the stream. Can you reach it without being seen?'

Faloon craned his neck to look round and shook his head. There was intervening open space.

'We've got to chance it,' Nuala continued hoarsely. 'You first. You're nearest.'

Faloon hesitated, not because Nuala was wrong, but because she was putting herself firmly in command at this juncture. She jabbed her finger in the direction of the stream and Faloon moved, inching his way carefully downhill and away from the cover of the low wall.

'It's no good, Nuala. We'll be completely exposed.' Faloon was staring at the patch of grass separating them from the comparative safety of the little trench. As if to reinforce the point, another volley splattered all around them.

'Did you see where the shots came from, Faloon?'

'I think from a wall about three hundred feet straight ahead. You can get a line by drawing from the marks on the wall through your own position. The shots went right over our heads.'

Faloon stared in bewilderment as Nuala looked forwards and backwards repeatedly, using the little hole in the low wall that Faloon had found moments earlier. Suddenly she reached for her large handbag and turned it upside down, spilling the contents on the grass. Her hand grabbed for the bottom of the empty bag and Faloon heard the sound of something being ripped.

When Nuala's hand reappeared, it was holding a small calibre pistol. Faloon blinked in astonishment.

'I am going to fire half the magazine at where I think this gunman is taking cover,' Nuala said crisply. 'By the time I stop firing, you must be in the stream. Leave room for me, because I'll throw you the gun. While you fire, I'll dive for the stream.'

Faloon appeared more stunned by the pistol in Nuala's hand than by Losev's first shots.

'Did you understand me?' She wore an expression that Faloon had never seen before. This was not the suave secretary, much less the gentle comforter or succumbing lover. This was a tigress.

'Faloon!'

'Yes, yes. OK,' he blurted.

She had begun firing immediately. Her head was close to the wall, canted over at an angle to expose as little as possible. Faloon rolled into the stream and moved down into the little trench. As soon as he looked back, the pistol was thrown to him. It landed in the water. He grabbed it, shook it as dry as he could, aimed and pulled the trigger, all the time praying it would fire.

It worked until the magazine was empty. By that time Nuala was in the stream with him.

'Now you can call a cab, funny man,' she said humorously, gesturing that he should start crawling.

'Have you any more ammo?' he asked as he half slid, half crawled in the mud and stones. 'We may need to frighten him again.'

Nuala ignored the sarcasm. 'No. So keep moving.'

Her words were cut short by another burst of firing, aimed at the point where they had entered the stream. Their enemy had not seen their progress on their bellies through the gurgling and extremely cold water. Faloon looked back at her and pulled a face. At last she smiled.

The bed of the stream led them diagonally down the hillside until they came to another wall, this time a substantial one.

'We'll leave the stream and follow this wall,' ordered Faloon, taking command once more.

'Why?' came the rebellious answer.

'Because as the gradient of the hill slackens, the bed of the stream is less indented into the hillside, so fifty yards from here we'll have our arses shot off.'

Nuala looked down the hill in the failing light and saw nothing to confirm what Faloon was saying.

'I know these hills, Nuala. Trust me.' Faloon tried to

snatch a glance back the way they had come without revealing their position. Had their assailant seen their escape route? Was he waiting for them in a new position?

There were no immediate answers to these questions. Faloon could see nothing. The growing darkness hid the man who was trying to kill them. On the other hand, the two of them were by now beautifully camouflaged, their sodden clothes liberally caked with mud and bracken. Faloon, crouching low behind the wall, began moving quickly down the hill. Nuala followed.

They half ran, half crawled. Every forty or fifty metres Faloon halted, alert for any sound from their attacker. Nothing reached their straining ears. They pressed ahead, wondering all the time if the man with the rifle was monitoring their progress, whether a single shot, aimed at leisure, would signify the end for one of them.

Faloon had decided to reach the road as fast as he could. He and Nuala could not return to their car directly without breaking cover, and neither wished to chance doing that again. Breathless and gasping they reached the narrow road and paused once more. Still no signs of pursuit. The ruined cottage where they had been attacked was lost in the gathering gloom.

'What now?' asked Nuala, beginning to shiver.

'I think he's lost us,' answered Faloon, never taking his eyes from the hillside. 'But I don't think we ought to go back to our car. If I were him, that's what I would stake out. We'll travel away from it, parallel with the road. Let's go.'

They jumped over a ditch and lost themselves from the view of the road. The waves on the beach masked the small sounds they made. After travelling about a quarter of a mile, both Faloon and Nuala began to relax.

Too soon. Faloon froze.

He sank slowly to the ground, all the time edging backwards. Nuala instantly did likewise. Neither spoke until they had manoeuvred themselves back into a cleft.

Faloon had his head above the lip of the ditch. 'A car. A parked car hidden from the road. I can't see if there's anyone in it.'

'It must belong to whoever was shooting at us,' ventured Nuala.

'Or to a courting couple looking for some privacy,' countered Faloon. 'Either way, let's wait here. If there is someone inside, they'll give themselves away sooner or later.'

'Or we will give ourselves away to them,' added Nuala through chattering teeth because she was soaked to the skin.

'But then,' said Faloon very deliberately, 'we are both trained agents, aren't we, Nuala. I work for G2.' He stopped speaking at that point and felt that his unsaid question had struck home.

Who was Nuala working for?

'I've saved your life, Faloon,' she said harshly. 'We have a common enemy out there and that's enough to be going on with. This is not the time or place for anything more. Agreed?'

Fleetingly Faloon looked as if he would argue, but the moment passed. 'I think I can guess enough about you for the moment. The rest of my mind is devoted to getting out of this mess alive, and trying to guess who that bastard out there is.' He looked in the direction of the hill. 'If it's Comrade Losev, then at long last I'm beginning to fit the pieces of this jigsaw puzzle together. I know where the last big piece is, and what it might look like.'

'So do I. We've got to get back. Grundy's depending on you.'

Faloon's face assumed a fierce expression which the blackness mercifully hid from her. They lapsed into a tense silence and waited. The hunted had become the hunters.

Sean nosed the inflatable boat into the shallows and cut the motor. In the darkness of late evening, he collected its trailer

208

from further up the beach, lifted the boat onto it and parked it well clear of the tide.

Sean didn't return directly to his home beside the garage. Carrying out O'Donnell's instructions, he drove over the border into Londonderry in the United Kingdom. He wanted to make the telephone call from as big a population centre as possible. Londonderry was the largest urban area in those parts. Large populations made tapping more difficult; frontiers got in the way of concerted action by different authorities.

He made the call from a payphone in the Everglades Hotel, straining a little because of the high level of background noise. A local young farmers' club was holding a dance. Plenty of people, just what he wanted.

The collect call was accepted and the connection made. Sean was mildly surprised to reach Martin Riley so easily until he remembered that the east coast of the United States was five hours behind. That would have made it early evening in Boston where Riley picked up the phone.

It had not been an easy conversation. Riley didn't know Sean and was at first unwilling to communicate. He suspected a trap.

'Tell me something about yourself before you say anything,' Riley had demanded.

Sweating a little, Sean gave his name and address and said that he was phoning on behalf of a friend.

'If you think that's an introduction, that's up to you, buddy. Call me back in an hour. Maybe I'll listen to you then.' Riley had then hung up.

Sean had wandered into the ballroom and lost himself easily for an hour among those who were suffering the effects of either too much alcohol or too much country music.

An hour later, he phoned again. Riley had by then verified Sean's credentials. As he delivered his message, Sean's voice dropped half an octave to accommodate his new authority.

Riley said that he would travel in the morning and had rung off abruptly.

Sean had then called his home to say that he was taking a short break in Limerick. Limerick was the nearest town to Shannon Airport and Sean was there for the first flight from Boston, USA.

Martin Riley's arrival in Ireland triggered no alarm bells at immigration control or among the G2 reinforcements. The picture on the passport accurately portrayed a man in his early thirties with a ginger moustache and short ginger hair, but the rest of the passport was forged. The name was wrong, the address was wrong and the occupation was wrong. All were innocuous to casual inspection, as was Riley's appearance. The leather motorcycle jacket and boots that Faloon had seen him wearing at LaGuardia airport had been replaced by a smart conservative business suit.

'Where's the car, Sean?'

Sean spun round to find his hand being shaken by a stranger. 'Man, you're putting on weight.' The man being familiar was unfamiliar to Sean.

While he spoke, Riley led Sean towards the bar.

'Are you Martin Riley?' blurted Sean.

Riley gave Sean a warning look. It dawned on him that Sean was new to this side of the business. Both an advantage and a disadvantage, Riley said to himself.

'What colour's your car? What's its number? What road will we be travelling on out of here?' Riley was as curt in the flesh as he had been on the phone the previous evening. Sean gave him the information. 'Now give me some Irish coins. I want to make a phone call. Go over to the bar and get us both a coffee.'

Sean did as he was told and Riley went over to a line of payphones. He looked about him to make sure that the phones either side of him were unused and that Sean was being obedient.

He dialled up a local number. 'Sinead, is that you?' said Riley's voice.

'Yes, Martin. Go ahead.'

He gave the woman the number of Sean's car, its colour and the road it would be on. She repeated the information back to Riley for confirmation and hung up without ceremony.

Riley went over to the bar where Sean had coffee waiting for him. Sean found it difficult to converse with Riley, who seemed human only when he was putting on an act.

They walked to the car park and to Sean's car. A yellow Datsun. 'Nice bright car,' remarked Riley. Sean raised an eyebrow but said nothing. They had driven only a few miles when Riley asked Sean to pull over. He offered no explanation and Sean, beginning to learn, did not ask for one. Riley turned on the radio and began reading a newspaper which Sean had bought at Shannon.

It was the beginning of the working day. By Boston standards, the traffic was a trickle but in rural Limerick it was rush-hour. Riley's eyes left the newspaper with the passing of each vehicle in each direction. Suddenly, he folded the paper and motioned for Sean to continue the journey.

After that Riley seemed to unwind a little. 'Tell me,' he said to Sean, 'what's happened over here in Ireland? Why the panic?' Sean began his account with O'Donnell's appearance with Moira and the stranger in the forecourt of his petrol station. He reserved great portions of the narrative for his own role, how he had become suspicious on the garage forecourt and how he had alerted the Provos. All this he spread thickly, insensitive to Riley's rising scorn.

Sean's narrative moved to the shooting at the road block, fudging how the tables had afterwards turned so that the stranger had become O'Donnell's prisoner. Riley sought no clarification. Sean then described how the area round Buncrana was now saturated with police and army, all searching for the stranger and O'Donnell.

Riley frowned. 'Where's this Russian now?'

Sean looked puzzled. He had never referred to the stranger as a Russian, either in the car or earlier on the telephone to Boston.

'Who said anything about a Russian?'

Riley smiled. They passed a single parked car as they sped through the countryside. Sean didn't notice it; Riley did.

'I got more information while checking your credentials last night,' said Riley, returning to Sean's question.

Sean accepted that and made another attempt at conversation with his taciturn passenger. 'We're all amazed that anyone got out of that helicopter crash alive. The others were all killed outright. Practically unrecognizable. Straight into plastic bags. But this character seems to have got away with minor scratches.'

He stopped talking when he saw Riley's perplexed expression.

'What helicopter crash? What are you talking about, Sean?'

'The helicopter crash in Inishowen that produced the Russian. It took off back there at Shannon and came down near Buncrana.'

Riley looked at Sean for a while without speaking. 'Where did you get that information, Sean?'

'Common knowledge, Mr Riley. It doesn't exactly rain Russians in Inishowen.' Then Sean asked, 'And where did you think he came from, Mr Riley? When the lads in Buncrana were telling you about the Russians, they must've told you where he'd come from. That would have been the first question in anyone's mind, wouldn't it?'

'You haven't made too many of these phone calls, have you, Sean?'

Sean shook his head.

'Well,' said Riley, 'you keep information to a minimum, just the way you did last night. And rather well too, I might add.'

'Thank you, Mr Riley.' Sean's face broke into the first real smile of the day, all other thoughts on the matter obliterated in the pleasure of a compliment from the hard man in the passenger seat.

It began to rain. The clouds dropped to meet the tops of the hills and soft drizzle fell without a break. Sean's pedantic driving slowed even further, making the two hundred miles between Shannon and Buncrana seem like five hundred. But Mr Riley didn't complain. He reclined his seat and dozed. At one point he sat up and snapped a question. 'We aren't going through the border, Sean, are we? Stay on the Irish side.'

Sean reassured him and Riley relaxed until they reached Buncrana. Nobody noticed Sean's familiar yellow Datsun pull into the forecourt of his own garage. They had arrived.

'Drive into the garage,' Riley snapped.

Riley climbed out of the car stiffly and made for the rear door, furtively peering out of the garage's main door. He entered Sean's house through the back door. All of this amused Sean. There were few secrets in Buncrana – and most of those were Sean's.

Riley changed into casual clothes and Sean gave him a yellow waterproof suit worn by fishermen in wet weather. The rain kept casual watchers away from the shore as Sean took Riley to sea. A woman watched, but not casually.

The visibility was reduced and it was no longer possible to see the far side of Lough Swilly. Though the sea was calm, Riley looked ill at ease. He did not like boats, or the sea, or the two together. Sean, with the control arm of the outboard motor in the crook of his own arm, looked in his element. And he continued to look happy until they closed on Macamish Point and its Martello tower.

Then the contentment left his face.

O'Donnell's boat was gone. The anchorages at Macamish were empty.

TWENTY

They lay in the ditch for a long time in the night, watching the car, unable to move. Their bodies became stiff, their mood despondent. Every wave on the shore, every rustle of a fuchsia bush became the approach of a creeping enemy. Every false alert took its toll of the cold wet Faloon and Nuala. The next sound they heard was real. It was loud. Unguarded. Someone was approaching the car with confidence.

The car door was opened and the courtesy light illuminated a man. He was thickset with dark hair combed straight back. He wore a car coat and dark slacks, both of which had suffered from crawling over the hillside.

But the eyes of Faloon and Nuala were transfixed by the rifle he held in his hand and the telescopic sight attached to it. This man was the enemy. Faloon tensed like a mountain leopard. The man closed the car door without getting in and the courtesy light went out. Faloon saw him as a shadow walk to the back of the car, open the boot and unsling the rifle from his back.

He began to dismantle the weapon by the small light in the bootlid but with difficulty, so he returned to the driver's seat. He sat half in, half out of the car, making use of the stronger interior light.

Viktor Losev was engrossed and clearly not familiar with the weapon in his hands. Faloon picked up a large stone and slipped out of the ditch. He angled his approach so that the door of the car was between him and his target. The target continued to sit sideways on the driver's seat with his legs outside on the ground.

Faloon sprang at the door. Losev screamed in pain as his shin was pinned against the car's valance. Just as quickly Faloon opened the door again.

Losev attempted to emerge, which was the wrong move. He was half out of the car when Faloon once again rammed the door against him, pinning his arms inside and leaving his head exposed above the door of the car.

Faloon's clenched fist holding the stone made good use of the opportunity. Losev's head was repeatedly and violently struck, as if it was a thick tent peg. When Faloon released the door, Losev slid downwards, allowing the enraged Irishman to bury his foot forcefully into the Russian's crotch. The final kicks to the bridge of the nose were unnecessary.

'Are you going to kill him now?' Nuala's question was so matter-of-fact that it brought Faloon's frenzy to a halt.

Losev was a twitching heap on the ground, making choking sounds. With the car door still open and providing light, Faloon turned him over. His face was covered in blood and unrecognizable. Nuala began searching him. There was a clip of rifle ammunition in the coat pocket.

'We'll take that, and the rifle,' Faloon said. 'Might come in useful since people are beginning to play rough.'

Nuala transferred her attentions to the inside pockets and yelped as she cut herself on broken glass. She withdrew a pouch of smashed phials and mangled syringes. 'Looks as if this was the nice man who thought you might be diabetic.' Faloon muttered something murderous.

She made another discovery in an inside pocket. Two passports. One showed Losev as a Swedish businessman. The other was a Russian diplomatic passport.

She opened the Russian one. 'Losev,' she read. 'This is extraordinary. Documentation in his own name!' Faloon reached down and grabbed Losev's inert hand, turning the back of it towards the light. There was the star-shaped scar he had last seen on the Boeing.

'Take everything. His passports, his money, his credit cards — everything. That'll keep him busy for a while.' Faloon was still in a bad temper.

'What are you going to do with him, Faloon?'

'Nothing more. There will be enough trouble because of

his diplomatic status, which he'll doubtless invoke. But we'll make it as difficult as possible for his status to be established. At the moment he looks like someone who has been in a pub brawl.'

'Diplomatic status doesn't apply if he entered the country illegally. Nor does it permit open season on the nationals of the host country.'

'These days it might very well do so,' said Faloon, recovering some of his humour, 'but most countries don't take up the option.'

Faloon put his foot under Losev and half kicked, half pushed him away from the car and away from the partly dismantled rifle. Using an expertise that Losev to his cost did not possess, Faloon dismantled the rifle fully and put it in an executive case adapted to carry it. He threw it into the back of Losev's car.

'OK. Hop in and we'll drive to our car.' As he was reclaiming the car keys from the boot lid where Losev had left them, Faloon saw an overnight bag and rummaged through it. Inside were normal overnight belongings – and more insulin.

Faloon grabbed the insulin with the intention of throwing it as far as he could into the undergrowth. 'Kill him outright, if you must,' Nuala challenged. After a pause, she added, 'Unlike you, I believe Losev really needs insulin.'

They drove off, leaving Losev lying in the grass, beside his bag – and his insulin. 'I'll kill him next time,' Faloon swore. They speedily travelled the half mile or so back to their own car, their mood now ebullient.

Their car was where they had left it, near the remains of the burnt caravan. Faloon slowed down and pulled the car off the road some distance short, illuminating their own car with Losev's car's lights.

'What's wrong?' Nuala queried.

'Losev was very relaxed. He wasn't expecting trouble. He may have a friend waiting here for us. Let's drive on.'

They drove on for about a mile, doused the lights and

turned the car. Faloon reached into the back, grabbed the rifle in its case and quickly re-assembled it. He tried the action out and finally snapped the magazine home.

They got out and climbed. When they stopped, they had a dim view over the area where their own car was parked. The light from a quarter moon gave them some visibility.

'Faloon, I'm going to catch my death of cold. I'm wet through and covered in slimy mud. I want a hot bath. Why don't we just take the car we have and check in somewhere?'

'Because if there's someone down there, they will carry on where Losev left off and we mightn't survive until your bath time.'

Faloon appreciated that Nuala's reserves of strength were beginning to fail. 'Nuala,' he said quietly, 'look how far these people are willing to go. Losev, in his own name carrying a diplomatic passport, willing to shoot a servant of the Irish state in Ireland! All the marks of a very hasty operation. The stakes must be extremely high. Have you any idea of what we found up at that house?

'An airman's survival gear, belonging to a Russian.'

'Right. A marine rescue beacon aerial, a lifejacket and flying suit.' Nuala nodded and Faloon continued. 'Out in that bay, Nuala, is a plane that the Russians have lost. It can't be just any plane. It's something very special. We're two of the few people who now know it exists and where it is.'

'Others probably know,' whispered Nuala. 'The IRA. The pilot, may God help him, escaped drowning only to meet up with bloody Provo. He may have been forced into . . .' She stopped. Faloon had his eyes to the eyepiece of the the telescopic sight and she had seen him suddenly take aim. The light was bad, but good enough to spot movement. In the long grass beside their own car, something lay hidden and had moved. It moved again.

'I'd like to talk to whoever's down there. A couple of shots aimed high. If he runs for cover, I'll shoot the legs from under him.'

'If you aim high from here, you'll hit my car.'

Faloon ignored her and squeezed the trigger.

The blinding flash of the explosion lit up the hollow below. They both reeled back. Their night vision was lost but they felt the wave of hot air and heard objects whistling past them.

Nuala's car had blown up.

The doors twisted off, the bonnet and bootlid flew like frisbees, the roof domed upwards and the floor downwards.

In the foreground, where Faloon had seen the movement, two foxes that had been stalking their way to the caravan's waste bin bolted terrified into the night.

Faloon stared at the silhouette of the flaming shell of their car. It was the only object he could still see, given that the flash had destroyed his night vision. 'Losev's accomplice was a booby trap, waiting for us under the driver's seat, by the looks of things,' Faloon snarled. 'Let's see what we can salvage of our belongings.'

Faloon leapt over a wall and headed towards the wrecked car. 'Why was I so nice to Comrade Losev? He wasn't much good at either shooting or fisticuffs, but he could turn out a nifty bomb at short notice.'

Their suitcases had been thrown clear from the boot, along with the spare wheel and a set of golf clubs. Nuala's clubs had taken the main force of the explosion, protecting their baggage to a limited extent. Faloon guessed from Nuala's expression that she wished their baggage had saved the clubs.

They went back to the car they had taken from Losev. 'I wonder if Michael Higgins could put us up,' Faloon said as they approached Buncrana.

'We can't turn up on the steps of a hotel or guest house,' Nuala groaned. 'Look at us, a mess of mud and blood.'

'Sergeant Higgins it is then,' said Faloon, turning to Nuala. 'His wife isn't going to like you staying in my bedroom.'

'I won't be in your bedroom. You will be on the couch

below, or the garage or garden hut. I am claiming the white sheets.'

Faloon pulled up outside the sergeant's neat house and rang the bell. Since it was now the early hours of the morning, it was a while before the Higginses could be persuaded to open the door. Both Michael and his wife Roisin nearly closed it again when they saw what was on their doorstep.

Roisin Higgins had always preserved a special love-hate relationship with Faloon. She had met him at the same time as her Michael. By presenting himself unannounced after the household had retired to bed – dropping caked mud on the floor – and with an equally dirty woman, that night's relationship with Mrs Higgins was heavily weighted on the hate side.

'We've had a bad night, Roisin. We're like this because of work, not pleasure. Put us up one night and we'll get out of your house. I know this is an imposition.' Faloon's apologetic tone was just enough to convince Mrs Higgins that something serious had happened, not one of Faloon's usual drunken escapades.

After they had both had a bath, Nuala went straight to bed, making it clear that she wanted the bedroom to herself. That further mollified Mrs Higgins, who also went to bed, leaving Michael and Faloon in the room below.

'Frankly, Faloon,' began the sergeant, 'I have rarely seen you look so rough. Anything you want to talk about?'

Faloon looked at the ceiling. 'Since you saw me today, or was it yesterday, I have been shot at, seen my girlfriend in a very different and unsuspected role, crawled along the beds of streams, beaten up a man carrying a diplomatic passport, stolen that passport along with all his money and his car – which is outside your door – and blown up Nuala's car after hitting a bomb inside it with shots from a stolen rifle.'

Michael Higgins began to laugh uncertainly. It was one of Faloon's jokes. Just had to be.

'Oh, and one more thing. I'm not official,' Faloon concluded for good measure. 'Grundy has suspended me for previous sins.'

Michael Higgins rose from his chair like a badly programmed robot. He poured two Bushmills and contemplated drinking both himself.

'Can I use your phone to call Dublin?' Michael nodded. Faloon tried two numbers for Grundy without success. He left a message with the G2 duty officer, who refused to give the call special priority.

Faloon's suspension promulgation was pinned on the office wall, the duty officer reminded him. 'It says you have no official standing in this organization until further notice.' The man said triumphantly, 'So your message will go through normal channels, Faloon. I suppose you've been drinking?'

Faloon swore down the mouthpiece. Higgins meanwhile had converted the couch into a bed and had dumped a quilt on it.

'Would you like me to sing you a lullaby?' Michael grinned as he spread the quilt. Faloon was his friend. He would stand by him. At least until morning.

'No thanks. When you last sang I was insomniac for days. The whiskey will do fine.'

'Goodnight then.'

Faloon fell into a deep curative sleep, filled with dreams of grateful Grundys, Irish helicopters, of rifle shots and cars and caravans blowing up, of Nuala covered in shampoo suds draped along a silvery fuselage with a star-shaped scar upon it.

The next morning the Higgins family left the pair undisturbed, and it was nearly lunchtime before Faloon eventually shook himself awake, staring at his watch incredulously. Had he really slept that much?

He grabbed a dressing gown and went in search of other human beings. There were none on the ground floor, and nobody except Nuala, still asleep, on the top floor.

Faloon sat heavily on her bed, expecting that would waken her. It didn't. She was lying on her stomach with her feet protruding from the bedclothes. He gently pulled the bedclothes away, starting at her feet.

Softly he began to knead her ankles, then her thighs. Half awake, half asleep, she began to move in concert and breathe more heavily. Faloon kissed the small of her back, all the time rubbing her with his hands. He wished he had more limbs at his command.

'I didn't give you permission to do that,' were her first words as she stretched and reached for the bedside clock. She was as surprised as Faloon had been to see how late it was.

'Come on. You need a shower.'

'Well you would know.' She swung her feet to the floor. 'And you could probably do with a shower yourself. You can have one after I've used all the hot water.'

In the Higgins kitchen they made themselves a makeshift brunch. Nuala stirred her coffee and looked across at an abnormally quiet Faloon. 'A penny for your thoughts,' she said.

Faloon toyed with the sugar bowl. 'Who are you working for?'

'None of your business!'

'It is now,' rasped Faloon. 'Is it for a foreign agency? I've got to know that.'

'I can't tell you anything. But I recognize that you will have to tell Grundy, if you haven't already done so.'

Faloon looked at her seriously. She stared back and said, 'Last night I demonstrated something about my loyalties. I'm no traitor, Faloon. But report me to Grundy, no one else.'

He looked at her again and thought painfully about her view of loyalty and disloyalty. Too many Irish espoused loyalty to the past, or the future, but not the present. 'That'll close the subject for the moment. If we aren't professional friends, we appear to have a common enemy. I'll settle for that.'

'We are friends, Faloon. I'll never forget that.'

Faloon sipped his coffee and smiled at her. 'Yes, we are friends.'

He stood up and went to the window. It was raining gently and the hills and mountains were beginning to blur into soft monochrome shades and shapes. He put the problem of Nuala's secret identity to one side and tried instead to fathom the meaning of pieces of the Russian equipment they had found.

There had been two separate incidents which had become confused with each other. Two aircraft, one Russian and the other an Irish helicopter, had fallen out of the sky. Two separate happenings.

'Or two consequences of a single happening!' he said aloud to a puzzled Nuala.

Faloon was groping towards the same theory as the KGB. If two aircraft fell out of the sky at the same place and at the same time, there was a fair chance they had collided.

There could be no proof without the missing helicopter tail pylon. The tail pylon would bear the marks of collision – or alternatively demonstrate that a faulty inspection hatch had indeed been the cause. It was a more comforting theory than Provos with surface-to-air missiles.

The day before, Faloon's thoughts had been locked into the premise that the Provos had been trying a new weapon and awkward facts which had not fitted this theory had been discarded. Sloppy thinking, he admonished himself. Start again with a more open mind.

But where should he start? And then he remembered what Higgins had said outside the pub. Something about the local police not giving their full co-operation to the tidal wave of officialdom and brass that had descended upon Inishowen.

He phoned the police station and asked for Higgins. 'Michael, I've got to see you.'

'What about? Can't it wait?'

'No. I want the tail pylon of that helicopter. I think you know something.'

In the police station, Sergeant Higgins blanched and put the phone down. His colleagues thought he had just been given bad news, which, in a manner of speaking, was true. He left immediately for home.

Faloon had a cup of tea waiting for him but Higgins was too angry to notice. 'Faloon. Your humour could get me into trouble. You don't run remarks like that through the station switchboard.'

'I know you, Michael Higgins. I know when you know something. Somebody local knows about that pylon, and it's bloody important, more than you realize.'

'It's vital,' Nuala interrupted. 'That's one reason half the army and police in the country are crawling over your patch. They'll not leave until they've turned over every stone in the county. So if you know something, tell him. If anyone can protect you from this point, he can.'

The sergeant rubbed his chin in thought and threw himself heavily into an armchair.

'I don't know where it is,' he began, 'but you're right. I know where it has been. And I suppose I could guess where it is now.' He looked up at Faloon, who had remained standing. And waiting.

Michael took a deep breath. 'The day after the crash I was driving between the crash site and the place where the caravan was burnt. I saw what looked like the tail part of the helicopter on a hillside, well away from the crash site.'

'So what did you do about it?

'Nothing. Remember, we had been ordered not to touch any part of the helicopter. The investigators wanted to pick over the bits themselves first.'

'But Michael,' Faloon said angrily, 'the investigators haven't got the tail section. Why the hell don't you tell them where it is?'

223

'Because it isn't there any more, that's why.' The sergeant stopped for a slurp of tea. 'He's a harmless soul. A bit of an eccentric, but well liked in these parts.'

'Who? You mean some lunatic has got the tail pylon?' Faloon asked incredulously.

'It's a guess, Faloon, just a guess.'

'I'll back your hunches.' Faloon was already grabbing a coat. 'Can we use your car? Ours might be on your stolen car list.'

'Faloon, I ought to have remembered just how much trouble you are in. Will I still be in the police force after all this?'

'Tell me, Michael,' Faloon asked as they drove away from Buncrana in the direction of the north coast, 'why should a farmer covet the arse-end of a helicopter?'

'Shit! Tell me I'm dreaming.' Faloon's gasp was the first alert to Nuala in the back of the car that they had arrived. McLaverty's small farm lay in the fold of the hills. Far above it, on the saddle of a low pass, was the evidence of McLaverty's hobby and obsession: windmills.

Half a dozen windmills of various designs – Cretan cloth sails, ones made out of oildrums, some on a horizontal axis, others on a vertical axis, large ones and small. McLaverty was a one-man research and development enterprise into alternative energy.

They stopped in the middle of the farmyard behind a modern bungalow. Mrs McLaverty came out to meet them and recognized the sergeant. They greeted each other.

'I suppose your man is up with the propellers,' said Michael, nodding in the direction of the hill.

'Oh no. He's away to Derry to shop. What's wrong?' she asked, slightly worried at the unusual deputation.

'I'm afraid that he can't keep that bit of the helicopter, even though it fell on his land. The accident investigation people in Dublin need it badly.'

224

'He'll be very put out, Michael,' Mrs McLaverty replied. 'He's ready to make another windmill with it.'

She turned to the strangers, Faloon and Nuala, and explained. 'He heats this whole house with the wind, you know. His new project is to have a heated barn for drying grain. He wasn't stealing anything. It just fell on our ground.' She was wringing a tea towel in her hands as she spoke. Faloon reassured her. Relieved, she led the party to an outhouse and flung open the door.

Faloon almost laughed. There it was, a gleaming piece of alloy in the middle of a jumble of ancient rusting turnip slicers and horse ploughs. McLaverty had raised the tail section on trestles, preparing to convert it into yet another wind generator. Three hens perched on it.

Faloon gestured for everyone else to keep away. He approached the pylon like an explorer discovering a fabled idol in a lost tomb. The tail rotor was badly bent but still firmly attached. The pylon inspection hatch, with its double clasps to prevent accidental opening, was still shut tightly. So his friend Brendan in the Accident Investigation Branch had been correct in his suspicions. The hatch was not the cause.

Faloon turned his attention to the line of fracture. The signs of impact and shearing were clear even to Faloon's untutored eye. The sheet alloy and support members had been sliced at the same point almost the whole way round the oval section. As he suspected, the tail had been cut off in mid-air and therefore had fallen separately to the ground some distance from the main fuselage.

Faloon stuck his head inside the pylon. Something odd had caught his attention. Securely lodged in a buckled metal rib was a small piece of rock-hard grey material. He dislodged it and pulled it out.

Mrs McLaverty saw his interest. 'There was a big lump of that stone rattling round the inside,' she explained, walking over to a workbench alongside the wall. 'And here it is. He was very puzzled because there's no rock like that on our hills.'

225

Faloon took it with mounting excitement. This piece was the size of a man's hand, roughly 'U' shaped and smooth on the outside. It showed every sign of having come into hard contact with the helicopter's metal skin.

'Thank you, Mrs McLaverty,' Faloon babbled. 'I'll take this grey piece with me. Someone else will come to collect the rest. You've been a great help.' And with that he walked briskly back to the car. The others followed, almost at a trot. Michael bade Mrs McLaverty a hasty farewell and began driving.

'What have you got there, Faloon?' asked Michael.

'I think it's a piece of RCC.'

'What's that?'

'Reinforced carbon-carbon. It can withstand temperatures over 1600 degrees centigrade. And that's very very hot.'

Nuala leaned forward to look at the material. 'And how would you know about stuff like that and remember so much about it?'

'I was once given a detailed guided tour round the OV-101. They boasted about this material, RCC. It stuck in my mind because it sounded like a super-Catholic who could go to hell and stay in one piece to watch all the Protestants burn.'

They all laughed. 'And the OV-101. How did you remember that? Sounds like an airship,' cackled Michael.

'No. It was an experimental machine. A test vehicle, used for atmosphere trials.'

'Atmosphere trials?' Nuala repeated, puzzled.

'OV-101 was the first American space-shuttle vehicle. Reinforced carbon-carbon protects the leading edges of space shuttle wings on re-entry. It's one of the most important parts of a heatshield . . .'

There was silence in the car as the implications of Faloon's words made their impact. They were holding part of a spacecraft.

TWENTY ONE

When Major Stukalin, cosmonaut, last wielded a screwdriver in the dark, it had been during his extensive training at Tyuratam in central Asia. The Tyuratam screwdriver had been as spotless as a surgeon's knife, his progress in using it had been monitored by a thermal imager and engineers had helped with advice through earphones.

In the fishing boat's forward cabin, conditions for Stukalin could hardly have been more different. The screwdriver he wielded was little more than a streak of rust and he was grateful that nobody was monitoring his efforts, particularly not O'Donnell or Moira. He had cleaned the tool as best he could, paying particular attention to the tip. Feeling with his fingers, he had located the hinges of the forward hatch above his head. If he could find some way through it, he would be ondeck.

Easier thought than done. The hinges had been painted coat upon coat, filling the screwhead slots with hardened varnish. Before he could begin removing the fastenings, the slots had to be excavated – a laborious and painful process, given the gunshot injuries which had stiffened his left arm.

The only help on offer to his relentless scraping was the gentle rocking of the boat at anchor. The lapping of the water, the rubbing of the anchor chain, the slight clink of loose items in the main cabin where Moira was asleep, all combined to hide the slight noise he was making. Several times O'Donnell came forward from the wheelhouse to put his ear to the bulkhead or the door, checking that nothing was amiss. Each time he left satisfied.

O'Donnell had pondered long and hard about what Stukalin had put to him. The offer of Russian arms was superficially attractive, but he had finally decided against dealing with the Soviets. Arms shipments in the quantities

O'Donnell sought would take time to assemble and deliver. In that case, he might have to deliver Stukalin to the Russians before receiving any arms in return and O'Donnell was not the trusting sort.

Then there was the question of Stukalin's plane – a subject upon which he hadn't been able to draw the Russian. O'Donnell was guessing that it was a fighter plane like those Stukalin mentioned in Afghanistan, and that it had come down on Inishowen. More likely in the sea near the shore, he argued to himself, since Stukalin's inner clothing was sticky with sea-salt.

The Americans might want a Russian war-plane, even a damaged one. With dollars, he could buy any arms he wanted. He had not yet decided on a price. That was why he wanted Martin Riley, first as a consultant, then as a go-between. The Americans would have to move fast if they were to recover the Russian plane, or the bits they wanted. They might pay millions of dollars in their haste.

The deviousness came with the second part of O'Donnell's plan. If he could manage it, he would sell Stukalin's plane to the Americans. Major Stukalin himself he would sell back to the Russians. Russian money was useless, but a small arms deal could be very valuable. Stukalin himself had suggested the currency: modern portable surface-to-air missiles. Even a small number of such weapons would multiply Provo firepower and many Russian naval ships would have sufficient for O'Donnell's purposes.

In the past, well beyond Irish territorial waters, O'Donnell had met ships which had sailed across the north Atlantic from Boston, Massachusetts. On board would be arms and ammunition, usually accompanied by Martin Riley. The cargos would be transferred to O'Donnell's boat.

He would have no problems pulling off the same trick at sea with the Russians.

Though the skeleton of the plan was simple, plotting the detail engrossed O'Donnell as he sat in the unlit wheelhouse of the unlit boat. Either by subterfuge or coercion, he would need to know precisely where Stukalin had ditched his plane. Bottom-mapping sonar, which he had fitted to the fishing boat, would make short work of finding the craft, or at least the major bits of it, but it could all take too long unless he knew precisely where to look.

Preoccupation was one of the reasons why O'Donnell failed to hear Stukalin scraping, failed to hear when he twice dropped the rusty screwdriver, failed to hear the groan from the wood as the first screw moved.

It took Stukalin six hours to remove six screws. When the last fell away, the hinges still remained attached to the wood, stuck with thick coats of paint. Using the screwdriver as a lever both hinges were prised loose with a loud cracking noise.

O'Donnell jumped from the stool. The sound had reached his ears over the deck, not through the cabin below. Quietly he opened the wheelhouse door and crept out. He peered over the low knee-high bulwarks, half expecting to see a small boat, perhaps Sean. All he saw was a piece of driftwood lying against the hull. Dissatisfied, he crept down the side deck to the foredeck. The anchor chain was rattling a little as it had throughout the night. His eyes fell upon the forehatch, the skylight to Stukalin's makeshift cell. He stepped forward and examined the heavy padlock securing it. He knelt on deck and put his ear to the hatch. Nothing suspicious. The hatch hinges had been attached to the underside and from above the hatch looked normal.

O'Donnell walked back up the side deck and stopped to look at the driftwood, slowly bobbing the length of the hull pulled by the tide, bumping gently as it progressed. He stared at it, and looked back at the foredeck. Tired though he was, O'Donnell was still not satisfied. He returned to the wheelhouse and armed himself with the pistol. Grabbing a bunch of keys he dived into the cabin where Moira was sleeping, heading for Stukalin's forecabin. Hampered by heightening apprehension, he found the right key, raped the lock with it and whipped open the door, gun in hand. The rectangle of

229

pale night sky through the open hatch told him all he needed to know.

In a frenzy of anger, he tried to thrust aside the hatch, which was still attached by the padlock, but it blocked both his view and his movement. He abandoned the attempt to reach the deck through it and thundered back through the main cabin and into the wheelhouse.

The glimmer of the approaching dawn bathed the deck in a half light. Major Stukalin was nowhere to be seen.

O'Donnell cocked the pistol. Inside the cabin Moira moaned a sleepy enquiry. O'Donnell ignored her. His complete attention was directed at the deck.

The wheelhouse, with its large windows, afforded a good view forward and to each side, but the rear view was restricted by a solid bulkhead with only two small windows. O'Donnell darted between the two. Stukalin had to be hiding behind the wheelhouse. He opened the wheelhouse door and propelled himself through it in a single whirlwind of movement onto the small sidedeck, the gun pointing from shadow to shadow. He stood stock still, listening only to his own breathing. There was no other sound; his eye could discern no movement. And yet, he thought savagely, Stukalin was on this deck. He couldn't have left it.

Very cautiously, O'Donnell began to edge towards the corner of the wheelhouse, the pistol held tensely in front. Still no noise. The afterdeck, its lobster pots casting long deceptive shadows, came into O'Donnell's sight. He kicked one of the pots into the shadows. Still no reaction. Stukalin was obviously not on the afterdeck. The Russian must be hiding somewhere towards the bows. He turned and pressed himself close to the side of the wheelhouse. That was his undoing.

O'Donnell had scanned backwards and forwards, left and right. But not up. Above him, lying on the flat wheelhouse roof like a stalking panther, Stukalin also listened and watched, waiting for his chance. In his fist, a winch handle. O'Donnell's head came within range and Stukalin put all the

230

force he could muster into the arc of a blow. Alerted by a slight noise, O'Donnell at last looked up.

The metal struck his head a glancing blow. Half stunned, half blinded, he staggered backwards. The bulwark of the boat caught him just below the backs of his knees and his feet stood on a rope which rolled on the deck beneath him. The combination of fulcrum, momentum, the loss of both orientation and grip sent O'Donnell into a backwards somersault over the side of the boat.

Moira's scream and O'Donnell's splash came together. Naked, Moira rushed out on deck and threw O'Donnell a lifebelt. The shock of hitting the cold sea had speedily revived his senses and he began fighting to recover his breath and stay afloat.

Moira suddenly saw the pistol which O'Donnell had dropped on deck. She lunged towards it. She hadn't seen Stukalin who was still on the deckhouse roof. He leapt, flattening her beneath him. The pistol slithered further along the deck. With his arm tightly round her neck the Russian hauled the winded girl to her feet. 'O'Donnell. O'Donnell . . . can you hear me?' the Major shouted. The answer was increased splashing.

O'Donnell had swum to the bows and was hauling himself out of the water and up the anchor cable like a rain-forest monkey. Stukalin threw a despairing glance at the fallen pistol. Having Moira to deal with, he doubted if he could reach it in time to stop O'Donnell reaching the deck. Already O'Donnell's hand could be seen above the bulwark fumbling for grip.

Stukalin could feel the strength of his wounded arm ebbing as he fought to subdue the struggling Moira. In a few more seconds, all would be lost.

With the last reserves of his strength, Stukalin turned Moira seawards and shoved. Her bare knees slammed hard against the low bulwark. At the same time Stukalin let go the upper part of her body and pushed hard between her shoulder blades. As she screamed and overbalanced on the low bulwark, he rammed his legs against her thighs, thus preventing her from going overboard completely.

Terrorstruck, she found herself upsidedown with her head only inches from the waves. She had wrapped her legs round those of Stukalin, who now needed to expend no energy to keep Moira exactly where she was. Moira screamed to O'Donnell that she couldn't swim, only stopping when a wave swamped her head.

'Go back, O'Donnell,' Stukalin yelled as the Provo's head appeared above the forward bulwark. 'Go back or I let her go. When I do I'll reach the gun before you. You'll die with a bullet. The girl will drown.' O'Donnell needed convincing. Stukalin, a hand round each of Moira's thighs, was ready to prise them further apart to release the grip that was saving her from the sea. Her screaming intensified.

'Yes.' O'Donnell was near but his voice was distant. He dropped back into the sea.

'Keep going in that direction, towards the shore. If you attempt to come back to this boat I'll let her go and then shoot at you.'

O'Donnell shouted defiance, but he was swimming towards the shore as directed, clutching the lifebuoy. Even above his own exertions, he could hear Moira sobbing. When he looked back he could see her white body against the black hull, her arms and hands flailing for non-existent grip on the slimy waterline.

When O'Donnell was a safe distance away, Stukalin put his arms round Moira's hips and pulled her inboard, gasping in pain from his wound as he did so.

She dropped on deck like a dead fish. Stukalin retrieved the pistol. 'Go into the cabin,' he ordered.

She struggled uncertainly to her feet and turned to face him, her arms by her side. He marvelled at how fast her distress had turned to anger, the same anger that Stukalin had experienced from her before. The residue of her tears was dripping onto her shivering breasts. Her nipples were stiff with cold, her wet hair plastered to her head and neck.

'Are you going to rape me before you kill me, or afterwards? Isn't that what the Tartars do?'

'Get dressed. Put something very warm on. First, where are the rest of those arms O'Donnell brought on board?'

She pointed at one of the lockers on deck. He threw the weapons into the sea as she watched. As the last weapon, except the pistol, plopped into the water, she pounced. Every ounce of her strength was directed towards Stukalin's right arm, the one holding the pistol. By clinging with both arms and using her whole weight she could prevent Stukalin bringing the weapon to bear.

'Come back, Dick. I'm holding him. He can't shoot. Come back. Come back.' Her shrill cries rang out over the water and still morning air.

Stukalin's wounded left arm was not sufficiently strong to free his other arm and the two of them wrestled on the cluttered deck until they toppled. Initially Stukalin had treated Moira's action more as a distraction than as a serious attack. A naked girl against an armed man. But he quickly realized that she could win if she managed to disable him long enough to allow O'Donnell to reach the boat.

Stukalin clawed for the rope on the deck that had contributed to O'Donnell's falling overboard. Wincing as he manipulated his left arm, he whipped a loop over Moira's head and round her neck. By twisting just like a tourniquet, he stopped her breathing.

In desperation, Moira tried one final wrench to free the gun from Stukalin's grip. It failed. She panicked in asphyxiation and released his gun arm to claw the rope from her windpipe.

Stukalin jumped to his feet, holding Moira by the rope like a prize cow. O'Donnell was by now within a few metres of the anchor chain. Stukalin fired. Three rounds zipped into the water round O'Donnell's head.

He dived. Stukalin waited. He could afford to wait.

'Don't shoot him!' It was a choking appeal from Moira. Stukalin shook her. 'Tell him to leave. You brought him

233

back, remember.'

O'Donnell surfaced. He gasped for a refill of air before going under once more, expecting more shots.

'Go away, Dick,' Moira's shrill voice penetrated. 'Go back. He's won.'

'Let her go, Major,' O'Donnell shouted between gulps. 'I'll bring her ashore in the lifebelt.'

'No,' said Moira in a whisper. Her fear of water was greater than her fear of Stukalin.

'You can have her,' Stukalin shouted, releasing the rope. 'Jump,' he said to Moira, pointing at the sea.

'No!'

Stukalin stood breathless behind her. She brought her hand down to her side and closed her eyes. Her tears were flowing silently. Stukalin's hand was flat between her shoulder blades.

'Then remember that I didn't push you. Remember that, Moira.'

O'Donnell turned for the shore, silently this time. He refused to look back until he had tottered past the first line of seaweed on the shore.

In the glow of a new day, he saw Moira, now wrapped in a blanket, standing on the foredeck looking at him. He saw the shadow of Stukalin in the wheelhouse.

And he saw his boat moving towards the mouth of Lough Swilly and the Atlantic.

* * *

On another foreshore stood a figure just as dejected as O'Donnell and considerably more injured. It was Viktor Losev.

He was breathing uncomfortably through his mouth because his nose was broken and because some ribs were cracked. While he'd been unconscious, a large blood blister had formed on his upper cheekbone. Blood from his nostrils and from a gash on the side of his head had matted his hair.

He had stumbled down to the waterline among the rockpools to clean himself up. The reflections told him he was not a pretty sight. The fresh seawater revived him enough to remember Faloon and he would have snarled if his face had been working. Then he remembered his duty. Painfully he climbed the hill towards the ruined cottage and found what he needed. He gathered up the flying suit, the buoyancy aid and the radio beacon aerial which Faloon and his woman accomplice had abandoned. He snapped the aerial into shorter pieces, used bits of it to puncture the buoyancy aid and wrapped the lot in a makeshift bundle using the flying suit.

Sometimes carrying the bundle, sometimes dragging it, he negotiated fields, walls, streams, and thickets of gorse until he found a fox hole big enough to hide his burden. Using his foot he rammed it well out of sight. At least the Irish would not be parading those artifacts at a press conference. By the time he reached the road, he was on the point of collapse. He took heart from the sight in the distance. It was the twisted, charred and mangled remains of his enemy's car. So the bomb had worked. He had got them after all. The secret was safe for the time being.

He lay down, drained and barely conscious. A passing farmer found him half an hour later and drove him immediately to a surgery in Buncrana. The doctor who examined him decided to call the police.

At the police station, Higgins had taken the call and decided to deal with the 'road accident' himself. When he arrived at the surgery, the doctor outlined the facts. 'The man who brought him thought from the condition of his car that this driver must have been doing a hundred miles an hour and then rolled on a bend. On that little road!'

Higgins wanted this case out of the way quickly. He knew what had happened to that car and he knew who the patient was. 'I suppose he could've been drunk at the time,' Higgins ventured, peering at the battered Losev.

The doctor shook his head. 'No, Sergeant Higgins. The

man is a diabetic. I think his blood sugar levels went badly wrong and he became disorientated, crashing his car as a consequence.'

'What identity had he on him?'

'Nothing. No money, no wallet, no driving licence. Nothing. Just an open air ticket, in his shoe, of all places. The rest was probably scattered as he was thrown clear.'

Higgins nodded gravely and wrote all this silently in his notebook. The doctor thought the sergeant ought to be a bit more energetic.

'On the other hand, he could be the missing Russian that everybody's talking about,' prompted the doctor.

The sergeant moved round the couch, away from the doctor's direct line of vision. 'No! Not possible,' he snapped. 'All the bodies in that helicopter are accounted for.'

'No,' echoed Losev, agitated. 'I'm a Swedish tourist. Unfortunately I crashed my car. My wallet, passport, credit cards have all spilled from my pockets.'

It was the best Losev could do in the circumstances, wanting speedily to reinforce the policeman's quick rejection of his being Russian. Losev's period of living and working in the United States now came to his aid.

'Some of my family are in America,' said Losev, watching the policeman. But he needn't have worried. This policeman seemed ready to accept anything he said.

'It's good to see tourists coming back here,' Higgins said. 'The IRA troubles have been chasing visitors away. I blame television. Many think that if they come here they'll be shot at or blown up.'

Losev examined Higgins anew using the eye he could still focus, wondering whether the policeman was playing with him. He concluded instead that this policeman was an idiot.

'I have a telephone number to call in case of this kind of difficulty,' Losev said. 'Would you mind if I made a brief call to Dublin?'

'I don't think you should move,' muttered the doctor, mindful that he would be paying for the call.

'I think that in the case of lost credit cards, a call needs to be made as fast as possible,' countered Higgins, already helping Losev off the couch. The doctor bowed to the inevitable and added his assistance to bring Losev to the telephone at his surgery desk.

The Russian dialled his Dublin embassy, now grateful that he had followed procedure and memorized an ex-directory number.

When the call was answered, he gave a codeword in Russian, followed by the name of the man he wished to speak to and the telephone number from which he was speaking. Then he replaced the receiver.

'I have asked them to call me back. That should save your phone account, doctor.'

The doctor smiled. 'Nonsense. You should have made the call.'

'Do either of you speak foreign languages? Swedish perhaps?' asked Losev, trying a simple sentence of Russian.

The doctor shook his head. 'Some French, some German.' 'French, German and Irish,' beamed Higgins glad to be topping the doctor's bid. The doctor scowled. 'Irish is not a foreign language.' The telephone rang. 'But not Swedish,' said Losev, feigning disappointment and picking up the handset.

No, nor Russian, thought Higgins to himself.

Higgins didn't care what Losev was saying down the telephone. If the Russian was not involving Faloon, was not demanding police or legal procedures and not invoking diplomatic status, he could play at being Swedish. The Russian was a spent force, scarcely able to walk, Higgins reasoned. It was evident that he wanted to leave Inishowen with as little trouble as possible. In that aim, Higgins was his accomplice.

So, unhindered, Losev told his masters what had happened on Inishowen and what had been found at the bay. He postulated that the spaceplane must be at the bottom of that particular bay and that its pilot was alive somewhere.

Losev was ordered back to Shannon to board the next plane home. He had fulfilled his primary function. Russia at last knew where her spaceplane lay and the final part of Bulgakov's plan could now unfold.

TWENTY TWO

Macamish empty!

Sean was incredulous when he saw that the Macamish anchorages were empty. Martin Riley only became aware that something was wrong when Sean began fruitlessly driving the boat up and down the same short stretch of coast. Sean could not bring himself to tell his passenger.

Over the sound of the rain rattling on the hood of his anorak, Sean heard an annoyed, wet and uncomfortable Riley bellow, 'Where is O'Donnell's fuckin' boat?'

'He's gone. Something must have happened,' Sean shouted back, pulling out the portable VHF radio which was to have been used at the final stage of the assignation. Repeatedly he made the call sign and put the set to his ear, hoping to hear O'Donnell.

Nothing but static. Sean turned back to Buncrana.

Inside Sean's house they peeled off their wet-weather gear and Sean produced a bottle of whiskey. He was relieved to see that Riley accepted a drink.

Sean went over to a writing desk and removed a false drawer front to reveal a VHF transmitter, the one by which O'Donnell had first contacted him. Watched silently by Riley, Sean tried the call signs again, but gave up after a few attempts.

'If he was listening, he would have replied,' Sean said. 'Something's gone badly wrong. We'll wait. People know to contact me here.' He looked at his watch. 'News time. Let's see if there's anything on the bulletin.'

They turned on the television. The news of the hunt for

bits of the crashed helicopter had featured for days, but after yet another day without dramatic results, the journalists in their boredom had finally dropped the story. There was nothing about a boat or arrests. The telephone in the hall rang and Sean answered it.

'For you, Mr Riley,' Sean sang out, surprised. 'A woman. Somebody called Sinead.'

Sean listened to the conversation but he learnt little for his trouble. Riley was even less talkative into the mouthpiece of a telephone. The doorbell rang. Riley turned in the direction of Sean, alarmed. Sean shrugged his shoulders to indicate that he was not expecting callers. Riley motioned him to delay answering. He bade a curt farewell into the phone and sped out of sight in the direction of the back door. Sean waited as the bell sounded again, more urgently and more impatiently.

He went to the door without haste, opened it and received a second shock for the day.

It was Dick O'Donnell. Without ceremony he pushed past Sean, straight into the living room. Sean closed the door fast and followed him.

'Who's here?' O'Donnell demanded, looking at the two whiskey glasses on the coffee table.

'Martin Riley.'

The name boomed through the house, and it was not uttered by Sean. O'Donnell spun round in the direction of the voice to see Riley framed in the doorway.

'You don't keep your appointments, O'Donnell,' said Riley, 'and that's damned rude for someone who's just crossed the Atlantic on your invitation.'

O'Donnell crossed the room and shook Riley's hand warmly. 'Things have gone badly since I sent for you.'

On the other side of the room, Sean was impatient. 'I turned up with Mr Riley as you asked. Right across the Swilly in this bloody weather. Have you any idea how wet it is out there, Dick?'

'Yes I have,' snapped O'Donnell. 'At least you were on

the Swilly. I was in it.'

'Is the boat sunk?' blurted Sean.

'Sean, why don't you go for a drink? The pub that lets you in after closing time will let you in now.' O'Donnell pointed Sean towards his own door.

Riley began speaking as soon as he heard the front door shut behind Sean. 'It was a good question, Dick.'

'Yeah. But the answer's bad.' O'Donnell moved over to the couch beside the coffee table and sat down heavily. He poured himself a whiskey from Sean's bottle and poured another for Riley. 'I need this for medicinal purposes,' he said.

Riley examined the abrasion on O'Donnell's forehead. He stayed quiet and let O'Donnell recount the story at his own pace. O'Donnell did not refer to Stukalin by either name or profession. Simply that he was Russian.

'He's slipped out of my hands. He's got my woman and my boat. What a shitty mess,' O'Donnell concluded.

Riley's face became hard. 'I take it you are referring to the Russian pilot.'

O'Donnell was jolted. 'Sean and his big mouth. But I didn't say anything about a pilot to him. Did Sean mention something about his being a pilot, Martin?'

'Sean didn't mention anything about a pilot, Dick. I knew what you were going to be offering before I left Massachusetts.' He sipped his whiskey while studying the effect of his remark on O'Donnell.

'You'll pardon the question,' O'Donnell answered slowly, 'but how the hell did you know this man was a pilot? What else do you know?'

'Enough to bring me across the Atlantic to help sell a Russian plane and its pilot to Uncle Sam.' Riley leaned forward. 'That was your idea, wasn't it, Dick?'

Almost, said O'Donnell, but only to himself.

'Only now,' continued Riley, 'Dick O'Donnell has let the live bait slip back into the ocean, eh?'

Any warmth that had crept into Riley's manner had departed. He had no intention of answering questions from O'Donnell. He wanted answers.

'Has anyone set out after the Russian?'

'No. That boat was our complete navy.'

Riley sat back to think at length, something he could do better than the tired O'Donnell, whose eyes had begun to droop from almost forty-eight hours without sleep. Riley went into the hallway to the phone and rang a number he had been given by Sinead earlier in the evening. Then he waited.

The ringing of the doorbell roused O'Donnell from a catnap. Riley told him to answer while he himself hid once more in the back room. O'Donnell opened the door to a woman he had never seen before, carrying a nylon sausage weekend bag.

'Martin Riley is expecting me,' she said without ceremony.

O'Donnell allowed her inside, eyeing her suspiciously.

'This is Sinead,' said Martin Riley, slipping back into the living room. He walked over to the woman and pecked her on the cheek. 'It's best that you know little else about her, except that she represents American Embassy interest in our proposal. Unofficial but real interest, if you understand me.'

O'Donnell was not sure that he did comprehend, but since his proposal had evaporated that morning, it hardly mattered. He nodded a greeting. Riley suggested coffee and he himself left to make it. He was purposely leaving O'Donnell and the woman to get acquainted. Their conversation began without polite preliminaries.

'Where is our Russian friend?' she asked simply.

O'Donnell smiled mirthlessly.

'I watched from the shore as Martin left to meet you on the boat,' she went on, her stare never leaving O'Donnell's haggard face. 'Something's screwed up. Your face says it all.' Her manner was cool and controlled. She and Riley were a matched pair, thought O'Donnell.

O'Donnell tried to rub the tiredness from his face before offering an explanation. 'Cutting a long story short, our Russian friend has escaped from me, taking my fishing boat. The boat has full communications and navigation gear. My guess, for what it's worth, is that he'll sail north and make contact with some of the Russian fishing fleet. The Russians are no strangers in these waters.'

She looked hard at O'Donnell and then said 'Fuck' in a clear, unemotional way. That was all she said in reaction to O'Donnell's tale of woe.

O'Donnell studied her as she glared at him. She was casually but well dressed in slacks and a high-necked jumper. She wore no jewellery, little make-up and her dark hair was pinned up. Whereas Riley's accent betrayed his Irish origin, Sinead, except for her name, seemed to O'Donnell to be pure home-grown American.

'He too has an American accent,' O'Donnell said suddenly.

She looked puzzled and O'Donnell realized that she did not know what he was talking about.

'The Russian, Major Stukalin,' he elucidated. Sinead looked interested and responded by pulling a notebook out of her bag.

'What was his full name?'

'Well his first name was Peter. That was the easy one. The middle name was a bit of a tongue-twister – something "ovich."'

Her pen was moving furiously. 'I need everything about him that you can remember. How well did you get to know him?'

'Not bloody well enough,' thundered O'Donnell, raising his hand to his pained forehead. 'I know that he's flown fighters in Afghanistan. But there's nothing else of great interest, except that he doesn't think very much of our struggle for nationhood.'

Sinead made more notes. 'So you spent time trying to make him into an Irish republican. Small wonder he hit you over the head.'

Riley reappeared with a tray of coffee. 'How far have we got?' he enquired.

She accepted a coffee and replied, 'I don't think at the moment that we've anything to sell. Unless, of course, your friend here can tell us where the Russian ditched his plane.' They both looked at O'Donnell.

'I know roughly where it must be. It must be in shallow water in one of the bays to the west of the headland, reasonably near the shore.'

'Not good enough,' Sinead snapped. 'We're in a race. We know that this plane is very special. Until it got into trouble of some kind, it flew very fast, very high and had the radar signature of something the size of a bath tub.'

She was agitated and began prowling up and down the room. 'You must understand that the Russians have a big advantage in this race. It's their plane and the salvage rights are theirs, if not legally, then through force of arms.'

O'Donnell was not usually slow on the uptake, but he was not at his best. He shook his head. With a note of exasperation, Sinead went on, 'Listen. We can't mount an open search of the seabed, even if we had the time. So we need to know within a small circle of probability where the Russian machine is. Then we might have a chance of achieving something. But we must be finished and be out of the way before the Russians arrive. I think we've less than twenty-four hours.'

It was O'Donnell's turn to be exasperated. 'I've told you, I don't know precisely where the Russian plane is.'

'So what was it you wanted to sell? The pilot himself I suppose. And you thought you had all the time in the world because the Russians would do nothing. Riley told me you were one of the best the IRA had. Well, God help them over here.'

'You listen, woman.' O'Donnell had taken as much as he could from her. 'I had every reason to believe that I was the only one who knew of the existence of Stukalin and that I had sufficient time to get the location of his aircraft out of him.'

O'Donnell was not about to tell her that he wanted to keep Stukalin undamaged for sale to the Russians, not to the Americans.

But the woman was not letting go that easily. 'And you thought that radars didn't exist and that the Russian wouldn't have given a position fix before he ditched?'

'Correct.' O'Donnell had moved to stand in confrontation before her. His mind was working faster now. He had thought of radars, but this woman seemed to know a hell of a lot about Stukalin's plane, including the fact that it showed up very small on a radar screen.

'You yourself said that the machine didn't show up too well on radar,' O'Donnell reminded her. 'Well I'm right. There's been a bloody big search for bits of the crashed helicopter, but to my knowledge, no search in the water for Stukalin's plane. They don't know it's there!'

O'Donnell had won a point and pressed home his advantage. 'Even if I could take you to the crash site right now, it would be too big an operation to raise the thing to the surface and carry it off. You would need the Dublin government's approval, then you'd need . . .'

'. . . An American armada to keep the Russians away,' Riley interrupted. 'The two would start shooting and a united Ireland could rise from the radioactive ashes of the world.'

Neither Sinead nor O'Donnell knew which of them was the target of Riley's sarcasm. O'Donnell was beginning to feel tired again as his anger receded. 'So what is everybody suggesting?' asked O'Donnell. 'Why was it worth Martin crossing the Atlantic just to tell me we're powerless?'

Riley spelt it out. 'The Americans can't have the whole plane. They want bits of it and photographs of the rest of it. Anything more is out of the question. And you, my friend, must deliver those things if we're to strike a deal. It's worth a lot of money to us. And that means to you and the movement.'

Sinead interjected, 'I stress that the government of the United States isn't officially involved. There aren't going to be any radioactive ashes over this.' She scowled at Riley and then at O'Donnell, pushing her message home.

Stepping round O'Donnell, she picked up her bag. 'Your friend won't mind a trans-Atlantic call on his phone bill, will he?' she asked, smiling as she went to the phone in the hall. O'Donnell thought Sean would mind a lot, but he could begin minding when the bill came through the letterbox. He watched her dial a long number as she said, 'Martin, I'm sure O'Donnell will understand if you close the door to give me some privacy.'

O'Donnell saw he had set in train events he no longer had much control over. He ran his fingers through his hair. 'If I had my boat, I could possibly search the most likely bays with the sonar. I could find echoes that might be the plane, but I wouldn't know whether I'd found it or some old hulk until I went down to see.'

Riley nodded, closing the door leading to the phone. 'I told her you've some diving experience.'

'For God's sake, Martin, that was a long time ago when you and me used to raid lobster pots and dream of finding an Armada wreck filled with doubloons. I haven't been down for years.'

'Not that long ago. Do you still have the gear?'

'Yes. But I don't have a boat, remember. The Russian has it. And he has Moira.' A shadow crossed his face and the two men remained silent. From beyond the door came the faint sounds of hushed conversation.

When Sinead came back into the room her expression had changed dramatically. 'When the Russian departed with your boat, he might've done us a favour.' Both men looked at her with renewed interest. Her previous coolness had completely gone. She looked and sounded excited.

It was O'Donnell who asked the question. 'I don't feel very favoured. What's happened? You've learnt something, haven't you?'

She turned to Riley rather than O'Donnell. 'O'Donnell's stumbled on something big, Martin. Very big. He didn't know what kind of man he tried to ransom. I asked for a file search through on the name "Petr Stukalin". I didn't expect much because I expected the name to be false. Well it wasn't, and the name Stukalin means a lot to us.'

It was Riley's turn to be hostile. He didn't like being dangled on a string. 'What does it mean, woman?'

'Major Petr Fedorovich Stukalin. Was that his full name, O'Donnell?'

O'Donnell nodded dumbly, and Sinead continued, 'Major Petr Fedorovich Stukalin was last heard of by our people at Tyuratam in the USSR. Tyuratam is near Baikonur, the cosmodrome for the development of their spaceplane.'

'Spaceplane!' erupted O'Donnell. 'What the hell's a spaceplane?'

'We would call it a space shuttle. The Soviets call it a spaceplane.'

O'Donnell's face was a mask. Riley threw his head back and laughed.

'So it's a Soviet space shuttle we've got on our hands, and a cosmonaut,' breathed O'Donnell hoarsely.

'Yes. Stukalin is one of their best men, a top test pilot and engineer. The Soviet have been testing spaceplanes for some time. The first ones were small engineless one-man jobs which landed on water. But we've known for some time they've been experimenting with larger versions with atmosphere engines. That's a difficult exercise.'

'If he landed on water, it was probably one of the small earlier versions,' Riley interrupted.

'We don't think so.' Sinead moved to a seat and sat down. 'They've just built a long runway at Baikonur. If this craft was a spaceplane which came down in the wrong place, at this latitude it may have been heading for the runway. That means it was probably one of the latest ones with an engine and undercarriage. However, Stukalin undoubtedly flew the earlier versions and had learnt the technique of landing on water. That's most likely why he survived a ditching in the sea near here.'

Riley scratched his head. 'Wait a minute. You said that the shuttle or spaceplane, whatever you call it, showed up very small on radar. That must mean it was the small one.'

'Not necessarily.' A superior expression settled on her face. 'It simply means it had a small radar image. This is why the people in the States are so excited about this. They think it's a big spaceplane made of a material largely transparent to radar signals. That's what we want to know about.'

'Very useful in a war,' said O'Donnell. 'An almost invisible plane.'

'It's still invisible,' she complained. 'It's only valuable to us if we get our hands on it, or bits of it.' She leaned towards O'Donnell. 'To date, I've not been very impressed with your organization. Need I remind you that so far, all I've heard is a catalogue of disasters. Any bright ideas, either of you?'

Neither spoke.

'In that case, I'll float an idea. O'Donnell, you think that the Russian is heading for a rendezvous with friends offshore, yes?' O'Donnell nodded agreement. She continued.

'And you, Martin, have no ideas at all?'

'Now listen. I've just arrived at this goddamned place and have hardly had time to get used to the situation.'

She waved her dismissal of him and his sentence withered on his lips. O'Donnell allowed himself a brief smirk.

'Then I've an idea,' she lectured. 'Our Russian crash-landed. Must have done. Certainly didn't mean to land here. If we've had trouble in locating precisely where he landed, isn't it just possible that the Russians, who don't have nearby radar, may be having the same trouble. Even Stukalin's last radio message, which had to be made while still in the air, could only be accurate within a few miles. And if the fault was electrical, then no message may have been sent – right?'

'What are you getting at?' O'Donnell asked.

'I think that the only person on earth who knows precisely where the bloody thing landed is Stukalin,' asserted Sinead. 'Therefore Stukalin may do one of two things. One, he may head out into the Atlantic looking for a friendly face, or . . .'

'Or what?' growled the increasingly irritated Riley.

'Or he'll simply use the radio equipment on O'Donnell's boat to contact and fix a rendezvous – I could guess where that might be.' She looked very satisfied.

'Know this coast well, do you?' asked O'Donnell coldly.

'No. But I think I might know my man. He'll not easily abandon his command. By now he'll have talked to the Soviet navy or the fishing fleet. They'll have but one question for him and his answer will be very simple. Follow me, he'll tell them. Then he'll sail your boat over the sunken spaceplane and anchor. His friends will meet him at the crash site.'

The two men looked dumbfounded and they had no better idea. She had taken charge.

'Let's start searching the likely bays near here,' she ordered. 'We've little time. Satellite pictures have shown a small fleet of Russian ships converging on this spot. One of them is easily capable of lifting the plane from shallow depths. But our information is not up-to-date. This low cloud has stopped satellite coverage and we're not anxious to alarm the Russians with aircraft surveillance.'

'How much time do we have?' asked Riley.

'Hours. We must be searching by first light.'

'And if we find O'Donnell's boat?'

'Bring Sean's boat on its road trailer. And bring as many weapons as you can lay your hands on.'

'Wait a minute. I've remembered something.' O'Donnell was rubbing his forehead. 'Something Stukalin said to me. He told me he'd stolen things from a holiday caravan. That must be near where he reached the shore!'

'There must be dozens of caravans dotted round this coast, O'Donnell.' Sinead was back on the warpath.

'Stukalin burnt this one to cover his tracks. There aren't dozens of burnt-out caravans round here.'

Riley smiled. 'A phone call in the morning will take us straight to the spot. Good idea, Dick.'

O'Donnell glanced at Sinead who said nothing. It went through his mind that she was going to fight for the last drop of his blood. O'Donnell would work with her only because Riley was doing so.

'You'd better snatch some sleep, otherwise you'll be useless,' Sinead said to O'Donnell. 'More useless than you are now,' she added contemptuously.

Useless to whom, O'Donnell asked himself as he settled down on the couch. He remembered that on two occasions Stukalin could've killed him to achieve Russian aims. It crossed his mind that this woman might grant no such quarter. He resolved to keep a gun within easy reach when she was in his vicinity.

As he drifted into sleep, distantly he heard Riley ask her, 'Anything more on Faloon?'

'A rumour.'

'Good or bad?'

'Good. I heard that the Russians blew him up in a car. Now why do you think they did something so drastic?'

Riley chuckled. 'Getting too near, that would be my guess.'

There was a pause before Sinead spoke again. Her tone was silky, her words deliberate.

'Laugh, Martin, laugh. That was the good news. The bad news is that if the Russians can do that to G2 agent Faloon in his own backyard, they'll be waiting to do the same to us.'

It took O'Donnell a long time to fall asleep.

TWENTY THREE

Thick curtains had been pulled across the triple-glazed windows of KGB headquarters, shutting out the dying warmth of the late May evening in Moscow.

'We can pinpoint, with reasonable confidence, the small bay in which our spaceplane lies,' the T Director reported, feigning an offhand manner.

Bulgakov beamed and members of his committee spontaneously congratulated themselves on their own achievements.

'I am happy to further report, chairman, that we have every reason to believe that Faloon is dead.'

Bulgakov's smile died. 'That could mean you've some reasons not to believe he is dead. Am I correct?'

The T Director's words tumbled over themselves. 'Losev has reported booby-trapping Faloon's car after a gun-battle during which Faloon had retreated . . .'

'Escaped, you mean,' chipped in Zotov, ever ready to be identified with the winning side. He received a glare from Bulgakov for his pains and the T director continued, nervously.

'Faloon then ambushed Losev and left him for dead. When he recovered consciousness, it was daylight and Faloon's car was in pieces, blown apart by Losev's device. In spite of his injuries, Losev was able to report by telephone to our Dublin embassy.'

He paused and the KGB chief continued his line of questioning. 'Did Losev report seeing a body?'

'No sir. Losev collapsed some distance from the remains of the vehicle. Before he could get any nearer, a local farmer had picked him up and brought him to a doctor.'

Silence ensued. When tension seemed at breaking point, the chairman spoke again. 'I can only ask for the best from our operatives. Losev was never trained for this type of work. I would like to meet him to express personal appreciation.' He stopped speaking for a moment and leaned back in his chair, savouring the abrupt way he could change the mood of the meeting.

Zotov thought that if Losev were given the choice between meeting the KGB chief or Faloon again, he'd go for the latter. Zotov was relaxed. He had watched Bulgakov at play before, just as he watched him now. Like Zotov, the T Director was accustomed to Bulgakov's methods. He looked at the floor, emotionally exhausted, but knowing that the boss had decided to call off the dogs for the time being.

'I don't know what devious game the Irish are playing,' Bulgakov speculated as he fingered a transcript of Losev's report. 'Losev saw Faloon handling the pressure suit and the remains of the automatic distress buoy. Grundy and G2 must now know to within a few hundred metres where our plane landed. Why isn't the bay thick with that diminutive nation's diminutive navy?'

The question was not rhetorical and Bulgakov looked about him for answers. There was a cough from the bottom of the table and an attempted answer.

'Unless Grundy got no report. Perhaps Faloon really is dead after all and the Irish are covering it up, like the way they're distorting the real reason for the helicopter crash.'

The T Director brightened visibly and the KBG chief scratched his chin as he spoke. 'But why? Too many questions, too few answers. I smell a rat.' Everybody nodded, because if the Chairman of the Committee for State Security smelt a rat, they all smelt a rat.

The mood changed again when Zotov spoke. 'If that was the bad news, chairman, may I be permitted to reveal some good news?' The KGB chief nodded his assent to the science and technology chairman. 'Western countries license their private citizens to own and operate radio transmitters and receivers. In the British Isles, these people are referred to as hams.'

There was a ripple of laughter because Zotov, translating literally, was talking about pieces of cured pig meat.

He ignored his colleagues. 'We, of course, do not permit unregulated transmissions, but we have found it expedient to operate some of these sets. They're considerably more powerful than their western private counterparts and from time to time, we indulge in amiable light conversation with westerners.'

'Oh do come to the point, my dear comrade,' interrupted Bulgakov, ostentatiously looking at his watch. The KGB knew all about these transmitters. The fact that Zotov was responsible for them was a cover for the true purpose of many of them.

'The purpose, of course, is to maintain an emergency channel of communication for your agents in the field,' Zotov said, peering mournfully at Bulgakov. 'A constant watch is kept on the amateur frequencies.' He stopped momentarily, partly to sip from the glass of water before him, partly to irritate the chairman.

'Early this morning, we received a voice transmission which included the cypher identification of a military operative. It was not an identification in current use. It was once that of Petr Fedorovich Stukalin – in Afghanistan.'

An avalanche of questions, expressions of relief, belief and disbelief poured from those who had not had previously known of this development. With a wave of his hand, the chairman restored order to hear more from Zotov.

'The person broadcasting spoke in English, said his name was Smith and made a good pretence of talking about the weather and scenery. Between such sentences, the cypher number was inserted several times, disguised first as distances, then as part of a telephone number which does not exist. Also included were the pet names of his wife, his dog, and above all, the slang name of the spaceplane. At Tyuratam it's called the Boomerang.'

Bulgakov sniffed. Zotov concluded his report with the fact that Stukalin's wife and colleagues all believed the voice on the recording to be that of Stukalin.

'Other than identification, was there any other message?' came the shouted question from a person who, in ordinary circumstances, would hardly have dared whisper in the presence of Bulgakov.

'We think so. He said he was going sea-fishing over a wreck where he knew there would be a good catch, that he was expecting friends in other boats to meet him soon and that he would be listening out on VHF, which is a short-wave close-range frequency very commonly used for marine communication.'

It was good news, but it was clear that the KGB chairman was not yet convinced that the amateur-band transmission was genuine. He suspected a trap aimed at provoking Moscow into revealing either what it knew, or more damaging, what it didn't know about Stukalin's craft.

'What do we do now?' someone asked.

The chairman answered the question with another, which he directed at Zotov. 'How long will it take the *Pericles* and its support to reach that bay?'

'About twenty hours for the *Pericles*, less if the bad weather moderates and the satellites say it won't,' Zotov answered confidently. 'But the support should be on station within hours.'

Bulgakov nodded. In spite of his reservations, he had no option but to accept the broadcast for the moment. 'So we should expect a fishing boat to be in the bay when you reach it. Stukalin may be on board, and may be a prisoner. Remember, the last we heard was that he was in the hands of the Provisional IRA. Those people may want to strike a deal of some kind.'

'Do we bargain?' the T Director asked.

'We'll wait and see,' Zotov said ominously.

Bulgakov gave voice to his misgivings. 'Alternatively, the whole thing may be a set-up. I'm being asked to believe that Stukalin escaped, that he gained access to an amateur radio transmitter, that Faloon is dead, and that the Irish and therefore the Americans don't know where the plane lies.' He paused to stroke his long nose. 'All of that could be true, but improbable. I've therefore arranged some unpleasant surprises for anybody trying to spring a trap, be they the IRA or the Americans or their Irish clients. Or the British.'

A junior representative of the Defence ministry, sent to the meeting merely to report, could no longer contain his curiosity. To him, the KGB chief did not seem to be making complete sense and he was afraid that his report might reflect his incomprehension.

'Forgive me, sir, but what is the *Pericles*? I cannot find it in our lists.'

Bulgakov laughed and began collecting his papers together. As he rose from the head of the table he replied, 'Talk to your superiors, young man. And I applaud your alertness. Let's just say for now that if you can't find the *Pericles*, it may take our enemies precious time to do so.' He made for the exit.

Halfway through the double doors he stopped and addressed a final order to the head of T Directorate. 'I don't care if the foul weather means clipping the fuchsia, tell the Aeroflot pilots to get us pictures of any boat heading for that bay.'

As he disappeared down the corridor he didn't hear the T Director asking colleagues, 'What the hell is fuchsia?'

'I think I'll go for a walk,' Nuala murmured in a small voice, as if she did not wish to be heard.

Faloon looked out of the window. The rain was still falling gently but it was not lashing against the window-panes of Sergeant Higgins' house as it had earlier in the day.

The sergeant and his wife were both out, so the house was silent as Faloon looked past the fuchsia growing wild against the low wall of Higgins's garden. The whisper of the wind past the sharp corners of the house was a fitting accompaniment to his bleak thoughts.

'Am I being a traitor, Nuala?'

Nuala was astonished. She was sitting on the carpet in the middle of the furniture, looking at the smoke of the peat fire curling up the chimney. She turned towards the window to face Faloon.

'I've never heard you say anything like that before.'

Faloon stuck his hands deeply into his pockets. 'Grundy won't talk to me. No one in G2 will talk to me. I've become a leper and I'm not sure why this is happening.'

'Grundy was pretty sore about the code chip you lost,' said Nuala. 'You can be sure the Foreign Affairs people, led by the Minister whose office I should be in right now, is emptying a ton of shit on his head for that reason alone. Add to that the combined diplomatic pressure from the British, the Russians and the Americans all trying to get their hands on that machine out there.'

Nuala waited in vain for some sympathetic reaction from her man. 'Has it struck you,' she went on, 'that Grundy and the Foreign Affairs Department in Dublin may not know why all this pressure is happening? They may still think it's all about a helicopter crash, poor bastards. No wonder they haven't the time or the inclination to talk to you.'

Faloon didn't turn from the window as he answered. 'Your boss, the high and mighty Minister for Foreign Affairs may be trying to get Grundy fired, or me fired – or both of us,' Faloon thought aloud.

'So why are you staying here, ex-agent Faloon? Answer that question for yourself,' Nuala quizzed gently.

Faloon took a deep breath. 'Because I hate the Provos and I think the Russian is in their hands. I hate the prospect of what the Provos might try to buy using him or his knowledge as currency. They would buy a greater capacity to kill people I want alive, to destroy things I want preserved.'

Nuala suddenly repeated, 'I think I'll go for a walk.'

Faloon turned to the window again and wiped an area of glass free from condensation. 'You'll be soaked on the way to the crossroads.'

'Then I'll go the other way, under the big trees.'

'No, Nuala, I don't think you'll go the other way. The telephone box is at the crossroads and that's what you need, isn't it, my dear Nuala? A private word with someone, perhaps the person who gave you the gun and trained you to fire it.' He turned to face her. 'Who will you be phoning? Who's your secret control?'

'I told you to put that question to Grundy before anyone else. I won't answer.'

A mist of helplessness swept over Faloon. 'And I'm isolated from Grundy. Very convenient! I'm feeling very alone, very exposed. When this is all over, I will be judged by people swaddled in a protective coat of hindsight.'

'Follow your instincts, Faloon.'

Faloon's eyes were once more roaming the wet landscape beyond the house. 'My instincts have been shaped by this place. By the sea, the hills, the heather, the sand.'

'And by the people, Faloon. Don't forget them. The good, the bad and people like yourself.'

Faloon laughed out loud and Nuala knew she had helped Faloon over a crisis of confidence, just as she'd done before.

He walked over to her and knelt beside her. 'If you stop talking about the people, I'll stop talking about patriotism.'

'But scoundrels like you need a last refuge.'

'If I walked into a Buncrana pub and told the drinking classes that a Russian space shuttle had landed outside, that the IRA had grabbed the spaceman, that the superpowers were locked in a secret cut-throat undercover race to snatch the spacecraft and that the country's leaders wouldn't listen to me, what would their reaction be?'

'The drinking classes would elect you their leader.'

Faloon leaned over, and gently kissed her on the forehead. 'I trust you, Nuala, so I'll go for a walk. You can use the phone here in the warmth. The rain's lifting; soon we'll be able to return to that bay, this time with scuba equipment. When I'm finished, the unbelievers will have evidence they can't refute. Tell that to your friend on the phone.'

Fine words, but Faloon couldn't help but wonder who was keeping the Provos one step ahead all the time.

If it was Nuala, then she could give her intelligence, telling them where the Russian craft was located. A secret that big would leak from the Provos to G2. It was just a more messy and time-consuming way of getting through to Grundy.

TWENTY FOUR

Low grey clouds over grey waves. Light rain fell ceaselessly, melting the horizon into seamless sea and sky.

The fishing boat chugged into the bay as if to escape the unpleasant weather, except that she didn't anchor. Instead she sailed in a search pattern for several hours, sweeping the bottom of the bay with her depth sounder. When Stukalin found what he was looking for, he secured his new command at a precise point, using two anchors, fore and aft. That way, the boat would swing to neither tide nor wind. She would stay exactly on station.

In doing so Stukalin fulfilled a commitment made to Moscow over one of the boat's powerful transmitters. He was also fulfilling the prediction of Martin Riley's woman, Sinead.

Stukalin knew that there was an outside chance that O'Donnell might rally his forces and come after him, but he had carefully led O'Donnell to believe that he would sail north to meet eastern European fishing vessels. If O'Donnell had agreed to Stukalin's proposed deal, that was what would have happened.

The decisive factor in Stukalin's decision to return to the point where his craft had ditched had been the IRA boat's unusually good electronic equipment – sonar, several different radio transmitters and a radar set, which wasn't working.

Stukalin had been unsure whether the sonar would locate the spaceplane until the echo showed up so sharply, exactly where it should. If the special fuselage was transparent to radar, would it also be transparent to sonar pulses, he had wondered?

The American space shuttle had a conventional metal fuselage covered with silica tiles to prevent it melting. Soviet engineers had adopted a different solution to the problem of extreme heat of re-entry. They had developed a light, extremely strong flexible heat-resistant ceramic, and built most of the entire airframe with it.

It was a radar-transparent material the West didn't possess. Stukalin wanted things to remain that way. As he waited for help from the Soviet navy, speeding towards him, he thought that if he ever met O'Donnell and Moira again, he should thank them. By capturing him they had effectively screened his existence from the Irish authorities.

In a manner of speaking, he was an invisible pilot from an invisible plane in an almost invisible boat. Only the Provos knew the boat existed, and they would scarcely be reporting its theft to the local constabulary.

Stukalin's race was against time. The longer he stayed in the bay, the greater the chance of a Provo sympathizer giving the boat's position to O'Donnell and friends. Furthermore, reporting the Irish authorities would be piecing together the crashed helicopter. Soon there would be a hue and cry to find what had hit it midair and brought it down.

The spaceplane had been in its death throes. He didn't have sufficient manoeuvrability to avoid collision. Stukalin absolved himself.

If O'Donnell turned up, he had one slight advantage. He had a hostage in Moira whom O'Donnell cared for and that might yet be useful. Stukalin had made her sit right up in the bow where he could see her. He knew she would not dive overboard. And she was useful when it came to anchoring.

Moira was very wet. 'What are we waiting for?' she yelled back at the wheelhouse.

'Friends of mine in the Soviet navy.'

'How long? I'm cold.'

'Three or four hours, I expect. But I'm not asking. The less I transmit the better.'

'What'll happen to me?'

'You'll catch pneumonia.'

'I mean you can't leave me here alone. I can't swim. I'm afraid of water and I don't like boats.'

'You could always defect. Why don't you come with me?'

'Stop teasing me, Major. Couldn't your navy people leave me ashore?'

'I don't think so. They're going to be very busy and they'll need to turn round fast.'

Then it happened. Too fast for a wounded Stukalin to prevent. He had left the wheelhouse so as to hear what Moira was saying. Not for the first time had he been enticed and diverted. A face appeared, peeping just over the edge of the bulwark. Alongside the face was the folding stock of a machine pistol, aimed at Stukalin's head. The man was Martin Riley. He was standing on Sean's inflatable boat alongside the hull.

Within a split second, a figure came from round behind the wheelhouse. It was O'Donnell, with an automatic also pointed at Stukalin.

'Stay still, Stukalin. Don't move a muscle or one of us will get you.'

Moira scrambled aft and almost hit Sinead climbing aboard. Sinead pushed her roughly aside. For a few seconds nobody moved.

Stukalin visibly sagged. 'How did you know where to find me, O'Donnell?'

'He didn't, but I did, Major Stukalin, cosmonaut from Tyuratam.' Sinead was peeling off sodden outer garments and settling herself on the seat in front of Stukalin. 'I know a lot about you and where you came from.'

'Americans? Are you Americans!' His astonishment was evident. He looked at O'Donnell. 'Who are these people, O'Donnell?'

But again it was Sinead who replied. 'We are the people who've bought you, Major Stukalin. You and your space vehicle on the seabed below us.'

Stukalin gasped. He was neither a trained spy nor an actor and the impact of Sinead's words was written all over him. Every position, every assumption upon which he had based his strategy had been torn to shreds in a single sentence.

The cosmonaut made an effort to pull himself together. 'I must warn you that my government will take the most serious view if there is interference with a salvage operation already under way. Are you sure your government knows what you're doing? Any attempt to interfere with my craft . . .'

'Shut up,' Sinead screamed. And then she added quietly, 'O'Donnell, get that woman of yours to make me some hot coffee or soup. I'm soaked through. I never want to get into another boat in my life.'

O'Donnell stared poisonously at Sinead before breaking off to go to Moira and hug her. Sinead had never taken her eyes from Stukalin, and was either unaware of or oblivious to O'Donnell's anger.

'We haven't much time, have we, Major?' Sinead said. 'But how much time? When will the Soviet navy turn up, Major?'

'I don't know what you are talking about,' he said.

260

'OK,' she grinned. 'Then the "salvage operation" you want me to keep away from – when is it due to begin?'

No response.

Slowly and almost casually, as if leaning forward to stub out a cigarette, Sinead pointed her gun between Stukalin's feet and pulled the trigger.

The Russian jolted and slid along the deck away from her.

The effect on Riley and O'Donnell was much the same.

'For fuck's sake, Martin, control your bloody woman. Take that gun away from her before she drills holes in the hull,' roared O'Donnell.

'O'Donnell, you're full of shit,' she snarled. 'If you'd had any balls I wouldn't be getting your boat back for you. Your part in this show is over, O'Donnell. Go and be sick if you can't stand the sight of blood.'

She turned back to Stukalin. 'You should know, Stukalin, I don't make idle threats. If you don't tell me how much time I've got before your friends arrive, I'll empty this magazine slowly into your kneecap. Then I'll start on your other kneecap and you'll never walk unaided again. You'll never fly again.'

'A matter of hours,' Stukalin hissed. He was breathing heavily and formed his words with difficulty.

'I said how long, Stukalin? I'm not a patient person.'

'I can't tell precisely. I had no contact with the ships, only with Moscow. I was ordered not to transmit any further messages.'

'That's right.' Moira had reappeared with the coffee Sinead had demanded, along with a mug for Stukalin. She now interceded on his behalf. 'I heard him make only one call on the radio, and he told me before you arrived that he had to wait here without transmitting.'

Fleetingly Sinead looked like a child whose teddy bear had been snatched away. 'You'd better be right, both of you, because if the Red navy turns up too soon, we'll have to rely on Stukalin as our only ticket out of the shit. Next time I won't be shooting to make him dance.'

She withdrew to the wheelhouse, where Martin Riley joined her. 'Get the air bottles out of the dinghy for O'Donnell,' she said quietly, pulling a package from a bag she had brought on board.

'O'Donnell,' she bellowed. 'here's a chance to redeem yourself. This is a waterproofed underwater camera with a powerful flash. It's completely automatic. Just point it and shoot. Maximum range about two metres, less if the water's dirty. Have you got that?'

'I won't be able to get the whole thing into the picture from two metres, will I?'

'Hardly,' she said condescendingly. 'Our customers want specific shots. Get shots of the nose and, if you can, the underside. That's where the main heatshield is located. Get multiple shots of the instrument panel and controls. The hatch that Stukalin escaped through will probably still be open. Get several shots of the edge of it. That'll give a cross-section through the skin.'

She dived into a bag and pulled out a short, vivid yellow ruler. 'And here, put this beside everything you shoot, but don't let it obliterate anything unique. It'll give scale.'

'How many shots on the camera? How do I wind on?' O'Donnell asked.

'It's really an ordinary 35mm camera with a motor drive. It will wind on automatically. You have 150 exposures. Any other questions?'

'Yes, madam, I have,' he answered aggressively. 'What is the benefit in this for the Republican Movement? I've heard nothing about the deal.'

'Martin,' she raised her voice again. He returned carrying O'Donnell's air bottles. 'Sort this man out. He's asking what's in it for him.'

O'Donnell turned to Riley to explain. 'Not for me. For the movement, Martin. Why am I doing this? I'd expected to be brought into the details of any deal, because I'm certainly not doing it for that bitch.'

'Not now, Dick, not now. Take it from me that the deal is a good one. Let's go.'

'Whatever the Americans have offered, we will top it,' Stukalin interjected. 'And to get what you want, you simply do nothing, nothing at all except keep me safe until my colleagues arrive.'

Sinead laughed. 'Don't be ridiculous, Stukalin. Your ships won't have what we want, and once the spacecraft leaves here, we'll have nothing to bargain with.'

'We could get something out of the Russians,' O'Donnell said. He was vacillating between wanting to impress Sinead and wanting to kill her. 'We can sell the photos to the Americans, and sell Stukalin to his own navy when it arrives. They'll have something we want. Shoulder-fired missile launchers and ammunition.'

Riley and Sinead looked at each other.

'Nothing,' Sinead emphasized, 'but nothing must stand in the way of the American deal. We can buy all you want with the American deal.'

Stukalin looked meaningfully at O'Donnell and shook his head. 'Don't believe her, O'Donnell. Once you get the photographs, she'll have no interest in what you want. One thing's certain. If you clash with the Soviet navy it'll smash you into little pieces. You're being used.'

'You may be right, Stukalin, but my suggestions may stop that trigger-happy American woman shooting you dead. Have you thought of that?'

Sinead smiled. She had impressed precisely the way she wanted to impress.

O'Donnell began to prepare. He peeled off his outer overalls to reveal that he was already wearing a wet-suit. Riley helped him strap on the bottles, a belt and a latex helmet. A mask and fins completed his outfit, except for the camera. Sinead clipped it to his belt with a lanyard. The ruler was tucked into the belt.

'Good luck,' said Sinead, as O'Donnell climbed down into the dinghy.

O'Donnell looked at her coldly. 'Why don't you come with me, Sinead?'

'Don't think I wouldn't, O'Donnell, but we don't have a second set of bottles.'

'I know. That's why I asked.'

Those words were the last the two of them would ever exchange. He lowered himself out of their lives into fifteen metres of water.

O'Donnell had forgotten what pleasure diving had given him years ago.

With strong strokes he pulled himself down towards the bottom and the familiar fronds of kelp wafting slowly in the current. He remembered that these giant seaweeds, with their closely-packed leaves up to three metres long, could hide even a substantial boat like his own from sight.

His first priority was to establish a base point from which he could orientate a search. Any prominent feature on the bottom would suffice. Stukalin's craft must be very near, perhaps in a large cleft in the rocks. Spinning himself around in a full circle, he saw in the murky distance a pinnacle of rock reaching out of the seaweed. That would be his start-point.

He swam towards the rock and, as he did so, his heart began to pump. Something about the rock was not right. It was a uniform grey, different from all surrounding features – and, except for its summit, much too smooth.

A patch of red betrayed the true nature of the object. It was the bottom half of a five-pointed red star on a tail fin. A jagged edge marked where the top of the fin had been torn off. The rest of the fuselage was indistinct, its outline masked by seaweed. It appeared to be lying in a natural trench where the sand of the beach began to tumble towards the deeper sea bottom.

O'Donnell was engrossed in his find. All his experience underwater had led him to believe that the search for the spaceplane might take longer than his American friends thought. And here he was, looking down on the machine that half the world was looking for. His heart raced.

But he had no time to lose. Many of the pictures Sinead had demanded, like ones of the underside, were not possible. The spaceplane was sitting the right way up and the infernal kelp got in the way of everything. The wing interested him. One had lost its tip. The end of the other was angled upwards, so he began with pictures of that. The lanyard attaching the camera to his belt persistently floated in front of the lens so he unclipped it.

Was this what all the fuss was about? O'Donnell asked himself. The machine looked very much like any other plane, except for an odd surface. It felt unusual.

The open hatch! That was where Stukalin had emerged to safety. Another photograph. Each flash revealed to O'Donnell for a split second the full colours in the monochrome world about him.

He was puzzled at the cables entwining the machine. At first he thought they were a species of seaweed, of which there were many. There must be a trawler wreck nearby. Flash after flash revealed detail upon detail.

The flashes also revealed O'Donnell.

* * *

He looked at the counter. Seventy exposures already. Was there anything else he should shoot? Not really. Time to leave. The bitch Sinead would probably throw a tantrum because he hadn't exposed the whole film.

The prospect of annoying her pleased him. Another reason for stopping, if he needed one. He turned into the forest of kelp in the direction of his boat's anchor chain.

There was never a chance that he would see the four shadowy frogmen who emerged from the hidden lip of the trench. Their breathing apparatus released no tell-tale bubbles, unlike O'Donnell's. Their equipment included yellow helmets with integral facemasks. Two of them carried harpoon guns. Another a coil of rope.

The frogmen armed with the harpoon guns led the group towards O'Donnell's back. One of the harpoonists and the figure with the rope broke off to take up a position three metres above O'Donnell's head. The unarmed man stopped behind O'Donnell. The second harpoonist made a final check that his colleagues were in position.

Then he moved slowly and deliberately into O'Donnell's field of vision, the harpoon aimed at the Provo's chest.

O'Donnell's limbs froze. In his shock he opened his mouth and tried to shout. His mouthpiece fell away and when he could not breathe, he panicked, dropping the camera. The kelp swallowed it up.

In disciplined formation, the frogmen fell upon O'Donnell as he began a desperate thrash towards the surface. In his frenzy for air, the threat of the harpoons was eclipsed. Strong arms gripped him, stifling his death throes. O'Donnell knew he was only seconds from the fatal act to trying to breathe water. The beginning of the drowning process.

Then the miracle.

His mouthpiece was being pressed against his lips. He almost ate it, gasping at its lifegiving air. While he was still coming back from the dead, a rope was tied firmly round one of his ankles. Suddenly his arms were released and involuntarily his hands shot to the mouthpiece, holding it firmly in place.

Only then did the panic decrease, but his captors gave him little time to recover his composure. The sharp barbed point of one of the harpoons was speared into the small of his back. O'Donnell spun round to see one frogman urging him to move.

He had no alternative. Another frogman had him tethered. He began swimming, following one man while the others took up station round him, like motorcycle outriders. They were leading him away from the spaceplane into the extension of the trench where another surprise awaited him.

At first he was unable to recognize what he was looking at. His first guess was some kind of storage tank. It was a long large-diameter tube with several bright yellow bands of colour.

Then he picked out details which helped him identify the object. A shrouded propeller; then a small conning tower. O'Donnell was looking at a miniature submarine.

Rails were fixed along the length of the hull and O'Donnell was tied to them with the rope stretching from his ankle. He began to wonder if he was to be the victim of a bizarre execution by his mysterious captors, except that they themselves gripped the rails alongside him. The handle of the harpoon was banged on the hull and the submarine gently floated clear of the seabed.

O'Donnell searched his memory. He had never seen a vessel like this in his life, but it seemed familiar.

Then it came to him. He had seen it in his dentist's waiting room, an old *National Geographic* magazine. What was the article? . . . deep-sea research off California. That was it . . . A bathyscaphe! He was tied to a bathyscaphe.

Fear gave way to a blinding and helpless anger within O'Donnell. The Americans! This was the double-cross. That harridan harpy Sinead! There wasn't going to be any payment to the Provos. The United States had already located the spacecraft, probably through his own efforts, as spied on by Sinead, with Riley as her dupe or partner. Sinead had sent O'Donnell into the water merely to separate him from Stukalin and to neutralize him. They had got the plane below and the cosmonaut above. Everything for nothing.

He was almost rigid with rage as the submarine hauled him away from the spaceplane. He remembered words from Sinead, telling him that his part in all this was over; words from Stukalin, telling him he was being used. He had been too tired to think clearly back in Sean's house. Sinead had known too much – far too much to be a simple messenger. She was an official ruthless arm of Uncle Sam and he had ended up as her prisoner.

TWENTY FIVE

'One miserable boat.'

Faloon was disappointed and perplexed. He had stopped the car at a point affording a view of the misty bay below. 'Frankly I was expecting a marine traffic jam in this bay by now.' Nagging doubts returned as he ended his survey of the placid seascape and passed the binoculars to Nuala.

'Probably just sheltering,' Nuala said, trying to wipe the lens free from water with the tip of a headscarf.

'I thought your telephone call would stir up a hornets' nest,' he said, looking intently at Nuala. Nuala stared steadfastly out to sea, her face expressionless, so Faloon persisted with his line of enquiry. 'Why isn't there one of our minesweepers out there? Why isn't the army smothering the beach? Why aren't the police blocking the roads? Why haven't I been arrested, if only for questioning?'

Nuala ignored him.

Faloon reached over gently and cupped her chin in his hand. He turned her head towards his. 'What are you trying to tell me, Nuala? All this peacefulness is driving me insane!'

'I'm trying to tell you we are still on our own,' she sighed.

It was Faloon's turn to say nothing. He reached for the binoculars and put them to his eyes. He cursed his profession, or was it the profession of both of them? Nuala could be telling the truth or she could be lying. He hadn't time to find out.

Faloon adjusted the focus. 'Not much sign of life on the fishing boat. Whoever he is, he's a belt-and-braces man. Got an anchor both fore and aft. It won't move no matter how high the wind gets. That could be useful.'

With that, Faloon cast an eye over scuba equipment in the back of the car. He had borrowed it from the police diving club – yet again through the good offices of Sergeant Higgins.

Faloon knew he was beginning to stretch the sergeant's friendship to the very limit. Faloon had promised him that if this final thrust was successful, the host of outsider policemen and troops, which were destroying Higgin's quality of life, would be speedily withdrawn.

But such promises from Faloon were beginning to wear thin.

When the sergeant had reported locating the tail pylon, the last vital part of the wrecked helicopter, a small army descended on the McLaverty farm. The hapless McLaverty family had been arrested and taken from their beloved forest of windmills for intensive interrogation, much to the embarrassment of the local police. Sergeant Higgins's reputation among his own people nose-dived, because the idiosyncratic McLaverty family were liked. The little community was even proud of the McLavertys. The final straw for Higgins in this matter had been a public compliment from visiting senior officers for his 'patient and painstaking police work'.

His life was further complicated by having to deal with the 'Swedish tourist' who had demolished a car which appeared to belong to a senior woman civil servant in Dublin who could not be contacted. Higgins had sought out the most lethargic, torpid and thick policeman and put him in sole charge of that investigation.

But what really annoyed, even embittered, Sergeant Higgins, was the reaction when he put Faloon's proposition that the helicopter had been struck by a space shuttle.

Senior *Garda* officers were embarrassed and offered Higgins some leave to get over the excitement. One of his brother officers reduced the small police station canteen to tears by parading among the tables with a clear plastic salad bowl over his head, droning a monotonous 'Leprechaun, take-me-to-your-leader.'

So it was a hostile, injured Higgins who was pressed into producing scuba gear for Faloon and Nuala. He eventually assisted the pair only because he secretly hoped that helping move Faloon's operations into the sea would reduce the mayhem on land.

But Faloon couldn't hire a boat. Local boatmen who knew Faloon refused because they knew Faloon. Those who did not know Faloon refused to hire boats to anyone when the weather closed in. So he had no boat.

'How could that fishing boat be useful?' snapped Nuala. 'It's out in the middle of the bloody bay.'

'If we go to the mouth of the bay, it's within swimming distance,' said Faloon enthusiastically. 'Especially with airbottles, wetsuits and snorkels. We'll ask the fisherman if we could use his boat while it's at anchor, as a base for diving on an old wreck.'

'They won't buy that story. Not in this weather. What's more, all serious divers have their own boat. Anyway, Stukalin's machine could be anywhere on the seabed.'

But Faloon's optimism was irrepressible. 'Mark my words, Nuala, that spacecraft is more likely to be in the middle of the bay, perhaps even right underneath that boat. If it had been in shallower water nearer the edge, the chances are that one of the searching aircraft looking for helicopter pieces would've seen it in sunlight.'

'If we swim out we could be swept away on the tide, Faloon, and the next stop is Iceland. It's a daft idea.'

Faloon's answer was to start the car and begin driving along a grassy track to the nearest point of land to the anchored fishing boat. The boat and the hills beyond faded temporarily from vision as another squall descended. It was not inviting weather for a swim, wetsuits or no wetsuits.

'It's just coming up to slack tide, Nuala. When it turns later, it'll be pushing us towards land.'

'You appear to have thought of everything, haven't you?' she replied morosely.

He had not.

From on board the fishing boat, the weather had hidden the movement of the car and the entry of two more divers into the waters of the bay. Using their snorkels to conserve the airbottles, Faloon and Nuala struck out on the surface for the fishing boat. Even in good light they would have been difficult to see in the choppy waves.

On the fishing boat, Martin Riley had stood for a while on the wet deck, waiting for O'Donnell to surface, but in the end had retreated into the cabin to escape the relentless rain. He was also apprehensive about leaving Sinead alone with Stukalin. He quietly shared O'Donnell's fear that she might shoot Stukalin if he annoyed her. Anyway, he was curious about what the Russian had to say about his spaceplane and why it landed in Ireland.

So when Faloon and Nuala reached the boat, there was no one on deck. Faloon wondered how he was going to climb the hull to get on board, and then he saw the dinghy Riley and his party had used. It had been tied to a point near the bow, on the side away from the shore.

Faloon and Nuala gratefully pulled themselves into it. From there they could reach the deck.

'Why don't you let me do the talking this time, Faloon?' suggested Nuala, fighting to get her breath back. 'Let's face it, to date your efforts to negotiate the use of a boat have failed miserably. You lack the negotiator's light touch.'

He grinned at her, while sitting on the dinghy bottom pulling the fins off his feet. 'Alright, but you'd better take your fins off too. The poor bugger is going to get a bad enough fright when you appear. You don't want him to think you're a mermaid from an oil slick.'

She took them off. 'I couldn't get on deck wearing them anyway, Mr Clever.'

With that, she nimbly heaved herself from the dinghy onto the deserted deck. 'Come on, Faloon. It's like the *Mary Ce-*

leste up here. Gives me the shivers.'

He joined her. They both unbuckled their airbottles and set them carefully on coils of rope on the foredeck. The wheelhouse was deserted.

We both must still look an odd pair, thought Faloon, as he watched Nuala's lithe figure, sensuous in its skintight wetsuit, incongruously topped with a face-mask pushed up to her forehead, making its way to the wheelhouse door.

'Ahoy there,' she shouted, trying to be nautical. 'Anyone at home?'

The effect of her shout on those below was electric.

Riley stood bolt upright, hit his head on a beam and said 'Fuck.' Sinead was equally startled, but pulled herself together faster.

'Hide the guns. Keep them handy. I'll deal with this.' She grabbed Stukalin by the throat. 'I don't need to threaten you, do I?' Without waiting for an answer, she sprang into the wheelhouse and out on deck.

Sinead was both amazed and dismayed to see a woman in a diving suit outside the wheelhouse. She was aware of the second diver further down the deck, but retained her main attention for the figure nearer herself.

'What do you want?'

Nuala had been hoping for a warmer greeting. 'We're underwater archaeologists. Could we use your boat as a diving base for an hour or two, if you're staying here, that is?'

Sinead never answered that question. Her first words had had an astounding effect on Faloon. As Nuala spoke, he had bounded along the deck until he was directly in front of the woman.

His mouth opened and closed wordlessly. He could feel the blood draining from his face. His heart pounded and choked on an intake of breath. He knew the woman before him. Sinead look at him, at first quizzically, then with deepening disbelief. With his head covered mostly in a wetsuit helmet and his face pulled slightly out of shape by the tension of the face mask, she did not immediately know who she was glowering at. But she knew the frogman had instantly recognized her.

Nuala was transfixed by Faloon's behaviour, and by that of the woman. Faloon was shaking, his arms were open wide, ready to embrace the woman. But the woman was backing away, just as shocked as Faloon, but repelled by him. 'Sarah . . . my God, Sarah,' Faloon finally stuttered and the veil fell from Nuala's eyes.

And Sinead's eyes.

But not from Faloon's. The woman looked every bit as shocked as Faloon. 'You're dead,' she said hoarsely. Faloon lurched towards her, his arms still outstretched. She backed further away.

Suddenly the woman screamed, 'He's alive, Martin. Faloon's alive . . . '

Faloon stopped trying to reach Sarah. He was shattered. 'Sarah. Please Sarah. It's me.' In the turmoil of his mind he could not accept Sarah's reaction at its face value. Not until Martin Riley appeared with a gun.

Faloon was in turmoil. Nuala's eyes widened at the gun and she began to understand a little of what was happening to Faloon. They had stumbled into the middle of their adversary's camp.

Faloon was finding it hard to collect his wits. 'Are you still in his hands, Sarah?' he asked incredulously.

'No, Faloon,' she replied, a slight smile playing on her lips. Now that Riley was beside her, her composure was recovering fast. 'If anything, it's the other way about.'

Martin Riley spoke for the first time. 'You're speaking to my wife, Faloon. You and the rest of the world know her as Sarah. To me she is Sinead.'

Faloon was having to cope with the complete inversion of his perceptions. Sarah as his enemy. And the friend of the Green Boys.

His expression changed from shock to horror as the ramifications sank home. 'You! You were the Green Boy source inside the FBI. You set me up, betrayed me, betrayed all of us. And that video, the electrodes, that was . . . '

In his emotion and bitterness, words failed him. Sarah completed the sentence. ' . . . play-acting. I played my Sarah part very well. Even had you believing the electricity was switched on.' She began to smile. 'Still watching horny videos, Faloon?' Sarah and Martin both laughed.

'I thought you were dead, thought I'd let Riley kill you,' said Faloon almost in a whisper.

'And I thought you were dead,' rasped Sarah. 'The Russians think they blew you up somewhere near here. And the FBI believed it because you'd stopped calling our computer. And you hadn't even tried to get into G2's computer, so we were all certain the Russians had finished you.'

'Are you still in the FBI?'

'She escaped, didn't she,' Riley mocked.

'Oh yes. I escaped, didn't I.' She went on, 'bringing out with me the intelligence that the IRA had got hold of a Russian pilot.'

'So she was given a free hand,' added Riley, unable to hide his glee, 'to see what she could produce.'

'No direct involvement by the American government,' she crowed, plainly pleased with herself. 'It's damn near foolproof, and damn near at an end.' She looked over the surface of the sea for O'Donnell.

And the final bit of salt into Faloon's wound. 'Poor Faloon. The FBI knew you were the G2 agent most likely to be rostered to this Russian business. They decided to let you leave with their chip and to use it to monitor your progress.' Faloon listened, both fascinated and devastated to hear confirmation of his suspicions.

There was a noise behind Riley. He whipped round. Sinead's smile disappeared and her gun hand kept a steady aim in the direction of Faloon and Nuala.

'Stukalin!' exclaimed Riley and they both relaxed. 'Come on out. Let me introduce Faloon, member of Ireland's fearless G2. Try not to shake in your shoes, Major Stukalin.'

Faloon raised his eyes to meet those of Stukalin. He saw the glint in them. Stukalin had been subdued but not defeated. Faloon nodded. The Russian nodded impassively.

'I don't know who the woman is?' said Riley, looking at Nuala.

'That must be Nuala,' said Sarah. 'She keeps lover-boy's bed warm when he's in Ireland.'

'The man's got taste.' He walked up to Nuala, looking her up and down. 'We didn't get the British codes with your bit of play-acting, Sinead, but if we began to cut bits off his live flesh, maybe Faloon would be more co-operative.'

Nuala paled. Faloon tried to play for time. 'Sarah – I'll call you that rather than the Irish name you disgrace. Does Riley know that you helped to put Green Boys into court. He might begin to wonder where your doublecross begins and ends. Does Riley know in the end who you're really working for?'

Sarah was stung. She was proud of her double role and its success.

'I'm a third generation American, Faloon. When I was a kid, I read a diary still in the family hands. It was written by my ancestor, forced out of his own land by the British who killed members of his family through starvation. He couldn't afford to pay the rent to English landlords and buy food to keep his children alive. God only knows how, but he managed to get them on a boat. More of his children died during the crossing to America and freedom.'

She had stopped swaggering. Her voice was low and hoarse.

'That diary was written so that his children, and his children's children, could summon the spirit to fight the British right out of Ireland, using a resolve born out of his suffering all those years ago. We want the Brits, their bodies, their influence, their legacy out of our land. Bastards like you are a Brit legacy. You soil our heritage by accepting the partition of our land. You're a traitor.'

Faloon lost control. 'You murdering sadistic bitch. The

English would march out of Ireland tomorrow if psycho-paths like you weren't on the loose. But don't let the facts get in the way. It's all shit, pure shit.'

Faloon shook his head in a mixture of disbelief and fury. He still needed time to think of some way out. 'Why are you thugs on this side of the Atlantic anyway? And why here?'

Stukalin spoke at last. 'They are here to steal the secrets of my plane. The IRA have arranged to sell them, through these people, to the American government for either money or arms. One of them is diving with a camera. I think they will kill you.' It was the first time Faloon had heard Stukalin speak.

'You too!' roared Riley, punching Stukalin viciously in the solar plexus and kicking him as he fell.

Moira suddenly came forward to restrain Riley. All eyes were following her when everything changed, abruptly and in terrifying chaos. First a deafening roar. Then the sea round them seemed to boil, rocking the boat violently and throwing everyone off balance. A massive curtain of white spray appeared, like a demonic waterfall flowing the wrong way. The noise penetrated their skin and bludgeoned their ears.

A wall of green water swept Faloon and Nuala down the ever steepening deck. Out of the corner of his eye, Faloon saw Riley and Sarah cling to the outside of the wheelhouse. Stukalin, with Moira in his embrace, remained crumpled up inside the wheelhouse. Further along the deck, Martin Riley and Sarah were looking over their shoulders in stark terror.

Faloon and Nuala clung to a fairlead to prevent the water and the jerking bucking movements of the boat flinging them overboard.

Faloon saw a tower of dark, grey metal, the water cascading down its sides. The sea was a maelstrom of whirlpools, eddies, surges and confused corrugation.

Without warning, the nature of the turmoil changed. A bang and shuddering tremor was felt through every timber

276

in the hull. A new motion replaced the old. The pitching and yawing stopped and the deck began to heel towards the steel wall.

'We're being rammed!' Faloon yelled with all the power at his command. 'Run for the bottles! Get the airbottles or we'll drown! Go! Go!' He wrenched Nuala's terrified grip free.

'Don't put them on,' Faloon shouted. 'Carry them and jump.' He thrust Nuala's bottles hard into her chest, shouting all the time. 'Jump, then stay under and get the mouthpiece working.'

They both plunged headlong over the bow. The water under the waves shut out the unearthly noise above. Amid the bubbles and churned up sand, they clung to their bottles and masks, waiting for the momentum of their dives to take them deep.

For both of them, this was the first time they had strapped on airbottles underwater since practising in a swimming pool. The training paid off and within minutes, both had the bottles on their backs and were breathing.

Gingerly, with Nuala following, Faloon began swimming upwards.

Protruding through the silvery surface above he saw female legs, swimming inexpertly and in frenzy. He broke the surface ahead of the woman. It was Sarah.

'Help me, Faloon. I'll never reach the shore.'

Her hair had uncurled itself and fleetingly she resembled the Green Boys' courier they had sent to him in Boston, the artless teenage girl who had died in a hail of bullets because she had been too frightened to stay still.

Faloon extended his arms and this time Sarah gratefully fell into his embrace. His strong limbs closed tightly, pinning her tightly. She looked into Faloon's eyes inside his mask for reassurance. His eyes were as cold as the water around them. He held her tightly, more tightly than he had ever done, waiting until the terror rose within her and until she opened her lips to scream.

Then he went under.

He kept her under until her movements became gentle once more. Until they stopped. Until the sparkle and the hatred had left her bulging eyes for ever.

On the surface, the Atlantic washed away Nuala's tears and drowned her sobs. Faloon surfaced alone, as she knew he would. There was no time for explanation, for regret, for justification, expiation or contrition.

The sight that met Faloon's eyes left no space for such things.

Silhouetted against the evening light lay the unmistakable shape of a large submarine. High and dry across the casing aft of the sail tower lay the fishing boat, tilted on her beam as if beached. Her two anchor cables were still attached, one each side of the submarine, preventing her sliding off her precarious perch on the abnormally high casing.

Thirty metres along the casing was another incongruous shape. It was like a thick sausage, but painted in bands of black and yellow, and seemed to have a small conning tower. Faloon identified it as a mini-submarine, carried in a special nest in the main submarine's casing.

'Holy shit.' It was all Faloon could think to say at first.

And then, 'My compliments to the submarine commander. He saved our lives by lifting the boat like that. Brilliant seamanship.' Faloon was gasping in a mixture of elation and relief.

Nuala regained her voice. 'They did it for their own man Stukalin, not for you. Look at the markings on the sub. Let's head for the shore.'

But before they could turn, another shape loomed up from behind the submarine. It was a ship, a small cargo ship somewhat longer than the submarine. Men on the submarine waved and cheered as it approached and swung round the submarine's bows. It passed the submarine on the same side as Faloon and Nuala, presenting them with the sight of a freshly painted hull and an equally fresh name, clearly readable. The *Pericles*. The Greek flag flew from its rigging.

278

With a splash and a rattle, the new arrival's anchor hurried to the bottom of the bay and she began paying out the chain, slowly edging herself towards a group of lobster pot markers. Lobster pots?

'Nuala. Go for the shore. Tell people what's happened. I have one last job to do.'

'Listen, Faloon, my lovely Faloon. They'll kill you if you get in the way. Losev proved that. Come with me. It's over. It's all over,' Nuala pleaded.

'I must see it, Nuala. It has cost me so much just to be here. Now go. If you stay, part of me will always be looking after you. That'll make me more vulnerable.'

She knew he meant it. She wept once more and turned away. Faloon slid beneath the waves in the direction of the group of buoys and the ship that called itself the *Pericles*.

TWENTY SIX

Faloon's eyes feasted on the strange sight. The fishing boat lying astride a massive Russian submarine. The newly painted ship was settling among marker buoys masquerading as lobster-pot markers.

For all that had happened, Faloon knew that he was empty-handed. Grundy would want something more than a good story as the price of re-admission to G2.

He thought hard. Stukalin had mentioned that the Provos had sent someone down from the boat with a camera. The buoys suggested that the Russians in the submarine had begun the process of recovering the spaceplane and had marked its position for the surface ship.

So Faloon dived. He expected company in the murky depths.

Faloon was so edgy that any slight movement in his peripheral vision caused him to dart into the kelp beds to hide. But this jumpiness, about which he felt so sheepish at the time, saved him from O'Donnell's fate. A shoal of small silvery fish caught the light and created a flash. This put Faloon among the kelp fronds again. He was about to emerge when another movement made him stop. He crouched low.

Approaching at speed on a converging course with his own, was a wasp-coloured mini-submarine identical to the one on the submarine casing above. Clinging to rails along its hull were half a dozen frogmen, all wearing bright yellow helmets.

Faloon noted there were no bubbles from their breathing apparatus. That put Faloon at a further disadvantage. He would need to keep to the seaweed beds as far as possible since the broad leaves of kelp partly dissipated the exhaust from his own air bottles.

All of this delayed Faloon's arrival at the recovery scene considerably. The lift was about to begin.

At last Faloon saw the machine which, over the course of a few days, had become central to his existence.

The damaged tail fin, now picked out by a spotlight on the mini-sub, stood proud of the wafting kelp surrounding it, like the pyramid of a lost city in a jungle. Off to one side, cables threaded upwards from, Faloon presumed, the main section of the fuselage out of sight in a trench. They looked as if they had been laid beneath the craft to form a cradle. The cables met at a hook which stretched down from the surface.

Russian frogmen swarmed, checking every cable, every point where the spaceplane would be supported.

Faloon found the extension of the trench in which the spaceplane had come to rest and it provided him with a hidden kelp-filled conduit to the centre of activity. The Russian divers had made use of it to ambush O'Donnell, but the trench had been a mixed blessing for the Russians.

In his struggle, O'Donnell had dropped the camera into its dark weed-covered crevices, which was precisely where Faloon was being forced. The Russians had tried to recover the camera, but failed. Faloon stood on it. He knew immediately what it was – and was both elated and depressed. Elated because it signified that something had happened to the IRA photographer. The Russians must have captured him, and probably learnt from him what was happening to their cosmonaut on the surface. That would explain why the submarine surfaced so carefully under the fishing boat.

The camera itself depressed Faloon because it was fitted with a flash which he dared not use. He disconnected the flash and attempted to photograph using the working distant lights of the Russians. A useless gesture. It might be better to try shots on the surface as the plane was lifted.

Faloon wormed away from the spaceplane until he could swim upwards without being seen. He broke the surface about two hundred metres from the *Pericles*, on the side away from the activity. Although the light was fading, he saw that from amidships a large crane had been deployed and was slowly bringing the spaceplane to the surface.

All attention seemed to be focused on that side of the ship, even by the crew who were supposed to be on watch. He looked again at the small ship. It was not a normal cargo vessel, though it had been very crudely dressed as one. From close-up the fresh paint was a poor disguise. Just forward of the bridge, Faloon could see that the gloves were off. Covers hiding twin 57mm guns had been removed and gun crews were in position. Further forward on the deck were shore bombardment rockets, also manned.

From the cramming done for various training exercises in G2, Faloon thought he recognized the class of ship. It was a large landing ship of a type known to NATO armed services as 'Alligator'.

Faloon looked for the submarine. It had gone. The fishing boat lay peacefully at anchor as if nothing extraordinary had happened, except that the stern anchor line had parted from the strain of being on the submarine deck. In the gathering gloom, no lights shone in her. She looked deserted.

Faloon noted that the weather was lifting. The rain that had fallen almost ceaselessly for the past few days had at last stopped and the cloud was beginning to break up. The wind had dropped. No wonder the Russians were in a hurry. Nobody could accuse them of not making the most of the opportunity provided by mist and drizzle.

Faloon had to make the most of his own opportunity. He had changed his position until he lay about sixty metres off the stern of the *Pericles*. The stern ramp was open and the yellow helmeted divers were boarding the ship through it. Some were carrying small bits of wreckage from the spaceplane.

He took several pictures, hoping that the camera inside the waterproof casing had automatic exposure setting and a fast speed film. The light was getting worse by the minute. Swimming just below the surface to avoid detection, he moved further round the ship, placing himself in a position to see the crane raise the spaceplane from the sea.

He could hardly have timed his arrival better.

First the damaged tailplane appeared, followed by the rest of the fuselage with the oddly shaped stubby wings.

But for Faloon, the most intriguing detail was the absence of thermal protection tiles like those he had seen on the American space shuttle. The skin was smooth!

Faloon immediately saw the significance of the smoothness. It was a strong indication that Russian aerospace engineers had invented a new method of heat protection during re-entry.

Faloon had to escape.

Even if his photography failed, he had a small victory to report to Grundy and a possible ticket back to G2 at last.

The Russians on the ship were cheering. All deck lights and searchlights were turned on the spaceplane. This was their victory. Faloon knew he was too far away for good pictures, but he kept his finger on the button. The automatic camera whirred away until it ran out of film. Only then could Faloon look at the spaceplane in its entirety. It was grey and white and glistening in its wetness. It was beautiful.

So that was the prize; that was why the Russians and the Americans and the British had been making life a misery for Grundy and G2. That was what had brought down the helicopter, what had brought down Sarah; what had almost brought down Faloon himself. He stared at it in awe, even in homage.

Faloon turned to go, suddenly feeling desperately tired. Since diving off the fishing boat he had been without fins on his feet. To conserve his depleted reserves of energy, he swam with his head just below the surface, making for the abandoned fishing boat.

Through the face mask, just underwater, he saw that a full moon had risen, rendering the surface a shimmering gold and silver. He thought of Nuala.

The first shell burst just ahead of him, followed rapidly by others. He jerked his head upwards. It was not moonlight. It was a searchlight from the landing craft. Dive. Dive. Dive. He dived for his life. Reserves of strength he did not know he possessed sent him to the bottom. In the Stygian blackness of night underwater, he could hear the rounds exploding, popping his eardrums. He swam until the noise had receded. Then his air ran out, exhausted by his exertion.

There was no alternative but to surface. The only preparation he could make was to unleash the camera from his belt. If they were waiting for him, he would drop it to the seabed. Maybe somebody would find it one day, but the Russians would not find it attached to his body.

He surfaced. It was quiet. In front of him lay the lifeless hull of the fishing boat, a waterlogged dinghy still attached to the bows. The boat was mercifully between him and the Russians.

Faloon listened, then re-attached the camera to his belt. Using the dinghy, he hauled himself to the deck of the fishing

283

boat, crawled across and raised his head above the bulwark on the other side. The Russians were leaving.

The ship was already under way, heading for the open sea. On its deck, just below the crane, lay the space craft, smothered in protecting covers. Behind it followed the submarine, half submerged. Recesses in her after casing now held two mini-submarines, like a mother with two calves.

Faloon would have raised his hat to the departing flotilla. For the Russians it had been a superb operation. Somebody in the West should have guessed that the Russians might use this highly specialized rescue submarine. The Russians navy had two of them and one was always on station in the north Atlantic.

Faloon walked into the wheelhouse and was met with shambles. The floor was spread with bits of transmitters. A fire axe was still buried in the radar. The engine controls and steering gear had also been deliberately wrecked. He could not move the boat nor make contact with anyone in the outside world.

He found O'Donnell's binoculars and trained them on the submarine's sail. The men on it were beginning to go below. One of them was distinctive because he was wrapped in a blanket.

The man in the blanket hesitated at the hatch entrance and turned towards the hills of Inishowen, silhouetted in a vermilion sunset. Faloon thought he saw him salute.

EPILOGUE

Grundy had received three crucial telephone calls. One from the accident investigation team at Baldonnel Aerodrome to tell him that the helicopter had been hit in mid-air by another object. The object had a heatshield and could therefore have come from space.

Grundy had put the phone down, clasped his hands together and said, 'Of course. That's why Semple's radar suddenly picked the thing up out of the blue. Before that, it had been too high.'

The next two calls improved his mood much more. One told him in a sweet familiar voice something new about the craft, and a position he had not known.

The third call came from Semple telling him a small Russian flotilla was heading for Inishowen. Grundy told him to drop what he was doing and fly to Dublin. Semple had not liked how happy the Irishman sounded.

In the small hours of the morning, the Soviet ambassador in Dublin was called to a meeting in the office of the Irish Minister for Foreign Affairs. Colonel Grundy was present, and the ambassador had brought the Soviet military attaché, but no interpreters.

Straight off, the Soviet emissaries were told that the Irish government suspected that a Soviet agent had set off an explosion in Inishowen with the aim of killing a G2 agent. The Irish government were formally protesting.

In a similarly low key, the Russians denied the charge, but the denials had petered out when Grundy told them to get Losev out of Ireland fast, particularly since there was no record of his ever having entered. The Russians were about to leave when the Minister asked them if they would now like to talk about their spacecraft.

Both Russians looked as if they'd choked on chicken bones. They sat in their chairs without uttering a word, just looking at the Minister and Grundy. So the Irish Minister for Foreign Affairs, who was enjoying himself hugely, continued.

The ambassador was told that the Irish government wanted the Russian machine out of its jurisdiction as fast as possible, and to that end, Russian ships were being invited into Irish waters for the purpose of salvage. Since these ships would be seen from the shore, and since the neutral Irish government did not want any more trouble, the Soviet government was asked to be discreet and use civilian vessels.

Irish forces on land and on sea would assist the operation only *in extremis*. It would be preferable if there was no Irish involvement. The ambassador, scarcely able to believe his ears, almost fell over himself to accept with gratitude 'the magnanimous gesture by the friendly Government and People of the Irish Democratic Republic', which Grundy thought a bit over the top.

The Russians could hardly wait to leave the Minister's office but were pulled back yet again by their host. That was when they were told that the Irish government believed that their astronaut was in the hands of IRA terrorists who were being aided in this nefarious enterprise by agents of the American government.

The Irish government was attempting by all means to secure the safe return of the pilot, and therefore to thwart any transaction between the Provos and the Americans.

At last, for the Russians, the penny dropped. The Americans had offended the Irish more than themselves. In retaliation, the Irish were making sure the Americans didn't get the spacecraft.

The Russians rose once more to leave. Grundy and the Minister watched amused as the two diplomats ran down the corridor towards the Foreign ministry door, followed with difficulty by the Minister's unathletic private secretary.

On the Inishowen peninsula, some days after the departure of the Russians, the bodies of Martin Riley and his woman, Sarah, were washed up on the beach. Post mortems revealed that both had died from drowning. Richard O'Donnell and Moira Strain were never seen again and were listed missing, presumed drowned. Only Faloon had doubts.

The recovered tail pylon of the crashed helicopter revealed minute traces of several compounds, which were given to the British.

The British were also given copies of the photographs which Faloon had presented to Grundy. The photographs Faloon himself had taken weren't worth the paper they were printed on. But O'Donnell had done a good job before being interrupted. Faloon, without actually saying so in as many words, gave the impression that all the photographs were his own handiwork.

When the photographs and associated materials were given to Britain, it was further indication of Irish displeasure at the United States. But it also happened in accordance with a hurried secret protocol concluded between the two countries. By its terms, Britain was to begin negotiating in earnest to find a way of involving the Republic of Ireland in the administration of Northern Ireland through an Anglo-Irish treaty.

The McLaverty family were given an Irish government research and development grant, laundered through University College, Galway, to build a professional wind generator, good enough to heat a barn. Nuala got compensation sufficient to buy a new car and a set of golf clubs.

In Moscow, Bulgakov's committee was dissolved after being showered with congratulations by the few who knew what they had done.

The head of T Directorate and his repulsive wife were entertained to dinner and dancing as the guests of Mr and Mrs Bulgakov at the ornate Praga restaurant in Moscow's Arbat Square. The recovery of the spaceplane placed Bulgakov in an almost unassailable position to take over eventually as General Secretary of the Communist Party of the Soviet Union.

At the end of it all, Faloon was a little dissatisfied. He felt the need of more protection, hoping to avoid ever being out in the cold again. Late one evening, when most of the staff had departed, he slid into Grundy's office.

The boss was having a sun-downer whiskey. Faloon sat down.

287

He came straight to the point. He asked Grundy what he thought the reaction of the members of the government might be to the revelation that G2 had planted an active agent in at least one Cabinet Minister's office.

Grundy nearly spilled his whiskey and uttered a curdling oath about Nuala and pillow talk.

Faloon quietly told him how he had arrived at this conclusion. When Nuala had left the department to work in a Minister's office, she had not been trained in the use of firearms.

How had Nuala produced a gun and the training to use it? Why would she answer Faloon's question only by referring him to Grundy? It could only have one meaning. She had become a G2 operative.

Grundy asked Faloon why he'd raised the subject and Faloon replied that he simply wanted one of Grundy's whiskeys. And the best jobs and overseas assignments in future.

There was a glint in Grundy's eyes as he poured a large Jamieson for himself and a Bushmills for his guest. Then he pulled a folder out of his top drawer and studied it for a moment.

'What's that?' Faloon asked.

'It's the instruction from my political masters – members of the government – to inquire into the loss of a code chip and fire the person responsible.'

'But you found you couldn't do that. Right?' Faloon raised his glass in a toast.

Grundy took a long sip of his whiskey. 'If I keep you, the implication is that you're too valuable to relinquish and you'd remain a credible witness on the subject of Nuala Gallagher. If I fire you, any accusation you utter would look like vindictiveness and would lack credibility. So by firing you I keep my bosses happy and protect myself.'

The confident smile left Faloon's lips.

Grundy raised his glass in farewell. 'Good knowing you, Faloon. Keep in touch.'